In Brady's Arms
Sweet McKenna Book Two

Christine Young

Published by Rogue Phoenix Press, LLP
Copyright © 2021

ISBN: 978-1-62420-629-0

Credits
Cover Artist: Designs by Ms G
Editor: Sherry Derr-Wille

Published in the United States of America

Chapter One

Scottish Highlands 1747

The last two years following the battle of Culloden had been turbulent ones for the residence of the highlands. Connal McKenna as head of the clan Chattan somehow managed to maintain neutrality between the combatant Jacobites and the English. As a clan they united in choosing neither side. A few individuals chose to fight with the Jacobites. There were not enough for the English to turn their hatred and vengeance against the entire clan. Still, the English patrolled the area searching for any man who might have fought against them. If found, they would be taken into custody.

Rumors abounded about a group of men who helped the wanted Jacobites escape Scotland to sail to America where they could live in relative freedom. No one knew for sure, however. No one could proffer a name. Part of the gossip revolved around a member of Parliament leading the cause. As far as Connal McKenna, head of clan Chattan, was concerned, it was all hearsay.

Brady McKenna, the oldest son of Connal and Wynnie, sat in a room adjoining the kitchen sipping a glass of ale. Relaxed, in his prime he searched for diversions, more exactly in the form of a pretty highland lass. His gaze was focused through the doorway on a newcomer, her hands deep in bread dough, flour smudged on her cheeks as well as the tip of her nose. Her eyes were the clearest softest blue, her cheeks, stained pink from exertion coupled with the excessive heat of the kitchen. Her golden-reddish hair was piled high on top of her head, a scarf wrapped and tied to keep the strands from falling into her face. He wondered what her hair would look like unbound, how it would feel against his naked flesh or if he threaded his fingers in the silken mass. She was tall for a woman, slender, almost too much to be attractive to Brady. She was though. He couldn't keep from gazing at her almost to the point of drooling. Her pale gray dress did little to reveal but was adept at concealing what curves she might possess. The apron she wore, however, hinted of a tiny waist. Still, there was a certain striking quality surrounding her, a haughty air that belied her status as a serving wench. Her back was straight, her chin held high pushing her nose into the air.

She was a puzzle to be figured out, his to put together one small piece at a time. Ah, but he looked forward to the solving, to the piecing together. *Ach, whit's fur ye'll no go by ye.* Of course, what will happen, will happen. Brady meant it to happen sooner than later.

Tonight would be nice.

He was an impatient man.

Until recently the clan accepted newcomers into their midst on a trial basis. Now, after the battle that left much of Scotland impoverished, Connal, the McKenna laird, was reluctant to even allow a wide-eyed innocent lass gain access to the castle and the lands. So, how did this particular female manage to secure a position inside the security of the castle walls no less? It was another puzzle for him to solve.

Roby, his brother, sat down beside him, a grin painting his starkly handsome face. His dark hair too long, his steel gray eyes sparkling he swiped away several strands that had fallen into his eyes. With a nod he began, "You seem distant this afternoon. What's got you staring into the kitchen with that besotted look on your face? It appears you mean to devour that sweet lass. She looks to be a tender morsel indeed, too innocent for you or me for that matter."

"What look?" Brady grinned, lowering his lashes in an attempt to keep at least a few of his seething emotions private. He understood exactly what his brother implied.

"That besotted expression you always get when you've seen a new conquest. Doubt if the lady stands a chance against you when you've set your sights on her," Roby said following the line of Brady's sight one more time. Then with a bland tone belying the light in his silver-gray eyes, "She doesn't look like one of your normal ladies. Not curvy enough, breasts a *wee* bit too small for your usual taste. You don't usually go for chicken breasted women."

"And what type of lady do I prefer?" Brady's voice was flat as the thought that Roby was correct in his assessment flashed through him.

Nor, at this moment was she readily available. His father frowned on dalliances with the hired help. Discretion would be the word if he decided to pursue the woman. Ah, if he first installed her as his mistress, his father would have no problems with what would be a short-lived infatuation. She was going to be his.

"Well," Roby leaned back, stretching his legs out, one arm negligently propped on the empty chair next to him, looking much the same as his older brother, thoughtfully stroking his chin, "short, lots of curves and blond," he paused then for breath, "Big bubbies too. That's what you usually prefer."

A frown marred Brady's face, his eyes narrowing as he looked at the chit again. Hell, she was nothing like the women he typically favored. So, what was it about her that drew his interest? Fascinated him? He grinned when she made a face, her nose crinkling, her lips parting slightly. She was unique. It was the differences that intrigued him.

She turned her head just then, sneezing. Most likely from the flour on the end of her nose. With the back of her hand, she wiped her forehead, more flour arrived on her tiny, perfectly shaped face. He realized it was a perfect oval.

He chuckled, amused by the scene.

"What's her name? Do you *ken* it?" Brady asked, turning to his brother in an attempt to put the lady out of his sight if not out of his mind at least until he discovered more about her. It wouldn't do for him to claim his feelings just yet.

"You really that interested?" Roby sounded surprised then in an ordinary tone. "Lillian Townsend."

"Sassenach."

"True, still she is striking in looks. It's too bad she is English.

Father told me she's living in the Fraser cottage." At his quick look of surprise and a shrug of his broad masculine shoulders, "She says she's a Fraser? The family hasn't been around in years. Heard tell one of them fought for the Jacobites. Father wouldn't want any of the clan settling into this area. Only bring trouble. So, what do you think he is doing? This is a puzzle to decipher."

Another riddle.

"She's lying, keeping secrets."

Brady was suddenly determined to discover what else the lady was not saying. Even though she intrigued and captivated him, he didn't trust her. Lust was never a reason to put oneself in danger. There was something else going on here. He would have to proceed with caution. By the way she kneaded the dough, she didn't truly *ken* how to do it. The kitchen was not a place she was used to. Homes of grandeur might well be her preferred domain.

"Suppose she probably is," Roby agreed with a smirk on his face. "Suppose you're going to make it your mission to find out what she hasn't told the laird. This should be entertaining to watch."

"That is a distinct possibility." Brady rose from the table.

Without looking back his long strides took him outside the castle walls. Curiosity driving him, he headed in the direction of the Fraser cottage eager to add to his knowledge about Miss Lillian Townsend, Sassenach. No one had lived there for almost fifteen years. The place should be run down and dirty, uninhabitable. If she was destitute and had to work in the kitchen, why wouldn't she live within the castle where it was safer and cleaner? There were rooms available for the servants. A woman shouldn't be alone, shouldn't be walking the narrow dark paths at night.

His fists clenched.

Anger simmered.

Fifteen minutes later he strolled around the small home, stroking his chin as different thoughts filled his head. First, he walked the perimeter then knocked on the door. A polite reflex, he chuckled since she was at work. When no one answered, he pushed open the unlocked door, discovering the door had no lock. He didn't expect the barrier to swing open with a turn of the knob. Neither did it have a bar to place over the opening to keep unwanted intruders like him from entering when she was at home, presumably alone.

He meant to make sure he was the only trespasser into her life.

Blood pounding furiously at her ignorance or nonchalance about her safety for a few seconds he stared around the room. The Frasers must have left everything behind when they moved. The place was clean, the furniture old and worn. He strode into the kitchen, opening cupboards and drawers to find utensils, plates and cups for two.

For two people? Roby said nothing about a second person. His annoyance as well as his curiosity blindsided him. Obviously, he cared too much. He would have to rectify both, her oblivious innocence as well as how much concern he harbored for the lass.

A broom. She had a broom. Well, the floor was clean and tidy. What more could a woman want than a broom?

He strolled into the bedroom. There was a large bed with warm quilts and pillows. The sight caused carnal thoughts to flow through his head as he pictured her long length stretched out on the bed eagerly waiting for him. When he closed his eyes, he could see her, entangled within his arms, her thick hair flowing down her back, wrapped sinuously around him. In the far corner a massive trunk sat. When he lifted the lid, he saw it was filled with gowns. *Gowns in silk, satin and velvet.* He delved deeper. There were all sorts of frilly frothy underclothing, corsets too. When he stared at her earlier, he would have sworn she wore only a chemise beneath her worn and very serviceable gray gown. *A gown that did little to flatter her body.*

He sat on the bed, running his hands through his hair, thinking, wondering at what he discovered.

What to make of it?

Still deep in thought, Brady wandered back to the main room. In the fireplace a stew simmered in a huge pot. Picking up a ladle, he stirred and tasted, examined the meat. Rabbit. When the hell did she have time to hunt and snare food to eat?

Clearly, she wasn't alone. A husband? A lover? His gut clenched at the thought of another man sharing her life. For the immediate future, he wanted her exclusively in his life. He would have to make sure this male in her life would be well persuaded to leave her alone.

A month earlier about ten red coats had ridden through here, searching. It seemed they never quit looking for Jacobites. They found no one. Brady knew there were rumors though, gossip that a handful of traitors were living near here in the woods. The last thing his family wanted were English soldiers traipsing over their land, enslaving people of the clan, discovering just how different they truly were. If that happened there would be no privacy, no way to shift and run wild over the heather throughout the ragged hills and cliffs. They would all be prisoners within their homes.

He was shaking his head as he turned toward the castle when a movement caught his eye. Stopping, he waited, holding his breath, sensing that whomever he thought he saw was doing the same.

For a moment his breath caught in his throat, his heart stopping. "Roby."

His brother grinned at him. "Thought I'd keep you out of trouble. Didn't like the way you looked when you headed out the door. Sure does look deserted doesn't it? What did you discover?"

"Thought you'd never ask," Brady said dryly, watching, hoping he would find the second person in this scenario.

Wishing there was no one else. From what he'd seen of her so far, her entire life was a lie.

"Well, you don't have to be sarcastic." Roby stuck his hands in the pockets of his coat as he fell into stride beside him. "Just here to help or give a second opinion, asked or not. I'm your eyes and ears so you can continue to think with your cock."

"Lillian does not live here by herself. She has a man with her if the rabbit simmering in the pot is any indication along with two place settings of everything."

"*Nay*, you've got that piece of information wrong. Heard father saying he sent her the rabbit with his blessings. Would help her with food until she was able to fend for herself."

Brady wasn't sure why he felt a small lift to his heart. He didn't like to think of her sleeping with someone or hiding someone either. The only person she was going to sleep with in the near future was him. If she was hiding someone, when caught the soldiers would imprison her just as quickly calling her a traitor as they would a man. Even though she was English through and through, they wouldn't care. They meant to make sure the past rebellion was completely squashed. There would be no upstarts to the English throne.

By the time he returned to the kitchen, she was nowhere to be seen. It was just as well. His emotions were in turmoil. He wasn't at all sure what he would say to her when he did get the chance to speak with her and he would. There was no question in his mind he would talk to her. The only question was when.

When he walked into the main room, his uncle Alistair was with his father deep in discussion. Kit, Alistair's middle son, occupied a chair nearby. He sat down beside them, listening. Much of their conversation was the same. Now their discussions were always about when they would have their first grandson or daughter. Who would be first? None of their children were married yet. Not even his sister who was of age. Problem was she needed to find her mate. Perhaps their father should send her to Glasgow or Edinburgh for a period so she could come out. A frivolous event that to Brady had no real meaning. All the debutants lined up, fluttering their fans coquettishly, blinking their lashes, until the man of their dreams swept them into his arm.

Foolishness.

Brady sat next to his father, unwilling to waste time listening to their idle, meaningless chat. He blurted, impolitely interrupting, "What do you know about Lillian Townsend? Why is she here?"

Is she keeping a man with her in the cottage?

Connal slowly turned his gaze to his oldest son, his brows drawn together, clearly displeased with the untimely interruption. "I don't believe that is any of your business, son. Unless she wishes to say anything directly to you it is not my place to tell tales. I gave her permission to live in the Fraser cottage for as long as she needs to do so. Her mother was a Fraser. She has every right to occupy the cottage. Why do you care?"

Brady heard the ice in his father's voice, giving him even more reason to seek out Lillian's truths as well as her lies. She was purposely hiding something from the laird, putting everyone in danger by the ongoing deception. He needed to put further discussion with his father aside. Connal didn't intend to give him information.

"Come, let's eat."

Together they walked to the table designated for the laird and his family. Wynnie was nearly finished with her meal. Brady didn't believe he should engage his mother in questions about the woman who seemed to be occupying his head. She would see right through him. If she discovered his intent, she would do her best to stand in his way.

He found himself leaning back in his chair, arms crossed in front of him, staring at the opposite end of the room. The food was unappealing tonight. He found he wanted to sample a bit of the rabbit stew with Lillian in her cottage. He could wait.

"Is there something wrong with the food?"

The sweet sultry voice next to him shook him out of his melancholy musings. He looked up into the soft blue eyes he noticed earlier. Felt his body become fully aroused. He shifted in his chair as he tried to hide the evidence she caused. She smelled of vanilla. He reached up and swiped away the flour on her nose.

She inhaled a sharp breath, stepping back so quickly she lost her balance for a moment. Brady reached out, stopping her fall. "My apologies. I only meant to rid your nose of the flour left from your baking today. It's charming," he said with mocking disdain, still wondering about her as well as her intentions. "You don't *ken* much about cooking, do you? Perhaps you're better suited for cleaning."

Lillian touched her nose, staring at him as if she thought he'd lost his mind. She was a skittish little thing, almost as if she wasn't used to men. He decided she was a good little actress. She had the emotions correct right down to the hand at her throat and the widening of her eyes, a deceitful little thing. Amused, he slanted her a mocking grin. Unraveling her would be interesting.

"You had no right to touch me," she blurted suddenly, her eyes fixed on Roby as if she couldn't bear to look at him or she saw something she disliked.

"I was just trying to help," he growled, no longer amused.

His gaze riveted on his brother who was grinning, clearly enjoying this encounter along with the woman's attention on him. His brother knew how he felt about the girl. Was using this opportunity to mock him.

"I beg of you, don't help again. I'm quite capable of getting the flour dust off my own nose."

She stuck her chin in the air, her nose higher. The regal tilt, the stiffness of her shoulders spoke of nobility.

Not a common serving wench. His thoughts returned to the silks and satins he saw in the trunk. The voluptuous pillows on the large bed, it was a bed designed for two.

Another piece of the puzzle that was Lillian Townsend he meant to vanquish.

She cleared her throat, looked at him with an imperious glare in those soft blue eyes, repeating her earlier question. "Is there anything I can get for you, sir?" she stood back, waiting. Her toe was tapping impatiently.

He reached out, confronting her earlier statement that he had no right to touch her as he placed his hand around her wrist, closing tightly, tugging her closer. "I want you," he said, his voice assuming a husky gentle timber.

The gasp of air, the sucked in breath was another good ploy. Her small breasts rose and fell at a frantic pace. "Food, drink anything of that nature."

She tugged on her wrist, seeming to ignore his statement. She would not ignore him forever.

"Tonight, when you are through working wait for me in the kitchen. I'll walk you home. Shouldn't be out there by yourself in the dark. *'Tis* not safe for a pretty lady." He knew she would not, at least he knew she would try to leave without him seeing her. She would not succeed.

"No."

"Yes. I believe you will. We've matters to talk over. You can't deceive me like you have my father. I *ken* what you're about."

He watched her eyes narrow to small blue slits. The soft blue turned to silver ice as she stared at him, never turning her gaze from his. She provoked him. Intrigued him to no end.

"I've not deceived anyone." She tugged again, her lips thinning into a straight line. Her anger was written clearly on her expressive face. "Leave me be."

This time he let her go, hearing Roby clear his throat behind him. Something else was happening in the hall. His guess was that he had the attention of his father. "Tonight. That's a promise. Don't leave without me."

Without confirming his request, she fled the room, her skirts swaying gracefully around her feet her back stiff as a board. He placed his hands on his belly, watching, anticipating what was yet to come. His next encounter with Miss Lillian Townsend would be interesting, fascinating indeed. He meant to determine her secrets as well as enjoy anything else that might come from their association.

"You're playing with fire, big brother. If father notices what you're about, he'll be displeased."

Connal sat down, his hands folded on the table. "She is not what she seems, Brady. For your own good, leave her be."

In a dry tone, "I've figured that fact out by myself. This has nothing to do with my own good, rather hers. What is it she is hiding, Father?"

"You should let her live her life. She is not your mate." There was a tinge of anger in Connal's voice.

"It seems, I can't forget her, she's found a place deep in my soul," Brady said in all honesty.

His voice was cold and hard, wondering why he felt so intensely connected when it came to Lillian Townsend. He thought on his father's words. "She is not your mate." How the bloody hell did one know if a woman was his mate? Ah, he brushed the thought aside. If he had to wonder, she most assuredly was not his throughout all eternity.

Thinking about that he decided once more it would not be unpleasant to have her for a few months. He would discover what he questioned.

She walked back into the hall, a tray of drinks and food in her hands. She was graceful when she moved. He liked everything about her except the deception and the lies. Lillian would be his, at least until he grew tired of her. He would begin the subtle coaxing he was known for this very evening when he accompanied her home. Perhaps they would even share a first kiss.

He turned to his father, "Did you snare a rabbit for her?"

His question seemed to surprise Connal. "What if I did?"

Brady lifted his shoulders in a slow dramatic shrug, more questions coming to mind. "Something you don't do for the crofters. Is she more than just a tenant on McKenna land? Is she really a Fraser?"

"Leave it be," the laird said harshly, rising.

He held out his hand for his wife. Together they exited the room, Wynnie looking over her shoulder, her eyes seeming to plead with him to do as his father asked.

He could not.

Normally, he would have given in to his father's wishes in a heartbeat. Something about this woman stirred his senses, provoking every masculine part of him; intrigued, fascinated, leaving him spellbound and needing more from her. He sought to kiss her senseless, possess her soft lips until she told him everything he wanted to know, until she gave him all of herself.

"I cannot," he whispered as Lillian whirled passed him another tray in her hand.

The breath he inhaled was long and deep. The scent of vanilla floated around her. "God help me, but I cannot leave her be."

The seconds and minutes seemed to tick by more slowly than they ever had in his entire life. The great hall slowly began to empty. The servers were few and far between. A few of the clan snoozed by the fire. When he watched Lillian slide passed him into the kitchen, he rose, following behind her.

Brady leaned against the doorjamb, arms crossed in front of him as he watched Lillian go through the process of leaving. If she realized he was there, she gave no indication as she wrapped her threadbare cloak around her slim shoulders. When she became his, he would make sure she dressed in the silks and satins she already owned, no more pretenses. What she presented here was a complete fabrication of her life.

As she left the room he pushed away, stepping at her pace until she was out the door. The darkness seemed to swallow her whole. Under his breath he cursed, wondering how many times she made the fifteen-minute walk to the cottage she was calling home alone by herself. Nights were not safe for a single woman, unprotected.

Anger simmered, annoyance at her flagrant abuse of her life flared deep in his soul. Did she truly think it safe for her to walk that distance by herself without a man's protection? After tonight, no longer would she put herself at risk. This was untenable. Furious strides ate up the ground between them until she noticed he was behind her.

"I told you to wait for me." His voice was cold with rage.

He held on to her arm, turning her to look at him, needing to tell her she would obey his commands despite her wishes.

She tried to wrench her elbow from him, her eyes darkening with her own anger as she stared at him, realizing she was helpless to resist his strength. "I don't take orders from you, Sir. Unhand me," she grit out between clenched teeth, her resentment with him simmering as hotly as his own.

"No?"

"No!" She swung at him.

He wasn't expecting her to retaliate. She moved like lightning. Her hand connected with his face so hard his head jerked back. He felt the fire on his face where she slapped him. He could even feel the imprint of her fingers forming on his cheek. Awe at her audacity filled him. Irritation at her inability to see the danger in the situation gave new meaning to his need to see this through to whatever end awaited them.

"You are an audacious piece of baggage."

He held both her hands, tugging them behind her back, bringing her against him, her breasts pushing against his chest. He heard each breath as she labored to draw in air, felt the heat of her body pressed so near to his, felt the lush curves he had not seen beneath her serviceable gown. She lowered her lashes, another ploy he thought to get the better of him. If anything, she was a consummate actress.

She looked up. *"Bassa!"* she spat out. "Let me go."

Yes, he supposed he could be a bastard at times. His smile hinted at mocking amusement. "You, madam, are in no position to make demands concerning me as well as my intentions. Perhaps it would be more prudent on your part to yield to my requests and humor me. What do you think, hmm...? a willing woman?" He changed tactics. Request seemed much more biddable than the words demand or command.

"Dodder! Bampot! Swine!"

"Sassenach." He spoke plainly, his voice very soft. He wasn't about to take her abuse.

She turned her head, seeming to school her features. "I'm a Fraser."

"Townsend."

He released her elbow. She continued walking as if he didn't match her step for step as if she hadn't sent foul words his way. The following silence permeated his thoughts, soaking into every pore of his body. Her back was stiff, her strides long for a woman while her fists were clenched tightly at her sides. An apparition of frustration and fury, if he didn't miss his guess.

If she were a man, she would be a worthy opponent. As a woman, she would fall nicely into his plans. He was confident to believe all he needed to do to make her his was meet her lips with his own.

Soon.

Rain began to fall, a few drops at first then turning into a deluge with gusting winds. It was turning into a *dreich* evening. She pulled the hood of her cloak over her head, pretending he wasn't there or perhaps hoping he would disappear if she couldn't see him.

He was sure the hood would blind her to him. A grin nestled in his heart sending signals of delight all the way to his toes. He didn't want to but he appreciated her stubborn infuriating courage. Still, she sought to win this game she was playing with him. Not by ignoring him she wouldn't.

A deer bounded across the path. She cried out, turning to him before realizing what she was doing. He pulled her close.

"*'Tis* nothing to be afraid of this time, Lilly. Next time the animal might be of human form," he murmured, his breath touching her face, his knuckles tenderly stroking her cheek in anticipations of more. "Much more dangerous."

Placing both hands on his chest, she pushed on him. He didn't move as he turned her. When she looked up, his mouth was so close to her own he could feel her rapid breaths against his lips. He watched her small tongue run across her full bottom lip that he knew would be soft and wet for him when he chose to kiss her.

"I'm not afraid."

"You must have been since you sought me out." His words were spoken with a bland indifference. "We both know how you feel about me. That will change."

"I was just surprised. That's all. A deer, nothing more or less. No harm, no foul." Her words were staccato like spoken quickly as if her lungs were still robbed of air.

"Could have been a man. Someone who wished you harm," he said softly. "I would not have liked that."

"You wish to do me harm."

"Nay, I only wish to give you pleasure." *As soon as you will allow my coaxing to culminate in something more.*

"I don't know what you're saying." She pointed down the trail where they were headed. "See, there is my home. You can leave now. You've seen me to my destination, and I thank you to go now."

"Not until I'm ready and I know there is no one dangerous inside waiting for you."

~ * ~

Earlier that afternoon, Lilly felt the heat from his insistent gaze before she saw him. When she turned her attention his way, he was sitting, his long well-muscled legs stretched out in front of him, one arm nonchalantly draped over a second chair. His eyes were the color of molten steel, his hair black as coal. The angles and planes of his face were hard and chiseled. Nay, all his body was solid, unyielding. Even sitting he was the personification of masculine grace. There was not one part of him that appeared soft. Every pound of compact muscle oozed male confidence. In part he terrified her on the other side he fascinated her.

In one hand he held a glass of ale. His gaze riveted on her, on her lips, her breasts even as the focus of his attentions roamed down her body assessing her. In London she'd known men who were so arrogant they believed they had the God given right to anything or anyone they desired. This man appeared to be cut from the same ilk. Though he made no move toward her. A sudden unexplainable wave of fire swept through her. She found herself undeniably attracted to him.

Not yet. Not now.

In part that was why she fled the horrid country as well as the more horrific town, littered with vices of every kind. Every nobleman kept a mistress or made use of the whores who dotted the waterfront taverns as well as upscale whorehouses. Few were loyal to their wives and vice versa. The stink of the town filled her with dread as well as revulsion. Even more so was the knowledge her stepfather promised her to a man three times her age. She could not stomach the notion of lying willingly in bed with the vile creature and allowing him to do what he wanted with her body. She fought the only way she could think of. She ran.

Her gaze returned to the man staring at her, joined by his brother. She knew who they were, recognized the McKenna brothers by the steely purpose of their long strides and broad, powerful shoulders. They possessed the same hard gray eyes as their father. The laird warned her to stay away from his sons when he allowed her to reside in the Fraser cottage. Not because he didn't deem her worthy of knowing her sons but to keep her from getting hurt. They would only wed their mate. She understood that fact. They loved women and never said no to an agreeable lady or one they could coax into their bed. Every unwed woman was fair game if they wanted a dalliance.

To avoid a liaison all she had to do was say no.

The moment she set foot in the kitchen she heard the rumors. A woman had hurt Brady a few years back. Believing her his soul mate, he fell in love with her, offering her a place by his side through eternity, offering her everything he was, all he owned. Later, he discovered what she wanted was his title and wealth. The lady was no more his mate than she was. She was here with a purpose, one she meant to fulfill. She would never allow a man such as Brady McKenna to dissuade her from her good and true commitment.

Inwardly, Lilly laughed. It seemed it was true of all women, even those living in the highlands. Until now, she thought it a trait of the women in London seeking to better themselves. Well, she didn't have the time or the inclination to form a relationship with anyone, let alone one of the brothers, especially not Brady McKenna who excited her in ways she didn't want to admit even to herself. She wiped her hands on her apron, finishing with the bread dough, allowing a heavy sigh to escape her lips. It wasn't as if she disliked the work. She dreaded it because she was so bad at it. The kitchen had never been her domain. No, she was more accustomed to the parlors and sitting rooms in the elegant townhouses of the London affluent, to being served not serving.

As the evening wore on, she'd been given the ultimatum that Brady would walk her home. She dreaded the upcoming moment. She wasn't afraid of him. When he touched her, held her wrist with his long slightly calloused fingers, she knew she was afraid of her feelings for him. He wasn't gentle by any means. She sensed he could be, suspected he could melt her heart as well as her body if given the opportunity. If she could only escape out the back door before he had a chance to know she left, she would be able to breathe a little more freely. Perhaps her heart would even stop thundering so harshly beneath her ribs. She would not have to worry that he would discover what she was about here in the highlands.

She understood the chance of escaping him was slim. He was a determined man. Had not been surprised when she spotted him leaning negligently against the doorjamb into the kitchen when she was ready to leave. She braced herself for the confrontation as well as his presence beside her while he escorted her home. She prayed her brother, Douglas, would hear them and leave the crofters hut just in case he insisted on seeing her inside. Her brother needed to remain hidden and unobtrusive for the next few weeks so he could heal, then resume their mission.

The rain began to fall, a few drops at first before turning into a deluge with gusting winds. She pulled the hood of her cloak over her head, pretending he wasn't there or perhaps more to the point wishing for her peace of mind he would disappear. She quickened her pace, hoping to reach the cottage before she was drenched to the bone. His presence beside her unnerved her, completely terrified her. A lump caught in her throat. Her knees quaked so hard she could barely place one step in front of the other. Maybe if she stepped inside the door, then slammed it shut in his face, he would understand she didn't want him to come inside.

Perhaps the world would stop turning.

A deer bounded across the path. "Oh!" she cried out, turning to him before realizing what she was doing. He pulled her close. His arms wrapped around her, warm and hard, inflexible, demanding. She had naught to give.

" '*Tis* nothing to be afraid of this time, Lilly Townsend. Next time the animal might be of human form," he murmured, his breath touching her face, his knuckles tenderly stroking her cheek. "Much more dangerous."

In her heart, she understood he was the most dangerous animal she would encounter. If given the chance, he could rip her heart right out from behind her ribs. She wouldn't give him the opportunity.

Placing both hands on his chest, she pushed on him. He didn't move as he turned her. When she looked up, his mouth was so close to her own, intimidating, yet strangely beckoning to her. Her lips parted. She moistened them with her tongue as she struggled against her fears as well as the strange heat of her escalating emotions. This was not something she was accustomed to. She had never been held so close, so intimately by anyone. While she danced and was held by other men, the sensations were never like this. The threat of his formidable body pressed against hers caused a strange ache as well as heat to gather inside. She was a tempest of seething emotions.

"I'm not afraid." She tried to swallow, tried to look away from him. His eyes were dark, fathomless as he gazed at her, imploring her to meet him halfway, to look at him. A half-smile formed on his lips as he watched her with that expression of his that accused her of lying. He knew her, understood how she felt. Understood she was struggling more with herself than with him.

"You must have been since you sought me out." His words were spoken with a bland indifference coupled with a mocking grin. "You turned right into my arms. It's exactly what I wanted tonight. You in my arms."

"I was just surprised. '*Twas* a deer nothing more or less. No harm, no foul." Her words were staccato like spoken quickly as if her lungs still were robbed of air. Once more she pushed against him, to no avail. He would not let her go until he was ready, until...

"Could have been a man. Someone who wished you harm. You might have been alone, defenseless," he said softly. "I would not have liked that."

"You wish to do me harm."

Even though she spoke the words accusingly she knew them to be false. He was experienced in the ways of sexual games between men and women, understood how to give and receive pleasure. She heard as much from her older brother when he warned her to stay away from the McKenna men. She just didn't understand what he wanted with her.

"*Nay*, I only wish to give you pleasure." His voice was whiskey smooth sending a telling shiver down her spine.

"I don't know what you're saying." She pointed down the trail where they were headed. "See, there is my home. You can leave now.

18

You've seen me to my destination. I thank you to go now."

"Not until I'm ready and I know there is no one inside waiting for you."

His hands encircled her upper arms. He leaned forward as if he meant to kiss her yet he did not. Disturbed, irritated with herself for wanting just that, she trapped her lower lip beneath her teeth. She didn't desire him in her home. He would see how little she owned then he would press his case.

I want you.

Those three words reverberated in her head, her entire being crying out no, no, he could not have her as his mistress or anything else. *Stay strong.* She would have remained in London if being used by a man was her intent or even her destiny. Here, she had a purpose, a job to accomplish. That wasn't true. She could have never let her brother flee without help. His only crime was that he pled the Jacobite cause in the House of Lords. He was not a Jacobite, barely religious in any way. He had soundly fought for the English, fought for the Duke of Cumberland during the war where the Scots tried to set James on the throne. He had simply felt that two years after the last battle it was time to put the differences aside thereby living in peace with the Scots. Now all he yearned for was to find a means to help those who were persecuted.

"Shall we?" He beckoned toward her home, his hand outstretched as if he wished for her to lead the way.

She heard his voice, felt the whisper of his breath against her cheek, jerking her back to the present. "What?"

She was shaking her head as he let her go. She had thought... What had she thought? That he was about to kiss her? Relief should be sweeping through her not this crazy disappointment.

"Go into your home. What did you think?" he asked as if he knew the answer before she could say.

Odious man. "N-nothing. I wasn't thinking anything."

At the blatant lie, she felt the flow of heat caress her cheeks.

He sent her a mocking all-knowing grin before nodding toward the door. "After you."

"Of course." She drew air into her lungs, felt the sting of the raindrops as she lifted her face away from him and his massive body no longer sheltered her. She stepped forward. At the door she paused to search his face. He was unrelenting, with only one purpose. She wished she understood the reasons he singled her out for this sweet torture.

Inside, a small fire burned in the hearth. He gazed at the remains as well as the pot hanging over it. "Must have been a large fire you made this morning for it still to be burning. Whatever you've got cooking in that pot is most likely burned."

"I don't go to work until the afternoon, if you must know. The fire would hardly burn down to nothing."

"I will see that you work in the mornings instead. That way you won't have to walk home at night."

She laughed at him, "What? You don't intend to walk me home every night?"

"If the lass would let me stay every night in her bed, I'd be more than pleased to walk you home."

Not waiting or seeming to expect an answer, he helped her with her cloak, shaking the drops off outside the door before closing it and hanging the coat on its hook then he slipped out of his coat. Her stomach churned. The rabbit stew should have been inviting. She'd not eaten since this morning.

"Would you like some stew?" she queried with a wavering voice all the while hoping for something to talk about before he pursued whatever plans he had for the evening.

"No, but don't let me stop you. Don't suppose you had a chance to eat," he said as he sat down, seemingly making himself comfortable.

"I couldn't eat a thing," she murmured, trying to look in any direction but at him. She needed to busy herself as well as her hands. "I'll clean it up and put the food in a container for tomorrow."

"It was nice of the laird to snare you a rabbit. Isn't something he usually does for a tenant."

She stopped, surprised, as she tried to hide her emotions. She lowered her lashes. "It was," she blatantly lied.

By the look on his face, she guessed he knew. Yet his scowl told her he was thinking over something. "Why are you here?"

"I live here. Why are you here?" she shot back as she poured a glass of wine for herself and him. "I don't have tea."

"You have wine."

She nodded. I drank the tea first. I've not been paid for my services so I can't purchase anything from the village. This is all I have," she paused for a moment. "And water, of course."

"Wine is fine. Tomorrow I'll see your cupboards are stocked."

"*Nay. Ye cannae.*"

"I can and I will."

"Why?"

"Because," he spoke slowly at first enunciating every word, "I intend on spending a great deal of time here—with you. I don't plan on being deprived of anything I want or like, beginning with you."

"I don't want you."

He rose, walking toward her, his smile firmly in place. "Let's see about that," he said softly.

"I would not like to see anything."

What an arrogant, self-centered bastard. He would do everything in his power to bend her to his will. She would do everything to prove he could not. Yet her hands were shaking, her breaths coming in tiny, miniature gulps as he pressed ever closer. The strange ache possessing her body was growing again centered in places she'd truly never thought of before this man appeared in her life. His gaze was upon hers. His eyes turning to dark silver, heated to a fine sheen.

He stood over her now.

"Did you realize that your fingers were moving on my chest just a few minutes ago when we stood outside in the freezing rain? You wanted me then. I'm gambling you still want me."

"They were not. You should leave now."

"In the freezing rain?"

One of his large hands wrapped around her neck, gently drawing her closer. Quickly, he undid the scarf holding her hair back. The length spilled around her shoulders. His fingers wound into her long hair. She felt the constant pressure at her nape. The other hand settled on her waist, stroking the curve of her hip. "No, I *dinnae* want this." Once more she lied.

"You will." Slowly his mouth descended, enclosing hers. He touched, stroked and nibbled across the width. His tongue moistened her lips, traced the crease between them. His teeth tugged with the suggestion she open for him. Her mouth was wet and hot, swollen slightly where he caressed. He kissed her again and again, nibbled on either side of her mouth, pressed once more before finding a sensitive spot behind her ear.

She resisted his subtle persuasion, refused to allow herself to be drawn into the delicate coaxing, to the fire smoldering inside. He barely touched her. It seemed she could not draw a breath of air.

"Relax, sweetling. Give into what you are feeling. All will be as it should be."

His hand stroked her back, up then down, gliding slowly over each tiny bone running the length. Each pass of his hand drew her closer to the hard length of him. She felt the play of his muscles against her breasts as they began to swell and throb expectantly. She had never been kissed like this, never been unable to resist the sweet intoxication of a man's lips. The men she'd been with in London were nothing like this man. Dangerous.

Lilly clung to him simply because if she didn't, she would crumple to the floor in a tiny ball of nothingness. Her fingers held on to his shoulders, her lips swelling under the fierce possessiveness of his mouth as he claimed her as his own. She stifled a silent whisper of expectations as he gently deepened the kiss, his tongue sweeping across her mouth finding entrance while he slowly parted her lips, his tongue delving inside, retreating then continuing the sensuous invasion over then over again, pushing inside her claiming her as his possession. His hand stroked her back again and again then settled on her rear to gently squeeze. As he pulled her between his legs, his hard arousal pressed against her belly.

"You want me," he whispered softly. "Admit it. Let me inside your sultry warmth. Melt in my arms. Let me dissolve in your fire."

Outwardly, she was still denying the feelings as well as the inferno he created within her. Inwardly, she was yearning for more, needing to feel the depth of his emotions as he enticed and lured her in ways she didn't understand to do his bidding. Refusing his insistent exploration was impossible as her hands rose higher, circling his neck drawing him closer. Her breasts pushed against his chest. It was everything she'd ever yearned for, to be kissed and treasured for who she was, not what she could bring to a marriage. Deep in her heart, she realized he wasn't treasuring her. He was using her for his personal needs. That fact made no difference at the moment.

This wasn't a marriage proposal, she reminded herself. If anything, it was a proposal to become his mistress, an invitation of sorts or perhaps an interview for the position. She would not give in to his demands. She would resist anything more he might ask except the promise of his kisses.

Once again she gave into his quest, opening her lips to his invasion. His tongue thrust inside then again as his lips molded to hers. He played her body as if she was created for him and him alone. Heat seared everywhere he touched then cooled when he withdrew. He nipped the corners of her mouth before stroking with his tongue and mouth across her chin to her ear. He placed tiny kisses down her neck as her fingers wound into his hair in an unconscious attempt to encourage him as well as to draw him closer.

The tiny moan of pleasure rippling from her was nearly her undoing as she still tried to withhold some part of herself from his expert coaxing. It was not to be simply because he would not allow her to hold anything back. When she tentatively touched his lips with her tongue, he sucked hers deep inside his mouth. With that simple gesture what she gave him was undeniable. His fingers clenched her body to his, tightening and squeezing her derrière until she could barely breathe, until she was pushing of her own volition against him as if she yearned to become one with him.

He pulled away as he looked down at her. Her head rested against his chest now. "Look at me," he said softly gifting her with a mocking smile that seemed to be meant to put her in her place. "Do you want me, Lilly?"

She stiffened at the thought he so easily played her, toying with her until she had no will of her own. She eagerly danced to the tune he set. This was just a prelude to the continuing games until he had her in his bed beneath him, her legs spread for him. She wouldn't be his plaything. Refusing his attentions in the future would not be easy. She knew she had to keep him from taking her innocence, from ruining her for a marriage.

And yet...

Lilly knew she had no prospects for a marriage, having knowingly left that part of her life behind her when she fled her betrothal and everything evil in London. The gossip surrounding her would put a stamp on her reputation that could never be erased. He would think less of her if he understood the extent of her lies and betrayals. Her stepfather entered into the contract with good intentions.

She defied him.

Would do it again in a heartbeat if faced with the same decision. She had no regrets. Perhaps becoming the mistress of a man such as Brady McKenna would not be so bad or humbling. Her fate could be worse. She might go through life without knowing the sweet pleasures a man could give a woman.

Brady McKenna was arrogant, a proud man who took what he wanted. He wanted her. Would that be so wrong?

"No," she told him. "No, I *dinnae* want you."

"Little liar, should I prove your statements are false?" He stroked her cheek, ran his fingertip along her collarbone.

She shivered in response, heat sweeping through her. Once again his mouth descended on hers, stroked and moved creating that same magical enchantment he crafted before. This time when his finger ran along her back he moved slightly. Now, his hand cupped her breast. Through the thin fabric of her gown, he caressed the hard bud at the tip, torturing her with the burning need his hands and lips generated. She should tell him no, push him away.

She could not.

"If you didn't want me, you would tell me to stop," he whispered, his teeth closing over her ear, biting gently as his fingers caught her nipple, tugging. "I could take your breast into my mouth, suck it deeply and still you would not say no."

The last words angered her, bringing her back to the reality of the present. He knew what he was about. She allowed him to seduce her into a state where she could no longer think only feel. "No." She pulled in a deep breath of air praying it would give her courage also. "Brady, stop. Please." Yet she heard the tone of her voice. It sounded as if she was pleading with him to continue not to cease.

He did stop then, sweeping her into his arms and striding with her to the large chair near the fireplace. Sitting down, he held her in his lap, continuing to caress her back, the curve of her hip then back to her nape. It seemed to Lilly that he was trying to comfort her not seduce.

"I want you, Lilly. I want you willing and begging me to kiss you, to touch you in places that only a man you care for will touch you. For now, perhaps we should sample that wine in our glasses and leave what comes next for another time. What do you say?"

"I won't ever beg," she told him lifting her chin, trying for an air of confidence she didn't feel.

Bloody eyes but she wanted to beg him right now to kiss her again, to stroke her with his long fingers until... Determined, she would never give that kind of power over to him.

"No, Lilly, you probably will not. Perhaps beg is the wrong word to use with someone so proud." Still his fingers continued to move on her flesh, finding places that heated her as she continued to dissolve into him. Each stroke of his hand created a new fire where it burned only to turn cold when his fingers left. She tried to still the violent shivering of her body but could not.

"Please, I can take no more of this," she whispered.

"Only one thing will ease the desire you feel for me. I can do that. Ease the passion and change those sentiments to delight. All you need do is ask," he told her as he placed his lips on the thundering pulse at the base of her neck, lingering, touching, kissing.

"I *cannae*."

"Then we must wait until you want me more than you've wanted anything else your entire life. Will you want me, crave me like that, Lilly?"

His silken voice caressed her to her soul, made her hunger for things a lifetime of teachings had told her were wicked, sinful.

She should not, could not tell him yes.

Her brother would certainly disown her if she gave in to this man's tactics. Her father had already done so. What did she care?

Her mind and body were weak.

"The rain has ceased." He swirled his tongue inside her ear.

She didn't understand his comment. Even now he was unfastening the front of her dress, moving the fabric aside so he could touch her, stroke her more intimately, flesh against flesh. She panicked "No!" She leapt to her feet, tugging the sides of her gown closed. "You must leave. As you said, the rain has stopped."

He smiled softly at her, his gaze moving from her breasts to the tips of her toes assessing just as he did when her hands were wrist deep in dough. "If that's what you want, Lilly. A good-bye kiss first. One that will warm me through the night.

Before she could inhale again, she was in his arms, his lips touching upon hers once more, claiming them asserting himself, leaving no doubts about his intentions.

Then, "I want you, Lilly. Don't ever forget that."

~ * ~

Brady left the cottage before he made the irrevocable mistake of taking Lily to bed before she would admit to wanting him. He never bedded a woman who was willing but hiding her eagerness behind the word no. Pulling up the collar of his coat to shield his neck from the wind, he chuckled softly. She was passionate, a desirable woman as well, an enchantress. Her hair was as silken and soft as he thought it would be. She melted into him when he kissed her. Her breasts weren't overly large but they fit his hands to perfection. They were soft but firm, her flesh silken fire. With a little patience, he would win this game, coax her into giving all of herself to him. She was a skittish little thing. He would fix that.

Ah, but he could envision her naked in his arms.

About five minutes down the path leading to the McKenna castle, he doubled back, taking a more circuitous route to the cottage. When he mentioned the rabbit and his father's part in gifting her with the meat, she appeared genuinely surprised. The two sets of everything still bothered him. She was hiding something. Before he made love to her, he meant to discover some truths, if he could wait that long. Perhaps nothing was amiss and what she presented to him was true.

He didn't believe that for a second.

Her home was in front of him now, the lights still shining in the main room. He hunkered down in the dark and waited. Minutes ticked by. The wind moaning around the trees surrounding him still he waited. He shifted his weight from one foot to the other, groaning at the tightening of his muscles. Rain began to fall again. Tempted to shift, his thick cat fur would be a better barrier to the water than the coat he wore.

Perhaps he was wrong about Lilly. Maybe there wasn't a second person living with her. Quite possibly she wasn't hiding her true identity or her purpose. He hoped what she showed him was honest and true. He heard the light tread of boots on the fallen twigs and leaves before he saw the shadow then the man. His breath caught in the back of his throat while he remained dead still, frozen. He watched. His breathing stopped. The man's fist rose to knock on the door.

"Douglas!" Lilly had thrown open the door then eagerly hurled herself into the man's arms.

"Deadly little liar," he murmured softly.

His anger at her deception filled him. The question now was just who was Douglas and what did he mean to her? None of the crofters he knew of went by that name. So, what would she tell him when he confronted her with this one's identity?

The man kissed her on the forehead, a chaste kiss that sent his fists into tight balls. Jealousy was not an emotion he expected or ever experienced. He never got that close to a woman. Even the woman he once thought was his mate never inspired jealousy. On silent feet, he padded cat-like to one of the windows. Setting his back against the wall, he listened to the conversation between them.

"You cannot stay here any longer," Lilly told the man, her voice soft a seductive murmur. He wanted to hear that same tone when he kissed her while she turned to liquid in his arms. "It's not safe and well you know it. You put me in danger as well as the clan if you continue. After all the McKenna has gone through to keep neutrality here, I cannot..."

"Hush now, Lilly. I would never do such a thing. Perhaps it is best I return and clear my name."

"Is such a thing possible?" she asked sounding breathless and out of sorts.

When he snuck a peak at the couple, Douglas was holding her, her long slim body pressed against his. The man's hands were around her waist. Rage he'd never felt before simmered, waiting to explode. He tried to remind himself she wasn't his, at least not yet. He needed patience to mold her to his desires.

"Perhaps not at this point." He stroked her hair. "If I leave, will you be safe here? This might be our last time."

"I *ken* it, Douglas."

"I saw you with one of the sons."

"I'm sure I'll be safer than you," she told him softly. "Where will you go?"

Brady wanted to laugh at her words. She wouldn't be safe from his attention, from his desperate need to possess her. No, she was acting to confident about her ability to tell him she didn't want him as much as he did her.

"Farther into the highlands, north where fewer people live. Mayhap I'll find a ship sailing for America. Leave this all behind. Start a new life across the ocean. I've heard a man can live there, pursue his dreams. I would miss London though. Would miss my betrothed even though I know she'll move on to another man." He kissed her again, a gentle kiss on her cheek. "Perhaps you could join me."

Over my dead body, Lilly, you aren't going to leave me.

"I will think of you. I love you, Douglas. Where ever you go take care." She reached up, placing her palm on his cheek.

Brady's breath stopped as he digested her words, telling himself it didn't make any difference how she felt about that man. He still wanted her, the little harlot. When he first saw her, it made no difference to him how well used she was. Now she confirmed his guess. He knew there had been at least one man in her life. He would erase this man from her memories.

"If my father finds you?" Douglas asked, "What then?"

"I won't go back to London. I can't live that way nor can I marry that man I'm betrothed to."

His gut tightened at her words. She was meant to wed another man. He would see about that, send out a few inquiries about Lillian Townsend. He meant to discover the truth about the woman. His woman.

"You might not have a choice," Douglas said, smoothing her hair from her forehead. "The contract has been signed."

"You could stop it."

"Nay, not even if I could wed you myself, could this nightmare for us end. If you were to wed someone else, well, perhaps then."

"Who would want me, or want to take a chance? Lord Claymore is filled with revenge as well as hate. He would kill anyone who took what he thinks is his."

"Lord Claymore cannot hold a pistol his handshakes so bad."

"He has the coin to hire the finest assassins. You take care, little one. Don't let anyone sway you to do something you don't want to do. Don't let the McKenna—"

They both turned, searching the woods for the sound they heard. "Go," she said. "What if it's the English searching for you? For us? I couldn't bear for them to discover your intentions."

"It would be a random bit of luck on their foolish parts. No one of any position even realizes your mother was Scottish. That she lived here before she wed Lord Townsend. No one will search for either of us here in the remote highlands."

Brady ducked down, moving silently behind a tree as he watched the couple from a greater distance, unwilling to give himself away as Douglas left the cottage.

"You will stop. Promise me you will stop."

"I cannot."

Chapter Two

The following day Brady had a lot to think over, his thoughts turning from jealousy to rage then back again, jealousy a new emotion for him. While Lilly was at work, he avoided the hall, unable to watch her moving from person to person, a seductive smile on her radiant face. She laughed and talked with all, seeming to enjoy herself thoroughly. She was poised, her chin tilted showing a regal air to all who watched. While he intended to confront her soon, he'd not settled on exactly how to go about that confrontation.

Best case she would tell him the truth.

Most likely she would lie.

Having made the decision to avoid her for the morning, he left for the village with every intent to restock her cupboards. Doing things for her pleased him. Whistling a jaunty tune, he made his way to the stables. Fifteen minutes later he was at the village store, buying all types of supplies to make Lilly's life more comfortable. He meant to deliver the goods then stretch out on her big bed in order to test its comfort as well as to wait for her to come home this afternoon.

Lilly, however, might not be pleased to see him. Ah, but perhaps she would be. She just wouldn't show him her appreciation, not yet. The little game of waiting had to be played out first, advance then retreat. He would enjoy only so much but he did intend to give her time. Patience, he repeated to himself over again and again. She would come around to his way of thinking in time.

For the first of summer the weather was unseasonably warm. Sweat beaded on his forehead, slipping down his face as he worked.

Outside, he continued loading the parcels he purchased for Lilly into the cart. Immersed in thought he didn't notice the changing surroundings.

"Whatever are you doing here, Brady McKenna?"

His sister, Crissie, stood in front of him, hands on her hip, toe tapping. Her grin wide, she appeared to know exactly what he was up to.

"Sis, nice to see you too."

Truly, he didn't want to have this conversation with his little sister. Didn't want to acknowledge his less than chivalrous behavior toward Lillian Townsend, a woman he couldn't purge from his mind, a woman who appeared to have bewitched him. It seemed he was a besotted fool where this lady was concerned.

"This cart is nearly full." Crissie tugged on the tarp he draped over his purchases as she examined the contents of the cart. "Flour? Salt and sugar? Tea? Looks as if you purchased more food than a lady can eat." She continued ticking off the items inside the cart. She slanted him a devilishly sinful grin.

Good God, she couldn't know his intentions where Lilly was concerned, could she? She was innocent, untried, couldn't possibly understand he meant to keep Lilly as his mistress or what that entailed? Perhaps he should pay more attention to what Crissie was up to.

"Imagine that." Brady wasn't about to explain anything to his little sister. She was much too observant.

"What's this?" Crissie held up a lavender silk peignoir.

"Wishful thinking," Brady murmured. "Put it back, brat."

"I'm sure father would like to hear about this." Her skirts swished as she made her way to the other side of the cart so she could look more closely at the items there. "What do you think? Should I tell him you disobeyed his request?"

"Keep your mouth shut," he muttered realizing his sister could cause a great deal of trouble if she wished. A bribe here might be in order. However, he was pretty sure his sister would never give him away.

He knew that.

She knew that.

Still the game needed to be played out to both of their satisfaction.

He needed to discover a secret of hers so he could hold it over her head. She grinned sweetly at him, lowering her lashes slightly. Blessed hell but he felt sorry for any of her suitors. With that look she could have a man wound around her so tight he couldn't breathe let alone think. She wasn't a shifter so her life mate might not be found the same as his. In any case, Crissie understood there was someone out there waiting for her. Would be special to her when she found him. Brady also knew his sister wouldn't settle for less than an all-consuming love. She resented the fact she wasn't a shifter. At times such as this, she used the fact to her advantage. A man would have to be found for her that she couldn't manipulate.

"Tell me more about her. This new woman in your life. You must think a great deal of her, must want her *verra* much." Rummaging through the parcels she pulled out another gown, simple but beautiful still made in a light shade of blue to match her eyes. "This wasn't meant for me, was it?"

Thinking about his sister as well as what she thought she knew, he hefted a few more packages into the cart.

"None of your business."

It appeared Crissie wasn't about to stop the interrogation. "Lilly, she's the woman father warned you to leave alone, isn't she? You're not doing that are you? All this is for her. Does she want it?"

Of course, Lilly wanted the purchases he bought for her. She was just playing with him, toying with him until he gave her everything she craved. She is using me. Just as I am using her. He could hardly tell his little sister the truth about Lillian Townsend. He didn't understand the deep penetrating draw she had on all his senses.

He wouldn't be her first lover nor would he be her last. Nor did he care.

That thought struck him hard. Telling himself he didn't care wasn't truly how he felt. Thoughts of Lilly beneath another man, giving herself to someone else sent a slow simmer burning through him, an urge to kill. The image of the man she kissed last night seared in his mind. For him, these feelings weren't normal. He should take a step back, reevaluate his sentiments, put his feelings for the woman in perspective. He understood from the beginning she wasn't a virgin. So, why was he allowing her infidelity get to him?

"She will be receptive to everything I give her, Crissie," he said softly, reliving the images in his mind of her stretched out naked on her big bed. Distinctly, he pictured himself entangled in her arms, her long silken hair wrapped around him. It's fire heating both of them. Every male part of him tightened, hardening with the need generated by his wicked thoughts.

"So, sure of yourself big brother? Seems the lady has a mind of her own," Crissie said appearing emboldened by what she saw. "After all, I noticed last night she didn't wait for you to escort her home as you commanded. What happened when you caught up with her?"

Brady made it a point to ignore most of what his sister said as well as what she thought she saw. This time he understood Crissie was wrong. He wasn't over confident where Lilly was concerned. No, when it came to this lady he was sweating with apprehension. "It's getting late. Why don't you tie your horse to the cart? You can ride home with me." He needed to see Crissie home before he set out for the crofter's cottage.

"Alright," she grinned shamelessly. "'*Twould* please father if you escorted me home. With what is going on behind his back, you should do this for yourself."

"You're all about pleasing father? When did this happen? Get in." Brady set the remaining packages into the cart. He wasn't entirely looking forward to the time with his sister. Answering her constant questions about Lilly until they reached home would not be tenable. Crissie would have to let her curiosity simmer simply because he wasn't going to enlighten her. He meant to turn the conversation to her. "I'll have you home before the sun dips behind those hills. What the devil were you doing here so late?"

She stuck her nose in the air, refusing to answer his question. He mulled that over for a few minutes, thinking she might have been seeing a beau. If that were the case, he would have something to hold over her head.

"Did father *ken* why you were in the village?"

"Don't have to ask his permission to go to the village," Crissie shot back.

"That's not an answer, Crissie."

Five English soldiers walked by them. Brady felt a shiver, a gut reaction to the men travel up his spine. Before something happened he couldn't counter, he needed to find out who Douglas was as well as his relationship with Lilly. He watched as they walked by, their attention focused elsewhere.

One soldier stepped away from the group, eyeing Crissie while she smiled at him, her lashes lowered slightly. She was of age. Blessed hell, did she have any idea what she offered with the flirtatious invitation? The pair acted as if they knew each other intimately. He prayed they did not and that it wasn't wishful thinking on Crissie's part.

"Crissie McKenna," the man said, nodding at her, his voice bland. Yet his eyes were darkening, shimmering with what Brady thought might possibly be desire. He nodded. "Nice to see you again."

Once more she lowered her lashes before sending a blinding smile his way. The man's attention shot to Brady. "Why, Walker Endicott, I'm sure we'll see each other again."

He looked as if he wanted to speak with Crissie. Instead, he nodded again, gazing at her, his expression unreadable.

Brady watched the man's long strides as he closed the distance between them and the soldiers he was catching up with. The man looked over his shoulder only to see Crissie boldly meet his gaze.

Ah, he assumed she was hiding something. This little not so subtle incident confirmed his guess. Well, let her have her secrets. It was up to Connal to watch his daughter not her brother. The ride home was silent, Chrissie's cheeks flushed prettily. When they reached the castle, he stopped long enough for her to hop out of the cart and get her horse.

"Will I see you at dinner?"

"Not tonight, brat. I'm eating elsewhere."

"Don't call me that," she told him over her shoulder as she turned her back to him.

Brady chuckled to himself as he watched her march away, her

nose in the air. Suddenly, he was looking forward to this evening with higher expectations than he should have. His time with Lilly Townsend would progress a bit more. He didn't mean to push her too far too quickly. It appeared to him, she had an agenda of her own making.

If he could manage his lust for her, he would pretend to fall in with her plans. That was the problem. He didn't know if he could do that, keep his lust in check.

When he reached the Fraser place, he set about unloading his purchases. By his calculations he had about an hour before she reached home. He bought dinner for them along with a couple of bottles of wine. They wouldn't drink both tonight. If anything tangible happened between them, he wanted her choice not to be muddled by alcohol. No, she would have a clear mind if she allowed him liberties.

After pulling out his watch, he set the table bringing the two crystal glasses to a side table in the main room. With the bottle opened, he strode into the bedroom and stretched out on the bed. Closing his eyes, he imagined Lilly next to him.

Ah, he sighed softly, putting his hands behind his head. He wondered what expression she would have on that lovely face when she first noticed him. He chuckled softly in anticipation, expecting her to be slightly flushed from the walk home, her cheeks a lovely shade of peach.

A few minutes later the door opened, her footsteps sounded on the wooden floor. She paused, he assumed to remove her cloak then hang it on the hook near the door. The tread of her slippered feet made their way into the main living room. Once more she stopped. Brady assumed she noticed the bottle of wine set with the two crystal glasses.

"Brady McKenna." His name barely discernible whispered from her soft lips. "What the devil...?"

He saw her in the doorway to the bedroom, her face flushed, fists tight at her sides, anger blazing in her eyes. When she parted her lips, they were moist, ready to receive a kiss. He wondered if she comprehended how seductive she looked framed in the doorway, her wild red-blond hair framing her lovely face. Little ringlets curled beneath her chin.

"Welcome home. Obviously, I've been waiting for you."

He knew the moment her gaze focused on his naked chest. Comprehended the instant she realized he was here to sweet-talk her into her bed, to lie with him. Understood she would have to give him a resounding no to stop him from pursuing his goal. A weak no would be telling him a hesitant yes.

Lilly surprised him as she turned, striding from the room. She didn't say a word. He heard the front door open then close. He decided to stay put for the time being, realizing she needed time to think, to process. A few minutes later she stood in the doorway again.

Her lips stretched to a thin line she stared at him for the longest time, seeming to stretch into an eternity. "I don't want you here."

She walked from the bedroom. He heard as she poured wine into a glass. She sat down. He wondered how long it would take her to turn up in the bedroom again. He wasn't going to say anything until she returned. Anticipation of how she might respond coursed through him.

Suddenly, she was beside the bed, the contents of her glass on his face. He sat up, sputtering, laughing as he reached out taking hold of her wrist, tugging her until she fell on top of him with a screech.

"That, my lovely, was a waste of good wine. Would you care to taste the drops on my mouth? I wouldn't protest."

He liked the way she felt against him. Enjoyed the sensation of her soft breasts pushing against his chest. One hand wound into her hair, purging the locks of the pins holding the strands in place, the other settled on her slim waist. He squeezed. Ran his hand up her spine. Tenderly, he brushed his lips across hers. He gave her part of the distance she craved, holding her so her soft pants of air, whispered across his face.

"Cad." She pushed on his chest to no avail, her eyes blazing fire, scorching his senses.

Brady had no intention of allowing her all the distance she craved, at least not yet. He wiped the drops of wine from his face, licked his lips. With a fascination that pleased as well as tempted him, she watched his tongue.

"Kiss me," he said softly, waiting for her to comply. He wanted to taste her sweetness again. "Put your lips on mine. Give me your tongue."

"You're joking," she whispered, her breath stealing softly across his lips. "I would have to be mad to want to kiss you."

"But you do."

"No."

She was so close to him her womanly scent enhanced by summer wild flowers wafted over him, enticing, beguiling. "Never joke about things like this. Kiss me. After that, I'll let you up."

"It's not a bargain I like."

"Ah, lass, you don't want to kiss me? If you tell me nay, I'll not believe you."

He ran a hand down her back, caressed the curve of her hips, lingered on the rise of her buttocks. She squirmed against him, her body molding perfectly to his. Deep in the back of his throat, he groaned. One hand traveled the length of her leg then back up, bringing fabric along with the stroke. The soft length of her leg met his caress. She squirmed again. With the continuing strokes of his hand, he brought the gown higher until his hand met the bare flesh of her bottom. She wiggled.

"Brady..."

"Kiss me."

"Promise you'll let me up?" she asked, a bit breathless.

Still, she didn't protest his exploration of her body. Once again, he ran his hand up then down her leg.

Against his chest, he felt the steady yet rapid beat of her heart seeming to meld with his. She ran her tongue across her lips, provoking him to a desperate need. As he stroked her hip, her lips parted even more. He knew she didn't truly object to him. Indeed, she must long for his possession as much as he yearned to possess. After all, it wasn't something new to her. She didn't say nay. He would be hard pressed to stop if she did.

"Kiss me," he wheedled, his voice husky.

Softly she brushed her lips across his before she looked at him, her lashes concealing most of her warm blue eyes. When she withdrew, he grinned at her, felt the devil inside him burst forth. He was touching her intimately where she was hot, moist, even swollen. She was allowing him an intimacy that would lead to the culmination of his cravings.

"For a well-practiced woman that kiss was a disappointment. I think you should try again. Make it count as a kiss this time."

Her brows narrowed, lips thinned. She protested with a push against his chest. "I'm not what you think I am."

"Still, it matters not. That was not a kiss worth calling a kiss. Try again if you want to eat and mayhap have a glass of wine. One that you drink though I wouldn't mind retaliating, dripping it across your breasts, tasting your silken flesh coupled with the wine. Would your taste meet my expectations?"

His hands never stopped their roaming even while one kept her in place atop him. He wasn't too sure why he prolonged this torture. In the position she was in, she was ripe for lovemaking. His body as well as hers was ready, in need. She wasn't denying him. He thought the dance between them would take longer. Now, he wasn't sure if he was disappointed.

"What is it you want me to do differently?" she asked as his hand closed over one perfectly shaped cheek, squeezing tenderly. "You should not be doing that."

"What shouldn't I be doing?" he asked blandly as if he truly had no idea what she spoke of.

"Touch me there." Her voice was whisper soft, weak with need. He heard the desire in the deep mellow tones.

"Where?"

"You know the answer to that." She gasped when his fingers explored once again finding more intimate territory. "Th—there."

Her eyes crossed as she looked at him while he continued to use everything in his means to tempt her closer to him. "I would like to hear it from your sweet lips," he paused for a few seconds. "Only after you kiss me. Kiss me, Lilly, then we can eat."

Brady kept his laughter behind his teeth when he heard the heavy sigh Lilly let rush from her lungs. He wondered why she continued to perform this show with him, toy with his need for her when she so very clearly wanted him inside her. She was not a virgin after all. Mayhap it was just the way she pretended her innocence to the men whom she meant to become intimate with.

Her past lovers must have liked this ploy.

Rapidly, he was losing patience with this scenario. He would much rather have her honest.

He watched her eyes darken, her tongue sweep across her lips as she slowly lowered herself so their mouths would meet. Sweetly, she touched upon him, moved her lips against his. He touched her with his tongue urging her to do the same. She did.

When he caught her tongue between his lips then pulled hers inside his mouth, a tiny ripple of pleasure mewed from her throat. Inwardly, he grinned. She took the initiative, playing with his tongue, nipping at his mouth just as he had done the day before.

Still, there was an untried innocence about her he didn't understand. Her pretense must be honed from years of practiced deceiving. This time when she pulled away, he reluctantly smoothed her skirts down around her legs. His hands dropped to his sides, wishing to roll her over while he assumed the upper position. He wouldn't, at least not yet simply because she fulfilled her part of the bargain.

Her eyes were glazed over with simmering passion, the desire clearly evident in their blue depths. "Was that good enough?"

"Aye," he said, his voice husky with the passion she generated in him so easily, "For now. Come, let's eat." He rose from the bed, holding out his hand for her to accept.

Lilly kept them by her sides, eyeing him skeptically. She was clearly shaken by the passionate kiss between them as well as his bold exploration of her body. He set his arm around her waist, ushering her into the main room where he set her in front of one of the ancient wing chairs. He built up the fire.

Smiling to himself, he strode into the bedroom to retrieve the crystal Lilly brought there. A few seconds later he poured them both a glass, "I will serve. You've been working all day. Relax now."

So far today, he felt pleased with his efforts to win Lilly over. She put on an exhibition, as did he. They both wanted each other to know who they were. She was more than receptive to his advances, his not so subtle wheedling her to come to him, give herself over to him. Even now she watched him, seemed to admire him.

When he returned with two plates piled high with the food he purchased in the village, her smile appeared reticent. He wasn't sure what to make of the expression. He thought she would be hungry, would be more than pleased at his attention to her needs.

"Shall we?" he asked, slowly lifting an eyebrow, searching her expression for information.

She nodded, the hair he dislodged earlier curling like silken fire around her shoulders. When she looked at him her usual warm blue eyes turned icy. He needed to know how the fire turned to ice so quickly.

"I am hungry," she admitted.

"As am I."

~ * ~

Lilly felt distinctly that Brady wasn't speaking about food but her. *I want you.* She swallowed the lump in her throat. Thinking of the kiss, the way his hands moved over her, she understood she should have told him no. Not about the kiss but the ardent, blatant exploration of her body. She allowed him to do what he wanted.

Picking at her food, she peered at him through lowered lashes all the while wishing she could read his mind. See his thoughts about her. He must think her brazen. Mayhap she could understand what he was thinking. It didn't take a mind reader to discern what he wanted from her was her complete submission. If she wasn't careful, she would give in to his gently yet not so subtle seduction. No there was nothing subtle about Brady McKenna. When or if she did say yes, he would know she didn't give her favors to anyone. He would be her first lover.

Silence generated a nervous edge as well as a fine trembling within her as she watched him from beneath lowered lashes. While she ate, her hands shook. Unable to eat, she set her fork on her plate.

"Who is Douglas?"

With his question, she jumped, startled by his words. "D-Douglas?" she asked parroting his question. How could he know about her brother? Fear at this knowledge rippled through her. Connal would never tell him something so private. It was her secret. She must keep it that way.

"Douglas." He grinned at her as if he knew something she didn't. With his elbow on the table, he moved his fork in the air in a tiny circle.

He couldn't possibly know anything about her stepbrother. Last night Douglas waited until Brady left to come into the cottage. He was very careful not to let his presence be known. Yet that had to be the way. He'd seen her with him as he must have doubled back to the cottage for some reason.

The meat she stabbed with her fork, looked unappetizing. She set her lips together in a thin disapproving line. Unwilling to tell him anything, she stared at the flames sizzling in the fireplace as they cast shadows. If she spoke of her brother, she would have to tell him why he was on McKenna land instead of his townhouse in London. She would have to tell him her purpose here.

"I don't know."

"Liar." He leaned close to her, his gaze riveted on her. Clearly, he was a man who would not take her dismissal of his question as a reason to stop asking. "Tell me who he is."

Once more, Lilly turned away from the man, from the subtle accusation in the tone of his voice. She stood, walking away from him to stare at the fire. "No. No, I cannot."

Outwardly relaxed, Brady leaned back, his hands across his stomach, the broad grin on his face disconcerting, confusing to her when she looked over her shoulder at him. She didn't want to have this conversation with a man she barely knew. With a man she just granted liberties to.

"A lover? Tell me now, Lilly."

"No!"

"Admit the truth, sweetheart," he spoke sardonically. His molten gray eyes simmering with anger that just now surfaced. "He is or was your lover. I won't share. Get rid of the man."

The sip of wine in her mouth spewed from her lips. He was angry over a man he believed to be a lover of hers. She marched back to her chair and sat down stubbornly, knowing he wouldn't believe her. Her mind spinning with words she'd like to call him. "I don't have any lovers," she told him despite the fact she meant to say nothing to him. She had not wanted to tell him anything she knew he wouldn't believe.

"Liar."

Her back stiffened, her eyes flashing. She felt heat shimmer up her body to rest on her cheeks. She lifted her shoulders in a futile attempt to show him her disdain. Letting this man get to her was not wise. "Believe what you will."

His breath left him in a long slow slide. "I will do just that. Believe me when I say I will discover the truth about you as well as the man you call Douglas. Lover or not, what does he have to do with you?"

"Nothing."

When she spoke, she saw his anger grow. All he wanted was the truth she couldn't give to him.

"Finish your meal." He stood, striding purposely to the kitchen. She heard the plate clatter on the counter. Wondered why he was staying in that room. Seconds turned to minutes. She closed her eyes, willing herself not to look for him.

When he stood behind her, she never heard the soft fall of his steps. His hands fell upon her shoulders. It seemed he meant for his questions to move in a different direction. "Why are you here, Lilly?"

"Not to become your mistress or whore, whichever word you would choose to use for my life. I don't care. My answer is no to both."

"A few minutes ago, you didn't tell me no, appeared to enjoy what we were doing together. Care to tell me why? What does it matter if you let me become your next lover?" he asked unemotionally, notwithstanding the tenor of his words.

While he spoke, his hands stroked her neck, along her collarbone. He ran a slightly rough fingertip along her jaw. The tremors coursing through her couldn't be stopped.

Despite or perhaps because of his lack of knowledge about her she was tempted to throw things at him. She didn't dare tell him the truth, so afraid for herself, for Douglas. They couldn't afford to be found out. She didn't have a doubt in her mind if he wanted, he would learn everything he was asking her now. Yet it would take time.

"Of course, what you think about me would make no difference if I actually wanted you." She was taken aback by the waver in her voice, the uncertainty, her confusion when he fondled her. He knew she wanted him, felt the desire in her kiss. For some reason when he looked at her, when he touched her, she lost all sense of herself all rational thought coupled with knowledge of right from wrong.

"Arguing will get us nowhere. Come, Lilly, tell me the things I ask. What have you got to lose?" He pushed the hair away from the back of her neck. She felt the subtle glide of his lips on her nape, shivered when his mouth touched the tip of her ear then the sensitive spot behind it.

She trembled, her body pulsing to his attentions, in tune with the tender movement. Her life as well as expectations could all be lost in a blink of an eye. If it was ever found out who she was, where she was from, she could be sent back to London. She would not be allowed from the betrothal contract her stepfather signed. Lord Townsend would go to great lengths to keep her confined to the townhouse until the wedding would take place. There was too much at stake to confide in a stranger, even a stranger who could wreak havoc with her body.

Before she could stop the words, "Everything," she said softly. To Lilly it was incredulous she spoke the truth to a man she'd known only a day. "I would lose everything. All that I am as well as all that I want to be." Aye, she would lose her heart as well as her soul.

"That sounds a bit extreme for a tumble or two," he murmured, watching her closely, too closely for her comfort. "Come now, explain yourself. Stop spouting generalizations that have no validity. Know that I would protect you, even from yourself if that became necessary. With me as your keeper you have nothing to worry about."

Lilly rose then, unable to sit still. For several minutes she wandered her home then left to walk outside. On the western hills the sun was setting. Vivid colors painted the sky crimson. In London it was rare to see such a beautiful display. A soft breeze ruffled her unfettered hair. She realized she loved it here, prayed she would not be forced back to London.

She stopped walking, staring toward the hills, silence surrounding the small crofter's cottage that had once been her mother's home. Her hands clasped in front of her, the life she once led vanished in a blur of fear for herself and a marriage she didn't want. No longer did she attend balls and fetes. No longer were days spent riding in Hyde Park showing off new gowns and finery with a man beside her. Her life here in the wild hills of the highlands was diametrically opposite. When he stepped behind her, his long fingers resting on her shoulders, she stopped breathing for a moment. Brady touched her in ways no other person had. To Lilly, it seemed he was already part of her she could never deny.

"Why do you resist me, Lilly?" He sounded perplexed, confused by her restraint where it came to telling him her secrets. "Why don't you trust me?"

Nothing he could do or say would convince her to tell him who she was. To reveal her personal trauma would leave her far too vulnerable as well as defenseless. He said he would discover who she truly was, what she hid. Days perhaps even months would pass before he would know the truth about her if he ever did. Even the few English soldiers passing through the territory didn't know her true identity. If they did, she didn't have a doubt that one or more would hand her over to Lord Claymore for the abundant reward he offered for information concerning her whereabouts.

Though, his father, Connal McKenna knew her, knew her mother when she lived here in the cottage. Was present the day she was born. Before her mother passed, she wrote to Connal, asked if he would help her daughter if she ever needed his aide or feared for her life. When Lilly needed Connal McKenna, he stepped up to the task.

His hands moved on her shoulders, massaging, lingering. An attempt, she supposed, to relax her, to bend her to his will perhaps. It would take very little for her to give into the not-so-subtle sweet-talking he employed against her will. He was an expert in what he did here. The fact of the matter was, he was charming, irresistible especially when he flashed his grin, when she looked into his compelling eyes. He was a well-practiced lover.

She wanted his kisses.

Yearned to know more of the physical pleasures he wanted to gift her with.

It was the other things besides the kisses she was unsure of. *Nay*, she dared not give her virginity away to a man who would not be her husband. A man who wanted her on his terms with no regard to her future because there would be no future between them. The thought sent a wave of despair into her gut. She didn't want to give her innocence to the old lecherous man she was supposed to wed. Didn't want to bear that man's children with the sole purpose of giving him an heir. Goose bumps rose on her arms. The thought of lying beneath Lord Claymore terrified her.

"You frighten me," she finally answered his question, not daring to turn in his arms to look into his eyes.

No, he terrified her but for far different reasons than why Lord Claymore terrified her. With little effort he could steal her heart and soul. Something she refused to give to any man unless he was willing to do the same for her.

Brady McKenna was not that man.

Ignoring her statement, he ran his hands down her arms, saying. "We should go inside. You're shivering."

She wasn't shivering because of the cold night air. She was shaking because with this tender touch he generated havoc within her. "Will you keep your hands to yourself?"

The question, she knew was pointless. Brady McKenna would do what he wanted when he wanted.

His chuckle confirmed her thoughts. "No."

She had not expected him to voice his thought so quickly. "I didn't think you would."

Perhaps it would be best to get this over with. If she gave herself

to him, would he go away, leave her alone to finish the work she began here? Most likely not.

"Come." He turned her, wrapping his arm around her waist, pulling her close. "I'm not going to take what you aren't ready to gift me with. Although when I kiss you, I know you're willing. Can feel the rapid, easy response to my kisses. Feel the way your pulse beats out of control when our lips are sealed together."

His body warmed hers, heated her from the inside out. She felt the solid wall of muscle against her softer curves. For a moment she set her head against his chest, wishing she could give in to his strength, allow him to give her the sweetest of pleasures perhaps even protect her from the dragons that might now be following her to this remote part of Scotland.

She could not.

"You don't know anything about me." After the fact, she understood he would pursue this. He would insist she tell him something.

"You could change that," he spoke softly, close to her ear. His breath whispered down her neck, sending another wave of shivers skittering throughout. "I would like very much for you to tell me all about yourself, every minute detail. Where do you come from, Sassenach? Why are you here? How many lovers have you had? The list would go on and on."

She shook her head, wishing life was different for her, wishing there was nothing for her to explain. "You don't understand."

"That's also easy to change," he spoke softly, sincerely, seemingly from the depth of his heart. "I'm willing to listen."

Lilly needed someone to listen to her, to understand the situation she found herself in. He wouldn't though. Brady McKenna would never allow her the freedom to continue escorting Jacobites to Inverness so they could leave Scotland. If he knew what she did in the middle of the night, what her brother was about, he'd find a way to put a stop to her endeavors.

"No, it is not. I cannot speak to you of anything."

"Perhaps I should change my mind, stay the night, or bring you to my rooms in the castle. Keep you from hurting yourself. I'm afraid for you. Suddenly, afraid you might do something foolish. What is it that you are about?"

Startled by his words she sucked in a deep breath of air. "You cannot."

"If I chose to do so, what would I discover?"

Pulling away from him, she turned to confront him. "No, you would discover nothing about me. There is nothing to tell you, no secrets, no intrigue, no lovers."

"Tonight maybe. What about tomorrow eve or the next?"

Brady was pushing her, challenging her until her very nerves unraveled. Despite her best efforts, he would continue to do so. Angrily, she strode toward the cottage. What would she do if he did settle into her home to keep track of her? For the first time in her life, she had the freedom to come and go as she pleased. He meant to take that from her.

Once inside, she poured herself another glass of wine. She sat down, gazing into the fireplace, watching the embers pop and crackle.

She drank deeply, hoping the liquid would give her courage. "I will not speak of my past nor the present or even my hopes for the future."

She realized then she didn't have much of a future to look forward to. It was too tenuous, could change with one tiny mistake.

He joined her but didn't drink the wine he poured. "Your past is the key to your future. Do you want to have a long happy life? I ask only because there are indications that you might be putting your very life in danger. I would not like to see anything happen to you. Tell me what you do? Talk to me of Douglas. If the man is not your lover then who is he?"

She watched his anger grow, saw the tick in his jaw where he clenched his teeth together. There was danger then there was extreme danger. Brady McKenna fit the latter category. He could not possibly have any idea what she was about. Lilly searched her mind for something, some tiny bit of information that would end his inquiries at least for the moment.

She could think of nothing he might believe or anything he might have heard to give this impression.

"I'm not leaving tonight until you give me something so I can trust you, trust that you will not do something foolish in the darkness."

"You've no right," she whispered, her voice unusually soft. "You walk into my life then try to take over it."

"I do have the right. If my guesses have any basis in truth, you put the life of my clan in jeopardy in more ways than just one. Why my father is allowing it, I don't *ken*, at least not yet. I will though. You cannot run from my questions forever, Lilly. I will know the truth."

She hissed in a swift breath of air, refusing to believe his words. "You have no idea."

His silver gaze focused unerringly on her. "I do. If I'm wrong, the only person who can change that fact is you."

"You would not believe me no matter what I say."

"Try me."

"I have already."

"Should we begin again, refresh my memory. It seems to me you've told me nothing of value nor have you hinted at anything that might appease me. If I didn't know better, I would believe you to be mute."

"No. There is nothing to refresh. You know everything I'm willing to give up. Which is nothing."

Desperate to remain strong, Lilly tried to keep her distance from this man who could so easily rip her heart into shreds.

Agreeing, "Which is essentially nothing," he reminded her, slanting one dark eyebrow upward.

Unable to meet his gaze she turned away from him, pushing her lips together, silencing herself along with her unwilling thoughts.

"Ah, Lilly, what's a man to do? You are a wee stubborn lass."

He swept her into his arms, dislodging her from the chair where she reclined, his intentions different from hers. All she wanted in the present was to impede his progress in taking her to bed. It seemed he was eager to dissuade her of that notion.

Gently, he pushed her hair aside. "It is so soft. Just as your skin, just as other parts of you. I'd like to leave nothing to chance where it comes to your body. I want you. But you know that." He pressed soft kisses along her neck, sending a tempest of fire pounding within. "Your heartbeat is fast, just as mine. Do they beat as one? Would you like that? To be as one with me, Lilly? I know I would like that."

Lightly, he stroked her shoulder then down her arm. His hand rested on her hip, caressing, squeezing tender, sensitive flesh. She sucked in a desperate breath of air.

"Brady..."

His name whispered from her lips in a soft caress against his cheek. Inadvertently, her hands rose to his chest, not to push him away but to draw him closer. God help her she couldn't, didn't want to say that single word which would stop him, desperate to learn what he sought to teach. If Lord Claymore found her, she would never know the touch of a gentle man, a man she wanted to love her more than just about anything.

"Do you want me, lass," he asked the question as his lips stroked hers, as his mouth sent fierce fire storms swirling in the pit of her stomach.

He stroked her, cupped her breast, his thumb traveling across the fabric atop the hardened peak.

She closed her eyes, wishing he would never stop while understanding she should say *nay*. Daring to answer him truthfully was not possible. She wouldn't give him that hold over her. If she did, she would be lost.

She was already lost.

His lips found more tender flesh, touched upon her ear, nibbled then sucked at the lobe. Sounds rippled upward seeming to come from deep in her belly. She found she moved against him, her hips seeking out something she didn't understand. In her most private places, she felt hot and wet. Shivers wracked her from her core within every part of her.

"Answer me," he told her, seemingly delighted in the affect he had upon her. "Tell me what I so need to hear. Lilly..."

His mouth slanted across hers, his tongue parting her lips before delving deep inside the dark recesses. She met his tongue with her own felt dark magic within his mouth as she became part of him with the kiss.

The heat of him, the strength of his body enchanted her, mesmerized and fascinated. He was so very different from her, hard where she was soft. "I cannot..." What she couldn't do was breathe.

"You can."

Just as he did earlier, he stroked her leg ever higher, caressed sensitive flesh until her body quivered, desperate in her need.

"What?" She squeaked as the palm of his had passed across the tender flesh of her belly.

Her hips moved to meet the caress, to encourage. In his arms she twisted. Her body quivering desperately for something she understood only he could give. "I'm so hot."

"That's the way you are supposed to feel, my sweet one. Just as you feel now, but of course, you know that. Play as many games as you will, Lilly. Understand though that I know who and what you are. I will give no quarter nor will I pretend you are something you are not."

His words were effectively a slap in the face. She woke from the tender cajoling that was Brady to realize he thought so little of her to call her a whore, well used. He meant to make her his mistress, nothing more, no tender feelings between them. All he craved was the physical side of this relationship. Her expectations did not exceed anything more than some man's mistress since she could be no man's wife.

Lilly found her voice. "No, Brady. No, you have to stop. I won't do this. I won't let you do this to me. You're plan on making me a rich man's whore. I won't allow it."

He leaned back, closing his eyes for a moment as he swallowed a long drink of air. "Perhaps it is for the best." He set his forehead against hers. "For now, at least we will wait."

"I don't understand," Lilly said, suddenly feeling as if the floor was pulled from beneath her feet.

"Don't think for a second that you won't be in my bed, my mistress. Not my whore. Don't ever say that word again." He ran his hands through his hair leaving it disheveled, standing on end. "I want you, Lilly. I won't rush your compliance even though you were melting in my arms just now. If I wanted, I could have taken you sitting on this chair."

She was shaking her head, attempting to defy him while she knew he was right about what he told her. "No."

"Yes, Lilly. If you continue to deny that fact you will force me to prove it to you."

Butterflies tumbled wildly around in her stomach. Thoughts of her betrothed changed those butterflies back into simmering desire for a man who had the ability to devastate her. She was suddenly very nauseous thinking of that Lord who wanted her only to conceive an heir.

At least Brady wanted her for her.

What she could give him. Were his intentions any better?

"What are you smiling at?" His voice was husky-soft, filled with desire for her yet clearly puzzled at the same moment.

A heady sensation swept through her as she unexpectedly decided she would gift him with her virginity. There were no more doubts. "I..."

Now that she made the decision, she wasn't at all sure how to tell him what she decided. It seemed too easy now. She ran her tongue across her lips, moistening them. He watched obviously fascinated.

"I?" His perfectly sculpted dark eyebrow rose skyward in question.

She swallowed her fear. Then she blurted in one breath. "I do want you, Brady McKenna. I'll be your mistress for as long as you want."

He sat back, blinking once as his gaze caught hers in a duel of wills. "Then we should come to terms with our expectations. There should be a contract, a verbal contract between a man and his mistress. What I envision as well as your expectations."

"I suppose we should." Brady was the man she wanted. Douglas would have been beside himself at what she decided, might even call him out if he heard. In the end her stepbrother had naught to say about her decision.

"May I ask why the sudden change of your mind?" Tenderly, Brady ran a long finger across her lips. His silver-gray eyes always changing color alight with questions.

"You very well know I haven't changed my mind. You sensed from the start I was yours. From the first time I saw you, I wanted you, knew I should deny the feelings. I wanted to touch your chest. Wanted to see you naked." She slowly lifted her shoulders. *I want to know what it is*

52

like with a man who is not old and fat, a man I desire. "The fight has gone out of me. Since the reason I was denying us both what we wanted has no value to me."

"What would that be?" There was curiosity in his eyes, the quirk of his lips. She understood he wanted more information.

"My virginity." She spoke bluntly even understanding her words would anger Brady. Even though he didn't believe her, she would always speak the truth if she was going to say anything at all.

"That statement is not worth a comment, Lilly mine." His voice dropped to a slow growl, clearly displeased. "We will put the notion of your innocence on the back shelf. I no longer want to hear those words from you."

She straightened, bolstering her courage to go on with this, at least for one more moment then she would do as he requested, speak of it no more. "You will discover I'm not lying."

"Perhaps I will. If what you say is true, when the time comes, I will apologize. However, the knowledge will not give me reason to wed you."

He rose then, carrying her to the bedroom seemingly intent on finding out the truth of her words. In a few moments this would all be over, all her fears, everything.

"You will be given reason to apologize." She smiled at him, touched a fingertip to his chin before settling it on his lips. With her decision a weight was lifted off her chest.

It seemed the discovery of her innocence was not meant to continue. The loud, boisterous knocking on the door along with his brother's voice interrupted them. He stopped halfway to the bedroom, swearing.

"This better be important," Brady mumbled as he set her back on the chair to stride to the door, quickly opening it.

Roby McKenna stood in the frame of the door, grinning as if he knew something he shouldn't. "Did I interrupt the two of you? Too bad. Father wants you, now. I'll stay here with your friend. Make sure Lilly is comfortable."

"No, you won't." Turning to Lilly, he spoke softly. "I will be back as soon as my business is finished. When I return, we can finalize our business."

For the time being, she didn't want either man in her small cottage, needed a moment to think over her decision as well as decide what she wanted from Brady. If he meant to dictate terms to her, she certainly could request a few things in return. With the news she breathed a bit easier. "I'm locking the door. You should return tomorrow."

"I have a key." His voice was low, smooth, provocatively impassioned. The simmer in his eyes told her arguing would be to no avail.

Lilly stiffened. Realities that could not be fought only dissuaded surfaced. Once again, her voice shaking, she didn't want to be in bed this evening to wake up to him crawling in beside her. As he said earlier, they had terms to discuss a contract between them. "You don't mean that. You would come into my home in the middle of the night, invade my privacy?"

"My home now."

"No." She was shaking her head while knowing if she dealt with him this way what he spoke was true. If she agreed to his proposition, he would own her.

"Sleep well," he said softly, reaching out to stroke her cheek. "If the time is unreasonable, I won't be back until the morning. Do not go into work. You no longer need to. I want you to stay here, in this house."

"What you want you get."

"In this case, yes."

The evening had barely begun. She didn't know what to think. Perhaps she could spend the rest of the night sorting out her feelings. From the purchases he made this morning, he would keep her in style. He told her she didn't need to work. She wasn't sure how she felt about that. Her work now was only to make her less conspicuous. She had more than enough funds at her disposal to live this life she adopted.

She didn't want his money or his gifts, deciding then she would dictate her terms in this arrangement.

He would do things her way or not at all.

~ * ~

The meeting with Connal McKenna was insignificant to Brady. It was meant simply to reinforce his father's request to leave Lillian Townsend alone. Brady had been candid with his father, telling him he wanted her. If Lillian was agreeable, they would become lovers. His father had naught to say over this despite the deep frown lines of disapproval creasing his brow.

"I will not make a promise to something I can't keep," Brady told the man who brought him up, set his values in place. "You cannot possibly understand since I do not either. Any other time I would bow down to your request. This time I will not. She is meant to be mine. And she will be."

After several seconds of reflection, "Is she your mate, son?" Connal asked even though he told Brady a few days ago Lilly was not his mate.

Brady suffered a deep sense of confusion where Lilly was concerned. He never felt this way about another woman. He lifted his shoulders shrugging, staring at his father, seeking answers. "How does a man know such a thing? All I know is that I have to have her. She is part of my soul, my heart. She belongs with me."

For the rest of my life? The question was too real to Brady. What he did *ken* about Lilly was that he wanted her more than anything he'd ever wanted his entire life. She sparked a flame deep inside him, created a magic he could not do without along with a desperate need he couldn't explain.

"For someone else, I cannot answer candidly or give you the answer to your question. I realized Wynnie was my mate almost to the moment I first encountered her. Once the dust settled around her feet, I knew I wanted her as I've wanted no other woman. I acted in ways that were foreign to me. Didn't truly understand."

"That does not tell me much."

Why would he consider a woman such as Lilly to be his mate? A woman who'd had lovers before him. He never thought his mate would be anything except a virgin. What brought her inexplicably to the highlands? Although his father's description of his feelings toward Wynnie matched what he was feeling toward Lilly, he agreed with Connal. Lillian Townsend could not possibly be his mate. She was simply a driving force within him for now.

"If you discover she is your mate, it is of course, something you will need to explain to Lilly. She is not a shifter. She won't understand."

"You're sure of that fact," Brady said, wondering how much his father knew that he did not.

"No, I'm not sure of anything where Lilly is concerned," he said softly. "She is an enigma to be figured out. If you wish to take the time."

When Brady left the sudden meeting with his father, he needed to run. The depth of his soul had just been jarred by his father's revelations. He was restless, out of sorts, perplexed a bit, disoriented as well. He wouldn't be fitting company for Lilly tonight, for their first physical encounter. Their first lovemaking could wait for tomorrow when he could give her everything she deserved. When he understood the questions plaguing his mind.

Brady reached a wooded area where he liked to run, understanding the need for isolation was important. This place was private, secluded. Quickly he disrobed, felt the usual tingling of all his nerve ending as he began to change form. The sensation incredible when he was all black panther, every animal instinct kicking in, the primitive drive so very important to his survival to who he was. He brought a deep breath of air into his lungs in preparation for the burst of speed that would soon take over his entire body.

Pausing for a few seconds, surveying the path he meant to take, he set off at an easy lope. Once the trail widened, he picked up his pace, running hard with the intent to exhaust his body. After many minutes, he slowed to an easy jog, realizing he had left the protection of the wooded area behind him. Still, he didn't hear or see another living soul. There were no foreign scents.

Despite his usual caution he continued. His destination was the nearby loch. No one was about, he was sure of it. The swim in the cold water would cool his ardor.

With his breath back, once more he ran. Mindlessly he raced with little thought to the direction. Forest gave way to rolling heather lined hills. Seconds turned to minutes as he continued his path. The nearby loch stretched out in front of him. The hills lost the decorative trees as they turned to rocks. Here he was vulnerable. Still, none of his senses picked up on a human. He heard no sound and there was no scent brought by the wind.

He drew up short then sat staring at the water as it rippled along the bank.

Ah, Lilly, what would you think of me if you saw me now? Did it matter? Perhaps not in the scope of things. Would she care if she knew exactly who he was? He'd been less forthcoming with her than she'd been with him.

They both harbored secrets.

The sound of horse hoofs in the silent night air coupled with the scent of man sent Brady into the loch. Beneath the water he shifted, hoping the person about to find him would not think twice about his lack of clothing. The situation didn't bode well in this instance. He would have to do a lot of fast-talking.

Chiding himself for his carelessness, he understood the risks. Even in this isolated part of the country there were dangers for a shifter. He was about to encounter the worst danger of all, man.

He rose, the water reaching his waist. Sliding his fingers through his hair, squeezing some of the liquid from the strands he remained where he was, waiting, evaluating the moment. He was at a definite disadvantage here.

The man staring at him was the English soldier he met earlier, the man who seemed to be watching his sister. *Nay*, mesmerized by his sister.

"Hello."

Brady didn't miss the laughter in the soldier's voice. "Walker Endicott at your service?" He would have strode from the water if there was clothing on the bank. Would have dressed quickly then gone about his business. Thinking of Lilly left him vulnerable. His innate caution vanished with the ever-changing winds.

Walker leaned on the saddle horn, sporting a crooked grin. "You always come way out here without clothing?"

"What makes you think I've nothing to wear?"

Walker spread his hands wide, searching the area for the evidence. "Not unless you've left them on the other side. You've nothing to dress yourself in."

Brady felt a wave of disgust with himself. He wasn't afraid of this Englishman, yet the man could make life difficult for him.

Walker reached into his saddlebags, tossing a pair of pants along with a shirt on the ground, his intent clear. "You should be more aware. A group of English soldiers approaches downwind a few miles to your left. Suggest you get dressed now. You have a horse nearby?"

Blessed hell, at least four miles from here. He'd run, but he needed to shift. At the moment, he couldn't do that. Swiftly he left the water, donning the clothes set out for him. Walker was larger. The breeches didn't fit him like a second skin as his did, his shoulders broader.

"Thank you." There was nothing more he could say.

Walker held out a hand. "Would you like a lift?" Walker was laughing again, clearly amused at his expense. "Point me in the direction of your horse and I presume more importantly your outer coverings. I'll take you there."

He mounted behind Walker. "Where are the other soldiers going?"

"Headed toward McKenna castle. I took a scouting turn. Needed to think. Told them I would catch up to them later."

"I see." Caution captured Brady's thoughts as he wondered what this man believed.

In less than an hour they stopped. Brady quickly dismounted.

"Don't worry about the pants and shirt. I'll pick them up tomorrow. I know what you are, Brady McKenna. You have nothing to fear from me." With that said Walker turned his horse, galloping from the scene.

Brady watched him go. As he mounted his horse, he shook his head as if the movement would clear his mind. Nothing helped. *I know what you are.* Blessed hell, the man *kenned* he was a shifter.

What to do now?

He had just put his clan into more danger than Lilly ever could.

Chapter Three

Lilly's presence in the kitchen the next morning didn't please Brady at all. He didn't want her to work since he planned on providing for her. He supposed that discussion would reach fruition when they discussed the contract between them, including what she could and couldn't do, incorporating the fact that she was not working in the kitchen. On his way out, he stopped long enough to whisper to Lilly he would be gone for several days, to behave herself as well implying she wasn't to take a lover while he was gone. After the rendering of his words, he saw the stiffening of her back.

Connal tried to convince him this mission to Inverness was mandatory, necessary in so many ways. He wasn't convinced. Roby was to accompany him on this fool's errand that didn't seem to have purpose. They would travel together, perhaps to keep tabs on him, perhaps for him to keep tabs on his little brother. In the past, a trip to the city meant they were given leave to play, to challenge their masculinity as well. In the city they both had mistresses. Brady thought to dismiss his on this trip.

All he wanted in the present circumstance was to reinforce his relationship with the blue-eyed beauty who mesmerized him, challenging him in more ways than he cared to admit. He wanted to make love to her, craved to hear her tiny moans of ecstasy she would garner beneath his hands. He wondered how Lilly would use her time during the next few days until he returned hoping her time spent would not be in the kitchen. Breath rushed from him as he realized she would show up to work every day he was gone. He understood the point she created. She would not be beholden to him in any way.

Now, he looked to the fading light, to the harbor along with the ships waiting to sail. For a moment, he could have sworn he caught sight of Douglas. His gut flipped over. The need to confront the man swamped him, along with the need to discover what he meant to Lilly. He started forward, stopping himself midstride.

He assumed a lover.

Brady knew he would have to deal with that fact, would have to learn to come to terms with the other men in Lilly's life, something he didn't like at all. In the past a woman's previous lovers meant nothing to him. What he did know was that there would be no other men in Lilly's life now and forever. That one word, forever, caught him off guard.

"What's got you frowning so," Roby asked, his smile stretching across his grinning face as it seemed he noticed a group of seaside whores standing in front of a well-known waterfront establishment.

"You should not be thinking of spending well-earned coin on the likes of them. You might come home with something you don't want," Brady muttered with the understanding both men had women they typically spent the night with when they visited the city.

"Just looking," he said shrugging his shoulders. "Can't fault a fellow for that. How about you? You going to your usual haunt?" Roby's voice held a dare Brady didn't miss.

For a fact, Brady wasn't sure what he would do when he left home. Now, the thought of bedding a woman other than Lilly was abhorrent to him. Something else that wasn't typical of his behavior. "No, think I'll find a room somewhere else for the evening. After we visit this tavern father sent us to. What do you suppose he thinks we'll discover?"

Roby let his head fall back roaring with laughter as he slapped his brother on the back. "You are smitten. Think she's your mate?"

Brady was in the midst of adamant denial. Not for one second did he believe his mate would be a well-used woman, one who gave her favors to anyone willing to bed her. "No. I do believe my mate will be a virgin. From all indication, Lilly is not." That was a truth he wasn't able to deny. Deep in his mind it was a fact.

"So, you *ken* for a fact Lilly Townsend is no innocent lass. You've had her then? You know for certain or are you still making assumptions?" Roby asked clearly amused at his expense. "Assumptions can get a man into trouble and then more of the same."

"Under the circumstances as sure as I can be," Brady murmured not wishing to discuss this one particular woman with his brother. Who and what she was, only something for him to *ken*.

"So, you've not made love to her. That's what has you so testy, on the edge enough to give up your current mistress? Seems that might be the resolution to all your confusion. Make love to the woman, in the process vanquishing all your suppositions." One eyebrow shot upward in clear disbelief.

Disliking the tenor coupled with the direction of his brother's questions as well as his comments, "None of your business. When the time is right, I'll make that decision to have her."

He laughed again. "You haven't."

"Perhaps we should put this conversation I'm not willing to have to the side. Go see your mistress. I'll meet you in the morning right here." Brady's slipped his hands through his hair, frustration the only feeling coursing through him.

"Not yet. We still need to check out the tavern father suggested. Said the men seeking to help the Jacobites from Scotland frequent this place. Seems we would just get ourselves into trouble if we're seen there."

"You're probably right. Father did tell us to take care. We are here just as observers. Our only mission is to report back to the head of the clan as to what exactly is transpiring in the city, specifically this tavern."

"So, we are spies. This is getting more interesting by the second. Who do you *ken* we are to spy upon?"

Suddenly Brady didn't like the direction of his thoughts. Before Roby and he left for the city, his conversation with his father had circled Lilly. Perhaps they were to spy upon her. Perhaps not, yesterday he left Lilly in the kitchen. What business could she possibly have here let alone at the dockside tavern whose upstairs rooms doubled as a whorehouse?

What indeed.

Once again, all his preconceived notions about the pretty lady were affirmed. He had taken too much time with her, letting her dictate their relationship. He treated her as if she truly was a virgin. She was not.

"If you're as thirsty as I am, we could go inside, find a dark inconspicuous corner where we can see without being seen. A pint of ale would be nice. Perhaps a bite to eat would not be out of order."

"Indeed, the more I think on this, the more I'm excited to see just what we uncover here. Could not be a dangerous mission or he would have told us more, given more information."

His gut told him he wouldn't like what he found inside, and his inner thoughts were seldom if ever wrong.

Inside, the place reeked of unwashed bodies and spilled ale. Laughter along with shouts and lewd comments echoed around the room. Scantily clad women sauntered through the main, candle lit room to disappear in the back before returning. A few would disappear up the steps for a bit. Their return to the main room took longer.

Brady and Roby found the secluded corner they spoke of settled in with a pint of ale, watching and waiting. A plate of warm bread arrived along with a bowl of fruit and chesses.

One of the tavern wenches sidled up to Roby, sitting on his lap. Brady shook his head at his brother even while Roby's hand found its way up her skirt to the delighted giggles of the lady. Roby winked at him silently telling him he could get a bit of relief from what ailed him if he so chose.

"You can't be verra old, lass. What are you doing working in a place like this?" Roby asked while he boldly explored bared flesh.

"You going to take me away from this fun, set me up as your mistress?" she asked leaning into him, her large breasts nearly spilling from her miniscule bodice, a corsage meant for just that purpose.

"No." Roby set her aside laughing but not before giving her a playful pat to her buttocks. "No, not today. I've a mistress."

"You sure. I'll give you whatever you want for the right price. I've got everything a man such as yourself could yearn for." She blinked several times as she bent over giving him a full-frontal view of her charms.

Brady was doing his best not to laugh while Roby tripped over his tongue to placate the little whore. "Not today, sweetheart."

After a second pint, Brady was beginning to feel as if they'd been sent on a fool's mission. Nothing untoward was happening. He sat back, closing his eyes for a moment, thinking about Lilly, the way her plush curves molded perfectly to his hard body. If he weren't here, he'd be in her bed with her tucked in nicely beside him or beneath him.

The sudden silence caught his attention waking him from his stupor of bliss. What had once been a raucous room seeped in pandemonium now issued little noise, the silence uncanny. A pan somewhere in the kitchen dropped. A bar maid giggled. More and more silence followed.

"Would you look at all that red hair?" a man said so loudly Brady sat up straight.

"Wouldn't you just love to run your hands through it? Wonder what it feels like?

"Would be enough to warm a man in the coldest night all wrapped around him," another man was heard from the front of the room near the stairs.

"Would rather see what's below that worn out cloak, have her long silky legs wrapped around me than her hair."

"Beneath the dress." Another confirmed what both men in the room where thinking.

Brady stretched to see the object of the men's attention feeling his gut twist, searching for the cause of the silence along with the woman these sailors were talking about. The mention of red hair caught his attention. What he saw stole his breath. He leaned forward, his heart lodged in his throat. The object of his imaginings was making her way up those very stairs to the rooms above.

His fists tightened. She was supposed to be at her home or in the kitchen. When he started to stand, Roby placed a hand on his arm. "Best you wait a few minutes. It would do no good to you or Lilly to go barging into every room above. Do you suppose this is why father sent us here? Do you think he *kens* something about her he wants you to know?"

He heard Roby's questions. While he had no answers, he certainly meant to discover why his mistress was visiting another man, "No, just one room. What the blessed hell is Lilly doing here? Why didn't she stay put where I left her? I thought she was safe."

"Calm yourself. Those are all questions you will be asking her as soon as you get the chance."

"Does she have any idea what could happen to her up there? Is she meeting someone?" Deep inside his blood pulsed, heated, his anger increasing. He didn't recall ever feeling this furious. His question was where his anger was directed, to the woman walking up those stairs or the man she was meeting. She had to know what to expect. He told her he didn't share.

"Again, things you will have to ask your woman," Roby said a tinge of amusement coating his voice. "If you listen really hard you might be surprised at her answers."

"She's not forthcoming with information."

"Oh?" This time Roby did chuckle softly.

"She avoids questions, refuses to answer anything. I've sent off several letters of inquiry pertaining to Lillian Townsend, but those might take months to prove helpful."

"Have you given it any consideration that those very letters might put Lilly in further danger. Haven't you *kenned* she might just be running from something or someone?"

Well, no, Brady had not thought anything of the sort. He cursed softly, wishing he wasn't so thoroughly involved he couldn't think straight. She was a witch, a beautiful disarming witch.

His very own enchantress.

"How long do I need to wait?" Brady gritted out having lost all pretense of patience, his gaze riveted on the stairway, praying she would descend before he could no longer contain himself or his anger before he went after her.

Finally, he saw her tiny black slippers at the top of the steps followed by the worn brown cape. Showed a hint of ankle as she descended. This time when he rose, Roby allowed him to pursue her. A few quick strides brought him to her side, his hand wrapped her elbow, pulling her away from the steps.

"Not a word," he told her while his fingers moved to her hand, tugging her toward the table where Roby still sat.

They didn't make it that far. A group of redcoats walked into the tavern silencing the room once more. Before their gazes were directed his way, Brady pulled her into his arms then pushed her against the wall. "Wrap your legs around my waist."

"What?" Her eyes were wide with confusion, her small body trembling against his. For a moment before he remembered where she just came from. He felt the cad.

"Now." His command was whispered but she clearly understood the urgency.

Her legs were wrapped around him. His lips took hers possessively while his hand cupped her breast, tugging on the fabric so it enclosed tender soft flesh. She squirmed against him, fighting him.

"No, Lilly, don't fight me, not now, not this time."

He pulled away from her to say the words before his mouth came down hard once more across hers. One hand held a leg to keep her from letting go of him. With a desperate breath, "This could be a matter of life or death."

To Brady she must have believed him at least a little. Her hands wound into his hair, holding him close, accepting the blatant actions he used to claim her as his. A soft sound of surrender coupled with what he hoped was pleasure despite the circumstance rippled from her throat. He made sure no one could see her behind him, or exactly what he wasn't doing.

Minutes later, "Now," he whispered, tugging at the corsage of her dress until it completely covered what it just an instant before revealed, "we're going to get out of here. You're not going to say one word. You're going to go with me without a thought or a moment of protest."

He looked toward Roby who nodded following them from the tavern.

At a brisk stride the three of them wound their way through the alleys of Inverness to the stable to their horses. Lilly didn't say a word. Brady was surprised she had not complained about the rushed exit and rapid pace he set or the way he blatantly took liberties. She was bent over sucking in each breath as if it was meant to be her last.

"Stay here, Roby. Go back to the tavern so you can keep an eye on it for a while. We will push for home. Follow as soon as you can get free. We'll stop for the night at the usual spot. Lilly needs to be far away from this place before all hell breaks loose."

His thoughts were all on Lilly's safety. He didn't know what she'd been up to, but he sure as hell meant to find out.

"You can't possibly make it tonight. Wouldn't it be belter to...?"

With a wave of his hand, Brady cut off Lilly's words. He knew what he was going to say. Brady wanted to get as far away from the city as soon as possible even if it meant he wouldn't sleep.

"We're going. If you can, meet us at the cave." He turned then to Lilly. "How did you get here?"

One hand was clasped over her chest, her breaths still labored. Her eyes were wide as she still struggled for a piece of normalcy. "I brought the cart. Ironically, the horse I borrowed from the McKenna stables is over there as is the cart."

"Roby, bring these home when you leave."

After saddling his horse, he lent a hand to Lilly pulling her up. She sat in front of him, his hands around her waist. He wanted to throttle her for this evening's deeds. Needed to find a way to tell her how much danger she put herself in, but he had the strange feeling she knew and would do it again. Instead, he let her lean against him. Her hands rested on his forearms. He felt each deep, ragged breath as she inhaled and exhaled.

Away from the city lights, the night was black. Few stars could be seen through the dense foliage. The darkness was a help as well as a hindrance. He knew when she fell asleep. He would allow it, for in a few hours' time she would have to answer his questions.

Still Brady wasn't sure how he could make her do that, respond to his inquiries. His breath rushed out in a soft laugh. She did confound him, this muteness of hers. At first, he expected her to tell him everything. Hours slipped by. Lilly was deep in sleep. He felt as if he would fall from the horse at any moment. He was so exhausted.

Turning the horse off the road, he followed a small trail to a creek then to the cave he and his brother often used. It was a secluded place. He decided it would be good to make camp and sleep a few hours before dawn. Well, he wouldn't sleep but he would at least not be sitting a horse. He meant to watch over her now, keep her from trouble. No one had followed, he was sure of that.

With Lilly in his arms, he slid off his stallion. He set her down. She woke up then. He wanted to see her eyes, read the expressions, the darkness too invasive for something like that. Perhaps it would be best for the answers to be discovered later. Nothing need be solved this moment. It would all wait until they were both more rested.

"Brady?" she asked. "What?"

"We are stopping for a few hours to rest."

"Here?"

"Yes, but inside this cave. Wait here while I make sure the place is safe."

She nodded as he strode to the cave. Inside it was dry and warm. Pulling a torch off the sidewall, he lit it, walking farther with his pistol drawn. There was nothing but silence.

Brady went back for her. Swooping her into his arms, he strode with her to the makeshift pallet that was set against a far wall.

He spread out a blanket. "Go to sleep." Blessed hell he could almost see her cringe at the harshness in his voice. He was angry, incredibly so. He wanted to shake her until she told him what she was doing upstairs in a whorehouse and who she was meeting. At this moment his patience confounded him.

He didn't have to see her face to remember how her mouth would form into a straight line while she turned away from him. Didn't have to have light to recall how her eyes shimmered with blue fury when he pressed her for the truth. The devil, when had he become so besotted with one red haired woman that he couldn't even think straight?

"Alright." She curled on the blanket, her hands beneath her cheek. "You going to go to sleep also?"

To ease his frustration, he bent over the small fire pit near the pallet. Within minutes a fire crackled, emitting some warmth to the area. He walked to the opening of the cave, bringing his horse inside. Rain now fell, constant and steady. Not wishing to stop when he did, Brady realized they might be here longer than he'd wanted. He pulled a plaid from his saddlebags, wrapping it around him.

He realized she must be exhausted as well as cold. She would have had to push herself to reach Inverness by this evening. A ragged breath rushed through him at the realization she traveled at night, in this darkness.

She risked too much.

This would not happen again. Damn his father and his wishes. If he stayed at home, she would have never left.

He might have to chain her to the bed to keep her safe from herself, either that or keep her there until she was able to do naught but sleep. That was the first lighthearted image he had since he saw her this afternoon waltzing up the steps of a tavern to meet a lover.

Roby held him back. By the look in his brother's eyes Roby didn't believe she was doing the obvious, going to meet a man or a paying customer. He should have taken matters into his hands. He might have discovered this Douglas fellow there. If this Douglas fellow wasn't one of her lovers, who the hell was he?

Watching her for a moment, he sighed softly letting all his questions rumble in his head. He pulled his plaid around him, lying down next to Lilly to pull her into his arms, wrapping the cloth around her to keep her warm. She was still deep asleep, but she snuggled next to him, looking for warmth he was sure. Lying next to him, she felt right. A fleeting thought that he wanted to hold her like this in her sleep for the rest of his life filled him, completed him with a joy and peace he didn't comprehend. Unable to help himself, he ran his hand up the length of her leg, stopping at her belly. He spread his finger from hipbone to hipbone. His thinking all too obvious, yet the thought of her carrying his child thrilled him.

He was getting ahead of himself.

Dawn came all too soon. He kissed the back of her neck, hoping to rouse her slowly. She murmured something he didn't understand, pushing back against him, her buttocks pushing against his arousal.

"Time to get up, sleepy head." He nuzzled her neck, his hand on her waist rose to cup a breast, his thumb brushing across the hardened tip. His other hand pressed gently between her legs, enjoying the soft swollen wet petals damp with need greeting him.

She was not averse to him.

He chuckled softly.

Her sigh of pleasure gave him reason to smile even more as he wished they were home in bed where he could pursue this to the most logical conclusion. That wasn't going to happen any time soon. He wasn't sure at this point if he meant to leave her at the cottage. He wanted nothing more than to take her to his rooms with the express purpose of keeping her there until she answered his questions satisfactorily. It seemed to him, in the light of everything he knew, she was an enemy to herself. He also understood that no matter what he did or what threats he issued, she would tell him nothing until she was ready.

"I'm so warm. Don't want to get up," she murmured then stiffened as if she suddenly realized where his hands were located. "Brady. No!"

"Hush, we've slept and we've loved. Now it is time to ride."

Inwardly, he chuckled at her seeming reticence. On the other hand, he was not thrilled with the idea a few hours ago she willing gave herself to another man and was at this moment rejecting him. Before his anger overcame him, he needed to come to terms as to who exactly she was.

"We've slept, milord, nothing else. I would remember if we loved. That is something I don't intend to forget nor to sleep through."

She sat up brushing stray wild locks of her hair from her face. Quickly, she pulled those silken locks back wrapping them around themselves until they were secured. When she gazed at him her eyes were wide, apprehensive. For the first time since he first met her, he saw her insecurities.

"Absolutely. Whatever you say."

She stood, smoothing her skirts, staring at the horse as if that was the last place she wanted to be. When she closed her eyes, he understood all too well the discomfort she must feel. He nodded toward a copse of trees without sharing what he was sure would bother her further.

A few minutes after she returned, the unmistakable blush on her cheeks endeared her further. The moment sent a soft shaft of compassion for her even though he well knew she wasn't deserving of his tender concerns when she slept with another man upstairs at that tavern. After she told him, she would be his mistress. She lied. Either that or she didn't comprehend exactly what a mistress's duties were.

~ * ~

Lilly understood Brady was going to demand answers, responses she could not reveal to him. She didn't trust the man. Had no reason to do so. The McKennas were well known for their neutrality. That wasn't the worst of her problems though. Brady was going to demand who she saw upstairs in the tavern. To tell him it was Douglas would only serve to make him angrier because she also couldn't tell him the man was her brother. Too much was at stake.

Douglas' argument with the crown was old news but well-known news. She wasn't about to risk her brother's life by giving information to someone she understood so little about. For all she knew, Brady would turn Douglas over to the crown. Given the right incentive he might turn her over as well. She couldn't let that happen. If Douglas had done as he said, he'd be on his way to one of the colonies. There would be no reason for her to lie to protect. He had not. Instead, he stayed to help more men escape. Last night he promised her he would leave. She wasn't sure he would do that, leave.

Lilly let out a long slow breath of air, realizing time would tell. He was a man so he did as he pleased.

She was more surprised when Brady dropped her into his suite of rooms then proceeded to leave her there. When she tried the door, she found it bolted from the outside. She didn't know how many minutes passed before the door was opened. Brady wasn't the person coming inside. No, servants walked in with a bathtub along with buckets of cold and hot water. Well, she would like a bath but not when he could turn up any second. She would also like clean clothing. That wasn't going to happen any time soon if she couldn't return to her cottage. Blast him, what was he up to?

The anger coupled with frustration she felt at the man simmered deep. He did everything in his power to embarrass and confuse her. Lilly didn't like the fact she melted in his arms every time he kissed her. Even though a few days ago she decided she would like to be his mistress, enjoy his attentions since she never meant to wed, she now changed her mind. The loathsome creature was not going to coax her into giving up her principles, exchanging the wild tempest he generated within her for her maidenhead. He could rot in hell.

When the servants left, she watched the steam rise from the water beguiling every sense she possessed. Telling herself she didn't give a damn if he walked in on her, she quickly stripped setting her gown near the bath so she could reach it quickly if things didn't go as she hoped. Liquid heat soothed every muscle, caressed her ravaged nerves, soothed her tramped upon heart. Sleeping on the pallet last night was better than the hard stone of the cave. However, it was not the same as a soft warm bed. *Ah, but admit it, Brady kept you verra warm*

Heat rose to her cheeks while she remembered where his hands were when she woke this morning. He was an audacious handsome rogue, too much so for his own good—or not. It seemed he received a lot from her. She didn't protest either. Some lady should refuse his advances, perhaps put him in his place. She would be willing to bet no one ever denied him anything. He was so incredibly debonair.

She set her head on the rim of the tub closing her eyes. Seconds ticked by as she listened to the ticking clock. Her breathing evened out. All seemed so peaceful. Suddenly, she sat up, looking around. Still, the room was empty. She could have sworn a sound, some inadvertent noise woke her. She must be wrong. She certainly didn't mean to fall asleep. The steaming hot water grew chilly. Quickly, she washed herself with the lavender scented soap provided for her. Even more quickly she ducked underwater in order to wash her hair.

When she surfaced, she gasped feeling fingers, Brady's fingers, massaging her scalp with the soap.

"Surprised to see me?" his whispered words sent a chill spiraling slowly inside to be replaced by the heat of embarrassment as she realized she was naked. Reaching for the cloth to cover her, she found it had vanished.

"I c-can d-do that," she stammered, trying to hide her breasts with her hands as she hunched over.

Didn't matter he held them in his hands whenever the opportunity arose. Made no difference he touched her even more intimately.

"Should hope so. I'm sure it is much more pleasing to have me wait on you, to feel my fingers massaging your scalp." His lips touched her neck, traveled slowly upward to her ear.

"No, truly..." She heard the panic rise in her voice, felt the shaking of her body.

He didn't say anything more. Continued to do exactly as he pleased. Without warning the bucket of water splashed across on top of her head to slide across her face. She sputtered, wiping water from her face. Lilly turned, forgetting her nakedness. "You!"

He sat back on his haunches, grinning, appearing to soak up the view she inadvertently provided for him. After a few seconds he stood, handing her a huge bath sheet.

"I brought you clean clothing. Hope you appreciate my efforts. They should fit. After all, the gowns are yours." With that said he sauntered across the room to settle on a large chair, his arms spread out, watching, his gaze fixed on her.

She turned her back on him then over her shoulder, "Would you be so kind to give me some privacy?" she asked realizing she had no grounds to ask for such thing since she agreed to let him basically own her for as long as he wished.

She heard his chuckle, felt a slow burn enwrap her. He had the upper hand and he meant to keep it. Before the tavern the control was hers. She meant to gain it back if at all possible.

"Some," he paused, "privacy will cost."

Once more what he said didn't surprise. He wanted information from her, knowledge she refused to impart to a man she didn't believe she could be straight forward with. With the towel wrapped around her, Lilly decided that was the most privacy she would receive for the time being.

She walked to the fireplace to sit on the hearth. Finger combing her hair, she attempted to rid the length of the tangles. She felt his presence before she opened her eyes to see him.

"Here." He handed her a silver comb. "Don't you want to know what the cost would be? The price I would ask? It is not much."

With a small sigh she lifted her shoulders. He would do as he wished when he wished. "Not particularly. I've a pretty good idea what it is you will want. To be sure, I'm not willing to pay the price. Privacy be damned, it should be mine out of courtesy, nothing more."

"Only your honesty. If you're not willing to be candid with me, I suppose you will have to stay here for the duration. I don't mind you know. Since you've agreed to share a bed with me. Matters not if it's this one or yours. Well, mayhap it does. Mine is larger."

"What is it you wish to learn?" It wouldn't hurt to ask. Perhaps this was something different than he asked her previously. Maybe it would turn out to be a question she could answer.

"Why did you turn to whoring when you agreed to be my mistress?" His voice turned harsh. When she looked at him, his eyes blazed. Clearly his emotions seethed.

"If I deem to answer, you will leave so I can dress?"

"Only if I believe your answer."

Firsthand knowledge from previous conversations told her he wouldn't believe the truth if it bit him in the arse. She could always embellish a lie. He would discover soon enough she wasn't a whore. She lifted her shoulders slightly, "I enjoy men. How they make me feel when they..." She lowered her lashes, studying her fingers along with the silver comb she held, waiting for a reply or a burst of anger. Either would suit.

"When they touch your breasts, Lilly? Is this what you enjoy? Do you like them to touch you in even more intimate places on your lovely body? You will have to tell me what you enjoy," he said, as the towel slipped from her body to pool around her hips.

His hands closed over her breasts. His thumb gently rubbed across a nipple. She inhaled swiftly, surprised by her sudden response as well as the fact he initiated this. Yet she knew he dared anything.

She could barely speak let alone breathe. "Yes, yes...and other things. I like to touch men too."

She had no earthly reason to provoke him. What the devil was she wishing for? To put an end to this to tell him she wouldn't be his mistress.

"This too, Lilly."

One hand dropped lower, spreading across her belly while she melted into him, leaning against his chest, her breasts rubbing against the fine lawn of his shirt. She felt him touching, caressing her exactly where she found his fingers this morning. Unknowingly, mindlessly, she spread her legs for him, giving him better access to the most intimate parts of her. "You like this don't you, sweeting?"

Dear God, she did. She wasn't going to tell him that. Finding her wits, "Don't!" She jumped up, grabbing the towel before pulling it around her. "I didn't invite your attention."

"You did. Perhaps I should ask another question. I didn't think you would be a whore if you didn't enjoy men. From now on, you will entertain only me. Do you understand?" Too many seconds passed. "Tell me you understand."

She was shaking so hard she couldn't think, couldn't speak. Didn't understand what prompted her to provoke the man who needed no provocation to mistrust her. Yet she reveled in the fact he would soon know she wasn't as he thought her to be.

"Tell me, sweeting. Do you understand?"

The lump in her throat didn't want to vanish. Instead, it grew. She looked at her bare feet then back to him. Finally, when she could speak, "I understand completely."

In any case, she didn't want to share herself with anyone but him. At the moment, she wasn't sure she wanted Brady McKenna in her bed. He unnerved her, confused and puzzled her.

"Good." He returned to the chair to sit again to watch. "That wasn't a satisfactory answer. So, let's try something else. Why did you go upstairs at that tavern? Before you give me some lie, no," He held up his hands. "Tell me something believable. Confessions I'm more likely to believe. The upstairs rooms are where women entertain men for coin. But you *ken* that, don't you, sweeting?"

For several seconds, she fiddled with the edge of the towel tempted to let it drop to the floor so she could see what he would do. Boldness in this situation was not an act she felt comfortable with. She changed her mind, decided to stick to the truth as much as she dared. "To deliver a message."

"You weren't seeing someone upstairs then? Sharing a bed for a bit of coin?" he asked, his voice taking on a bland tone.

Brady didn't hide his emotions well. Lilly was positive inside he was boiling. "No. Not the way you're thinking."

"There was no one upstairs you would enjoy?"

"No."

"I must truly be a fool. For some reason I can't explain, this time your words have the ring of truth. What was the message?"

The last question surprised her. She tucked her bottom lip beneath her teeth. Still staring hard into his eyes with the hope he would accept the fact she wouldn't give over a confidence. "I cannot say. It's not my place to tell. If you knew the truth, the knowledge might put you and others in jeopardy."

"Get dressed or I'll do it for you."

He stood, leaving the room, walking swiftly away from her as if he couldn't stand her presence. In his wake, the door slammed. A second later, he was back. "You've five minutes. I'll wait out here."

She scurried. The towel fell to the floor. The chemise and gown slipped over her head. Unfortunately, she couldn't fasten the dress despite how she squirmed and stretched to reach the tiny buttons. The gown was

Christine Young

one of hers, from her trunks. He didn't take heed to the fact she might need help to dress. Her shoulders slumped. She didn't want his help right now but she needed his hands. If he touched her again, right now, she might beg him to make love to her. She didn't understand but she was so thoroughly aroused she couldn't think clearly. All she wanted was more of his tender seduction.

When she wasn't outside the solar in five minutes, the door burst crashing against the wall. Brady stood in the opening framed by the light. "What's wrong?"

"I—" she began before she quickly spoke. "Didn't mean to make you angry. The gown you picked out for me well..." Once again, she paused.

Unable to think, unable to form a coherent sentence, she turned, presenting her back to him. What she was trying to tell him obvious.

She heard the soft chuckle. Didn't, however, want to see the look in his eyes. Before he said a word, she felt his knuckles provocatively graze her back before sliding slowly down her spine. His hand slipped beneath her dress, squeezing her buttocks. She couldn't help the tiny mew of pleasure he elicited from her.

"Very nice," he spoke softly as once again he took the opportunity to coax her to his ways.

"Please."

"Please what?" His laughter now had her fuming.

"Fasten my gown for me," she told him indignantly.

"I'd much rather take it off." His gentle murmur along with the graze of his teeth across her shoulders had her thinking the same way while forgetting any possibility of anger.

"Then," she swallowed the apprehension in her throat that sex with him was going to happen sooner than later if she wasn't careful, "whatever you were in such a hurry for won't happen."

He did roar with laughter. "I was in a rush to get you to your cottage where I could do just this. Explore every tender, exquisite inch of you without being interrupted by some well-meaning soul like my brother."

"Oh."

Brady laughed again. Heat rose to her cheeks. Yet he fastened the gown. "You are ready. Shall we?" Gallantly, he extended an arm.

"If you meant what you said, it won't be possible unless you meant to carry me the entire way. I suppose if you are riding your horse, you will only have to carry me to the stables."

Blessed hell, she was rambling again speaking so fast she didn't remember a word she was blurting. If she didn't know better, she might have told him everything he wanted to know. Hopefully, he wouldn't ask her anything important.

"Why is that?"

She lifted her skirt to show him her bare feet. "You forgot shoes."

"Indeed. Then I will carry you. While doing so, I'll take great pleasure in the way you feel against me. Do you give me permission to touch every inch of your silken body? Should I set you on fire? Turn you into liquid heat?"

In his arms, cradled close to him, they stepped into the main hall. Whenever anyone passed by, she pushed her face against his chest. She really shouldn't have asked him to carry her. It would have been nothing to walk while still inside.

Set her on fire? The devil but she didn't want him to do that. Not until she had her emotions under control where it came to him. When they turned the corner into the great hall, she gasped in surprise. Truly, she shouldn't be surprised. Had known it would be just a matter of time. She wasn't ready to see him, wasn't ready to leave. Lord Townsend, her stepfather, would demand she honor the betrothal contract even though she never gave her consent, never agreed, never would.

Lilly needed to convince Brady she wanted back in his room. They would never escape the hall without her father seeing her. He would force her to return with him. *Nay*, she couldn't let this happen. She would not go back. Panic swelled inside.

"Stop! Stop now, please."

To her immense and pleased surprise, Brady did so. Perhaps it was the fear in her voice, the absolute terror that caused his quick action. In any case, she couldn't have asked for a swifter reply. When their gazes met, his held a look of surprise coupled with confusion.

"What is it?" He didn't hide the concern he obviously felt at the sudden, unexpected command she issued.

"I cannot go in the hall." When her father turned to look this way, she buried her face once more in his chest, praying the man didn't recognize her.

"Why? You're terrified."

The question was certainly simple enough. He deserved to know what she feared. So, she blurted, "My father is down there."

Without asking another question, he returned to the bedroom. Once inside, he bolted the door. He set her gently on a chair before pouring them both a glass to fortify. She swirled the brandy around the crystal watching the amber colors in the candlelight of the room. She would have to tell him something. Would have to give him at least one good reason why she didn't want her father to see her other than the fact she just agreed to become his mistress.

A father wouldn't want that for his daughter, especially not when she was betrothed to a wealthy lord.

He didn't say anything. Didn't push her to reveal well-kept secrets. Her father, of course, was not a secret. His appearance on McKenna land would be questioned when he was known to despise travel. He followed her here. She supposed it would be a logical conclusion for him to search for her where her mother once lived.

When Lilly looked at him, he was sipping the brandy. His gaze resting upon her was thoughtful. She knew he was waiting for answer to his unasked questions.

"I sense a long story in the making. We have time, sweeting. Should I send for a bottle of wine and some nourishment? I trust you will enlighten me eventually. As soon as you feel comfortable." His words held a wealth of sarcasm.

She grimaced understanding he wanted more honesty from her than she was willing to give. What she really wanted was a proposal of marriage and a wedding to take place this instant. However, he would never agree to wed a whore.

Looking at her folded hands still in her lap, "Yes, food and wine would be nice."

For the time it took for the requested food and wine to be brought to the room, the pair said nothing. The silence stripped her nerves raw. She listened to his even steady breathing. Heard the occasional click of his glass as he set it on the table, the rustle of his massive body as he changed position on the chair. All the while she was sorting out the facts she could tell him from the ones she could not.

Lilly knew she should start the conversation before he lost patience with her. She just wasn't sure how to go about getting the words past her lips. When she finally finished eating and pretty much singlehandedly finished the bottle of wine that was brought to them, she decided she had no more excuses.

"He never leaves London, not for anyone," she began in such a soft voice she noticed Brady leaning forward in order to hear. "He despises traveling. I never actually thought he would come for me."

"I assume the he you are speaking of is your father. The man you witnessed in the great hall."

She nodded waiting for the barrage of forthcoming queries. When nothing happened, she swallowed another glass of wine from a new bottle. "Stephen does not like to travel," she said again having forgotten what she already told him.

"His visit here must be important." Brady's voice held a touch of amusement. "Hunting for a long-lost daughter?"

He couldn't possibly understand how difficult this was for her to discuss. She wasn't going to mention Douglas. He was undoubtedly more interested in finding his son than his stepdaughter.

Lilly nodded silently wishing this conversation could be avoided. She would tell him everything except about Douglas. "He is looking for me."

"Let me get this straight. You left London, by yourself without informing your father of your whereabouts. Seems he has good reason to look for you. He must know what you are about and wishes to stop you before you can ruin the family name."

"Yes, you're right. His honor is at stake or so he believes," she murmured. "I can't do it though. I would rather die than honor the contract he made with that pig." She couldn't tell him the man only wanted her because she was a virgin. If she wasn't, her betrothed would have made Stephen pay in some other foul way.

Still, he twirled the amber liquid, watching her his eyes narrowed waiting. "Death is an extreme measure."

Still, he didn't ask a question, just left her dangling. "Not in this case."

~ * ~

Crissie stood in the rose garden waiting for Walker to show up, sure he was bringing bad news. Well, she would weather anything if he would just tell her he loved her. If he would tell her, he wanted to marry her. He warned her earlier he would have to return to London. Walker also told her that in time he would come back to the highlands to figure out their relationship.

In her mind what they meant to each other was obvious. She had nothing to discern where he was concerned. She loved the man. She loved him from the first instant she saw him when he turned and smiled at her.

For long minutes, she roamed the garden breathing deeply of the scent of roses, her heart fluttering wildly beneath her ribs. The sun was beginning to set, a soft breeze cooling the air. If her father or brothers knew what she was doing here, they would make sure she never left the castle by herself again. She wanted Walker in the most elemental ways, had kept him at bay for the past months, giving herself so many reasons to deny his sensual advances.

"Crissie?" Walker strode toward her, smiling, holding out his arms for her to run into them as she always did. He was so handsome her breath gathered in the back of her throat to stay there for the longest time.

Today she held back, hesitated. In his red uniform, he was so debonair, cavalier. His coat fit his broad shoulders as his pants molded to the thick powerful muscles of his long legs. His eyes, a deep very tawny brown, compelled her to give him anything he wanted, anything he asked her for. Every time she saw him, he stole her heart. He was larger than her brothers, more handsome in her mind, more dangerous.

She inhaled a shaky breath as his eyes narrowed, most likely wondering why she hesitated to run to him. It was simple. She just was not herself today. Moisture threatened, clogging her throat, filling her eyes. His leaving today would be the worst day of her life. The emptiness assailing her threatened to overwhelm every sense she possessed.

"Is it something I did?" he queried as he reached her tugging her into his arms. His hands roamed the length of her back, just as he did every time she met with him. He stroked the curve of her hip, moved higher to cup her breast in his hand. He'd stroked her, touched her, never too intimately, never taking her innocence even though she knew it was difficult for him to hold back. Even though she would have given it to him if he asked. He had not asked.

Walker was an honorable man.

Damn honor!

Gazing up and into his eyes, "No, it's just that I *ken* you're going to leave me. That's why you wanted to meet me here today. The fact *doesnae* please me at all. *Nay*, it terrifies. I *dinnae* want you to leave."

Quickly he kissed her, "Is there anywhere we can have privacy? We do need to talk. I need to kiss you where no eyes excluding our own will see."

"Both my brothers believe there is something going on between us. They have kept me in their sights all day. Truly, I can do nothing about them. They are protective of me." She found she was hedging, afraid of her feelings, terrified of being alone with him. Both brothers were nowhere near. Though she wanted nothing more than to have a private place with this man she was terrified of what she might do if they found a secluded spot to be alone. What she would give him today if he asked.

"If I had a sister as lovely as you, I would feel the same." He ran a finger along her jawline, touched her lips, parting them slightly. Her tongue touched the tip, eliciting a groan from him. "Perhaps they should have kept a closer eye on you, on us before today."

She saw the passion in his eyes, the desire simmering hot and clear in the ebony depths. The tempest he created in her grew with the mercuric magic generated by his touch. She could not, should not be alone with this man she loved. Knew she loved with all her heart although her father might dispute that fact. Might tell her she was too young to know how love felt. She was of age though. Walker could wed her if he so chose.

I love you. "You are leaving. When? I *cannae* bear the thought. I will miss you each breath." Moisture pooled in the depth of her eyes. She pushed the hot liquid back, refusing to shed tears in front of this man. The trust she felt when he was near went beyond her common sense, what she understood of men, what her brothers instilled in her. Still, she lost her heart to Walker. If he asked, she would give herself to him.

He didn't ask.

"Now, as soon as we say our goodbyes. Let's walk." His arm circled her waist as he pulled her closer.

"What is it you want from me? I don't want to cry yet..." She swallowed hard. "Not until you are gone. Truly, you should leave before I make a fool of myself."

His arm around her tightened, "I would have you smile at me when I leave, place a chaste kiss upon my cheek, perhaps wave that tiny hand of yours that fits so perfectly into mine."

"You are coming back." So unsure of his intentions, she made the words a statement instead of a question.

"Yes." His voice was stiff so unlike himself.

"Tell me the problem. I hear a maybe in that one word."

She was determined to get the truth from him until she told him her truth. It was something he should know. Not if he didn't want her, not if he was lying to her now. As if she finally realized the information, he was trying not to tell her, "You are not coming back."

He cleared his throat, running his hand once more down her side, brushing the curve of her breast sending a shiver of desire through her. She wanted him even now when she sensed he had no intention of returning to her. He didn't want her. Gifting her virginity to any other man was untenable.

"My father is sending me to Paris on business. I'll be gone several months. That's after I return to London. I can't tell you when we'll see each other, just that we will. I cannot ask you to wait for me."

His words did nothing to ease her fears despite the tiny bit of sincerity she heard. She stepped back from him, deciding her anger would overcome her sadness if she allowed the emotion. It was as she assumed it would be. Blessed be all the saints, but she should have trusted her instincts. Still, she looked at him and yearned for his touch, the stroke of his long-bronzed fingers needed it as much as she needed to breathe as her heart to beat. Even while she stood in front of Walker, she mourned the loss, which she felt deep in the depth of her soul.

"I brought you a gift."

The only gift she yearned for was a proposal, an assurance he loved her. When he brought out the long slender box, she understood what she yearned for would not be forth coming. He tried to hand it to her.

She could not bring a smile to her lips let alone her eyes. With a shaky hand she accepted, didn't want to open the box. Drawing in a long deep breath of rose scented air, she lifted the lid.

The necklace was beautiful, a heart shape with a small sapphire embedded inside.

"To match the color of your eyes when the silver darkens to blue," he spoke softly an expectant look in his gaze as his knuckles gently brushed the side of her face.

He took the necklace from the box, placed it around her neck fastening it for her.

"Thank you," she murmured wishing she dared throw the gift in his arrogant face. Her anger built as she watched him, realizing he meant to leave her, never to return. She didn't trust his words. This was a parting gift, nothing more. He wooed her too easily. She should have put up more of a fight. Still, she wanted him more now than ever before. She needed to steal her heart against him. To take back his possession of her heart and soul.

"You don't like it?" he asked, his voice telling her he might be hurt by her curt dismissal of the gift.

"When I look at it, I'll remember you. As well as what you meant to me."

She was angry, furiously so. By giving in to the fury rising inside, she would lose the last few precious minutes she might have with him.

"Somehow I'm not believing you." His eyes darkened, his confusion at her reticence simmering deep inside.

"Believe it, Sassenach." With that said she turned striding away from him, unable to contain the anger or the fear her future now held, unable to keep the tears from tumbling from her eyes.

What would she do? What would he do?

She didn't look over her shoulder, knowing he wouldn't be standing there when she did. Nor would he follow her. A long shuddering breath of despair swept into her lungs. She couldn't allow him to leave like this, believing she had no real feelings for him. Collapsing to her knees, she let her head fall into her hands. "No. No, not like this." Somehow, she held back the sobs.

Seconds turning to minutes swept by while she tried for the courage to go after him, to show him what she felt for him. She couldn't tell him. She could show him though.

Crissie raced to the stables, hoping to get there before he left. When she reached the horses, she saw him riding down the lane. He truly was leaving, his back stiff, a perfect soldier.

"No..." the whispered plea was lost in the highland winds, the rustle of the leaves overhead.

The time it took to saddle her horse would take an eternity. With only the halter and reins on Muire, she leapt on her mare's back. Racing after Walker, tears in her eyes, she couldn't let him leave her this way. He had to know how she felt, exactly what favors she was willing to grant. What he meant to her. If she didn't do so, she would never forgive herself. If he never returned, she would have this one last memory with him.

Finally, she reached him. He must have heard the pounding hooves of her little mare as he turned his horse to watch her approach. His smile was broad, accepting of her. Today, before he left, she meant to give him everything, all of her. She would hold nothing back.

"Crissie...?" His voice trailed off as she pulled up next to him.

He leaned over, drawing her from the mare to settle her gently across his legs. His lips found hers in a long searing kiss filled with all the promise she could imagine coupled with ones she couldn't. "Why are you here? I thought..." Again, it seemed he wanted to touch her, kiss her more than listen for answers.

"Make love to me." She was barely able to whisper between kisses. She heard his groan of desire rumble from his chest, felt his arms tighten even more. "Please, Walker."

"No."

"I..." She swallowed her fear of rejection. "Please."

"Where?" he asked as his horse began to move slowly from the lane. He held the reins of her mare in one hand. It seemed he knew where he was going even before she could say.

They traveled farther into the trees toward a tumbling creek. A small pond was situated just north, secret, protected on three sides. While they moved, he pulled her so she straddled him. His hands roamed along her body, touching the length, caressing her breasts. Urgency possessed them.

"Are you sure?"

Unable to form the words she nodded.

"Don't tease me, sweeting. I want you too much, have waited so long for you to say yes."

"I want to see you naked, Walker. I need to touch you beneath your clothing. I want to see that hard part of you that I feel when you pull me against you."

"Crissie..." he moaned softly. "You unman me."

Keeping her in his arms he slipped from the horse. Gently he settled her on the ground. Soft moss lay beneath her. His kisses generated a tempest, tested her will. "I want you," she murmured as his fingers quickly divested her gown from her body.

She tugged at his shirt, unsure of herself now that they were pursuing uncharted territory. He was a practiced lover. She was sure of that. He was eager, his hands and lips roaming everywhere, touching on sensitive, erotic spots she never guessed existed. She arched into his stroking fingers, twisting in his arms.

He rose above her, slipping from his shirt, sitting then to tug off his boots before removing his trousers. She watched, mesmerized by his form, by his jutting arousal. She reached out to touch him, quickly having second thoughts withdrew her hand.

He chuckled softly, his charming grin encouraging. "You can touch me anywhere you like. It might be prudent though, this first time to not provoke the animal in me."

Crissie blinked, trying to understand his words. Gave it up when he lowered himself atop her, spreading her legs, his weight comfortable atop her. He sucked a nipple then drew most of her breast into his mouth, his tongue curling around the tip. She gasped at the sensation, her back arching against him.

The time slipped by as his explorations grew bolder, ever more intimate. When he touched her women's part she jerked, surprised, unsure of what he was doing. Almost told him *nay*.

"Easy now, sweeting. This is to give you more ecstasy than you've ever known before. "Let me give you that pleasure."

"Will it hurt?"

He paused a moment, a strange smile on his face. "*Aye*, it will but for a moment only. Your cream is making you wet and so very ready for me. This place here," his thumb caressed her intimately, jerking her hips again. She twisted in his arms. "Will give you such delight, you will beg for more. Do you still want me Crissie?"

"Yes." *More than ever.*

He slipped a finger inside her then another. She closed her eyes, reveling in the sweet bliss he created. "Good then let this come, just let me work the magic that will have you begging for so much more. I don't want you to forget me while I'm gone. You will have this day and what we are doing here to remember me by."

As if I could forget.

Tremors began to build inside her as he stroked and caressed. His lips moved upon hers. His tongue dancing and playing inside her mouth before he moved to caress her breasts, her belly lower still. She reached upward, shudders filling her, pulsing within until she couldn't stop them, had no control of the spiraling of her body or the fire pulsing through her.

She felt him, stretching her more as his finger withdrew to be replaced by his rod. He thrust forward. She cried out, the pain intense, achingly so. A tear ran down her cheek. He sipped it away.

"You will be fine," he chuckled softly my virgin flower. "Is the pain over?" he asked as he placed nipping little kisses across the corners of her mouth before angling down her neck.

"Walker, please," her voice was whisper thin.

As he began to move within her, she felt the beginnings of that same pleasure she just experienced, the tremors growing with each hungry plunge of his hard male body.

He thrust inside, deeper, harder until she was sure he reached all the way to her core. Once more, the world vanished to be replaced with spiraling sensations ripping through her thrusting her higher and higher still until she cried out. He took his name within his lips. She couldn't think all she could do was feel.

Moments later part of his weight was atop her while he braced himself on his forearms. His fingers were running through her hair, all the pins dislodged. His body was sweat sheened, glorious.

"Regrets?"

"None."

Chapter Four

Brady felt as if she would never say a word to help herself. Over the years, he heard rumors abound about Lord Townsend. None of them attesting to a gentle or bending character. When Lilly showed up here as Lilly Townsend, he never equated her with this man who was unforgiving to a fault. Lord, but he needed her to explain. Didn't like the probing questions. He wanted her to tell him on her terms but she didn't seem capable.

"Why would death be preferable? What is this contract you speak of?" He set his glass down before leaning forward, his forearms resting on his thighs as he concentrated on her eyes.

"Stephen signed a betrothal contract. I haven't agreed to marry the man, but my father will find some way to force me. You see, he's getting something for me. Don't know what it is."

"So," he leaned back. "that is why you turned up here. I'm guessing that because my father knew your mother, he is willing to give you a place to live as well as hide you if necessary. My involvement with you makes it ever more complicated. He knows more than he lets on."

"Yes, the Fraser cottage. He knew mother when she was young, they were young."

Still, it seemed she didn't want to say anything. At least this time she was talking. Her lips weren't drawn in a thin line. He suddenly realized he would help her avoid this marriage anyway he could. She belonged to him. "Tell me about the man you were supposed to marry."

She wiped her hands down her dress. All he wanted at the moment was to pull her into his arms to give comfort. When she looked at him, moisture filled her soft blue eyes. His heart went out to her. To be a pawn in a father's game could not be pleasant.

"I'm afraid there is nothing you can do to help. Well, there is but you won't."

"I'm not going to ask what it is you are thinking I won't do. Tell me about the man. Why don't you want to marry him?"

Certainly, he had his guesses. Many betrothals were not made with the woman's best interest or consent.

"He is old enough to be my grandfather. All he wants is a virgin and an heir." Her lashes lowered. It seemed she hid from him.

"That's all?" Brady kept his smile behind his teeth along with his laughter. "That is what men wanted when they wed, a virgin along with an heir. Why else would they succumb to that institution?"

She nodded seeming to feel as if she told him everything. Several minutes ticked off the clock. Her fingers wound into the fabric of her dress.

"You have nothing to worry about since you are not a virgin. You don't have the qualifications he is looking for."

He heard the swift intake of her breath. So, he hit upon a nerve. Perhaps there was more. "All you need do is prove the fact to him."

She didn't say anything, but the glare she shot him told him his comment was not appreciated.

"I would fix that problem for you," he told her with all sincerity, "but obviously someone beat me to it."

Her eyes were narrowed on him, flaming with the passion he wanted to tap into. "You are the only man of my acquaintance who believes that."

"You are still protesting my words, claiming your innocence. I rather liked our conversations better when you did decide to become my mistress. Well, Lilly, if you are a virgin, I cannot take you to my bed nor will I claim to do so. I do not defile virgins." He was surprised at his words as everything he thought previously about Lilly belied that fact. His jealousy at the other men she'd known simmered.

She waved a slender hand in the air. "You are right. I've protested too much. I'm not innocent. I've had dozens of men."

He was surprised at her easy capitulation as he realized he was wrong about his earlier thoughts. If she was a virgin, he wanted her even more. Oh, he told himself too many times he didn't care about her status. He did.

"I'm glad you have finally accepted the fact and have stopped lying," he said as he stood holding his hand out to her. "Shall we make sure your father finds you in bed with me? Or would that be too crude."

Her eyes widened. She placed her hand in his. "I'm giving you half of what you wanted. The rest, a marriage, is not possible. I can only wed my mate, no one else. As of yet I haven't found her. You will be mine until she makes her presence known."

She didn't hide her relief along with her dismay at his words as she placed her hand in his. Still, he felt the fine trembling within his. He didn't want her fear. He craved her passion.

"How are you going to go about doing this? My father finding me in your bed?"

"As much as I don't want our first time together to be interrupted, I'm going to make sure it is. Undress. When I return, I want to see you in my bed naked."

For a few seconds he watched her fumble with her clothing. With a sigh and the realization he would have to help, he quickly unfastened the buttons it seemed he just fastened. He did tell her he'd rather take the damn dress off than help her put it on. He left.

In the great hall he found Roby. After imparting his intentions, he returned to find Lilly just as he commanded. She was in his big bed curled onto her side. He hoped she was indeed naked. He wasn't sure how much time he had before they were interrupted.

Quickly, he rid himself of his clothing. Naked, he slipped in beside her. Blessed hell, when he drew her to him, she was soft and warm. She fit into his arms quite nicely. He understood all too well this ploy might just backfire, resulting in a marriage he didn't want. She wouldn't object though. He understood a marriage was the only way she would permanently acquit herself of the betrothal.

He was twenty-seven. Didn't believe he would ever find his mate, not unless he left the highlands. What would it matter if he wed a woman he was attracted strongly to?

He could do worse?

"Brady?"

"What?"

"Are we just going to lie here until someone comes?" Her voice cracked at the end of the sentence.

He chuckled softly. "We could do other things while we wait. Don't want to be interrupted when I do make love to you." He kissed the corners of her lips, felt the soft brush of the hardened tips of her breasts against the muscles of chest. His breath left in a slow swish of contented air.

He turned her then put her beneath him. "Is your father a man who will demand marriage when he finds you in bed with me? Because if he is..." Second as well as third thoughts pierced his brain.

"You will tell him no. You will tell him you don't want to wed me."

His mouth found hers, danced and played with her lips then her tongue. He plunged inside groaning, as they seemed to play hide and seek with each other. The dark sultry core enticed magic, generating smoldering heat. A raging hungry fire erupted in his loins. He didn't know if he could wait until after they were discovered.

"Will you?" he asked as he pulled away unable to put the feel of her breasts pushing against him from his mind. They fit into his hands perfectly. The tips were a soft coral and the taste of Lilly reminded him of spring and wild flowers that abounded in the fields amidst the heather. Carrying this too far too soon was not his intentions. This moment could so easily get out of control.

What had he done?

He'd taken this action, remembering how his father forced a marriage with Wynnie, his mother. If Lord Townsend were any kind of a man, he would insist they wed. Strange that he didn't want to deny it. Suddenly a marriage with her didn't sound so horrible.

Lilly was his.

"You are mine, Lilly. You belong to me."

The truth was in his thoughts. He stroked her side, the curve of her hips, the flat plane of her soft belly where his child would grow. His heavy arousal pulsed against her as he moved her legs apart so he could settle between them. He was so close to heaven. So very close he felt the warmth of her core, the heat of her body, the rounded curve of her breasts.

Brady nibbled her lips then down her neck, placing smoldering wet kisses across her collarbone until she was writhing and twisting beneath him. Roby, damn his perfidious soul, was purposely delaying this. He would have his revenge when his brother wasn't looking. The devil but he would. This was torture when he wanted to push inside Lilly, give her all the ecstasy she deserved. Yearned to show her he was the only man she needed. Craved to show her he didn't care if another man took her innocence. That was all in the past.

The knock on the door echoed in his head. It took several seconds for the realization to settle into his brain. The door burst open. Light from the hall lit the room. Now turning back wasn't possible. What they set in motion could not be stopped.

"We are discovered," he whispered to Lilly. "You must let me do the talking. Know that I will say we've been lovers since you arrived. That is why there is no virgin blood on the sheets." Beneath him he felt her stiffen. Her nails curled into his shoulder. This is it then.

She didn't say anything. Her face turned a deathly white, yet he saw courage along with relief in her eyes.

What the devil did I just get myself into?

"Sorry to interrupt."

It was Roby's voice he heard. Brady pushed away to see his brother framed in the doorway. No one else stood nearby. He pulled the covers around Lilly as he wondered where their fathers were.

"What is it?" Brady asked as he rose from the bed, quickly slipping on his britches.

"Nothing. I'm afraid Lord Townsend is not downstairs. He isn't here."

Brady looked to Lilly. He wasn't sure at all about the emotions playing on her beautiful face.

"Nothing? I-I saw him. I know I did." Lilly whispered. "He isn't there? Who is it then?" she asked her confusion evident in the tone of her voice.

"A lord yes, but not Townsend. Said his name was Fuller. He's here on a vacation of sorts. Has a hunting lodge farther east. That is where he's travelling. Just stopped in for an evening. Although rumor has it a Lord Townsend was here earlier but left."

"Lord Fuller?" she was still whispering. "Thank you."

Having delivered the needed information, Roby backed from the room. Brady closed the door then leaned against it staring at Lilly, wishing he could see inside her head. Was this some new ploy she played with him, getting him to dance to the music she set.

He pushed away slowly striding across the room to pour them each a glass of wine. When he returned, he handed the liquid fortification to her before sitting on the bed. He watched as she drank long and deep finishing half as if the glass had a hole in the bottom. Aye, perhaps it did. This time, as he did the last time they spoke, he wanted her to begin, didn't want to barrage her with the hundred questions swirling within his head.

With his wine in hand, the bottle in the other he sat down next to her on the bed, stretching his legs out in front of him. After setting the bottle on the stand, he sipped slowly while he waited for her to ask for more. How could she mistake some man for her father? The fact just was not tenable.

With pleasure, he recalled she was still naked beneath the covers. Maybe that would give him an upper hand in this next set of questions. He wasn't going to allow her to dress until they got to the bottom of this situation, which grew more and more complicated as the minutes passed.

The silence didn't unnerve him, but he was pretty sure it did Lilly. Indeed, the room wasn't silent at all. The pop and crackle of the fire sounded cozy along with the methodical tick of the clock. The sound of servants moving around outside the bolted door was normal as well as reassuring that nothing untoward was going to happen.

How long would it take her to give him some tiny piece of the puzzle he was waiting for? The complicated puzzle was taking too long to put together.

"More wine?" he asked as she emptied her glass.

Even while she was telling him no by shaking her head, she was holding the glass out for more. He would have to ask for more wine as well as some food. Going to her place tonight would probably not be a prudent endeavor. She would be wary as well as guarded in her dealings with him. This first time they needed no threat of interruption. Despite all that happened tonight, he still wanted to seal the deal between them.

After all, they had a verbal contract. She was his mistress now in his mind if not in deed.

"Care to tell me who Lord Fuller is?" he asked, sardonically, realizing she would have to have more wine if she was going to impart any information at all.

Relaxed, she might forget she didn't want to reveal anything about herself.

Her dark lashes fanned across high cheekbones as she seemed to study the red burgundy in the glass she held. When she drew her attention away from the liquid to look at him, he thought he saw a shimmer of truth in her gaze then she said, as she once again shook her head, "I don't know him. Doesn't mean my father didn't send him though. You told me you made inquiries. Those alone could bring my father here to make sure his word stands."

Brady grunted his frustration. "Honestly, Lilly, I don't know what I can believe."

With huge soft blue eyes that seemed to melt him when he looked at them, she lifted her slim shoulders saying, "I've never lied to you. Everything I've told you has been the absolute truth."

The chuckle he meant to hide he couldn't stop. "Except about your virginity."

"Are we talking about that again?" she asked sounding miffed. "I believe you said the topic was off limits."

"No, my apologies. You're right of course. So, since you haven't lied to me then truly you don't know who this Lord Fuller is. Think, Lilly, I'm sure your father has a great many friends." He meant to probe, to get her to think of anything she might have seen or heard while she lived in London.

"He does," she acknowledged

"So, we are back to one-to-two-word answers."

"I'm sorry. I don't know him. Have never heard of the man."

He let out a long slow breath of frustration. "I'm going downstairs. You should get some sleep. I'll bring back food and wine when I return. If you're still awake, I'll let you know what I've learned."

A few minutes later he was dressed and striding into the main hall. He picked up a glass of ale from one of the serving maids as he walked through the room. Roby greeted him, waving his hand. He sat down beside his brother.

A retainer handed him a sealed letter.

Before Brady could open and read it, Crissie joined them. Brady wasn't sure about anything when he looked at his sister closely. It seemed she'd been crying. Her eyes were red and puffy. Crissie never cried. He wondered if he had the strength to deal with his sister's problems along with his.

Before he could question Roby about this Lord Fuller, Crissie's sob caught his attention.

"He's gone." Crissie's words came out in a thin wail turning to a frantic sob.

"Who?" Brady asked, perplexed by his sister.

Roby shot Brady a baleful glare. With a bland tone, "Who do you think, big brother?"

Brady searched his mind for everything he knew about Crissie. Still, he came up with nothing. "Haven't the faintest idea."

"Walker, he left," she said, stifling a sob as if she was trying to keep her tears at bay. Of course, she was failing at the task. "I don't think he's ever coming back."

"You're too young for him, brat," Roby said, beating Brady to the same comment. "It's for the best before you do something you can't take back."

Those words started more tears. Brady was sure Roby said the worst things he could have told their sister. It was obvious exactly what he referred to had happened. She'd done something she couldn't take back.

Well, hell.

Both brothers stared at Crissie. She looked up shooting them a glare that left both baffled. "I don't regret anything," she told them fiercely her eyes blazing. "He loves me."

No, she wouldn't regret giving herself to the man she loved. The problem here was whether or not Walker truly loved her. "There might be consequences. Are you prepared?"

Brady was thankful for the momentary diversion. He didn't want to think of his little sister alone and pregnant.

"It was only one time," Crissie blurted before she had the wherewithal to keep from saying what both brothers guessed.

"Should we escort him to the altar?" Roby asked grinning his devilish grin while he spoke. "I'm sure with a bit of determination we can catch up to him. We know the land better than he does. There are shortcuts he wouldn't *ken*."

"I won't say I do to any man who doesn't want me. Besides, he promised to return. Please don't tell father." She was begging now with her eyes as well as her words.

"If anyone would understand, he would," Brady said, as if he knew what a father would think if his daughter's virginity were stolen. Crissie was Connal's only daughter. He would be possessive, furious as well if she was violated. Even if she was willing. Would blame himself for failing to protect her. Connal would make sure he caught up with Walker Endicott before he left the highlands.

"I was the aggressor," she said softly. "I pleaded with him. Begged him to make love to me. I wanted the memory to hold on to while he was gone."

"That doesn't change anything," Roby said aggressively, his fists tight. "The man should have known better. He's a cad, a rogue. He had no right. Now he's gone. He waited until there was no one to answer to before taking your innocence then leaving."

"You're telling me you wouldn't have done the same thing?" Crissie was suddenly more herself.

"Wouldn't have," both brothers said in unison.

"I don't believe you." She crossed her arms in front of her belligerently staring at both of them. "You both have had numerous lovers."

"Would never take a virgin unless she was my mate," Brady said his voice even and steady, hoping he impressed this upon his sister. Didn't know why Walker, a man he thought to be upstanding until now, went against this code of morality. "Even then I would wait for the wedding. It's a matter of principle. All my lovers have been well-practiced in the art of love."

"Couldn't have said it better," Roby told her, taking on the same steady tone as his brother. "Any man worth anything doesn't dally with virgins."

Those words seemed to deflate her. "I love him," she protested in a seeming attempt to defend the man who didn't deserve defending.

"Well, that's a given, Crissie. You wouldn't allow liberties such as those if you didn't. The man doesn't love you or he wouldn't have made love to you a few minutes before he left the territory." By the immediate look on his sister's face, Brady knew he should have never said those words. "Sorry." He was sure the apology came too late.

"You're not making me feel better," she spoke softly moisture brimming in her soft gray eyes. "He asked me if I had regrets. I told Walker no. Now I do." She sat up straighter her chin tilted upward then. "I'm not going to think about it one more minute."

Both brothers watched as she strode from the room, her back stiff. "What if she's carrying his child?" Brady asked, his fear for his little sister suddenly very transparent.

"She was raised too gently. She is stronger than she looks. We will worry about a possible addition to our family in another month. We will also make sure she knows we don't care if the father is not around, will continue to love her as well as the babe."

Brady stayed in the main hall, hoping Lilly was sleeping peacefully. He knew the night before had been exhausting. Roby left, following Crissie in hopes of speaking with her further, easing her fears. Hell, she had to be terrified. The McKenna women didn't get pregnant before they were wed.

Ah, but there had been so few of them.

Brady was deep in his thoughts when a man sat down across from him.

"I'm Lord Fuller. Heard you were asking about me," the man said as he relaxed confidently back in his chair, his hands clasped, resting on his soft belly. "I'm an open book. What do you want to know?"

Inside Brady ran over everything he knew as well as what he wanted to ask. Without harming Lilly, he had to keep his questions in check. It wasn't the scenario he wanted but it was necessary to keep her safe. This man could seriously threaten her. His light blue eyes held evil, his chin weak, although Brady was sure the man understood how to hold power especially over a woman.

He lifted his shoulders in a nonchalant uncaring gesture. "Just curious about strangers. You haven't been here before. Sassenach don't usually travel this far north without a purpose. What is yours?" he asked leaning forward.

The man seemed evasive even before he chose to answer.

"I've a hunting lodge in the hills. Hoping to do some rusticating." He grinned then and Brady felt there was so much more the man wasn't saying.

"Rusticating?"

"Don't care about the hunting. Just want to relax for a week or so. Need to put the cares of London behind me. What better place to do that than in the wilds of Scotland?" Fuller answered as he searched the room not giving away his intent, at least at this moment.

"You looking for something?" Brady asked, wishing fervently he would allow some vital hint about his intentions. He knew full well that until this man left, he could not allow Lilly out of his room.

"Just a willing bed partner for the night. Are there any of those around? Heard there was a lovely lass with wild reddish-blond hair working in the kitchen. Would she perchance welcome a man to her bed?"

The unease Brady felt before multiplied. He hid the stiffness in his voice "No. The women here are protected by the men who care for them. About the lady working in the kitchen? Well, she left a few days ago. Heard she went into Inverness looking for a job. You might find her there, perhaps the whorehouse near the docks."

"Ah, come on, you cannot tell me there are no whores on McKenna land?" He sounded incredulous. "There are always willing women."

"If you go on to Inverness you will find enough lusty wenches to satisfy your needs. We don't welcome men like you here."

Brady understood he was not playing the gallant host as his father would expect. In this case there were extenuating circumstances. No good feelings about this man caused him to be abrupt.

"A virile man like you? You've never dallied with a whore or even a virgin?" The man's voice turned to a sneer. "Don't even think to tell me otherwise. I wouldn't believe you."

Rather than giving answers the man was looking for, Brady responded. "What I've done or not done is none of your business. Stay the night but be on your way as the sun rises."

His anger showing, reverberating through him, Brady stood so quickly his chair toppled to the floor. Before walking to his solar and Lilly, he took one last look at Lord Fuller. Striding toward his solar, he read the letter handed him earlier in the evening.

~ * ~

Lord Fuller? Lilly had forgotten about the old crony of her betrothed. The two had always been inseparable. Many of the rumors circling around her betrothed included Fuller. While Lord Claymore would never physically be able to make the trip to Scotland, Fuller could. He would come here to bring Lilly home for both of them to use. She should have thought to tell Brady but he left so fast. Until a few minutes ago, she hadn't remembered the man.

Her father gave her to these two men. Her stomach turned sour, bile rising to her throat.

She was deathly afraid the two old men meant to share her. What her father had in mind when he settled the contract was beyond her. They must have offered him the moon along with all the stars as payment for her. While she knew her father never loved her, she never believed he would go this far.

Her skin crawled just thinking of the two men pawing her, their sagging bellies apparent. Perhaps they would not take their clothing off. She could only pray as she realized now that if they found her, she would soon be wed to one, a plaything to both of them. Stories about their perfidy abounded in London. She never thought to be the recipient even when Lord Townsend apprised her of the contract. Yet she understood how binding a betrothal was. When all that sunk in, that was when she fled.

Too embarrassed, she didn't want to tell Brady any more than necessary. Tonight, he would claim her. He told her as much. Yet, he'd been gone now for hours. In his suite of rooms, she was still naked in his bed, waiting for him. Since when did she take orders?

From any man?

Her laughter sounded weak, pathetic. She had nothing to laugh about. Especially not Lord Fuller waiting downstairs for her to show herself. No, maybe she could find a way to slip from the castle. Where could she go if she succeeded?

Certainly not to her cottage.

Or back to London.

With those thoughts in her head, she tried to put on the gown, giving up in disgust when she couldn't fasten it. A few seconds later, searching his clothing, she found one of his shirts to wear. She would have to wait for Brady to come back while he left her in the dark to wonder what he discovered below. Grabbing the bottle along with her glass she poured herself a drink willing now to wait for him.

She waited.

When the clock chimed the hour, she woke with a start. He'd not returned. Restless with the bottle in one hand, her glass in the other she roamed the room. Finally, she settled by the fireplace, sitting on a fur rug before tucking her feet beneath her. The flames were dying. She should have stayed in bed and slept. She could not have slept.

Now, she added more wood to the fire, watching the flames burst higher.

This was not the way the evening was supposed to have ended. She thought by now, she would no longer be a virgin. By now, he would understand her words were true. She didn't lie to him. At the moment, it seemed this evening would pass with him still believing she was a well-used whore.

For more reasons than she could enumerate, she didn't want him to think that way about her. If she gave herself to him, she would be a whore with the lofty title of mistress. Damn, she already debated with herself about that status. She just couldn't make up her mind.

Curiously, she saw him the day before he first noticed her. He'd arrogantly strode through the kitchen with his brother, talking earnestly, their heads bowed close together. So, he didn't raise his head nor did he see her. His was a unique face. She was also discovering he was a unique man, even if she couldn't understand what made him that way. His eyes were sometimes molten steel, sometimes a soft gray rimmed with blue. She never really knew what color they would be. She supposed they changed with his moods. His hair was the darkest black just as all the McKenna men possessed certain qualities, gray eyes coupled with black hair. There was strength in his face, the set of his jaw. Everything was put together pleasantly. He was tall, over six feet she guessed. He seemed to be a creation of lean muscle and lithe sinew.

With a puffy little sigh, she decided it was his eyes that attracted her to him. The essence, that magnetism the made him unique, so unusual that always left her breathless when he gazed at her sometime with such an inscrutable expression in his eyes she wanted to punch him then ask him what he was thinking.

Lilly wasn't sure why his gaze was so sensual. It was a look that seemed to dismiss a woman even as it assessed her. He could act so many different ways where she was concerned. Sometimes cordial, courteous, his manner flawless. Other times, when they were alone, he could touch her. It wouldn't matter what he thought of her or that he didn't know her at all. No, she knew something. She'd known it from the beginning before he ever followed her home or kissed her.

He was dangerous.

Denying his appeal was impossible for her. It was stronger than the morality she'd grown up with, and far stronger than reason. He was indeed a sensual man. From the first time she saw him, she felt the draw, a magnetic pull she couldn't deny no matter how she tried. From the first time he touched her, she knew it could not be repudiated. In his arms when he held her, she felt the swift quickening of her heart. Something raw and powerful shimmered around him, encompassed him. Despite all the warnings of her mind, she wanted him.

The bolt slid on the door. She didn't realize he locked her inside. Just her luck, she thought of leaving a few minutes earlier. Escape would not have been possible. Of course, dressing wasn't possible either. So, what did it matter? She could hardly leave wearing his shirt and nothing else.

"Lilly?" He stood in the light cast into the room from the hallway. "Where are you?" he asked a note of panic in his voice.

She heard the tone, didn't want to do anything to make it worse. "Over here. By the fire."

He turned his head. Finding her, he closed and locked the door then strode to her. "Thought you would be asleep in my bed. It's where I would have liked to find you." Now his words held a sensuous tone that couldn't be refuted.

She made a little grunt, "I was worried. Couldn't sleep. Needed to think about this man. Who he is and why he's here?"

"What did you remember?" he asked seeming to guess she recalled something.

"Nothing good," she muttered. Nothing that didn't reinforce her decision to become this man's mistress. Shivering, thinking about wedding with either of the two lords coupled with lying in bed with him made her stomach churn.

"All I learned is that he is looking for a virgin, for you I presume. We both comprehend you won't do for him," his mocking tone didn't go unnoticed. "What did you recall?"

Deep inside she cringed. Lilly didn't want him to mock her or think about her in that light. Until she truly became this man's mistress, his view of her could not be changed.

He was also a very stubborn man.

"As I said nothing good. He's a friend of the man I'm betrothed to." The shudder sweeping within could not be controlled as her imagination brought unwanted terrible visions to her.

"Who is your betrothed?"

Waving her hand in the air she tried to put all her musing about Brady to the back of her mind. Even while he stood in front of her, the draw was unquestionable. "It wouldn't matter if I gave you the name. I'm sure you've never heard of him."

He leaned back in the chair where he sat, his long arms stretched across the back. "Would be nice to know whom I'm dealing with if and when the man decides to show up here."

She laughed, thinking of the portly old man who could barely walk down the steps in his home. He had to be helped each time. What difference if Brady knew the man's name? "Lord Claymore. While he has visions of siring an heir, he couldn't travel all the way to the highlands. He barely leaves his home."

"So, you say." His tone was casual yet questioning.

"The man needs help walking."

"Sitting in a carriage takes little strength."

"It can be exhausting though. Most likely he would not be able to get out once he got in."

Without changing his expression and very blandly, Brady said, "He could always roll out."

Lilly laughed harder. "I suppose that is true. I've a feeling though

Claymore sent Fuller to bring me home. Don't suppose they trust my father now that I fled London. They might think he had something to do with it."

"That won't be possible. Bringing you back to London."

"Why is that?" Lilly caught her breath at the look in the silver eyes now shimmering as if they were burning.

He stood, slowly moving toward her. "I won't let anyone take what is mine."

Standing beside her, he was lifting her into his arms, drawing her so close she felt his heat radiating from him. With her breasts pushed against his chest, his hand on her buttocks pressed her to his length. She felt every potent masculine part of Brady McKenna.

"I don't believe I'm yours, at least not yet." She was breathless nearly panting with the need she felt for this man.

"Should we fix that little problem?" he asked as his lips met hers over and over again, nibbling with his teeth soothing with his tongue.

Lilly knew she could drown in the volatile passion that so easily invaded her when he touched her, stroked her. She wanted to feel the magnetic hunger when he became a part of her.

"If that's what you want."

Suddenly she felt so shy she could barely swallow. He'd touched her intimately, stroked and caressed her. This time was for real. There was no turning back for her.

"Is it what you want, Lilly?" His teeth touched her ear, bit gently as his hand slid up her back, stroked the curve of her hip, higher still to cup her breast before running his thumb across her nipple. "You have to want me Lilly."

"You *ken* that's true. I melt beneath you."

Her breath caught in her throat as he lifted the shirt over her head. She didn't know when she lifted her arms to aid him. His lips against her flesh were wet, searing, hot. A tiny cry of pleasure escaped her throat as his one hand held a breast, stroked the hardened tip before his mouth sucked the rounded globe into his mouth.

"I *ken* nothing of the sort. Do you want me, Lilly? Tell me true.

Don't leave me guessing." Coaxing gently, he moved closer to the bed. "You have to say the one word."

She ran her fingers through his hair, unexpectedly delighting in the power she held over him. He wanted her, needed her, wouldn't finish this unless she told him yes.

"Perhaps I do then maybe I don't," she whispered then sucked in air as he bit the tip of her breast before he let her down gently on the big bed.

She'd been there earlier this evening. They were interrupted. Otherwise, he would now know the truth about her virtue. He would be the man claiming her tonight, making her a woman.

His woman.

"Don't tease me, sweeting." He straddled her; his shirt unfastened by her fingers only a few minutes earlier. Gazing at her, the light in his eyes heated her, melted her set a tempest swirling within.

"Yes," she spoke softly. "Yes, I want you. More than anything, I need you."

Her hands rested on his chest. His hard unyielding muscles rippled at her touch. Amazed she could do that to him, she smiled.

"We will suit well together, you and me." He spread her hair out around her head, sifting his fingers through the strands as he did so.

Until you need to move on to someone else. "Yes." She sighed into his mouth as his lips molded against hers, pressed knowingly to draw the deepest response. She didn't want to think about tomorrow or the day after that even the next month. Tonight was about this moment, nothing more. The decision was made. For as long as Brady McKenna wanted her, she was his. She would give herself willingly to him with no regrets.

There would be no misgivings.

He withdrew from her. She watched with fascination as he disrobed. When he turned to her, she shuddered, the reflex involuntary as she saw him fully aroused. True, she'd seen her brother naked when he was a boy and obviously not aroused. Despite Brady's beliefs, she'd never seen a grown man in this condition.

When he was on the bed with her again, he pulled her to him. "Are

106

you alright?"

"Why?"

Her voice trembled quivering despite her attempts to calm herself. His rod pulsed against her, with what seemed like a life all its own.

"I've..." She stopped herself swallowing the words she couldn't say to him. "You're *verra* large. *Dinna ken* if you will fit."

His laughter echoed around the room. "Of course I'll fit inside you Lilly. Never doubt that. But then, you've known men. Know how it works."

He sounded pleased with her words. The smug expression on his face gave credence to the fact.

He pulled her on top of him, his hands stroking, caressing every inch. Suddenly, she was on her stomach. Searing, wet and very heated kisses traveled the length of her spine, stoking a desperate need inside her. She wanted to yell at him to finish, to be done with this because she could barely breathe. His hands fell away from her. She no longer realized the inferno he generated. Her hips pressed upward, searching for his touch.

His laughter rang out clear and strong, "I'll not abandon you, sweeting. Never that. This loving of ours will take the entire night. I promise you that."

Baffled by his words, she turned to ask. He stopped her when he ran a finger down her back then upward to stroke the curve of her hip. The need and heat, what more would he do to her? The yearning for all these sensations and more sent her blood racing while her heart pounded. His teeth and lips touched her buttocks, kissed and laved coupled with tiny nips with his teeth. He explored all of her, leaving no part untouched, unloved.

She was quivering with need, helpless. Frantic. "Please..."

"Don't you worry. I won't stop." The passionate ardent assault on her body continued.

She moaned with pleasure, couldn't help the soft mewling sounds. Images began flashing through her head. It seemed as if her body floated outside herself. While on some deep level she understood the body she saw was hers, it was not. She cried out, surprised when he turned her to her back. His lips touched upon hers again and again, insistent, captivating melting all of her.

He was on top of her now, her legs spread apart as he settled between them. "Wider, sweeting spread them wider just for me. Let me feel the depth of your heat, your passion, your dark velvet core. This will be magic for both of us." Sparks flashed between them while she did as he asked the magnetic pull undeniable.

She felt the tip of his manhood at her woman's core. Ecstasy seemed to curl and rise within her, deep within her in places she never realized existed. She arched and twisted against him, silently begging him for something she didn't understand. He continued his assault on her body, sucking biting, kissing. His mouth closed over hers again, his tongue dancing and playing with hers until she joined in the uncompromising sensual ballet between them.

The feelings exquisite, he was exquisite pure male animal.

"How do you feel?" he asked as his kisses found each tight bud then moved lower to kiss her belly. The tremors she felt shocked her. Still, she knew there was more. He was denying her something. His hands were beneath her buttocks, lifting as he pressed his mouth against her most intimately.

"No! Brady, please." She was terrified, embarrassed, certain this was not something he should be doing.

He lifted his head, his grin stretching across his face more endearing than she'd ever seen it before. "What? No one has ever done this to you before? You taste just as a woman should yet unique. All Lilly"

No one had done any of this to her before. Everything was new. The silver of his eyes drew her into his magic. He bewitched her. Enchanted her. This was something he would believe. "No, no one has touched me like that, like you touch me."

Once again, he appeared smug, pleased with himself. "Good, that is truly what I wanted to hear from your sweet lips. You can tell me that over and over again if it pleases you."

He returned to kissing her yet this time it wasn't his mouth upon her. His fingers worked their magic, stroking, teasing until she thought she would come undone. More flashes, more images, the pain she felt again and again yet it wasn't her pain. It was buried in centuries deep inside her mind.

"Brady..." His name on her lips was whispered. Small tremors began, increased as she reached for him, her hips seeking him for something only he could give her. She knew this but didn't understand anything.

"Sweet Lilly, soon you will have your release, your pleasure, you will feel the ecstasy only I can give you. Remember *'tis* only I who can give you this. In a moment I will enter your soft velvet depths. You will know heaven in my arms." His lips found hers in another long drugging kiss while his long fingers stroked, as the desperate need he generated in her body increased tenfold. She was beside herself, frantic in her need.

Just when she thought she would die of the pleasure, pass on to another world if something else didn't happen, he thrust inside. She cried out, the pain blinding. For a moment he stopped, pulling away his eyes wide with amazement coupled with confusion coupled with the smug expression she saw before.

"Are you...?"

The question was left unasked. Once more, as if he couldn't stop himself, he was thrusting into her harder and faster. He was deep inside her. Suddenly, he grasped her by her shoulders.

More pain, his nails dug into the backs of her shoulders. The sensation felt as if he grew claws. She cried out for him to stop.

She didn't want him to stop. Again, she saw flashes, more images, soaring through time while all this happened to her over and over again. Her body pulsed, writhed as tremors raced through her in a never-ending wave of delight, the bold ecstasy something she never expected. No longer did she feel any pain only the sweet joy of his lovemaking, the delight coupled with the pleasure he gave.

It was over. He lay still. Brady groaned as he moved to help shield his weight from her, pulling her close. He didn't speak yet she wanted him to say something. Never in her life had she thought this first time would be anything like this. He was still inside her, his hot length filling her. His sweat sheened body heavy atop her, she didn't want him to move.

Still, she was sure something out of the normal happened.

The clock was ticking, the sound almost sweet in the eerie silence. She stroked his back. Ran her fingers through his hair.

"What?" she began. "What just happened?"

The soft masculine chuckle surprised her. "I just made love to a virgin I thought was a whore. In addition, this beautiful woman I've wronged with my thoughts is my soul mate."

He kissed her quickly, rolling to his side taking her with him. She was astonished at what he said, more actually than he ever let on before. "Soul mate? I don't understand."

He sat up before pulling her to a sitting position, "I suppose I've as much explaining to do as you."

She nodded, agreeing completely with him. "I never lied to you."

Laughing, he pulled her closer, caressing her gently. "I'm so sorry. It was not well done of me. I will spend the rest of our lives making it up to. You did tell me you never lied to me. I chose not to believe you. From this moment forth I will always believe what you say. Since you *ken* the one thing, I never tell anyone, perhaps now, you can tell me some of the things you held back."

Lilly couldn't help but look away. In her mind, nothing very much changed these last few minutes. He was still a person she could not trust with the lives of the people who came to her for aid. To Lilly it didn't make one bit of difference what he thought she knew. She could not reveal her brother to him until he left the country. How would she ever know?

When she looked at him, she saw the shimmer of danger in his eyes. "Nothing has changed," she murmured softly lowering her lashes to hide her eyes.

"No, my love, everything is different."

"Tell me how. Tell me why I should trust you, reveal secrets that might put others in terrible danger."

"Because, you and I, we are tied irrevocably together throughout eternity. What happens to one of us will happen to the other. Never would I do anything to harm you or anyone you hold dear."

"So, you say." The unthinking words were blurted before she could stop them. By the look in his eyes, she would give most anything to hold them back.

He said nothing else but walked to retrieve the washbasin and cloth a grim expression on his handsome face. When he returned, he sat down, the bed dipping slightly with his weight.

"Turn around," he spoke softly as he dipped the cloth into the water. "I'm sorry I hurt you twice. It will never happen again."

She closed her eyes as he gently dabbed at her shoulder to remove the crusted dry blood. "What did you do to me?"

"I claimed you. If I could have waited, I would have explained what was happening first. It seemed I had no control, lost what little I had when you began to climax."

"It felt as if you had claws," she murmured still holding the sheet to cover her breasts.

When she looked over her shoulder to see him, his smile was small. Nevertheless, it was there on his face. "I do have claws. Lilly, I'm a shifter. The McKennas are shifters. That's why we don't take sides in political battles. We must have this land to survive for our very privacy. Without it we would not be free. We would all die."

"Shifters?" Her eyes were wide, focused on him. "Mother spoke of such things before she died."

Brady tugged on the sheets while she clung tenaciously to them. "I need to clean the blood from between your legs." He didn't let go but waited, a patient but grim expression on his face.

She sent a shaky breath his way, slowly letting go of the covering. Watching him as he gently touched her, cleaned his seed as well as the blood.

"I have seen and kissed all of you, Lilly." He sat back letting the cloth fall into the bloodstained water. "Now, will you marry me tonight?"

For a moment her heart stopped. Her voice quivering, she stared at him. "Tonight?"

His grin broad, he nodded in agreement with her. "Tonight."

"Do I have a choice?"

Truly, Lilly didn't know where the questions came from. She needed to marry him. A marriage was the only way out of the contract. Did she love Brady McKenna? She didn't know but she wanted him.

"No, no other options."

"In that case, I suppose I will have to do so." Butterflies seemed to flutter deep in her belly.

"Stay here. Don't go anywhere. I'll be back as soon as I can make arrangements. It will take about an hour if all goes well."

She watched as he dressed and left the room, her heart in her throat. It was what she wanted. The air she drew in was filled with his scent where it still clung to the sheets she held tightly.

~ * ~

Lord Fuller paced the tiny room he'd been given. Dirty little secrets nagging in his head, his fury reached an all-time high. Lord Townsend owed him. Lillian was the payment. The fact he had to chase her all the way to Scotland did not sit well with him. Now, he was in danger of losing her.

Brady McKenna was hiding Lillian. He wasn't going to get away with this. The wench was his, promised to him by her not so doting father. The man despised his daughter. If his wife tried to pawn a daughter off as his, he would despise the girl too. Lady Townsend should have known better.

Lord Claymore sat in a chair near the fire. He stretched his legs out in front of him. "You know for a fact the girl is here?" he asked as he fondled his crotch in clear anticipation of having the girl. "We've spent weeks searching for her. Why would she come to this desolate part of the country?"

"Not for a fact," Fuller said rubbing his chin as he paced. "Yet, I've every reason to believe she is in Brady McKenna's rooms. I'd also be willing to bet she is no longer a virgin. So, that much of the bargain must be paid for by her father. We are not getting our money's worth. If Townsend did not prevaricate, Lillian would have been ours the night of the contract. The time we wasted getting here could well change our plans. I did search the cottage where she was supposed to be living. Her trunk was there, the gowns were cleanly owned by someone of wealth. It has to be our Lillian."

"Once we have her, we will just have to wait until we are sure she doesn't carry McKenna's bastard. If we sire an heir, we do want to make sure the brat is yours or mine." Claymore laughed heartily as he sipped his whiskey. "Yes, the thought of having her warms me all the way to my toes. I even feel my rod rising in anticipation. Something that doesn't happen very often these days."

"She will have to do all the work if you are to have her," Fuller sneered, fully intending to manipulate her time. He would make sure Lillian was in his bed more often than not.

"Before you start making all your lofty plans, you need to find her first. Now that McKenna knows why you are here, he will guard her even more closely. Getting her out of his rooms will be the trick." Claymore was staring at the door. "You say you found a willing woman for tonight? One who knows there will be two men to service? Not just one?" Claymore asked.

"Indeed, she should be here any moment."

"Good. I'm famished for a willing wench."

'Yes, well, there are ways. Back to Lilly, I'd rather not resort to anything rash before we try to cajole her from the room," Fuller said. "Perhaps if she learns the truth and what will happen to her father if she doesn't come with us willingly, she will concede, come along without our using force."

"Cajole?" One eyebrow lifted thoughtfully. "Have you ever known Lillian to be cajoled? She has a mind of her own, a free thinker that one. She's a little spitfire. I doubt if she cares what happens to her father after what he did to her. She might care what happens to the McKenna lad."

"Which will make it the more fun to bend her to our ways. I like spitfires. A fighter is all the more fun to have in bed." Fuller guffawed at his comment, clearly imagining all the wonderful things they could do to bend Lillian Townsend to their sordid ways.

"Ah, there she is now," Claymore grinned. "Do you get her first or do I?"

"Perhaps we can have her together. That is a lot more fun. Can be downright challenging."

Fuller opened the door. The girl was young, perhaps even a virgin. All the better. They might keep her until Lilly was ready and willing.

Chapter Five

Brady stepped inside his room to speak to Lilly before seeing to the wedding plans. "Lock the door behind me, Lilly. Whatever you do, don't go anywhere. Don't answer the door to anyone but me."

"I won't," she said her voice soft as she nodded.

As he sauntered down the hall, he whistled so very satisfied with the revelation. Irrevocably content for the first time in his adult life. He didn't think he'd ever been quite so pleased with himself. The moment he first set eyes on Lilly he knew she was special, unique in so many ways, magnetically drawing him to her. He needed to know more about her, all she would allow. Her soft blue eyes whispered of seduction seeming to mesmerize him. Without even knowing what she was doing, she enchanted him, bewitched every sinew and nerve. The soft lines of her body whispered of feminine allure, secrets he needed to uncover. She knew she was special, a gift to be treated gently, treasured with expertise. She was so beautiful he couldn't imagine she was innocent. All he knew was that he wanted her. Even warned away by his father, he could never stop thinking of her.

Lilly was his.

He'd believed that fact from the very beginning. Known he would never rest until she was his mistress. Now, she would be his wife. Finally, he found his father and mother in their rooms.

He knocked before calling out, "It's Brady. Can I come in? Hell, I have to talk to the two of you now. This matter won't wait."

A few seconds later, Connal with his shirt unfastened opened the door. "You can't be put off from this conversation until morning? A reasonable hour?"

Sauntering into the room, he knew he interrupted his parents when he saw his mother finishing with the securing of her gown. "Sorry, Mother. This is indisputably a matter of life and death. The news can't wait until morning. Has to be taken care of as soon as earthly possible."

"Could be your life we're talking about here if the situation isn't as dire as you make it out to be, Brady," Connal growled as he motioned for Brady to sit. He poured them both a brandy.

Brady waved away the drink before saying, "No time for any of that. I'm getting married. Tonight, as soon as I can arrange everything. You and mother need to be there. Could also use your help."

One dark eyebrow arched upward, silver eyes questioned. "A marriage is life or death?"

"Lilly's, yes and mine if I lose her." He was inordinately satisfied with himself, looking forward to the hasty nuptials then the wedding bed afterward. He didn't know if there was time to explain everything. In any case unless he was forced to spill the reasons, he wasn't going to do so.

"Thought I told you to stay away from her," Connal said speaking softly. "She has hidden baggage. There are secrets about her that complicate her life."

"I could not. Told you that from the beginning. She's my mate, father. I know that for a fact now that I've bedded her. I've already marked her as mine. I also *ken* something about the issues that brought her to the highlands. Not enough. Once she trusts me, she will tell me everything." He felt confident in his words, his assumptions.

Brady watched closely as his father took the time to sit down before pouring himself a stiff drink. Wynnie refused but she was smiling seeming happy with his news. It was almost as if she knew before he did that Lilly would come to be more than just a woman, a mistress to him.

"I see. So, you were making her your mistress. Now, that has backfired," Wynnie said, her lips thinned as she seemed to think. "She is to be your wife. Do I have that right?"

"That was the honest truth. I'm not sorry about it. Would have never come to realize who she was if I didn't bed her. All the signs were written plainly for me to see. What can I say? I didn't *ken* anything except the fact I wanted her. That sensation was so intense I couldn't think of anything else."

"Our lust sometimes works in strange ways," Connal laughed again seemingly amused as he looked at his wife. Then back to Brady, "Tonight? What's the rush?"

"I would be honored to plan my first child's wedding," Wynnie said. "You don't have to question why."

Brady didn't have time for any of that nonsense. The planning would have to take place in the next fifty minutes. "Lord Fuller is here. He's looking for Lilly. Her father signed a betrothal contract. I'm sure he means to take her home to London. If she's my wife, he cannot."

"So, would you like me to speak with Father Damian?" Connal asked, downing the drink he just poured then wincing as the liquid fire burned down his throat. "He's probably asleep."

"Yes. Bring him to my room in about an hour. I want to go to the cottage to find something for Lilly to wear. She has a trunk filled with gowns and all those frilly pieces of underwear to go with them. She should have a negligée for the wedding night."

"An hour it is. Should I rouse Roby and Crissie?"

"Just Crissie. I'm getting Roby to go with me to the cottage. Don't want to take any chances."

"I will find her a bit of the McKenna plaid for her to wear with the gown you choose, a sash perhaps," Wynnie said. "I know it's forbidden but perhaps, since no one but family will see you, would you wear your plaid?"

Brady wanted nothing more than to be dressed in the manner of the clan, his heritage. "Yes, I'll make sure I'm dressed appropriately." So many of the highland traditions were curtailed by the British government since the battle of Culloden. Many more would be curtailed tonight because of his haste.

Roby was in bed with his latest paramour when Brady knocked on the door. Once he explained the circumstances along with the reason for the intrusion, Roby was more than willing to mount up to accompany him to the cottage, making the lady promise to be there waiting for him when he returned in a few hours' time.

"You're getting married, laddie. I'm pleased it's not me who found their mate. Not quite ready to give up all the willing maids who find their way to my bed. Believe it's my smile," Roby said laughing. "Or perhaps it's my charming personality. What do you think, big brother?"

"Must be your great rod," Brady chuckled, joining his brother's mirth as he spurred his horse forward, bent on finding an appropriate gown.

The quicker they accomplished the task the sooner he would lawfully be wed, the sooner Lilly would be safe from Claymore and Fuller.

When the pair reached the cottage, the door was open, swinging on its hinges. A sharp breath of air caught in his throat.

"What the devil?" Roby asked as the two men dismounted both, drawing a pistol.

Approaching cautiously, Brady called out, "Anyone here?" He was sure last time he was at the cottage with Lilly the door had been locked. He remembered her hasty and unexpected trip to Inverness. She had not been home since. Blessed hell, he swore beneath his breath. She can't even remember to lock a door. He supposed she was too used to people waiting on her, doing the obvious for her. To live and survive here in the highlands there were a few things she would need to learn.

Inside, the room was a mess. Furniture was moved as well as upended. Lilly's bedroom was a pile of clothing as the intruders had ransacked her trunk. Velvets and satins were scattered across her bed as well as on the floor, frilly very feminine underthings assumed the same disgraceful position. He somehow knew Lilly wasn't the cause of the mess. Brady had the sudden thought he would love to remove those frothy underthings from her body, one he would get to know better later tonight after they were wed.

Roby whistled softly, seemingly surprised by the wealth of clothing. "Lilly never wore any of these dresses, did she?"

"Would you if you were working in the kitchen?" Brady asked

stuffing his hands through his hair as he surveyed the mess.

Roby sent him a sideways glance. With a soft chuckle, "Wouldn't wear them if I wasn't working in the kitchen. What are we looking for?"

"A white or off-white ball gown. If there is nothing like that a pale blue would be nice. Close to the color of her eyes." Brady knew the blue would go nicely with her hair as well as help her eyes to shine bringing out the softness. A darker blue would make them sparkle with the passion he read in them just before he kissed her, when he looked deeper than the surface.

For several minutes they sorted through the vast array of gowns. Finally, Brady settled on a pale blue confection decorated with lace and pearls. The corsage was cut deep which would show off her bosom. The matching chemise and corset were soon discovered as well as the slippers. If his mother succeeded in finding a sash of the McKenna dress plaid, it would go nicely with the gown. He sucked in air thinking of how beautiful she would look when she wore this. His bride. His mate. His fingers twitched with the need to take the clothing off slowly, kissing each tender portion of exposed skin.

Christ, but the wedding couldn't take place soon enough.

When he looked up, he found Roby leaning against the doorframe, his arms crossed over his chest studying him clearly amused. "Should we go or would you like to continue to daydream about your fiancée?"

"Go."

Displeased to be caught in the act of imagining his soon to be naked wife's body, he sauntered to the hitching post. His exit was followed by his brother's laughter. "Just thought you were impatient to get the wedding done since you've already done the bedding."

Brady wasn't going to answer the jest. What he and Lilly already did was none of his brother's concern. Roby's mind was racing in assumptions. His brother had no solid facts that he already made love to Lilly. The man was guessing in any case. Even though he was right made no difference to him at this point.

The ride back was silent except for Roby's songs about the woes of marriage, the loss of freedom. If Brady wasn't so afraid for Lilly, he might have found his brother's antics amusing. As it was, his mind was filled with thoughts coupled with the questions she still did not answer. Tonight, he didn't intend to pursue those questions as they could wait until the morning. What the devil would it take for her to tell him what she was up to here in the highlands? Why he found her in a tavern in Inverness, coming from an upstairs bedroom?

Perhaps she was no longer up to anything.

He could hope.

As they grew closer to the castle, his excitement grew. He was about to make Lilly his wife. A few days ago, he only wanted to bed her until he tired of her. Now, he wanted to spend his life making her happy knowing she would never bore him. They would raise their children here in the highlands. Roby would feel the same way eventually. He just had to find his special and very unique lady.

One who would fulfill all his dreams.

Once they reached the yard, he handed the reins to the boy who came out to take the horses. With the dress in hand, he raced up the steps to his room. Roby followed sedately behind him. The door of course was bolted from the inside.

He pounded on the door. "Lilly! Lilly, open the door. It's me."

The silence unnerved him. He didn't like being locked from his room. The only consolation was that she was safe behind the secured door.

"Brady?"

It pleased him she asked before she opened the door. Maybe she was learning to be more careful. "Yes, we've only got about fifteen minutes to dress. Think you can do it?" The door slowly opened. He grinned to see she was dressed in one of his shirts, most of her long shapely legs showing beneath the hem. Perhaps they should put off the wedding for a few more minutes so he could taste her sweetness again.

"You brought something for me to wear?" she asked, reaching out for the gown along with the other things. "You do realize I will need help getting into the clothing you brought. Do you have time to be a lady's maid?"

"He doesn't but I do." Wynnie along with Crissie stepped into the room. His mother reached out taking Lilly by the hand. "We will be in Crissie's room. Have Connal come for us when father Damian arrives."

Disappointed to have the control wrenched away from him while he watched his woman disappear into another room, Brady swore softly beneath his breath.

"Patience, brother, you'll have her beneath you soon enough. You'll have her for the rest of your life, a long one God willing." Roby stepped into the solar, Connal only a few feet behind him.

Servants bringing food and drink appeared seemingly from nowhere. A tub appeared with hot water. A quick bath would be nice. Speedily he stripped. By the time the water was in the tub, so was Brady. Making swift work of the soap and the water only a few minutes passed before the towel was wrapped around him and he was drying himself off.

Connal brought his kilt to him along with the matching velvet jacket. The shirt he donned was made of the finest lawn with ruffles down the front as well as on the cuffs. Around his waist he fastened the sporran. The knee-high socks added the perfect touch. He looked every bit a highlander.

"Now, we wait for the bride." Connal handed his sons each a glass of brandy. "She is indeed lovely. I'm glad I don't have to reprimand you for disobeying me. The whole thing was a puzzle."

Brady's throat felt clogged, his hands were sweating. The devil, but he already bedded her and claimed her. What did he have to be nervous about? Not the sudden marriage. "Thank you," he murmured barely able to get the words out.

"Hope I show better on my wedding day," Roby laughed as he downed the brandy in a single gulp. He stopped suddenly, a darkness seeming to pass across his eyes. "I've the sudden and strange feeling my wedding day won't be as happy as this.

All Brady could hear at that point was the shuffling of feet as they waited then the sluggish tick of the clock as time passed so slowly, he wanted to roar. More seconds rippled by. He heard each breath each beat of his heart. What the devil was taking her so long?

He stuffed his hands through his hair.

He walked from one side of the room to the other.

It wasn't as if...

It wasn't as if she had a million pieces of clothing to put on, the same million he, a few minutes earlier, thought he would delight in taking off her slender frame. Women shouldn't wear so damn many clothes. A gown was all they needed, nothing underneath. Yes, from now on that was all she would wear. That way he could get to her so much swifter. If he kept her in his bed, he wouldn't have to wait for anything. She would always be naked.

"Father Damian," Connal said with a chuckle as he looked at his son who was now pacing the room like a caged panther, his hands fisted a fine sheen of sweat on his forehead.

"More than ready to perform this service. Hoping the rest of your children will be following suit soon. Ah, but we would like to see another fine generation of McKenna children before *verra* long."

Children? Brady winced. He made love to Lilly, not giving one thought to the conception of a child. He never did that. To his knowledge there were no illegitimate children in his past who might look like him. He was always careful. He had no McKenna bastards.

"Children would be nice." Connal laughed a blessing indeed. "Alistair and I have a bet as to who will get the first grandchild. Since we've a marriage taking place this eve, I think I'm going to win. He doesn't stand a chance. Houston hasn't shown any interest in settling down. Nor have any of his other children."

"Should I tell mother that father Damian is here?" Roby asked as he started to do just that.

"No," Connal held up his hand stopping Roby. "Give them a few more minutes to prepare. I'm sure they aren't ready yet. Have another drink, Brady. You too, Father Damian, if you'd like."

"Don't mind if I do," Father Damian said with a laugh. "Does your lady know all she should *ken* about you?" He held up the drink. "A toast to the oldest McKenna. May you have many beautiful children?"

Brady felt the heat of the liquid sear his throat. All this happened so fast he was bemused as well as stunned. He wanted nothing more right now than to see Lilly walking through the doorway.

The men finished the drink. Another few minutes drug by. Brady looked to his father who was grinning, laughing at him as if he knew something that he should.

With a nod to Roby, "See if they are ready. No, I believe I will do the honors. If she is willing, I'd like to give the bride to my son."

Brady was now standing in front of the fireplace, Roby to his side. Crissie would take the other side as a maid of honor for Lilly. He wondered if Lilly had friends of her own who might have wished to be in attendance.

"Did you forget something, big brother?" Roby was whispering even though there was no one to hear the words except the father.

A slight flush of heat rising on his cheeks, "You know I have no ring. Didn't give it a thought until this moment when you asked. Perhaps you have a solution. I for one certainly do not."

"Seems father thought of everything." Roby pulled a slim gold band with a beautiful sapphire surrounded by diamonds from his pocket. "It was grandmother's wedding ring. Both mother and father wanted you to have it."

The persistent lump in Brady's throat made its appearance again. Truly, he tried to push it down, to swallow, to breathe again. Moisture clung to his eyes even while he tried to blink the tears away.

A noise in the doorway caught his attention. His mother stood, her hands clasped in front of her, a beautiful smile on her face. She mouthed the words, *I love you*, to him. Slowly, she walked toward him, stopping and moving to the side when she was a few feet away.

Crissie, dressed in a gown made from the McKenna dress plaid followed behind. She stood in a place opposite him with room for the bride. When he looked to the doorway, his father and Lilly were walking toward him. The sight of her stole his breath. A sash of the McKenna plaid was wrapped around her waist and draped over her shoulder. Her hair hung loosely around her face, the unbound reddish curls falling to her waist.

Was it only a little over an hour ago when he spread the red-gold strands across his pillow? Was it only a little over an hour past he made love to her, claiming her as well? Even in the dim light, her eyes sparkled with the passion he remembered, her lips twitching slightly as if she recalled something amusing. Maybe she was also recalling their lovemaking.

Connal beamed with fatherly pride as he stopped in front of them before handing her to him. He took her hands in his, accepting her then and for always as his wife. In his mind, this ceremony was a formality, nothing more. He had to remind himself, in the eyes of God as well as the clan Chattan, the ceremony was so much more than a formality.

Father Damian cleared his throat. "We will proceed now in the ways of the ancients and the Clan Chattan." He turned to Lilly. "No matter what happens do not be frightened. All will be fine. Do you understand? Nothing here will hurt you. Trust in your husband. That is your duty as his wife."

Eyes wide, Lilly nodded her understanding as she nervously moistened her lips. "Wynnie explained a few things."

"You are here under no coercion?" Father Damian asked.

Brady held his breath. There had been coercion of sorts but he didn't think she protested. The pressure had not come from him but from her need to be rid of Lord Claymore.

"I'm here freely. I want to marry Brady McKenna." Her voice was soft yet it carried far enough for him to hear.

His breath rushed out. Finally, he was able to inhale again.

Father Damian turned to Brady. "This is all such a rush. I assume this is what the both of you want. When this is done, there will be no regrets between the two of you."

Brady squeezed Lilly's hands, a slight smile on his face. "It is. It must be. There are no other choices."

"Very well then."

Father Damian began to chant, the words nonsensical at first. Brady assumed this was what he meant in the ways of the ancients of the Clan Chattan. While he had witnessed clan marriages, he never realized what might be taking place with the spouse who was not a shifter. He never prepared Lilly for this, never could have since he didn't know.

Lilly's eyes grew wide, her face gradually draining of color. He felt slightly dizzy as the room began to spin on its axis. He closed his eyes trying to keep his feet planted firmly apart. He was worried about Lilly. She was leaning into him, clearly having difficulty standing. He needed to open his eyes, needed to be there for her, support her. Hold her up if she were to fall.

The soft chanting faded away. Father Damian returned to a normal voice. He smiled at Lilly then at him. "Do you take this woman...?"

After both Lilly and he said their respective I dos and Father Damian pronounced them married, he bade him kiss the bride. Brady's breath hitched in the back of his throat then he flooded his lungs with a long deep breath, steadying his nerves. When he pulled her close, her breasts pushing slightly against his chest, he kissed her softly. By his standards the kiss was chaste yet endearing. The scent of her filled him, teased him with the originality.

Roby exuberantly was cheering, his mother and father clapping. Smiles were wide. "You can do better than that," Roby called out generating a momentary spotted pink blush on Lilly cheeks, which swiftly changed as a few seconds ticked by. "Kiss her like you mean it."

Brady shot his brother a baleful glare intending to get even as soon as possible. How he kissed his new bride was no one's business save his.

Father Damian cleared his throat. "I now present to you the Lord and Lady McKenna."

Now, Lilly was leaning against him, her expressive face void of any emotion, deathly pale. She appeared terrifyingly exhausted. Brady was frightened for her, concerned, puzzled as well. He wanted to shoo everyone from the room so he could be alone to speak with her, discover what happened to chase the color from her face.

His family had other ideas, a celebration being in order for the next few hours if they had a say in what was about to happen. He would have to wait to speak with his new bride, the devil how he liked the sound of that, Lilly McKenna.

Champagne corks popped. The cook brought a small cake into the room along with other tasty delicacies. Alistair, escorting Connal's sister, Brenna, appeared suddenly as if they were outside waiting for the ceremony to come to its end. Kit arrived grinning as did the other Stuart siblings, Houston and Riley.

Glasses filled, hands in the air, everyone raised their voice to wish them good luck. Two clansmen entered with pipes blaring a lively Scottish tune. It seemed his mother and father outdid themselves on such short notice.

"Dance!" The call surrounded them. "A first dance for the newly married couple," Once more Roby called out. Kit joined in with the call to dance.

Brady pulled her into his arms with a whisper, "Are you alright? Can you manage one dance on your wedding day? Our first dance ever."

"If you hold me up so I don't fall flat on my face," she told him looking at him with her soft blue eyes. "I would dance with you. You must know I'm still a bit dizzy headed."

For the first notes of the song, they moved slowly around the room. As the seconds passed by, Lilly seemed to grow stronger, a soft rose color returning to her face. They picked up the pace whirling until she was breathless and laughing.

"Should we have a piece of the sweet confection our cook baked so quickly for our special day?" Brady winked at her thinking about just how singular it would be when he could usher all the well-wishers from his suite of rooms and he could have Lilly all to himself. Strangely, he wasn't the least bit tired. He wanted to hold Lilly on his lap, visit with her, drink the celebratory champagne while he enjoyed his new status as a married man with his wife.

"As soon as I catch my breath." She punched him in the arm, a soft twinkle in her eyes. "Need to talk to you about what happened during the ceremony. It was passing strange."

"I suspected you would. It is the way of the clan. Weddings such as ours are always," he paused, "distinctive. Each one is different because all the couples are also unique. No two couples have the same story to tell."

"That would be one way to describe what happened to me when Father..." Closing her eyes she waved her hand in the air. Several seconds rippled by as she tried to suck in air.

"Damian, Father Damian," Brady reminded her softly with a grin accompanied by a kiss to her forehead when he wanted to mold his lips on hers.

"Father Damian was chanting." She ran her hand up his arm, still leaning on him but this time he suspected it wasn't because she needed his support.

"When everyone is gone, after I make love to you again, you can tell me what you saw as well as how you felt," he bent low to whisper close to her ear, noticing the ripple of shivers the gesture created.

He felt her subtle heat, appreciated the sight of the rapid rise and fall of her breasts. He wasn't sure when but he wanted to show her his cat. Wanted to see her reaction to him.

What seemed like an eternity passed before his family along with a few additional friends who wandered into the celebration began to leave. Finally, he was alone with Lilly. For a moment, he wasn't at all sure how to proceed. This had all happened so quickly it quite stole his breath. When he woke up this morning, he'd not expected to wed anyone let alone Lilly.

"Would you like to get into something more comfortable?" he asked, smiling as he poured champagne then dished up plates of food for them to eat while he remembered the lavender negligée along with the matching robe he brought with him from the cottage.

Her nod of agreement sent his body into a heated tailspin as he imagined the barely hidden curves the silk would reveal. Then he offered, "Suppose you'll need help with the gown." Her smile wrapped around him, delighted him in so many ways he couldn't count.

~ * ~

"Suppose you are right. I don't have anything comfortable to put on except the shirt I was wearing, which is in Crissie's room. Should I go get it?"

"You stay here."

The knock surprised her. The door opened. Wynnie poked her head inside, the merry twinkle in her eye obvious. "I've something for you, Lilly." She stepped inside before handing a pale blue peignoir to her. "Something special for your wedding night. I'm sure Brady will appreciate it more than you will."

Brady grinned wickedly as he accepted the gift, running his fingers through the silken fabric. "Thank you, I will no doubt appreciate this more than my bride."

With a wink, he turned to give the negligée to Lilly. "I will save the one I brought from the cottage for another time."

She felt heat rise swiftly and suddenly to her cheeks, her thoughts wanton, erotic too. He was so very right. As to enjoyment, he would obviously be pleased more by the peignoir than she. Indeed, the obvious heat of her embarrassment was readily apparent to anyone looking at her face. At this moment, however, Brady's wanton gaze reflected off her breasts. It wasn't difficult to recall the feel of his mouth at the same location where he stared.

"I will be going."

With a smile that spoke of bemusement, Wynnie left them, the door closing softly behind her, the click of the lock falling when Brady reached the door.

Lilly's heart thundered beneath her ribs. While she knew she would need help with her gown, she hoped he would give her a few minutes after unfastening the dress to adjust to the newness of marriage. Something she didn't have one clue as to how to proceed. Beneath her ribs, her heart thundered while she realized she wanted to see him naked, probably more.

With no hint that he was behind her, his fingers caressed her neck then down her spine as each tiny button slipped from its holdings. With each newly uncovered place, his lips pressed tender kisses. The fabric slowly fell away. His lips followed until he met the soft silk of the chemise then her corset. She held the gown to her breasts lest it would tumble to the floor.

"*Dinna* be shy, sweeting." Still, Brady lingered, his lips touching softly on her skin, stroking with moist caresses generating a swift response, her body tingling in awareness of every moist stroke. "Ah, I feel that you are. I'll wait in the other room. Don't take too long."

The heat from his body coupled with his spicy scent disappeared as quickly as it came a few seconds earlier. She drew in a deep lungful of air, reminding herself he'd seen all of her, wondering how many times in her future she would have to tell herself that. The gown fell to her feet. Quickly, she donned the peignoir as well as the more concealing robe that went with it.

A gift from her new mother-in-law, a very wicked woman one who must know how to please her man. Brady's father would have tutored Wynnie in the ways of love.

When she stood in the doorway to the main sitting room of his suite of rooms, he looked up, a devilish smile on his face. He stood. Holding out his hand, Brady strode toward her. When he reached her side, he captured her in his arms swinging her up so he could carry her to the chair where he sat down with her. Unable to help herself, in any case not wanting to, she draped her arms around him. His sparkling gray eyes coupled with a hint of mischief met hers.

Sitting down with her on his lap he offered her a glass of champagne. She was holding it, looking into the clear bubbly liquid speculating about what to say. Lilly didn't have one idea what might be appropriate conversation for an event such as this. While she'd been in the changing room, Brady had removed his jacket. His lacy shirt he'd unbuttoned so it revealed his chest where her hand now rested on soft dark hair. She spread her fingers, appreciating the way he felt to her touch, relishing the solid male heat springing from his muscled strong body.

It seemed he was also at a lack for words. His teeth and lips found her ear then the column of her neck charting an erotic path that sent fire raging within. Delightful shivers consumed her, spiraled through her all the way to her toes only to find their way back up. His hand ran the length of her side, stroking her waist then lower to the curve of her hip.

She closed her eyes, moistening her lips, afraid of the next question yet compelled to ask, her curiosity brimming with the need for knowledge about her new husband. "Are you ever going to show me what you look like when you've shifted?"

His chuckle sounded softly amused yet tolerant at the same time. "You want to see my cat?"

"I would not be surprised if you showed me now. What would happen if you suddenly shifted and I'd never seen you before? I could die of fright of sheer terror," she told him, her voice filled with concern yet she also felt a sprinkle of amusement sift into her words. "Will our children be shifters too?" Immediately, she lowered her lashes, horrified she might have said something untoward. Perhaps it was too soon to think of a family.

"First, I would be happy to show you my cat if you promise not to scream then run from the room in this flimsy gown. No one except me should see you in this. Second, our children might be shifters. There is a chance they will not. Since you are not a shifter, there is a fifty-fifty chance. We shall see, won't we? Suppose we will need to conceive first. Should we get started sometime this night?"

By admitting to her he was a shifter, he gave his life into her hands. He trusted her. She didn't see how she could do any less. Still, the thought of revealing her brother to him as well as the mission to send homeless Jacobites oversees was too much to ask of her.

Not yet, not until...

Not until when? What more did he have to do to prove to her he could be trusted with every aspect of her life? Perhaps tomorrow would be a good time to begin this conversation.

"Could you do it now? Change?" She turned into him, tracing his jaw with a fingertip relishing the soft stubble there.

He mimicked her caress doing the same to her. "Actually," he brushed his lips across hers, "I would rather wait." He paused seeming to think. Then, "No harm, I suppose, in doing so now. Are you ready?" He set her on the chair, slowly undressing until he stood in front of her naked.

His tall body muscled, so beautiful the sight stole her breath, her heart rattling around beneath her ribcage. "If you keep looking at me like you want to eat me, I won't be able to change form. I'll have to have you right now, this very instant. It wasn't my plan for the evening to consummate the marriage immediately. Although under the circumstances, the consummation might be appropriate sooner than later."

She tucked her bottom lip beneath her teeth lowering her lashes in what she hoped was a provocative manner. She didn't have any idea how to flirt even though she'd watched some of the most practiced courtesans in London do that very thing. Lilly didn't care if he shifted for her this moment. After watching him disrobe and now stand in front of her, his perfect male body presented for her to feast on, she wanted him to make love to her again. She wanted to touch parts of him she'd not stroked before.

"You're doing it again," he murmured softly, one of his long-callused fingers beneath her chin.

"What?"

"Making it blessedly difficult, *nay* impossible, to think or move except to gather you into my arms. Best I do this before it is no longer possible." Now, he didn't hesitate.

Lilly watched fascinated as slowly he began to take on a different form, so immersed in the process, she couldn't take her gaze from him. After only seconds, Brady sat on his haunches in front of her. She was sure he was cocking his head and grinning at her. Padding to her, he set his chin on her lap, looking at her through his beautiful cat eyes. She was sure he was asking her to pet him. She stroked his head, rubbing his ears. Softly, he purred for her. The breath she sucked deep into her lungs was wobbly weak at best. This was far more than she expected. His tail twitched.

In one bound his front legs were on her lap, his nose inches from hers. "Oh."

A moment later, he settled down, lying half atop her, still purring. She stroked his back, watching him arch contentedly. "You are ever the rogue, now aren't you? Even now you are taking advantage of me. You are a very crafty cat."

Lilly continued to stroke him. It was enough for now. She grinned despite the way this set her nerves a kilter.

Once again, she was at a loss. Not for words but for something else, some kind of communication. He rubbed his head on her breasts, purring even more loudly. "Brady?" Her eyes widened at the subtle caress. "*Nay.* You stop that. It's not right. I *ken* what you are thinking. If you want to do that, you have to change back right now."

He looked at her, his raspy tongue touching her chin for less than a second. She could have sworn she heard him say "Hmm...."

"You're enjoying yourself far too much. Now that I've seen you in your cat form, I want you to change back and stop teasing me. It's not right or fair of you to do so."

She clearly heard him tell her he would be naked. Did she want that? Well, he was naked when he changed to his cat. Of course, she wanted him naked.

Well, no, not yet. He stripped in front of her in order to change. Sternly, she said in the most authoritative voice she could summon, "You can dress just as easily as you undress. You *dinna* have to remain naked."

With that said, he jumped off her landing lightly on the floor in front of her. He changed back, rapidly wrapping his kilt around his slender hips.

His grin sinfully wicked, his voice as soft as butter, with his hands on his trim hips, he asked, "Did you like that?"

She nodded while he set her across his thighs once more just as if nothing untoward just took place. "You are magnificent."

Lilly could have sworn he beamed while he arched one perfectly shaped dark eyebrow toward the ceiling.

"Well, you are." She defended her words.

"So are you." He nuzzled her neck down to the rapidly beating pulse at its base. He sat up abruptly, handing her the glass she set on the table earlier. "Since I showed you something about me, showed you who I am, perhaps..." He let the sentence land on thin air.

It wasn't hard to understand what Brady was asking her. She

should tell him something. She couldn't remember what he knew and what he didn't. "I told you about Lord Claymore. Did I mention Lord Fuller?"

"Yes." The ensuing sigh sounded dissatisfied perhaps even frustrated. "You *ken* what I want to know. I'm not going to pursue the questioning on our wedding night when we can pursue things much more pleasurable. However, I am going to ask you what drained the color from your face during the ceremony. At the sight, I was deathly afraid you might faint."

"Even though Father Damian told me not to be afraid, I was terrified. Had no idea what would happen." She remembered the rushing of the wind, the twirling of the room so fast she couldn't keep her feet beneath her or her knees from buckling. Somehow, she did though. "Did you hold me up?"

"*Nay*, lass but you did lean on me. Your fingers left tiny little marks on my arms where you gripped so tightly I thought you would pierce my skin."

His remark seemed to amuse him as he chuckled. The look in his eyes was sweet, so very caring.

Her eyes widened. She felt the shimmy of desire enfold her tenderly. "I'm sorry. I didn't mean to hurt you."

He chuckled, showing a smile of even white teeth. The palm of his hand settled on her cheek, his thumb lightly stroking her lips, enticing, luring more intense feelings to surface. "After what I did to you earlier, suppose one could say I deserved a tiny bit of pain. Lilly, it was nothing."

"Are you sure?"

"Nothing to worry over. Why were you terrified?" he asked, bringing the palm of her hand to his lips to caress softly with his lips to moisten with his tongue.

He held her there for the longest time.

"Everything was moving so quickly I couldn't breathe. The sensations so intense they stole all thoughts. A wind threatened to whip me off my feet. Yet all the while I heard his singsong voice, chanting words I didn't understand. It was the voice that reassured me, gave me strength to continue despite the way the ceremony unnerved me. He constantly reminded me all would be as it should be, to be patient. He said you and I would endure through time, through all eternity to always meet again and again. Nothing and no one could ever keep us apart. It was the same as you told me after you claimed me."

"It is as I thought." Reverently, Brady kissed her fingertips, smiling at her each time he took one between his lips then sucked it into his mouth. "Sip your champagne, sweeting. Are you hungry?"

He was changing the subject, taking her mind off his not-so-subtle coaxing to his bed. Yesterday was surreal. She didn't know what to expect now. "I'm hungry and thirsty. Afraid if I drink too much of this, I'll fall asleep."

"Not a chance in hell of you sleeping on your wedding night, at least not until we are through satisfying each other, completely irrevocably sated, so exhausted we can do nothing except sleep. I want my wife begging for more and more."

He set her on the chair again. This time when he left, he filled a plate for her. "You have to eat all of this then we will proceed with the wedding night." Lovingly, he ran his hand along her arm.

Her amused laughter stopped him, his brows drawing together. "I couldn't possibly." The plate was overflowing with food. "Not unless you wish for me to turn into a roly-poly ball or get sick."

"A roly-poly ball, hmm...I see. I think I would like that. Perhaps we have already begun that process." His slow lazy gaze sent a spiraling of wicked sensations down her spine.

Truly, she didn't have one idea what he spoke of. "Are you mad? Whatever are you talking about?"

"Pleasantly besotted would be a better word. Father Damian put a thought in my head. Can't seem to get rid of it."

"What was that?" she asked as she fed him a piece of cheese off her plate instead of herself. "What notion did the good father set in motion?"

"Children."

"I have not accustomed myself to marriage as of yet. Now, you speak of babies. Whatever would I do with a baby? If we have them, I hope you know what to do. I do not."

She fed another piece of cheese to him, her fingers touching his lips prompting a tiny groan to rumble from deep in his chest.

"Figuring it out could not be too difficult."

He laughed looking pleased with himself as well as her inability to decipher his true meaning. Eventually, she would figure everything out.

"Speak for yourself," she muttered feeling a deep-seated embarrassment with herself. "I've no idea what you speak of," she chatted as she fed him another tiny morsel of food.

"I see your ploy. It is a game of food. However, I guarantee you if you don't also feed yourself, you won't have the stamina for the night to come. Sleep is not a necessity on a wedding night. My intention is to keep you up the entire night."

"You changed the subject," she said unhappily wishing he didn't tease her with his words. It seemed they were speaking of two different things. "And," she hesitated thoughtfully, "I'm not playing any games with you. I simply cannot eat all this food you gave me."

"Very well, perhaps we should proceed with the next step in our evening."

Lilly wasn't at all sure how he did it, but his agile fingers undid the robe, slowly robbing her of all inhibitions. When the blue fabric pooled around her hips, she caught a tiny gasp in her throat as she tossed her head back giving him more flesh to stroke and kiss. Brady's eyes simmered, danced with desire, his passion building. Bending his head, he sucked a still veiled nipple deep into his mouth, his tongue curling hotly around the sensitive bud, teasing and shaping it. Her sounds of appreciative delight could not be curtailed as her body writhed and arched responding to his sensual wheedling.

He did know exactly how to play her body, the dance sensuous heating her from the inside out. The tempestuous storm he generated within her blazed to an inferno. Still, he held back. Her fingers unfastened the kilt he wore. He was naked beneath. She threaded her fingers into his hair. Felt his face cradled against her breast. Slow simmering ardor flashed faster and higher. He turned her so she straddled him. Her long slender legs wrapped around him. Murmur followed whisper, gentleness tempered urgency. All the things he said, the things he did, movement and measure, she would remember.

Delight upon ecstasy...

So, would she recall with vivid imagery the sweet enchanting beauty of this night. So, would she recall the tender concern he treated her with.

The evening passed too swiftly, too sensuously. Before the night should have ended, morning sunlight filled the solar with its soft promise of a new day. When she woke, his arm was around her a hand cupped her breast, flicking the nipple, playing once more with her body. One of his long muscular legs was thrown over hers holding her in place.

"You are an insatiable animal," she murmured softly as she tried to turn to meet his gaze.

"You a greedy wench. Whatever should I do with you? Keep you in bed all day?" he asked a delightful amusement hinting in his voice. "Would you like that?" His lips teased her ear, her neck, the shoulder peeking out from beneath the sheet.

"Everyone would know what we did." Heat rose swift and true, touching on her cheeks as well as the rest of her body.

"Is that such a bad thing? We should stay here until you are with child," he murmured as he slowly slipped inside her body.

Lilly didn't know what to say to his words or his actions. Obviously, what they were doing would create a child. It was his wish. So, it might not be as fearful as she thought it might. "Don't you have work to do?" she queried her words spoken so very softly as she arched toward him, urging him to continue instead of stop. She didn't want him to leave.

"Not today, not this morning."

As he moved slowly within, he nuzzled her ear, fondling her breast, teasing her intimately as she slowly felt the rise of passion and pleasure. "Where is your heart, sweet Lilly?"

If she knew, she still couldn't find the words to answer. The little mew of ecstasy spilling from her lips caught her by surprise. As always, the tremors slowly grew until she could hold back nothing. She closed her eyes, letting the intoxicating delight overwhelm her. "Brady!"

He laughed. With another hard thrust, he too climaxed. He pulled her against his broad chest. She felt replete, satisfied. He ran a finger down her arm then back up stirring more warmth. The movement was idle, not meant to seduce. She pushed back against him, enjoying the slow loving moments, feeling secure in his arms. These seconds were as fulfilling as the climaxes he brought her to.

Lilly didn't think she ever felt so safe and protected as she did now, with this man his body entwined with hers sharing each slow breath with him. How did she ever get so fortunate to find a man such as Brady McKenna? The sting of his hand on her bare buttocks brought her away from her wistful musings.

"Brady!"

"Would you like a bath this morning?" he asked softly as if he didn't just swat her on her bare bottom.

"What do you think?" she answered with another question, his eyes on her, teasing, resting on the naked flesh revealed.

His wicked smile, his voice purring softly. "Share?"

"A bath?" Her eyebrows rose in silent question. Never in her wildest imaginations had she thought of something so decadent.

"Yes."

"Doubt if we would fit," she told him strangely disappointed at that thought. "It would have to be an extremely large tub."

"That is exactly why it will be so much fun to share. Our arms and legs will be nicely tangled together."

"If you think to get anything done today, we will have to take separate baths. If not, we will never leave the room," she said the prude in her shining clear in her voice as well as her words.

"I don't plan on doing anything today except bedding my wife, embarrassing her thoroughly so I can witness firsthand the beautiful blush stain your cheeks as well as your breasts a rosy color. It's even more enticing when your belly turns that remarkable shade of pink."

She hit him over the head with a pillow. "We have to go down to breakfast. Your parents will miss us."

"They will not expect us to appear."

She hit him again, laughing, kneeling, unwilling to stop.

"So, you would like a tussle," he said ignoring her statement just as she knew he would.

"No."

Yet she hit him again.

"Little liar."

He grabbed her hands rolling over so he lay atop of her, her hands above her head, stilling her more with the passionate hot simmer to his eyes than his brute strength, appearing too pleased for his own good.

Lilly was breathing hard, wondering what his next move would be. She bucked trying to dislodge him. He grinned. His eyes twinkled with laughter before they turned dark again with desire, the sensual passion in him so evident in all that he did.

"A bath," she blurted as if that would stop him from his primary intent.

"Later, sweeting, much later. You managed to bring out the animal in me. It seems I cannot let you go right now."

Several hours later they emerged from their rooms. Hand in hand they strode downstairs. Lilly understood all too well that the presence of Lord Fuller would unleash a barrage of questions. Most of them had been answered. What of the ones no one knew to ask? She didn't intend to answer anything.

There were two very important questions that had not been satisfied.

When they sat down, Connal was there, his steely gaze so much like his sons unwaveringly focused on her. His meaning was unreadable yet penetrating.

"Lord Fuller left the inn where they were staying with his companion, an older man. I'm going to assume it was Lord Claymore," Connal said as he sat back, relaxing with his cup of hot tea.

"That news is for the best," Brady murmured, scrutinizing Lilly, his thumb rubbing tender circles on the back of her hand. "We don't want those men walking around here seeking out my wife."

"They will be back," Connal said with a look in his eyes that brokered no argument.

"How do you know? Won't the news of the wedding send the two men home? Nothing is left here for them."

For some reason Lilly thought her troubles except those surrounding Douglas and the fleeing Jacobites were over. From the set of Connal's eyes, it appeared they were not.

"Their kind don't usually give up," Brady said, agreeing with his father. "We could always send them through the Kinnel Stones and be rid of them forever."

"Only as a last resort and only if they persist in their intentions against your wife. You need to discover the hold they have over Lilly." Connal directed his hard gaze her way. "She knows things she is not telling you."

"What are the Kinnel Stones?"

She watched the men looking between each other wishing Connal did not put forth that particular statement. Brady would push harder for her to tell him what she wasn't.

Connal leaned forward, his forearms resting on the table. "Rumor has it, if a person enters the circle they will disappear forever."

"That would solve my problems," she said softly her gaze on the floor.

"Perhaps, perhaps not." The question was still unasked and unanswered.

She stiffened her back. "I've no idea what they hold if anything over my father's head. Obviously, he must have gained something by selling me. Don't think he despised me enough to sell me without his own gain."

~ * ~

Lord Stephen Townsend paced the tiny confines of the Silver

Moon Inn in the village near the McKenna castle. The rustic inn was owned by the laird, operated by the McKennas, cousins and second cousins of the laird.

Sweat beaded on Stephen's forehead. As he paced, he searched for a way out of this dilemma he found himself in over a year ago. He tried everything to win the money he lost back. Each time he was sure he had a winning hand or the winning horse his luck backfired, the addiction evident and growing since Lillian's mother died. She'd been the sole person who could curb his desire to gamble. She was gone. Now he had no one.

Selling Lillian was the only way out of the predicament. It was either give her to the doting old Lord Claymore for the amount he owed all his creditors or find himself in debtor's prison. Thoughts of his daughter beneath that man made his skin crawl with loathing. However, after weeks of threats, he'd found no way from his predicament.

Luck abandoned him.

Douglas was his last hope. When his son fled London only to disappear, he lost what little confidence he had in solving his financial problems. Disgusted with himself, his breath rattled slowly from his throat.

He didn't approve of Douglas or the cause his son put himself in jeopardy to support. Douglas was supposed to be the next Lord Townsend, his heir. Douglas would have found a way to right this predicament, to pay the gambling debts he accrued. Now, he was hiding in the northern wilds of Scotland to escape demanding creditors, hoping to find Lilly and convince her she could still solve his problems.

He sat down on a chair, facing the fireplace. A snifter of brandy sat nearby. His shock at discovering Lillian had followed her brother here left him unable to defend his position with Lord Claymore. When Lillian discovered the betrothal, she fled leaving him to make excuses.

Now, rumors here in this village were ripe with news of his daughter's marriage to the oldest McKenna boy, making her nearly untouchable. The clan defended their own to the death. Although with the right amount of coin coupled with knowing the right men, a man could have a marriage annulled easily enough, especially since a contract was signed.

The knock on the door didn't surprise him, neither did the man who stepped inside. "Lord Fuller." he murmured without looking up from the flames licking the charred logs in front of him. "To what do I owe this unwelcome visit?"

Fuller didn't say anything. Townsend heard the shuffle of his feet along with the splash of brandy filling a glass. Silence lingered in the small room while both men sipped the amber liquid and stared at the flames.

Finally, "How do you expect to get the girl back?" Fuller asked as he examined his nails. "I don't like waiting for what I've been promised. She should have been in Claymore's bed as well as mine months ago. Instead, we had to traipse all the way to this god forsaken place just to find out she's wed another."

"I don't know."

His broad shoulders lifted in a shrug of despair while he thought of the game downstairs. Perhaps one more try would win him enough cash to stall Claymore and Fuller. He had enough money to purchase a spot. The stakes were high. With luck, he could win everything back.

With luck...

"Best you figure something out," Fuller said, his voice quite calm, unnerving in the delivery. The threat was quite evident.

Townsend knew the underlying anger was held behind the man's teeth. Fuller rarely showed emotion. He was furious he lost the girl more than the loss of the coin, which was little to nothing to him. Whit a slight lift to his slumping shoulders, "I'm open to suggestions."

"Heard your son Douglas hasn't left the country as he planned. He's been hanging around Inverness, the harbor. He's a wanted man. Turn your son in to the authorities. The bounty on his head would go a long way in covering the debt to me. If you do that, perhaps we can work out some sort of payment. Lillian would have to play a part in that scheme however. I want her and won't rest until she's away from McKenna and in my bed."

"Hand over my son? Never!" Stephen felt the noose tightening around his neck. The sweat that previously beaded on his forehead now slipped down his neck onto his back. His son meant the world to him. Lillian came into his life with her mother. While he brought her up, she wasn't his blood. Lilly meant nothing to him except a way out of his troubles.

Fuller rose, resting an elbow on the mantel above the fireplace, nonchalantly sipping the brandy. "It's a choice you'll have to make, your daughter or your son. I wouldn't find any difficulty myself if faced with the decision. One is worth the coin she will bring the other is your heir."

"My daughter is married now. I'm sure no longer a virgin. Doubt if Brady McKenna will hand her over, give her to Lord Claymore without a fight."

"No, I don't suppose he would do anything like that. Ah, then the son would have to be exchanged. He's already abandoned you. Heard he's sailing to America to start over. He won't be too useful as an heir so far away."

"I won't give up my son."

"Your daughter."

Tears welled in his eyes even though he still harbored thoughts of the game to start in less than an hour downstairs. "They would lash him before they tossed him in *gaol*. He might never see the light of day again. Would that be better than handing over his son? He would have to first find his son."

"Ah, but he might be able to escape," Fuller said. "I would, however, prefer your daughter in my hands as well as at my beck and call for as long as a I choose. Think on it, Townsend. You've 'til tomorrow morning to make your decision."

With his head in his hands, Townsend listened to the door bang shut. "Bloody hell." He knew he had one choice. He stood. Before he headed out the door and downstairs, he downed the remainder of his brandy.

It was the same choice as he made months ago.

Chapter Six

Brady stepped into the rose garden searching for his illusive wife, scratching his head. There were not a lot of places she could be. He hunted everywhere in the castle. Whenever he looked for her, the garden was where he would find her. Heading in that direction, he discovered this time was no different. Caught by surprise when he saw her in the shadows speaking with a man, he stepped against the wall circling the garden. His breath catapulted to his gut as he watched.

Two weeks had passed since their hasty and unusual wedding. Lilly still didn't reveal any of her secrets, keeping everything close to her heart. He didn't know what he had to do to win her trust. What little patience he had left was quickly coming to an end. However, the sight of her intimately whispering to this man sent his steady but calm reserve to an explosive level. He'd been a patient man, too patient. He needed to know the identity of this man who she trusted more than her husband.

His fists clenched and unclenched with the need to hit the man and perhaps talk later. Jealousy united with anger then pooled in his gut submerging him with feelings he had never experienced before Lilly. This situation untenable, he cursed softly, hitting the brick wall he was standing beside instead of the man. His life seemed to revolve around two distinct categories; before Lilly and after Lilly.

Shaking his head to ease the pain of his stupidity, he realized the loving pair must have moved on. While Brady wanted, no yearned to trust in her, he didn't. Ample opportunities were presented to her to confide in him.

She didn't.

Instead, she chose to continue to hold herself back from him, constantly reverting to silence when confronted with a question. Her reticence spoke of distrust, of secrets, of complications he didn't want to deal with. If she would just tell him what the devil she was up to, he would believe in her, aid her if necessary. He had the sinking sensation he would not be pleased, but he would deal with his raw emotions. Perhaps that was the reason she didn't want to confide.

He couldn't help her if she didn't reveal the complications presented to her. As the weeks passed, they should have grown closer. Instead, a chasm between them seemed to open growing ever wider. He could not abide the secrets. He would have it no more.

The pair walked farther into the shadows distancing themselves. Hell, but he wanted to wrench her away from the man, shake her until she understood how much he cared, needed to find out the reason for the apparent affection these two people had for each other. While he knew first hand now that she'd never been with another man, the fact didn't change that she might choose to give herself to the Englishman now.

Deciding to put an end to this tryst once and for all, he strode angrily in the direction the two had disappeared. When he rounded the corner, he was greeted to the sight of his wife with her nose buried in one of the yellow roses on the grounds. Her erstwhile lover was nowhere to be seen. Instead, she appeared to be making love to the flower as she gently stroked the petals down the long column of her neck.

"Lilly!"

His gruff voice seemed to startle her. She looked up, her soft blue eyes wide the color ever-changing with her moods. Good, she should be surprised. Where the devil did the man vanish? He stepped closer not meaning to intimidate though he knew he did just that. "We need to talk."

"No," she murmured turning from him, her attention once more on the flower she held beneath her chin.

"Now."

She looked up again, still, her eyes wide, startled pools of blue. They continued to darken as he approached until they were a deep sapphire. With a breathless voice, sounding guilty she asked, "Brady? Wwhat are you doing here? I thought you were with your father."

That was why she had the temerity to meet with this man. She thought he was busy, would not discover her duplicity. "Was wondering the same about you," he said his voice smooth, tinged with all the pent-up anger he felt when he saw her with the man who was rapidly becoming his nemesis.

The air in the garden instead of sweet smelling offered up a rancid scent to him. Bile rose in his throat. He didn't want to mention the man, needed for her to tell him of her own accord exactly who he was as well as what he meant to her. Yet he'd given her more than enough opportunities to do just that.

She had not.

She plucked the rose from the bush. Focusing her attention again on the inanimate object, she held it to her nose, let the velvet, soft petals caress her cheek. The repetition of this erotic delight unnerved him. His body reacted violently and immediately to the sensual scene she inadvertently created. He wanted to follow the path of the petals with his lips, his teeth, moisten the path the rose took.

At least he thought it was unintentional.

With a look that bespoke of questions, she tolerantly asked, "What does it look like I'm doing?"

Her sarcastic words enraged him, touched a part of him he didn't know existed. "Perhaps you would like to enlighten me."

Still, he didn't want to mention the man unless she brought up his name first. Even with his burgeoning anger coupled with the lust she created with the damn flower this was still a matter of trust between them and their fledgling relationship. How the devil could he trust a woman who didn't trust him?

"Smelling the flowers," she spoke softly, almost whimsically while her wide blue eyes skimmed his body. "The roses to be more exact if that is what you want. I wouldn't think to disappoint you."

Blurting out a question about the man and what she was doing kissing him was almost on his tongue. As she stepped closer, he caught the scent of roses in her hair. He knew the scent very well. She bathed in it every day. He picked up a strand of her hair, holding it close, inhaling the scent that was Lilly.

He leaned closer, his breath whispering heatedly against her cheek, knowing it floated across her mouth, her lips, her cheek. "I want you to be even more exact. What were you doing before you were smelling roses?" he asked his voice harsh, his grip on her arm tighter than he wanted.

Quickly, he loosened his fingers as he stood his ground, so close to her he felt the heat from her body the shiver of desire he knew he generated.

Her eyes simmering with questions, she stepped back, rubbing her wrist where he'd grabbed her. "Before? Before what?" she asked her voice wobbling with her burgeoning fear.

She was playing with him. He didn't like it. "Before."

"I *dinna ken* what you mean?"

She blinked a few times as she turned away from him, leaving the sweet curve of her back for him to ogle. He could do nothing more than imagine her naked, her soft flesh ready for his caress. He wanted to run those flower petals across her breasts, watch as the tips hardened. Then the velvet soft petals he would have them travel lower, across her belly, the soft inner part of her thighs.

"You do. You just don't want to tell me."

His bitterness rang loud and clear in the tone of his voice, angry at her but angrier at himself for the lust he couldn't deny. He turned away, rapidly striding through the gardens his fury written clearly in every tight movement of his body. He had to get away from her.

He needed to leave the keep and Lilly behind him for a few hours before he did something he would regret. Needed time to release the unexpressed frustration he harbored when it came to Lilly and her secrets as well her body. In the stables he discovered Roby had followed him there. A slight curve formed on Roby's lips as he approached with seeming caution.

"What do you find so amusing?"

Brady saddled his horse swiftly wishing to ride out of the

suffocating confines he found himself in. The open air of the countryside would prove to be a welcome distraction. Perhaps he could breathe.

"Nothing," Roby said as he followed suit, saddling his horse with every intention of shadowing him.

"You're not coming with me."

"In your present state of mind, you need me whether you want to admit it or not. Maybe I'll hang back, give you the room you are seeming to crave at the moment," Roby declared with wry amusement coupled with a crooked half smile on his lips. "Marital paradise not to your liking? Suppose soul mates can give you just as hard a time as any wife."

"Don't need anyone right now. Not fit company."

He set his horse to a gallop leaving the castle behind and he hoped his little brother.

He did not.

The two brothers rode without speaking, this stillness between them just as suffocating as Lilly's silence. When he finally slowed his horse to a walk, Roby spoke up.

"Perhaps you should beat the truth out of her," Roby said sardonically. "Might make you feel better."

Brady had no words. He shot his brother a look of distaste, his eyes showing all the emotions he held back for weeks now. "You might have a point. Too bad I could never lift a finger to hurt her."

"Then you should keep her in your rooms and make love to her until she is so exhausted she doesn't have the strength to betray you. That is what you fear? Betrayal? Is it not?"

Those easily spoken words caught his attention along with the ragged breath he tried to suck, without success, to sweep into his lungs. "Betray me? What do you know about her?" He was instantly on edge. What the devil did his brother know that he didn't?

Roby reached into a pocket drawing out a folded piece of parchment. "Here, you might be interested in this." He handed over the missive. "Doesn't mean she has betrayed you. Doesn't mean she hasn't. It's just an interesting bit of information for you to mull over. I'm guessing you'll recognize the man."

Brady pulled his horse to a stop, unrolling the paper. He stared at it for the longest time, his air held inside his lungs. When he finally looked at his brother, "The hell you say. Beat her? I'm going to skin her alive."

He turned his horse intent on racing back to confront his wife. Roby reached out to stop him. His stallion reared his legs pawing in the air.

"Hold on," Roby said softly. "We should discuss what you intend before you do something you'll regret."

"Already regret what I'm thinking." His wife was involved in the Jacobite revolution. She would end up in *gaol*, lashed. They could hang her for her part. He couldn't let that happen. In the short time he'd known her she was sunshine and light, a melody he couldn't stop humming. To put her in a dark place to live out her life would kill the sweet breath of air that she was.

"Did you happen to notice the name on the warrant?" Roby said blandly, holding back any emotion that might trigger him.

Brady knew the tact well. He used it to help his hotheaded little brother whenever his temper flared uncontrollably. Now the technique was being used on him.

Brady pulled the crumpled ball of paper from his jacket pocket where he stuffed it. Somehow, he overlooked the name when he recognized the face. "Douglas Townsend."

"Who is he to her?"

"Damned if I know," Brady said softly with a whistle of air escaping him. "Damned if I know. I'm going to find out though."

He would sit her down. Before she could prevaricate, he would demand answers. As her husband it was his right to *ken* what he was going to have to rescue her from. Now, however, he had something with which to confront her. She would explain. Frustration ate at him, filled his soul to overflowing with pointed barbs. Where was her heart? It certainly wasn't with him, her husband.

"He's wanted for aiding and abetting the men fleeing from Scotland. The few men who survived the battle of Culloden, a good and noble cause, one worthy of any Sassenach," Roby persevered even though he must see his eyes smoldering with fury. "He's most likely a good and fair man. A man who deserves loyalty."

His wife would not get caught up in this deadly game this man played no matter who he was to her. He wouldn't allow it. If it became necessary, he would chain her to their bed. "I don't know anything. Only what you've read there and told me. How did you discover this?"

"Walker, Walker Endicott, before he left for home spoke of the man. Guess he knew him when he was a member of Parliament. Douglas Townsend dared defy the House of Lords. Dared to put forth a memorandum that would give those men asylum, saying they should be forgiven for the part they played and the forgiving was long overdue."

"He did."

That was something else he could speak of with Lilly. Time to wait until she became forthcoming was over. The matter too important, time too precious. She would tell him her part in this scheme of Douglas Townsend's and what part the Sassenach played in her life. If he could do anything, he would keep her from the British. "My God, does she have any idea what could happen to her if she plays any role in this treasonous scheme? Does she have any idea that the English are set to kill any man who took part in that battle or who in any way supported the Jacobite cause? Does she?"

Roby cleared his throat, his apparent concern for his brother obvious on his face. "I would guess she does and has chosen to play a role in this misadventure. What that is remains to be seen."

Brady peered down the road toward his home, her home. This time fear for his family surfaced. "She could bring the British army down on our heads. We could lose everything."

"It would not take much. There are those who resent Connal McKenna. Would love to find a way to place him with this conspiracy, in the process taking all he owns. All he holds dear. As we both know, he has nothing to do with it," Roby said with heartfelt sincerity echoed in the manner he spoke the words. "Except providing Lilly with a place to live. I'll wager father knew all that you do not. I think Lilly was forthcoming when she asked for his help."

"Do we?"

Brady was beginning to question everything about his wife as well as his father. The devil if he didn't know she was his mate...

"No," Roby now spoke with a deliberate calm. "We don't. However, what we will do is we will proceed as if all our thoughts about our father's dealings are as they appear to be and how he wishes us to see them."

"She's a treasonous bitch," Brady said softly, wishing he didn't *ken* how she used him for her gains.

He thought it was the betrothal to Lord Claymore. For all he knew that could be fake. A means to use so he would let his guard down. Well, that was exactly what he'd done. He believed in her; was so sure she would come to trust him.

Let his guard down.

"She's your mate," Roby pointedly reminded him. "What are you going to do? You can't set her out."

Brady started back. He thought to run first. Now, after seeing all this for himself, he decided a confrontation was in order. No, he couldn't set her away from him but there were other ways to see she behaved. "I'm going to keep her locked in our suite of rooms until she can do no more damage to herself or our family."

Roby chuckled as he trailed behind him down the path. He heard the sound of his horse as the hoof beats pounded gently on the forest floor. Mayhap he should run tonight. It might be the only way he could relieve the radiating tension that consumed him. The only way he could rid his soul of the dark demons swamping him.

"Pray that she didn't leave." Roby's words from behind him sent a spiral of fear and anger into him.

He struggled to inhale the warm highland air, fought for the scent of heather. It rattled into his lungs with a catch. This was a coil he had no idea how to solve. "If she did leave, I'll go after her, hunt her down. Even if I have to follow her across the ocean, I'll bring her back to this land. She's not going anywhere that I don't personally put her."

Brady hoped he had his escalating and confusing emotions under some semblance of control. As he continued toward the argument awaiting him, he went over the words he would use, the questions that had not been answered that he would ask. The long slow steadying breath escaping his lungs calmed him. His heartbeat slowed tangibly.

He would tell her what he did know, would show her the wanted poster then pray she would explain the rest.

When he entered the keep, a servant came out to greet him. He handed the reins over to the boy. Where to look for his wife? He started through the myriad of rooms on the main floor. Wandering into the dining area, he was aware of his mother and father.

Seated next to his sister Crissie, Lilly was sipping ale, laughing as if she had not betrayed him along with the rest of his family. He prayed she had not. A slow burning anger simmered as he approached her. She was careless of her life, too careless. She wasn't going to be thoughtless of anyone else's. He would make sure she would no longer put herself in jeopardy or the possible child she might even now be carrying.

By God but she had a great deal of nerve this woman he wed. More than any female he'd ever encountered. Who the blessed hell did she think she was?

Sassenach.

A born and bred lady.

Even if she did spout the views of a woman born and bred in the highlands, she'd begun her life raised in England. She didn't see him approach. He now stood over her, staring at her audacity.

When she looked up to meet his gaze, the little gasp of surprise and the narrowing of her eyes gave him reason to smile at her. She would rue this day if she didn't tell him the absolute truth. He knew much of it now. Still, he needed to hear the words from her lips. All the blank spots needed to be filled in so there would no longer be any doubt about her intentions for good or for bad.

"You're coming with me," he gritted out harshly as he watched her eyes widen in question.

He held out his hand. She would not defy him in this.

Crissie looked from one to the other, a strange questioning look in her eyes. "You better do as he says. Hope you know why my brother looks near to boiling."

Lilly lowered her lashes before peering at him from beneath the dark fringe. When she finally looked up, her eyes were wide shimmering questioning pools of blue. They weren't warm or soft. Slowly, the blue was turning to ice. She rose, ignoring the hand. A shaft of sunlight across her form drew his attention to her dazzling beauty, the ever-changing colors of her hair. Tonight, it seemed she personified both fire and ice.

He wasn't going to allow disobedience from her. No longer would Lilly challenge him. Before she could protest, he took her elbow, holding it tight. Bending close to her ear with a soft whisper, "Don't give me reason to haul you over my shoulder. It would be best if everyone here thought there is nothing wrong between us when we both know there is a chasm to fill in."

"Brady?" she queried softly, feigning ignorance about his seething anger. With a mocking tilt to her head, she asked, "What are you talking about?" Then, "Well, of course, there is nothing wrong between us."

"You *ken* more than you're letting on." He couldn't help the harsh tenor of his voice, the fury coating every syllable of every word.

"I'm sorry but I don't."

The pace they were walking increased until she was running to keep up with his much longer strides. The fragile peace existing between them the last few days and weeks vanished with each step forward. Brady was eager to leave the prying eyes of his family and friends behind. Before he said anything more, he needed the privacy of his rooms. Despite the rapid pace, the walk there seemed to take forever.

He didn't speak again.

Neither did Lilly.

When they finally stood inside his room where no eyes or ears were present to listen or gainsay his wishes, he gave her a tiny push. She stumbled slightly. Guilt at his behavior coursed within. Quickly, Lilly regained her balance turning to meet his gaze head on, her tiny hands fisted by her sides, her ample breast heaving with the obvious agitation she was feeling. She could not, would not claim ignorance now.

"What the devil do you think you are doing?" Her voice shook with the distress she couldn't hide.

"Sit down."

He thought for a moment he was even angrier at her seeming façade of innocence coupled with the pretense of ignorance. The fact she was the cause of this didn't sink home with her.

She did sit on the edge of her chair, her hands placed tightly together in her lap, nose in the air. He paced the room, running his hands through his hair, reviewing all the words he planned to say, all the questions he needed to ask. The breath he inhaled shook with the all-consuming fury residing in his chest. Still, the scent he sucked into his lungs was musk and roses. The same scent that wafted around her when they made love.

Despite his objections, his body hardened with need, his arousal insistent and recognizable.

"You will stay here, madam, until you answer to my satisfaction every question I ask. Even then you might remain in this room for your good as well as the clan." The anger simmering inside was dark and black. He shook with fury her actions so easily spawned.

She sucked her bottom lip beneath her teeth eyeing him as if she was figuring out what lie to tell next. Her darkened lashes lowered briefly against the whiteness of her cheeks, hiding her eyes from him.

When she finally looked at him, her gaze was bright, intensely disturbing. "What is it you want me to tell you? I've been forthcoming about everything you've asked. I've not lied to you."

"You've told me only expedient things, information that is common knowledge. Nothing more. I've given you ample opportunity to tell me the truths as well as the secrets you hold close to your heart."

He stole a long even breath from the stuffiness of the room. The air seemed stifling. She appeared unaffected, a picture of calm serenity in midst of chaos.

She lifted her hands in a gesture of confusion before letting them settle once more in her lap. "Tell me why you're so angry. What have I done?"

"Treason."

He didn't see any reason to dissemble. Her feelings no longer made a difference to him. Her life did. If he said something she didn't like, too bad. Here and now, there was no reason to speak subtly to ease tender sensibilities.

"I don't understand," she murmured yet he saw the draining of color from her cheeks, watched her swallow desperate for air now that part of the truth was out in the open. She couldn't think to deny him the facts of her elusive actions much longer.

He tossed the wanted poster at her. Watched as she slowly smoothed it out. Saw the look of abject horror crease her brows.

"Don't lie to me, Lilly. Not now. Not ever again. You understand very well what I'm talking about. Tell me about Douglas Townsend."

Her sudden stillness confirmed she knew more than she wanted to admit. There were many truths here coupled with silence.

"Douglas Townsend?" she asked with a soft polished tone of unawareness as if she hoped to hide her nervousness by denying awareness.

Briefly, he thought to laugh at her very audacity, her quick wit. Still, she stupidly meant to refuse him what he asked. "I saw him kiss you, hug you a few weeks back. Today I saw him in the gardens with you when you pretended nothing was happening. When you strove to tell me all you were doing was smelling the roses."

"If you know so much then you should tell me who he is. Since I've no idea what or who you are speaking about." Condescendingly, her chin rose another notch.

He longed to pick her up and shake her until she understood the eminent danger she courted without a thought. After that, he wanted to turn the man she was protecting over to the English when next he saw him. He didn't have one doubt the man would show up again.

"You're a terrible liar, Lilly. Who is Douglas Townsend?"

He wished he understood what he could do or say that would drag the truth from her. He did not. Not for a moment did he believe threats would do the trick, unless of course he offered to turn the man over to the soldiers who were searching for him. He would if she didn't tell him the truth.

Timeless seconds passed while she gazed toward the one window in the room. A tiny ray of sunlight lit a pathway along the rug ending at her feet. Dust motes danced happily in the shaft. If she thought she could delay the truth, she was most likely right. Delay tactics would change nothing in the end yet Lilly was a master of them.

Her words shook belying the truth, "He is no one. Nothing to me."

Her lashes lowered again. The small gesture was simply a ploy to hide the depths of her emotions.

He knew she was unwilling to allow him insight into the truth by letting him see her eyes. Without a doubt, he understood she lied to him. The more important question was why. None of his letters to places in London bore fruit. Still, he knew nothing about her family, only that her mother was gone, died years ago and her father sold her to an aging decrepit old man.

The why was not forthcoming. For one so small and delicate, Lilly lied as easily as she inhaled each tiny sip of air. His wife was most likely involved in treason against the English.

"If he is no one to you, you won't care if he is wanted by the British. Won't care if he hangs for the crimes he has committed. Won't care if you and the McKenna clan are entangled in that crime."

With each knew accusation she flinched, drawing farther into herself and her thoughts.

"If I see him again, I swear to you, I will turn him over to the Sassenach soldiers. At the moment his life means nothing to me. Give me a reason to care."

Her eyes fluttered shut as if she willed all this to go away. It would not vanish unless she gave him the knowledge to make it do so. If he knew who this man was and what he meant to her, he could find a way to help him. Despite the reservations, despite the implications that might be drawn, he had resources, people who would lend aid if he asked.

She needed to learn how to trust. Something he supposed that had been ripped away from her.

~ * ~

Lilly understood it would come to this someday. Comprehended her brother risked his life and all he held dear for a cause that could not be won. Except with each life saved by sending the pour soul who chose the wrong side of the battle, the wrong man to be king, to America. She flinched with every word and every vile allegation Brady shot at her. For the longest time she yearned to tell him everything. From the first moment he touched her, kissed her, held her in his strong arms, she realized she would eventually give him her very soul.

Why couldn't she explain this to the man she loved more than life?

His presence next to her unwrapped her soul, filled her heart until she ached with the need for him to possess her. Even now when he caused her to bleed, she wanted to enfold him in her arms. She yearned to stroke the hard angles and planes of his body. By the dark fury in his eyes, he wouldn't accept her tender care. This was a coil she knew would come; knew too she wouldn't be able to talk her way out of it.

Revealing Douglas' crimes was not something she would bring herself to do lightly. By not betraying him, she was doing the same to her husband and new family, the clan Chattan.

"May I see...?"

She wasn't sure what to ask for. With a slight lift to her shoulders, she looked at him with hesitancy.

He had picked the poster up after it drifted from her hands to the floor. "I understand."

Brady handed the poster with Douglas Townsend's likeness drawn on it to her waiting fingers. His anger undiminished, he watched her seeming to study him. She too searched for things she might find in his eyes.

The telling parchment rested on her lap. Biting her lip, she stared at it while she listened to the sounds in the quiet room twirl and spin around her. Dizziness assailed her. Life as she knew it flashed past her for the second time in such a short period. The first circumstance being when she discovered her father's perfidy, the betrothal contract.

The seconds ticking by on the clock filled her with dread. If she could just stall, keep her fingers from unraveling the paper, perhaps the death knell ticking away her life could be forestalled. The tiny sips of air she inhaled were not enough to sustain life. She closed her eyes willing herself to breathe long and deep. Still, she could manage nothing more than tiny drops and bits of air.

"Look at it, damn you. I want answers before it's too late."

His voice was harsher, more commanding than she'd ever heard it. "It's just too late, Lilly. What the hell do you expect me to do?"

She didn't dare disobey. She didn't dare obey. Despite the fact he claimed her, acknowledge her as his mate, he could set aside their marriage leaving her at the mercy of Lord Claymore. A salty tear slipped down her cheek. Furious with her weakness, she dried the moisture with the back of her hand.

"A very handsome man," she told Brady gazing at him through her moisture clouded eyes, her lashes sparkling in the light with the unshed tears clinging there. "I don't know him."

The growl springing from his lips unnerved, ripped her apart. She stood, her body weaving slightly, knees threatening to give out. The world tilted, spinning away from her feet. Slowly, she crumpled to the ground. Voices pummeled her, etching into her subconscious as she tried to return to the present. Present, past or future, nothing would be the same when she opened her eyes. If only she could remain in the dark, escape her husband, run from the truth of her mission here in the highlands.

She could not.

She was an unwilling participant. Pushed into the role through chance.

Smelling salts brought her to a startling wakefulness. Her eyes open now she stared into Brady's concerned face, Crissie's behind him. Blinding light from the lantern hanging near her gave her reason to close her eyes again. The world was too bright, too vivid.

"I think she's fine." It was Crissie's voice she heard.

"Aye, she is. You can leave now."

Lilly yearned to reach out a hand to stop Crissie from leaving her with her husband's wrath. Needed to tell her to stay. She needed someone to protect her. Brady would never allow anything such as that. Truth, all he wanted was the truth. If she didn't tell him, he could learn everything from the next British patrol to wander onto McKenna land. Perhaps it was time. With any luck, Douglass would escape on the ship out of Inverness. For so long he seemed loath to leave this land.

He helped her to sit, tucking a pillow behind her. She found he placed her on one of the huge chairs facing the fireplace. The door clicked shut. Crissie was gone. Once again, they were alone.

"You should start from the beginning? It will all make more sense if you do," he told her, his voice gentler now.

"I don't know what that is."

"If we do, will you faint again?"

I never faint.

Another lie she supposed was no longer true. With a heavy sigh that left her feeling drained of energy, she nodded as she curled her bare feet beneath her where she sat. "The beginning..."

"Was that a yes to starting afresh or a yes to fainting a second time?" he asked sarcastically seemingly holding none of his raw emotions back, "Are you comfortable?" He handed her a glass of wine. She drank deeply before setting what was left in the glass on the table.

Her laugh was brief holding with it a wealth of disbelieves. "Douglas Townsend is my brother, step brother, heir to the Townsend fortune and titles. Something it seems now he will never inherit. He doesn't care. His life is about the cause he has supported for so long."

When Lilly looked at Brady, she saw the incredulity in his eyes. Knew it wasn't at what she told but that she told him anything at all.

"Was that so hard?" he asked blandly, mocking her all the weeks she kept quiet about the man. "What was there to hide? I would never turn against you in this case. Why was it so hard for you to tell me about your brother, your kin? You understand family is everything to me."

"Terribly hard," she told him smoothing her skirts. "What else would your highness like to know? Perhaps we could have another glass of wine or something to eat while the inquisition continues."

The ever-ticking clock told her the hour was nearing seven. Breakfast this morning was the last meal she'd eaten. That being only a slice of bread and a cup of tea.

Brady rang the bell, calling for food as well as more wine. He sat down across from her, appearing relaxed without a care in the world while her body shook with fear as well as fatigue. The predatory glare in his silver-gray eyes bound around her, entangling her in the web he wove.

He didn't say anything more until the food was devoured and a generous portion of the wine consumed. All the time, he created a seething inner fear she didn't know how to vanquish. Then...

Brady began, "From the wanted poster I discovered his plot, one that leads me to believe you are deeply involved with it also. It was why I discovered you in the tavern in Inverness, why you turned up with a wagon in the same town when you should have been safely tucked into your cottage." Each word was spoken with more venom than the last.

"All true."

Her whisper floated in the darkening room, dangerous and foreboding until they filled her body with wrenching shivers. Thoughts of her brother along with the horrific things that would be done to him when he was caught chilled her.

He would be caught.

If he didn't flee, he would be caught, flogged then worst of all would be sent to spend his final days in a dark dreary dungeon filled with rats. He could hang for the treason he committed.

So could she.

"So, what were you up to today in the garden?" He was standing beside her, bent low so very close to her.

The blazing heat from his hard body spiraled into hers. The mint clean scent of his breath whispered across her cheek, slithering down her neck. His long-bronzed fingers rested on her shoulders. Touched her escalated her anxiety.

The truth as she knew it would have to satisfy him for the next few hours. The truth was all she had. Didn't know if it was enough.

Douglas needed to be given time to reach Inverness and the ship sailing to New York.

"Money. I gave him coin to reach his safe haven."

She closed her eyes while the strength of his fingers pressed into her, heat penetrating, reminding her of better times.

Slowly, he ran those same tantalizing fingers along her neck. The air she gasped inside caused her to stiffen as he tightened his grip. He would not strangle her. She was his wife.

His lying, betraying wife.

"You best pray he reaches that ship before the British find him. Best send up prayers that you will not find yourself caught up in these schemes with nowhere to run. I can only protect you so far. Is there evidence?"

His touch vanished. Sounds carried to her from outside as well as in the room. He walked across the floor, settled onto the big bed they shared. She didn't want to lie with him when he was so angry. He threatened, albeit subtly, to strangle her.

"I pray constantly for his safety, my lord."

The breath she sucked inside smelled faintly of spices and man, which he left behind floating around her when he walked away.

"For yours also? What part, madam, have you played in his schemes all the while telling falsehoods to me?"

His calm demeanor in the face of treason unsettled her. True, she had played a part. At first, she was unwilling. "I..." she moistened her lips, the tip of her tongue running along the expanse of her dry mouth. It did little to ease.

"I?" His question was too close to her.

He lifted her. Held her beside him, his lips molding over hers, touching. Even the kiss threatened repercussions. He would hold her responsible if anything happened to his family.

"Men, the ones who came for help seeking a new life."

"Men?" One of his perfectly sculpted dark eyebrows lifted heavenward.

"Yes," she wrenched herself away from the force of his hold. "In a wagon I took them to Inverness, took them to the ships waiting for them. Most had no money. It was arranged for them to work their way across the ocean."

"You drove the wagons at night?"

"Yes."

"By yourself?"

"I did."

"To the docks? The worst part of the city. Do you *ken* what could have happened to you? Little fool."

The questions now coming too fast for her to answer, she resented everything he insinuated. "I'm no fool."

"My wife needs to be shackled to my bed."

This second, he left her, paced the room, his strides quick and harsh pounding against the wood of the floor, the noise thudding through her brain.

"You would not."

This was archaic even though she knew, as her husband, he had that very right. She was his. He could do anything he wished to her even shackle her to the big bed.

"Give me a reason not to." His frustration was obvious in the tone of his voice.

Heaving a huge breath of air, Lilly grimaced. The trickle of courage that drawing air into her lungs gave her was not nearly enough to stand up to her husband. "With any luck Douglas is gone. I no longer have a need or a reason to protect him."

"It was Douglas who sent the men to you."

The sudden revelation seemed to clarify a lot of things in Brady's mind as the emotions charging across his face took on an even darker fury. "He found them and sent them to you. You were smuggling men."

The answer, the condemning response to that question failed to make it from behind her teeth. She didn't have to answer. Brady knew the truth just by looking into her eyes.

Without saying anything she heard the door close, the bolt slide against the wood. Taking a few seconds to compose herself, she closed her eyes. Thoughts of Brady and the next days crumpled her into a desperate heap. A low wracking sob tore through her.

Facing the reality of this day was too difficult for her mind to handle alone. She wanted to talk to Crissie, to anyone who might listen to reason. Brady certainly would not. She didn't expect his sister to interfere just perhaps lend comfort to her tattered heart. Essentially, she was a prisoner within the McKenna castle, within Brady's rooms. The night assumed an eerie whisper of dark and very black danger. The clock ticked solemnly on the shelf. Wind whistled mournfully across the leaded windows.

Lilly walked circles in the bedchamber, silently moving into his office then the main sitting room. She slept on a large chair. Finished the first bottle of wine. Started on another one. Paced then slept again.

Brady was out looking for her brother. She knew it as a fact better than she understood the motives driving Douglas. The two men were much the same, stubborn to a fault, confidence at times turning toward arrogance. She should have dealt better with Brady. She'd know exactly what he was about, in temperament almost a mirror image of her brother.

When sunlight hit her square in the eyes the next day, she understood Brady had not returned during the night. He had indeed gone after her brother. Looking out one of the small windows, she discovered the sun was nearly at its zenith. Still, she was left alone to wallow in her guilt or think over her transgressions. She wasn't sure which. More than anything she wanted out of his rooms.

A little after the noon hour, a bath along with food and drink were delivered. When everything was brought into the chamber, the door was closed and the bolt slid home once more. The sound sent shivers of guilt up her spine. By her very silence, she brought this on herself.

Little nigglings of doubt swept through her to culminate in her stomach. The food presented to her sent bile to her throat even while her stomach rumbled discontentedly. She found herself thinking about the way his hands felt when he stroked her. The sweet tenderness of his kiss had her sipping tiny gulps of air while her body flamed with need.

Thoughts and memories. Ecstasy coupled with delight. Tremors shooting through her body until she was left with no control save to cry out his name. A fire that burned brighter than the sun.

Would he ever hold her again, touch her with intimate tenderness she'd learned from him? He was angry with her.

Desperately so.

She'd wanted nothing to do with the schemes and plans of her brother. Yet she'd come to believe in them with all her heart. If given the choice, she would change nothing about her past. Together they helped weak and world-weary men find a new beginning in a different land.

Was that so wrong?

Where her part in this was concerned, she had no regrets. She believed as her brother did the cause was noble.

The day wore on, turning to evening. Still no sign of Brady McKenna. More food was brought into the room along with more wine. This time Crissie entered, the bolt sliding home behind her.

"I can't stay very long. Bribed one of the guards Brady set at your door with a lemon tart from the kitchen. He won't tell. I promise," Crissie said with a giggle. "If I were you, I'd be going crazy right now. How are you holding up?"

"Did my husband give orders that no one was to come see me?" She made a face. "I'm about the way you described yourself if you were a prisoner." Even though in some ways she might deserve his wrath, she didn't deserve prison. Didn't deserve to be kept from everyone.

"No, father did."

"Connal?" she asked shocked that the older man would do such a thing. "I don't understand."

Truly, she didn't. Why on earth?

"*Aye, 'tis* for your good, your preservation. There have been British soldiers prowling the grounds all day, last night too. Couldn't risk any of them seeing you and perhaps recognizing you. None of us actually know how visible you've been in the goings on of Douglas as well as the others helping. Don't go blaming this on your husband."

That was exactly what she was doing, blaming her isolation on Brady. "Looking for Douglas? Brady is looking for my brother or he just doesn't want to see me," she queried praying they weren't also searching for her.

"Douglas is gone," Crissie said. "You've no need to worry about your brother. Brady tracked him to Inverness and the ship he booked passage on. He is safe unless he returns here or to England. He will not be able to claim his inheritance or title it seems."

"Does everyone know about him now?" Brady might even hang for his part in this although innocent.

"Only the family. It is you Brady is worried about. He's terrified you will do something foolishly stupid, putting all of us in danger, especially yourself. He did, however, agree with father you should be kept in his room until he could talk to you some more."

"I would never..." She had, several times.

"You have. As long as my brother knows where you are, he can concentrate on what needs to be done. He doesn't want to worry about you and what crazy scheme you'll concoct next."

There had been no crazy schemes. She did her part as asked. The only one crazy thing she did was to try to warn Douglas of the British presence in that alehouse. "I only wish to help," she murmured, thinking about all she could do, all the ways she sent men in the opposite direction.

"You are helping by staying in the room," Crissie said, reaching out to touch her hand, granting her the first genuine smile she'd seen in quite some time. "We've discovered Lord Fuller is still nearby. He is still a threat to you. If you were to wander even to your cottage, he could get to you so easily."

The gesture was encouraging, heartfelt. Still, she wanted to see Brady, feel his arms around her one more time. She had the strangest feeling that might not ever happen. He'd been so furiously calm when he walked from this room last night.

"Where is Brady?"

Crissie looked away. It seemed she didn't want to answer the question hovering in the stillness. When her gaze shifted back to her, "Downstairs."

"Which is the only reason you were allowed in here." Lilly was bristling with anger at her husband. How dare he?

"Yes, and I should probably be going soon since I don't seem to be able to keep a secret. Where you are concerned, my mouth seems to run on and on. I suppose it's because of the way he is treating you. I don't understand men. How can he possibly think staying away from you could be beneficial to your relationship? *Dodder,"* she said sharply.

She supposed he could be an idiot at times. "Was he here last night?" Lilly asked, her voice shrill floating on the late afternoon breeze wafting through the open window.

Crissie's eyes widened. She didn't hide the answer. "He was but he chose not to come to his chamber."

~ * ~

Downstairs Connal watched his son repeatedly stride from one side of the room to the other. When he stopped, his gaze would travel up the steps toward his rooms, a smitten expression rounding his rugged features. Connal grinned, understanding some of the predicament his oldest son was entwined in. There was more to his and Lilly's problem than the wanted poster suggested. It had to be a matter of trust. Given time, they would come to terms with what exactly they mean to each other. The journey to accomplish that feat might not be too easy.

True, Douglas Townsend played a role in the schemes of the Jacobites. The man was now safely away from the highlands and threats of prosecution. The question at hand was if Lilly would be safe. The soldiers searched for a woman. They didn't, however, have a name or even a description. There was no wanted poster. If Lilly stayed put, the soldiers along with the problem would vanish with time.

"You should go to her," Connal said, stopping Brady in his mad pacing. "She will need you to help her understand what is happening out there. You are the only one who can put her at ease."

"I can't."

"It seemed a few weeks ago you could not leave her alone. Forced a wedding in the middle of the night because you insisted, she was your mate. Has any of that possessive need for her changed?"

Inside, Connal was chuckling at his son's inability to control the lust along with the growing love he felt for his new wife. If he didn't miss his guess, his son was sexually frustrated, confused as well as hurt by his wife's duplicity. Albeit it was before they met.

"She is lonely." Crissie walked into the room joining the conversation. "You need to find a way to forgive her. She doesn't know what to think."

"She lied to me," he gritted out his hands fisted by his sides. "I can't trust her. What the devil am I supposed to think?"

"By omission, she lied by omission" Connal reminded him softly. "She might well be your mate. We both know. However, this was not a match made in heaven. It did not start out with love. Love needs to be nurtured before it can blossom. So far all you've done is threaten her and bed her. That is not enough."

"She did lie to me. Told me she didn't know who Douglas was," he gritted out between clenched teeth while he looked up the stairs to the south tower where they resided.

"If you make love to her, you'll feel better and so will the rest of us," Roby let his laughter rumble from his chest. "That permanent scowl you've fostered might vanish for a few hours."

"I might throttle her by mistake. Heaven knows that's exactly what I would like to do."

"Did you ever discover what Lord Townsend is doing at the village at the Silver Moon Inn?" Connal asked, seeking his own answers while setting into act his own diversion. "Lord Townsend's presence might well solve one of your problems." Or complicate it farther.

"Losing money, quite a bit of it. The proprietor has threatened to kick him out if he doesn't pay for the room," Roby spoke up. "It does nurture some intriguing ideas. Don't you think?"

"Should we offer him a room here at the manor? So he can be near his daughter?" Connal directed his question at Brady, searching to read an answer in his eyes.

"The man who sold her to Lord Claymore? Never! Don't have one redeeming thought when it comes to that man. If he had the opportunity, there is not a doubt in my mind he would gift her to that man."

"Sometimes it is wise to keep your enemy nearby. Perhaps Lilly will be safer if we discover the reason a father would sell his only daughter to an old man for sexual pleasures." Connal had his ideas but the proof of them was not in his hands yet. A visit to the Silver Moon Inn along with a meeting with the British Lord might be in the McKenna's best interest, Brady McKenna to be specific.

"Would not mind a meeting with that man. Would like to put my fist down his throat," Brady grated out, his eyes filled with the anger he must feel. "I'd like to tell him what I think of his crude and evil tactics."

"You cannot murder the man. He is your father-in-law. His efforts where Lilly was concerned to marry her off were unsuccessful. All you can do now is discern the truth. Lilly has been running for a long time. I for one would like to see the both of you settled to concentrate on my grandchildren." Connal's gaze centered on Brady then lingered on the younger son. "If the two of you keep this up, Alistair will have his first grandchild born first."

"Perhaps there is one on the way as we speak," Brady offered giving the conversation a lighter mood. "We've been working devilishly hard at siring one."

"I pray it is not too much work," Roby laughed, winking at his father before he widened his smile. "Would think the process would be an enjoyable one. If you headed up there right now you could continue with your labors. Wouldn't want Alistair to win this contest."

A slow rise of color flowed to Brady's face giving his brother reason to chuckle again and Crissie to send him a look he couldn't read.

"Nay, should not be too much work to bed your new bride," Roby said almost wistfully.

"I find her disloyalty distasteful," Brady mumbled as he looked above once more. "Her lies worse. She would protect her brother over her husband."

"Take my advice, son, put those thoughts to the back recesses of your head. As it turns out Douglas is her brother. She knew him and was loyal to him before she ever met you. Now, he is on his way to a new life. In the present it is up to you to make your new life here successful. Forget the past discretions, decisions that occurred primarily before you met your sweet lady. She was trying to protect her family, those she loves dearly. You would do the same in her case. Don't judge her too harshly."

"Sweet? More like a pariah," once again his words were mumbled, left sourly in the back of his throat.

Connal heard them loud and clear. Knew that as soon as their lives turned to an even keel, they would fall into love. She was his mate but love between them didn't exist yet. It would have been nice for love to come before the bedding and the marriage.

When Brady started up the steps, a set expression on his face, Connal hoped the ensuing argument would result in peace between them. Somehow the two would be able to forgive and forget. After that they could truly begin their new lives.

As it was for he and Wynnie, it appeared it would be for Brady and Lilly. Love would come but it would blossom later.

Chapter Seven

Brady stood in front of the barred door, his hands resting on the wood while he contemplated his future steps. Guilt coupled with recriminations undulated through him with a rapidity he couldn't control. Lilly's frame of mind when he finally entered the room could be anything. Knowing her as well as he did, he supposed she would fling whatever object she could find at him. One thing his lady wife wasn't was meek. It was not well done of him to leave her alone to brood for this long.

The breath he inhaled for courage stuck in his throat then dropped like a lump to his belly to turn acrid. He spun away starting for the spare room where he spent the night before. He would meet her tomorrow. It would be safer then.

"Thought you had more fortitude than that big brother," Roby chuckled, clearly still amused with his brother's plight as he thumped him between the shoulder blades. "You can't make a prison for a woman, as pleasant as it may well be, without a few nasty consequences to contend with. Own up to your discretions and she will go easier on you."

He had no words, no way to explain the coursing, swelling possessiveness he felt for the woman behind the door, proof of his lust growing beneath his trousers. His need overpowered common sense. If he stepped inside that room, saw her, breathed in the sweet scent of roses, he would be lost to the ardent desire for her that simmered in his loins. He would give in to whatever she wanted.

Brady didn't know how to change the fierce sensations barging through him. Sleeping in another room would be the best course for him. For his peace of mind, he needed to keep his wife at arm's length.

"I have more fortitude than a sane man should have." He eyed the bolt critically, thinking it was all that stood in the way of him and his bride, his mate. If he let his imagination flow, he recalled every rounded curve, the moist juncture between her thighs along with the dark rosy tips of her breasts.

"What are you waiting for?" Roby asked, still smirking while refusing to leave him behind and seek his own bed.

"For sanity to return," Brady said before lifting the bolt and entering the dark room.

Surprised, he thought for a moment that she'd gone to sleep. Slowly, he closed the door hoping his eyes would adjust to the darkness. The first missile hit him in the side of the head, the second in the chest. He put his hands in front of his face to protect himself. Gradually forms began to take shape. He thought he saw her near the bed.

She was yelling at him now. *"Dobber! Bassa! Bampot!"*

He supposed at times he was all of those things. He didn't like to believe his wife thought he was a jerk, a bastard as well as an idiot. This time he saw the book as it tore through the air. He batted it away, approaching the woman on the other side of his bed, a smile of amusement curving his mouth. If she meant to keep him out of her bed, she was doing the opposite. This moment he relished a good fight, a much-needed expenditure of energy before taking his wife to task. He couldn't think of a better way to accomplish that than to bury himself deep inside her willing feminine body.

He ached for her.

Missed her passion and warmth.

All he longed for was to protect and cherish Lilly. So far, she had not allowed him the pleasure, keeping herself aloof, so very distant he couldn't penetrate the walls she built around her.

With long dangerous strides he pursued her relentlessly. It seemed she ran out of missals to throw his way. He grinned, warming to the conclusion of her fiery temper. Her breasts were heaving with the exertion, moving and swaying enticingly beneath her gown.

He stopped to light the room with a nearby lamp.

She was running from him again, darting between pieces of furniture. All the pins fell from her hair, leaving the length falling in tangled disarray around her shoulders, curling provocatively at her slim waist. This was how he needed to think of Lilly. He banished her treachery from his thoughts while his body, heated and aroused longed for fulfillment within her sultry velvet heat. This diversion would be more pleasant than it would be work.

"Stay away from me, Brady McKenna." She was breathing hard, pointed a slender finger his way. "After the time you've ignored me, don't even think to tuck me into your bed and use me for your carnal delights. I won't have it. I warn you, stay away."

"Or what, wife?"

He kept his laughter behind his teeth, pleased that at the moment he was no longer simmering with anger. His body was aroused beyond pain. He needed her now. He would have her.

With the air of a pagan sacrifice, she was kneeling on his bed her arms extended as if that would ward him off. When he drew closer, she leapt from the bed. The chase was what he needed before he enfolded her in his embrace. Before he sated himself inside her lush woman's body.

"Or..." She was panting for air, sucking in tiny gulps while she darted different directions to avoid him.

"Or?"

One dark intimidating eyebrow rose skyward in question. He wondered what threat she would use against him. Nothing would work but it would be vastly amusing.

Scrambling across the bed, once more she managed to elude him but only because he allowed it. Yet she was wearing herself out. Across the room, he poured himself a snifter of brandy a second glass of wine for her. To watch her more carefully, he sat.

He waited.

"What are you doing?"

Her voice squeaked softly wavering as if it was a soft patch of candlelight sitting in front of an open window. With both hands she pushed her hair away from her wide eyes, blue eyes before she used the bed to rest upon.

"Resting, sipping my drink calmly while I watch you. I enjoy this immensely."

He realized he did too.

She sat down cross-legged, her arms across her chest. "I don't want to be watched. Not tonight. Not by you."

"A glass of wine?" He held it up for her, his smile so wickedly sinful she shivered in anticipation of the rest of the evening. "Have you eaten?"

"You would care?" It seemed to Brady her anger was simmering deeply about to explode. He wanted it to explode when he was deep inside her. Well, his was at the same level. Looking at her, he wanted her. The feeling the same as when he first saw her working in the kitchen.

Nothing changed.

He had to have her.

"Come sit by me," he spoke softly seeming to note the wariness in her gaze. "Have your glass of wine then you can tell me how your day was."

On hesitant feet she came to him unsure of the direction of his thoughts. She took up the glass of wine before sitting down in another chair opposite him, guarded, ever cautious.

"Boring," Lilly said her voice seeming to recover from the physical battle. "I had nothing to do all day. No one to speak to. I was confined in here as if I was a caged animal. You had not the right."

At the revelation of her thoughts, he grimaced. "I did not have you locked away."

"You did nothing to change the fact."

She was looking over the rim of the glass with her wide blue eyes. Eyes he could very easily drown in. Tonight, he didn't want to talk about anything that was between them. He only wanted to relive the erotic lovemaking of the nights before.

Tonight, he needed to forget everything revolving around Townsend. Tomorrow morning would be soon enough to discuss what was to be done. How he would keep her from *gaol*. Tonight, he wanted to stroke the soft curve of her hips, squeeze gently the lushness of her buttocks, fill his hands with the rounded firmness of her breasts suck them deep into his mouth.

"You never said if you needed anything to eat."

"No, I didn't and no, I'm not hungry. Have not been hungry since that door was bolted shut from the outside."

She downed the wine before pouring herself another, this time filling it to the very brim.

His lips quirked with humor as he tried to hold his laughter back.

With the ensuing silence, Lilly squirmed in the chair. She watched him beneath lowered lashes. The very scent of her, roses, swirled around her teasing his nostrils until he wanted to roar.

"I'd like you to take all your clothes off," he said blandly watching her for a reaction. "Will you do that for me? Take off everything you are wearing?"

"Why?" In her eyes there was a dark look of distrust. "You c-can't expect..."

His smile was wicked, his words soft as butter, flowing smoothly from his lips and "You truly have to ask?"

She set the glass down too hard, red droplets slipping down the crystal. "What game are you playing with me, Brady McKenna?"

"I want you, Lilly. I've always wanted you. The first time I saw you, I knew I would have you."

He stood, holding his hand out to her, praying she would set her small one in his.

For a few seconds she held back, her breaths ragged beneath the gown she wore. While he held his breath, waiting, she did as he hoped. She set her small hand on top of his, palm to palm. "No questions?"

"Just love between us, nothing more, nothing less," he murmured gently drawing her into his arms.

His lips touched upon her forehead, made delicious forays down her slender neck to the spot where her pulse thundered for him. She ran her hands up his sides to his chest across then back down tantalizing ever part of him.

"I've missed you." Her voice was soft, thick with emotion. "You left me. Didn't come last night. I was terrified for you. Where were you?"

"Gone for your protection."

He unfastened her gown, pushing the fabric from her shoulders. Watched as her breast bounced and jiggled with their freedom. He could watch this forever and beyond.

"I wasn't in need of protection. Except maybe from you."

She slipped her hands beneath his shirt, stroked his chest, brushed her palms against his hardened male nipples.

Fire inside burned hot and true. He didn't know if he could wait to give her pleasure to hear the delicious sounds of delight he could fashion so easily within her.

"Your father was invited to stay here, in the McKenna castle."

She stumbled backward. He caught her in his arms, striding quickly to the bed. "You can't mean it. He-he sold me to that lecher! You're going to offer him a room in this manor?" She was angry now, her slender body vibrating with the fury.

The devil, but he hadn't meant to bring up that disturbing bit of news at least not until the morning when he would have no choice in the matter. "He has no funds, Lilly. He's a gambler, addicted to the game. Could he have gambled everything he owns away? Lost everything?"

With a heavy sigh he sat on the bed, holding her close, stroking her hair as she leaned into his shoulder soaking up all the comfort he could give her. This would all have to be discussed before he continued with this sweet persuading of love.

He misspoke. He would pay the price.

"That can't be possible."

She was looking at him, now her moist pink tongue running across her mouth, enticing seductively. Coaxing him wasn't necessary. He was harder, more than ready.

"Maybe not."

His lips closed over a sweetly puckered, crinkled tip.

She tossed her head, arching her back toward him, giving him more access to that part of her. He wanted her to forget everything but the night and how she felt in his arms.

"Raise your hands," she murmured, her breath floating across his chest hot and sultry.

He helped her with his shirt as her hands ran the length of his chest while she took it over his head. Her breasts were pressed against the width of him. When she moved, every part of his body came to instant arousal. With every caress he grew harder. Now, her hands rested on his waistband. She fumbled with the laces. He was free, pushing the encumbrance down his legs before he kicked them to the floor.

When she reached to touch him, "No, not yet." With gentle purpose, he held her hand away.

"I want you, Brady McKenna."

She touched him with her mouth, trailed kisses down his chest to his arousal. When she would have taken him with her lips once more, he stopped her.

"And I, my fine lady, want you begging."

He turned her onto her stomach. Pressed kisses along her spine, darting wet kisses followed by nipping bites to her soft, tender flesh. Her body quivered with desperate need as he continued this heated assault.

"Please, Brady."

Her soft purr of delight filled his senses, generated a greater need to please her, to give her the ecstasy she craved.

"Not yet, sweeting."

He bit gently. Sounds of pleasure bubbled up inside her with each daring stroke of his hands the moist pressure of his mouth, teeth and tongue.

"When? I will surely die if you don't finish with this, if you don't allow me to caress you in return."

He lifted her, his mouth finding purchase in the delicate soft swollen folds between her legs. Lingering there, languorously he stroked her with his mouth, delving with his tongue, nipping tenderly with his teeth. The pleasure built, grew with increasing speed, the intensity overpowering as she spoke her delight with the constant rumbles of her deepest pleasure.

She was beside herself with blinding need as she moved against him, pushing herself toward him, arching and writhing. He entered with a finger then a second, felt her close around him, drag him deeper into that dark, mysterious part of her that pulsed around him. She was moving against the magical rhythm he set, her body quivering, trembling with the delicious ecstasy. She felt ragged and raw with her need for this formidable man she hungered for.

No one else had ever touched her so. No one else would. Swiftly, he flipped her over. In a second he was deep inside her, enjoying the tremors as they swept from her into him. Seconds passed while he held himself still. He set his lips upon the tip of one delicate breast, bit gently while her back arched taking his pulsing rod ever deeper inside.

She was his heaven and hell.

Delight and miracle.

Ecstasy and bliss never ending.

She was his. He would protect her with his life.

Slowly, reverently, he continued to move inside her. She responded just as he knew she would. Eagerly she met him stroke for stroke. The moment was ripe with her hungry body waiting for his to fulfill hers with delicious pleasures. He pushed inside her until his length filled the hot sultry core she gifted him with. Holding back was no longer possible as her tremors of delight pulsed and tugged around him. She wanted his seed. As she cried out his name, he roared with the sheer pleasure of possessing his wife, his mate.

He lay replete on top of Lilly, the weight of his body pressing down on hers. Her body was moist with the pleasure he gave as was his. He pushed up lifting his body from hers. He trailed a finger across her finely sculpted brow. She was so tiny and delicate, fragile.

He found he wanted her again.

Not now, not until they figured out a few irritating truths.

Lord, but she had no business pursuing the things she did, no business allowing her brother to talk her into the dangerous business of treason. He rolled to a sitting position, leaning against the headboard. She curled her body, settling beneath the covers her eyes closing dreamily.

He swatted her bottom. "Not yet."

She sat up, holding the sheet against her. Her eyes flashed. She was angry with him. Too bad. "We are back to the beginning then."

"*Aye*, that we are. I watched your brother board a ship to God knows where. I don't. I only pray he is not headed to London."

She inhaled a swift and sudden gasp of air, seeming astonished by his remark. "He would not do such a foolish thing."

"Truly? Seems your brother is naught but foolish tagging you along with him, endangering your life. He had no right to do that. He should have dissuaded you. While I don't so much care about his fate, you are important to me. Don't care to lose you as I've only just found you."

"You say he boarded a ship?"

"*Aye*."

"We agreed he would go to Baltimore." She ran a gentle fingertip across his jawline, a provocative smile on her tender kiss swollen lips.

The constant inferno within his body escalated. When had she learned how to flirt so outrageously? "Then perhaps he did go there. I can check the manifests at the shipyards. There will be some notation as to his destination. Did he have anything in England to go back to?"

Her hand fell to her lap as did the slant of her eyes. "Yes," the one word was softly spoken. "His fiancée was waiting for him." She looked up. "You see, we did not expect any of this to happen. Did not plan to help men reach the ships. Did not plan on defying the crown so intently. We left London only to give respite for those who didn't like the laws he tried to write."

"He will be caught if he goes to the city. Will said lady agree to go with him to America?" A bad feeling sat in the pit of Brady's stomach, souring further the more he thought on this issue. If Douglas was caught, would he give Lilly away? Was he too much like his father who cared nothing for Lilly?

Lilly was shaking her head, the look in her eyes sad, tears spiking her lashes. "He loves her very much."

"Yet she doesn't return the sentiment."

Brady's question was truthfully a statement. He'd known too many men, nobles, who gave their hearts to a money-grubbing title-hunting lady whose only care was for themselves.

"Never thought so. He was the heir to a fortune coupled with a title. That was all she wanted. I pray he had sense enough not to put his life on the line to return for her. As an outcast and a man who could no longer give her what she wanted, she would never follow him to Baltimore."

"Shall we speak of your father?" His gaze fell to the swell of her breasts hiding behind the white linen sheet. He learned one thing. Perhaps they could play a little longer before attacking the subject of Stephen Townsend. He heard the long breath of air spilling from her lungs.

"I would rather speak of dragons."

"Dragons?" he queried slightly amused by the vivid description. "Is that how you speak of the man who raised you, a fire breathing dragon or did he just blow smoke?"

"Sometimes I heard rumors. I don't know if the man was indeed my birth father. He never seemed to love me. Tolerated me at the best of times as well as when he wanted to impress Douglas. He always seemed to put me in the background unless he could get something for bringing me into the light."

He mulled her words around in his head for a few minutes wondering if Connal knew of her birth father and if that was why he seemed so elusive and secretive when it came to Lilly. Perhaps it was also why he allowed her to live on McKenna land.

He waved those thoughts aside. "Your father has a gambling problem. He can't control himself. Did you know about any of that?"

"No, yet there were times when I overheard Douglas arguing with him. My father spent an inordinate amount of hours betting on horses. I never knew him to win or lose. Around me, he kept silent about what he did at the track as well as the night, at least most of the time. However, one night months ago, he was yelling about the amazing luck he had."

With a wry half smile, "Good or bad luck? Did he say?"

"No, but I do recall watching Douglas leave the house swearing a blue streak. He didn't like father gambling. Called him a wastrel."

"If I were to venture a guess, I would assume the luck bad," Brady said, eyeing Lilly critically for a response to the statement.

The wealth of emotions sweeping across her face surprised him. It seemed to Brady she realized a few facts as the aftermath of his statement. The ensuing silence left him slightly unnerved. The wait, he understood thoughtfully would bear fruit.

She finally looked up and said with sure knowledge coupled with stunned disbelief, "He sold me to Lord Claymore to pay off his gambling debts."

"At first glance it appears to be so." Even to Brady, a man who thought he'd seen or heard everything this realization disgusted him. Even if he wasn't Lilly's true father, what man who raised a daughter could do something so horrible?

"Do you think Douglas knew about this?"

Quickly turning her face away, she swatted at the moisture sliding down her cheek.

"What kind of man is your half-brother?"

He held her chin between his thumb and forefinger, gazing into her eyes refusing to let her look away. The truth, he knew, could be read within the depths of her soft blue eyes.

She snagged a quick breath of air before she could find the words she was looking for. "I always believed him to be true and honest. He didn't know. I'm sure he didn't. The one time we spoke, he was as baffled about the betrothal as I was. That was why he encouraged me to come here. Helping with his cause was my idea not his. He understood I would do what I could with or without his approval or consent. Douglass believed it would be wiser to keep me close rather than have me work on my own."

~ * ~

When Lilly woke the next morning, she was alone. Outside the window, storm clouds seemed to brew, turning blacker with each passing second. She sat up pushing a wild tangle of hair from her eyes. Beneath the sheets she was naked. She had slept with the warmth and comfort only Brady could give her.

She rose. Slipping on her robe she found a pot of tea as well as some rolls with sweet butter and honey left on a table near the bed. There was also a note.

Lilly,
Meet me downstairs whenever you are ready.
Brady

No words of love were espoused but at least she was to be let loose from her prison today. She was his mate, his wife. She wanted his love. Years had passed since she knew her mother's love. Douglas cared for her but he didn't love her even as a brother should love his sister. It was quite obvious her father never loved her.

Ah, but it would do her no good to dwell on the past.

Needing a change of scenery, she decided not to waste time with a cup of tea and a few rolls. In a matter of a few minutes, she was dressed and walking down the stairs to the main floor below prepared to meet Brady and whatever challenges the day might bring her way.

With a winsome smile on his handsome face, Brady met her at the bottom of the steps. Holding out a hand, he led her to a table in the dining room. "Did you just wake?"

"Yes, and I didn't want to waste time upstairs when I could come here to be with you."

She thought she heard him chuckle softly. It was not as he thought. She wasn't about to enlighten him.

"Didn't expect you would. Your father should be arriving shortly. You can stay here. If you want to disappear for a while, we can ride to your cottage. When we feel it's safe, I'd like to move there."

She eyed him warily believing he must have some ulterior motive for going to the cottage. Everything she owned had been removed and brought to his rooms. "What is it you're looking for?"

His broad masculine shoulders lifted slightly as she shook his head. "Don't know. If I see it, I'll know it."

"Then..." she began but he cut her off mid-thought.

"Truly, I don't know what it is I'm looking for or would like to find. As I just said I'll know it when and if I see it."

Lilly didn't want to admit to the fact. She felt the same way. There was something they were missing. Something that turned acrid in her stomach and niggled her mind, pestering her to no end. She'd told him everything she knew. He still didn't believe her though. As they walked through the manor, she felt ill at ease. People turned to stare at her. They all must know Brady had locked her in his rooms, their rooms, she told herself but that fact didn't have an impact on her feelings. With each person who stared at her, she wanted to melt into the walls. The man had no idea how her confidence suffered from his unthinking actions. By his actions everyone knew how much he distrusted her. Yet she could only tell herself the suspicion was laid solely at her feet.

Finally, they were outside and riding along the trail leading to her old home. She had not been there since her trip to Inverness, the near confrontation with the British soldiers, the night they spent in the cave. When they entered, she was appalled at the sorry state of the cottage. What was left of her things were all scattered willy-nilly around the room She realized her mouth was open. "What happened?" She stepped inside, moving furniture that had been upended, setting the pieces to rights.

"That's what I hoped you would know. The house was like this weeks ago, before we were wed. I came to bring you a few gowns until we could have your trunk moved to the manor house. This is the way it was."

"Who?"

She found herself questioning all she knew, all she held dear. No answers occurred to her.

"Again, I hoped you would have an idea. Would be able to shed a bit of light on this oddity. Could it be the people you were helping?" he asked putting the thought out there.

Anger bristled to the forefront. His accusation stung. "None would have reason to do any of this. They were all so appreciative to be granted the possibility of a new life. Some had spouses as well as children who waited until their husbands could send for them."

He arched a brow in speculation. "Your father? Could he have been looking for money?"

She was shaking as she wrapped her arms around herself. The gesture was futile. "Suppose so, if he thought Douglas was staying here. I don't have much. That's why I was working in the kitchen. Brady, when I left London, I left quickly taking only the barest of essentials."

His look of disbelief didn't go unnoticed by her. "The trunk of satin and velvet gowns were a necessity?" he queried softly as if he tried to get to the rest of the facts straight in his head.

"Suppose one could say I was vain. No, I discovered when I arrived here, they were of little to no use. That trunk was all I took though. I didn't have any idea what I would or would not need."

"You had much more?" he asked sardonically, a tender smile slanting lips she longed to kiss. "Suppose a lady of your standing would have closets full."

At his casual words, Lilly felt the swift rapid rise of heat to her cheeks. All he said was true. She winced trying with a desperate need to say something that would make sense. Instead, she shrugged knowing at this point what she did or didn't do back in London when she fled made little difference. He held a certain opinion of her. Only she could change it. She knew full well the changing of Brady McKenna's stubborn mind would be a difficult task.

Stepping into the bedroom, the trunk he spoke of was gone. It had been taken to the manor. The bed was rumpled, the covers appearing to have been slept in since she was last at the house. Lilly thought Brady was behind her. She thought when she turned to find him framed by the sturdy door. When she turned, he was lying on the floor. Her gaze flew to the man standing behind him.

"You!"

"Yes, my dear it is I. I'm ready to claim you not as a wife but as my mistress, or maybe whore would be the better term as it denotes hard use. You were bought and paid for, my dear. Not going to let a simple wedding to a Scotsman stand in my way of having you," Lord Fuller said. "Come along, I've so much to teach you. I intend to get started as soon as we reach my hunting lodge."

"It was Claymore I was betrothed to not you," Lilly informed him wondering if she stalled for time Brady would gain consciousness.

"For legal purposes, yes. He doesn't have the power to enjoy you though. When you conceive, if you haven't already, he will have his heir but the child will be sired by my seed." Fuller flicked a piece of lint from his frockcoat, his smile filled with lechery.

"I won't go with you. You've no rights where I'm concerned. I'm legally wed."

Lilly knew her words echoed of false bravado. She stiffened her spine, her chin lifted. The man could overpower her with not too much trouble. She wasn't going without a fight though. If he wanted to have her, he would have to work hard to gain, what did he say? Enjoyment?

"You think not? Well, McKenna can have you back when I'm through with you. If he wants you then."

Fuller's leer revolted Lilly. Bile rose in her throat at the notion he wanted her in the same ways Brady had her. She could not let that happen. He would not defile her.

"Why?" she asked wondering if what Brady guessed was anywhere near the truth.

"Why do I want you?" he asked, his steps taking him ever closer to her. "I would think that's obvious. You're a very lovely woman. One any man would like to call his own."

"I will never be yours." She meant to stand her ground.

"On the contrary, my dear. You are mine. I bought you from your father for a tidy sum."

She backed up, found herself against the wall. Shaking her head, "No, why did father sell me to you?"

"Oh, my dear girl, that's, a simple bit of good luck on my part. You see, he lost everything he owns in two turns of the cards." He paused to make a point, his broad grin showing yellowed teeth, "To me. I wanted you more than I wanted his holdings. Stephen didn't care about you, his bastard daughter. You were another man's get. You know that fact, don't you? Ah, by the look on your face you didn't know. Perhaps you guessed though. You could have heard the rumors. I digress. So, in order to keep what was dearest to him, he gave Lord Claymore you, and in the process, I will reap the benefits."

Fuller just gave her a lot of things to think over even while he confirmed one of her guesses about her parentage. She tried to stand tall, square her shoulders. Courage to outlast this man was hard to come by. "What are you going to do?" she asked as she tried to keep her voice from quivering.

"To begin with, I'm going to tie up your husband. So, even if he's inclined to go after his wife, it will take him awhile to get free. By then I hope to have a substantial head start. He won't be able to follow the trail we leave."

Vaguely, she wondered if a panther could follow its prey by the scent that would be left behind. Lilly looked around Fuller with the hope of rushing to the horses only to find two men blocking her passage.

Her frantic heart knew no peace. It thundered behind her ribs obsessed with the fear gnawing at her. There was no immediate escape for her.

She looked at her husband lying on the floor, now bound and gagged. He'd never told her he loved her. It had been too soon she supposed. Maybe he didn't love her. She was, however, falling deeply in love with the man who first wanted her as his mistress then claimed her as his wife. The healed marks on her shoulders throbbed painfully. She wondered at that. Something she could ask him if she ever saw him again.

For the last few weeks, Brady had touched her, held her, while he coaxed her to feel magic and enchantment with each soul-shattering caress. Each day he burned her with the desperate passion of wanting and needing her. With each mating it seemed he held her closer, his muscled arms a sheltering heaven of comfort and strength.

Never had he admitted to loving her.

With her mind stripped bare of her memories, she focused on the present. Lord Fuller held tight to her arm, ushering her from the room, from her husband. With no more than the passage of a few seconds, she found herself inside a carriage. She half expected to see Lord Claymore inside.

He wasn't.

At her look of confusion, Fuller laughed, his grin so very evil it sent shivers snaking down her spine. From head to toe her body shook with loathing. "Lord Claymore will not be joining us at the moment," his sugar sweet voice belied the vicious look in his eyes. "He is indisposed."

Lilly didn't want to dwell on Fuller's words or the way he said them. In truth she was relieved the old man was not going to bed her. That wasn't what Fuller said but she had the feeling that was what was in his mind. She wondered then if Claymore lived.

One less man to force her.

No, she would wait on rescue as she looked to see if there was any chance at all of a way out of this dreadful loop. It pained her to admit she was terrified of what Fuller meant to do. He could quite easily turn her over to the authorities once he was finished with her. Perhaps he had no idea what Douglas had been involved with.

No, he told her he would allow Brady to have his wife back.

The future terrified her, petrified her Brady would never come to love her, might never find her, might not even try. She never failed to make him angry. He could be relieved she was gone and no longer a responsibility to him.

I want you.

Time and again she remembered his fervent words that long-ago night. With the sweet taste of his kisses and long tingling strokes of his fingers. The night when she let him have her body and soul. Dear Lord, she craved him.

She dared not let him know how much she cared. Never did she speak those reverent words of love to him, lest she give too much of herself. Deciding from the first night unless he vowed his love, she would indeed hold back.

She was a fool. Probably always would be.

Never would she willingly confess her love to him—not when he neither wanted nor needed it. He was a force by himself, confident and arrogant in every possibility. Indeed, he wielded more power over her than any man, even a husband aught.

He snatched her will from her along with her heart and soul. She wasn't going to give him more power. Now she wished she had. She was sand falling through his fingers at every command. His sweet caresses turned her to liquid in his arms. Her life was no longer hers to control. Nay, now instead of her husband, she was in the hands of a man who would use her for his foul purpose, a man she despised.

She had no choice when Brady had been determined to make her his mistress, no choice when he told her he wanted her. Now, it seemed she was still a pawn meant to be used by a man for his selfish purpose.

Nay, she decided over and over again, she would not love Brady. She could not love him. Loving him would make this union with Fuller viler than she could live with. She must not weaken. To survive she would have to forget the love she felt for one man so she could harden her heart against another. Perhaps she had it wrong. Maybe her love for Brady would see her through all the trying times she was sure lay ahead of her.

She would not admit to any love for Brady in front of her captor. Fuller would use that love to torment her further, to threaten her into submission. For all she knew he might have already ended his life. Showing a sign of weakness could be her downfall. Yet she prayed Brady truly did love her, would come for her. Reach her before Fuller could defile her.

The thumping of the carriage wheels broke her from her thoughts. She looked up to find Fuller staring at her with a bemused look, his evil intentions shining clearly in his pale eyes

"Thinking of your lover?" he asked with a sneer. "He won't be coming for you. Won't know where to find you. Did you believe otherwise? Were you dreaming of his valiant rescue? He will be no knight in shining armor for you."

"Brady McKenna is my husband. Even if you have him killed, his father will send men after me, his brother along with his cousins will surely search. They will long for revenge. You will not fare well against the strength and power of the McKennas."

When she mentioned the family, Fuller's face paled slightly, his Adam's apple bobbing in a nervous pulse. She struck a chord with her words. He was afraid of the clan.

"They won't find you," he repeated showing much less confidence than before. "There will be no way he can follow you. No one in these parts knows where my hunting lodge is."

"Where are you taking me that is so difficult to find?"

She would know her destination. Mayhap she had more time than she thought to keep him at bay. While they were riding, he would do nothing. He was too old, his body too bulky to try to seduce her in the carriage.

"Ah, so you are curious as to your fate. I like that. Curiosity is a rare gift in women."

He shifted on the seat, settling his ample girth in what appeared to be a more comfortable position.

"You won't hold me."

"You think not? I've men outside who will keep a guarded eye on you when I cannot. Did you think I would take this on by myself? No, of course not. They will be handsomely paid for doing as they are told in the ensuing weeks. If they serve me well, I might even allow them to enjoy your womanly charms before I allow your husband to buy you back. If he wants used merchandise, that is."

She wished Douglas had not left the country. Wished Brady was not lying on the cottage floor unable to help. Wished also her father had not betrayed her. She closed her eyes on a ragged breath of fear. Men had this ability to let you down when you needed them most.

"I repeat. You won't hold me. Your men will grow tired of waiting, grow less vigilant. You're a fat old man, Lord Fuller. You don't have enough strength to keep me for very long."

His cheeks reddened at her words apparently not liking what she called him. He leaned forward grabbing her by the wrist then wrenching her onto his lap. "Even if I'm an old man, I'm still stronger than you. You cannot fend me off when I decide to have you beneath me in all your wanton splendor. I've coveted you since the first time I saw you years ago. You were barely fifteen but you showed signs of becoming a rare beauty. You, my dear, are even more beautiful than my imaginings. I will tame your arrogance. Arrogance is not seemly in a woman. No, you will become meek and biddable in time."

To no avail she pushed at his chest, trying to remove herself from his deceitful person. The man was right. He was stronger but she would still get away. This would not end up a matter of strength but cunning. She was smarter.

"*Nay.*"

"You were fifteen. I waited for you, my dearest. Waited for a chance to get the upper hand where Lord Townsend was concerned. I knew it was just a matter of time before he gambled his fortune and lost. My wait paid off. You grew into a beautiful and very desirable woman. I now have you in my control. I do believe I will enjoy this immensely." His hand stroked the curve of her hip, higher to cup her breast in his hand, weighing the rounded globe as if he meant to sell her.

She bit her bottom lip to stop from crying out her rage. Her body shuddered in revulsion even while she struggled with the panic flooding through her. It seemed he felt the heat of her distaste for him. He shoved her to the floor.

"You will not always feel this way about my tender touch. Mark my words. In time you will beg for me for whatever pleasures I want to bestow upon you. I will make sure of it."

Siting on the floor of the carriage, staring at him with hatred simmering in her entire being with a clogged throat she managed a resounding, "*Nay*. I'll never beg for anything from you," she tossed out the vow only to see his body grow rigid with anger, his eyes narrowing in wretched regard.

She should learn to watch her unruly tongue.

"Regret those words, I will make sure you do. You don't know who you are dealing with," his low snarl gave emphasis to his threat. He settled back against the seat, his fingers laced together across his sagging belly. For a few minutes, he closed his eyes as if daring her to do something stupid.

Vividly, she recalled Brady's words. He kept her locked in his rooms to keep her from doing something foolish. It was not her idea to visit the cottage. Nor did she take any responsibility for her capture. None of this was her doing. She was not a foolish or stupid woman.

She would do her best to escape this man. He could not watch her constantly night and day. All she would have to do was remain vigilant, bide her time until the right moment was upon her. Now was not the time. She could not jump to the forest floor and vanish therein. The coach was travelling way too quickly. He had men riding alongside the carriage.

It seemed they turned off one narrow rutted road to find themselves on another then another after that. The passing of time eluded her. She started to rise from the floor. His foot hit her back, keeping her in place.

"I like you on the floor groveling, my beauty. It is a place I deem you'll become accustomed to."

He pushed. Her arms gave out. She found that her face was now forced against the floor mat, one shoe neatly pressed against her neck. At that moment she understood what he wanted.

Her complete submission.

He would have to try a hell of a lot harder for her to give in to the subjugation he tried to enforce. She vowed she would not bow down easily. If he wanted a fight, he would have it.

They traveled for hours, her position beneath his foot unchanged. She tried to calm herself with long, deep breaths unable to gain anything but ragged shallow puffs of air. Her body cramped. Nothing seemed to work. When they stopped for a moment, he purchased food in a small village. His men drug her to the bushes so she could relieve herself. The abject humiliation he forced her to endure was unbearable. She swore once more she would withstand any torture he might conceive. She would survive if for any other reason than to seek revenge.

This wouldn't last forever.

They were in the carriage again. He ate. He drank the wine he bought. His burp of satisfaction left a foul smell in the small vehicle. When he finished with the roasted chicken, he tossed the remains out the window. So, this was how it was going to be. He would starve her. Well, if he wanted to force her, he would have to make sure she was still alive. Lilly willed herself to ignore the rumblings in her stomach, ignore the headache that was beginning to pound in her temple. She closed her eyes with images of Brady making love to her along with the images of their other lives together. She would stand strong.

Night turned to day then night again. He continued in the same pattern as the first day. On the fourth day he allowed her a slice of bread and a sip of the heady wine he always drank. That was all. Sometimes he kept her on the floor, his foot pressed against her back, sometimes he drew her up to sit on his lap, his hand stroking her, fondling her breasts, insinuating themselves beneath her gown. Whenever he didn't like her response, which was all the time, he tossed her to the floor again.

This time when the carriage came to a blinding halt, he shoved her through the door. She stumbled. Hit her knee then her face on the ground. Tried to stifle the cry of pain by sticking her fist in her mouth. His men sat on horses surrounding the coach. He mounted the third horse. He stared at her for what seemed an eternity.

"You may walk or ride in front of me. Your choice milady," he spoke slowly as if she was a small child unable to understand.

She pushed her hair from her face. Dirty and tired, all she wanted was to be left alone to sleep and forget. She tried to swallow the acrid taste of fear. She couldn't, wouldn't ride in front of him. He would fondle her. Caress her intimately. She could not bear his touch. With her nose pointed skyward, she said very softly, "I'll walk."

Once again, she defied him. One more time her simple words angered him. His brows drew together in fury. His jowls wobbled as they turned a fiery shade of red. "You'll regret your decision. However, this defiance of yours might manage to tame you sooner than expected. Hold out your wrists."

When she didn't one of his men leapt from the horse he was mounted on, tied her wrist together before handing the long leather strips to Lord Fuller. She cringed realizing now what he intended.

He tugged on the rope. His voice soft, he spoke with a decided relish, "Come along then, my dear. Before I'm done with you, you will beg to ride in front of me. You will have to be very sweet and biddable. I won't allow you the privilege if I see defiance in your spoken word or your eyes."

The horses started at an easy canter. She stumbled behind, pulled by the leather holding her. Exhausted from lack of food and no sleep, she faltered, falling to the ground to find herself dragged a few feet before Fuller stopped. She expected him to say something, to have one of his men help her.

She thought death might be preferable.

For the longest time she stayed in the prone position. He waited for her. Didn't move or tell her to get up. He could rot in hell.

She heard the slow steady beat of the horse's hooves as they approached. They stopped inches from her head. Heard the laughter echo around the trees shading the path they followed. Her stomach turned sour, acrid as she fought to keep the tiny crusts of bread inside her belly. Maybe now there was nothing inside her not even water. He withheld all liquid except a few sips of wine every few hours.

His voice was clear and arrogant above her. She heard the anger in his voice. Felt the raw displeasure. "You have three choices now, my dear girl. Either get up and walk, let me drag you or ride with me. What will it be?"

Go to hell, fat old man.

She heard the shifting creak of his saddle. Listened to the moaning keen of the wind in the trees while the silver backed leaves danced to the breezes tune. There was really no choice. Yet she could not allow herself to be held by him. Could not bear the touch of his arms around her or the smell of his ample body. With what little strength was left in her arms, she pushed from the forest floor standing now on unsteady, weaving legs. She was exhausted. This was the foolishly stupid action Brady was afraid she would commit. She could not bear his touch. Tilting her chin high and with a confidence she didn't feel she said, "I'll walk."

"Stubborn bitch, you'll regret that decision. I'll make sure of that." he grated out before turning his horse. The canter was a bit slower this time. Still, she was hard pressed to keep up. What little air she sucked into her lungs burned tight and hot until she thought she could breathe no more. Time and again she stumbled. More than once she was sure her face was about to meet the ground.

Her time on her feet was shorter, more erratic as she staggered waving along the path. Finally, she fell again, landing on her hands and knees, her head hanging, her hair framing and hiding her face, salty tears sliding down her cheeks. Unable to help herself she sobbed, gut wrenching sobs she could not hold back.

"Get up." He tugged on the leather straps binding her wrists. "You belong to me, Lilly. You'll do as I say or suffer the consequences."

It was too late. She could not do as he said. Nothing within her worked, neither her arms or her legs would move. Wretched pain swamped through her from her head to the tips of her toes.

"*Nay*, I cannot. I cannot move. You cannot expect..."

Her breath was barely a whisper on the wind. The sun had begun to set. Darkness would follow her to hell before she would sit beside that man.

"Then...?" Fuller questioned her again. "What I expect is for you to sit in front of me. You will do that or once more you'll suffer the penalties of your disobedience. You can sit with me, walk or..."

"Drag me. I don't care if I live or die."

The despicable curse gave her little reason to delight in the fact she defeated him for the moment. She knew he would not harm her that way. The leather tightening while it stretched her arms in front of her belied that fact. Slowly, her body moved across the earth until the horse picked up speed. She hit rocks and branches, brambles along with rutted out holes in the earth. She bounced along the trail as each toss of her body created sobs into the darkening sky she couldn't control. Bushes whirled, snapping by her as her face and arms were bloodied and torn. *Close your eyes and forget the pain* she willed herself to think. Remember Brady. Still, the black horrifying moments turned one into the other until she finally lost consciousness the world turning dark and black around her. It was with welcome relief she gave into the blessed oblivion.

~ * ~

Roby looked first in Brady's room before making his way to the floor below in search of either his brother or Lilly. Brady told him they would stay the night at the cottage. Time to exclusively to be by themselves was what he sought. While he wouldn't be surprised if they intended to make it a honeymoon get away, he half expected them to return to the manor for food and wine.

From what little Brady told him of the cottage and Lilly's sojourn there, food had not been plentiful. He strode through the kitchen, sampling some of the delicacies. He stole a few kisses from the serving wenches, listening to the satisfied giggles following in his wake.

In the main hall he found his mother, sitting pleasantly by the fire, speaking with Crissie. Their heads were bowed close together and it seemed to Roby they were sharing secrets over their needlework or some feminine accomplishment. One of the manor dogs sprawled at Crissie's feet while she absentmindedly rubbed the dog's ears.

"Either of you seen Brady or for that matter Lilly?" Roby asked as he sat in a chair across from the ladies.

One of the girls he gave his favors to in the kitchen brought him a glass of ale. He nodded with a smile and a glance to his room upstairs. "Later," he whispered, hoping his mother had not seen the blatant invitation.

"Tonight?"

Once more he grinned his approval.

"Truly, Roby, you need to curb your baser instincts with the servants or at least not be quite so obvious," his mother said with a bit of chastisement in the tenor of her voice.

"Was I obvious?" he asked his chuckle warm, thinking perhaps Wynnie had a valid point. "Until I find my mate, I don't intend to be celibate. If you want, I can buy a small house in the village." He watched the color of his mother's cheeks blossom.

"*Nay*, your father wouldn't like that." She waved a slender, delicate hand in the air. "As long as they are all willing lasses. I just don't like to be in the middle when you are arranging your dalliances. It's truly embarrassing for a mother to watch knowing they will be with you for the night in the south tower."

"Point taken," he said, vowing from this moment forward to be more discreet, especially around his mother. "Back to my first question. Either of you see Brady this morning or yesterday?"

"He hasn't been around this morning or yesterday afternoon. Did you check his room?" Crissie asked. "I thought he took Lilly somewhere to be alone."

"Yes, and I wouldn't be worried except I've this strange gut feeling that something is terribly wrong. My gut is never wrong. Felt it since yesterday but chose to ignore the sensation." He sipped the heady brew, staring at the door hoping his brother and wife would walk through, in the process end his brooding thoughts as well as the niggling seeds of growing unease.

"I'm sure your brother is capable of taking care of himself," Wynnie said as the focus of her gaze seemed to track her son's. "It wouldn't hurt to check on them."

"Of course, he is but that's not the point. He is with Lilly. That fact alone will make him vulnerable," Roby spoke as he ran his hands through his hair. "At the moment there are more British soldiers. We don't know the whereabouts of Lord Fuller. There are a host of other factors to consider." To Roby this was clearly not something in the realm of normal.

"You sound like a mother hen afraid of shadows," Crissie laughed darting a curious look his way. "When have you ever been worried about our big brother?"

Roby cleared his throat, thinking about his sister's question. "Since the number of redcoats in the vicinity seemed to have doubled. Since we took Lilly's father under our roof. The man is vile. Since we discovered Brady's wife was betrothed to Lord Claymore, a fat disgusting pig of a man. Do you want me to keep going? Nothing around here has been as it should be for well over a month."

Crissie sucked in a gasp of air at his brother's comment. "If you're so worried, go look for him. Didn't you say he was going to spend the night at the Fraser cottage? If nothing is wrong, they should be there."

"Don't think I did say that."

"Well, maybe I overheard them talking. They just want to be alone where no one is going to interrupt them. Isn't that what lovers want, to be alone?" Crissie asked keeping her face on the work in her trembling hands.

"What do you know about lovers, brat?" Roby asked then was shocked at the rapid drain of color to his sister's face.

Perhaps more than she should. Well, hell, at least Endicott was no longer in a position to compromise Crissie. His gut turned over. The devil but he hoped she wasn't increasing.

"I suddenly don't feel well." Crissie set her stitchery to the side, quickly leaving the room without a backward glance.

"What did I say?" Roby asked his hands rising into the air as he watched the angry swirl of his sister's skirts as she stormed away.

He knew though. He just wanted someone to tell him she wasn't with child and that he wouldn't have to find Endicott.

"She's overly sensitive these last few days. Don't worry. I'll go talk to her." Wynnie followed after her daughter leaving him alone to brood over his feelings along with his sister's condition.

Roby watched, a puzzled expression on his face. Well, that conversation didn't garner him information about his brother, but he was terribly afraid it told him a myriad of things about his sister.

"Perhaps you should give this another day." Connal sat beside him, a puzzled expression on his face also. "Suppose the ladies will tell us what is going on with them when they are good and ready."

"Suppose."

Roby still didn't like the feel of unease lurching through him. He decided he would give his brother until this afternoon. If he wasn't in the hall by then, he would at least ride to the cottage to see what was happening there if just to relieve his mind that all was well.

Chapter Eight

The groan hammering in Brady's head woke him. The floor pressing into his shoulder sent a jolt of fear straight to his core. He didn't understand but he feared for Lilly. The devil, what happened? With his head thumping a rapid staccato, he tried to open his eyes, tried to move his arms and legs. He was bound as well as gagged. Seconds passed turning into minutes still finding no success in his endeavor. He had to wait even longer to garner the strength needed to open his eyes.

Once his eyelids slanted open to welcome the sunshine, he groaned again, desperate to right whatever was wrong with him. Brilliant light shining in his newly opened eyes was the last thing his head needed. The throbbing doubled in time as well exploding in its intensity. What the devil happened? One second he was watching Lilly rearrange the bed chamber, the next...

...Well, the next he was complaining to himself about sunshine and the drums beating nonstop deep in his head.

Lilly?

"Lilly?" his question flowed through the empty room meeting no answer. She wouldn't leave him like this. Then he realized his mouth was gagged, his hands and feet tied.

Townsend?

Fuller or Claymore?

No, Lord Claymore could not have done this. Fuller then or Townsend. Suddenly very real fear for Lilly swept through him. A terror he'd never felt before swamped him with terrifying dread. She had not done something foolish. He had. He brought her here to be alone with her when his suite of rooms was certainly sufficient for his leisurely seduction of his wife. He wanted more though. Resented the constant interruptions.

Now, where the devil was his wife?

She would not have tied and gagged him. For what purpose? Doubts coursed through him, suspicions he forced to the back of his mind. He trusted her. Maybe that trust was misplaced. *Nay*, he refused to believe she did this or was a part of this. She was in trouble, his wife dark, dangerous misfortune. He was trussed up ready for the spit over the fire and could do nothing to help. All he could pray for is that someone would miss him then look for him.

Overwhelmed by the blinding headache, he closed his eyes. Counting to ten he tried to relax, attempted to will the pain to the back of his mind. A few deep breaths helped. A few extra seconds helped more.

He scooted to the fireplace hoping to find a jagged edge to unravel the rope around his wrists. Almost there, the sound of boot steps thundered on the hard floor. He prayed it was a savior not someone to do more damage. He wasn't much use in this condition.

When the boots stopped close to his nose, he swept his gaze up the long legs of the man standing in front of him. A long-spent breath left his lungs.

"Roby." His voice croaked unintelligently through the gag so quietly he wasn't even sure if he heard the word.

His brother lowered to his haunches, quickly pulling the knife he kept sheathed in his boot before he set to work on the bindings and gag. It was a matter of seconds before he was sitting up, rubbing his wrists to work out the numbing effect.

"What happened here?" Roby asked as he helped him stand then walk to relieve his muscles of the kinks.

Brady was shaking a perplexed head, aware of only two things. "I don't have any idea. Where is my wife?"

"Lilly have anything to do with this?" Roby asked, voicing his question as well as ignoring Brady's.

He didn't want to believe she would do anything against him, not after the last few weeks of wedded bliss and sexual delight. "There is always the possibility but no. No, I doubt it. She was coming to terms with the perfidy of her father and the thought of lying with Lord Claymore was abhorrent to her. She would not side against me and with either of them for any purpose. At least I cannot think of a reason."

"*Aye* with Douglas gone, there is nothing to hold over her head except perhaps your life."

Roby chuckled softly staring at him as if he just woke from the dead. The devil, he felt if he had. "

They left you here so they must have thought you were more of a risk if they took you with them."

"They?" Watching his little brother, he arched an eyebrow skyward. "What do you know?"

"I was lumping Lord Claymore and Fuller together as one. If they are a team, they might well continue to be one. This is at their door not your wife's."

"Then we have two opponents to contend with," Brady said, listening to the heavy fall of horse hoofs against the trail leading to the cottage. Brady pulled his knife.

Both men strode to the front. Connal along with Kit were bearing down on them. Connal leapt from the horse before it came to a full halt. Breathing hard he took a minute to catch his breath.

"I see you found your brother fine. Where is Lilly?" Connal asked repeating the question most prevalent then searching the inside of the room as well as the exterior for her.

"We don't know," Brady said, fear for his wife pooling in his gut. The sight of his father racing here did not help ease the tension. "Don't even know who is responsible. One minute I was standing watching her the next I was trying, unsuccessfully mind you, to open my eyes. I was hit in the head from behind. Just woke up a few minutes ago to find Roby hovering over me."

Both Roby and Connal exchanged glances. "Do you *ken* what day it is?" Connal asked.

"I'm assuming it is Tuesday. By the looks on your faces, I'm wrong. Blessed hell, how long have I been out cold, dead to the world?"

"Since yesterday morning, I'm assuming," Roby said quietly. "We all wanted to leave the two of you alone on your honeymoon of sorts. No one dared come interrupt to find out how things were going. I was worried this morning when I didn't see either of you come for food. No one in the kitchen saw you. Then there was this sick feeling in my gut, an unease I couldn't explain away, the tiny hairs prickling on the back of my neck. Father bid me wait until the afternoon to come check on you." Roby turned to their father, "Why are you here?"

"Lord Claymore was found dead"

"Foul play?" Brady asked wishing all the talk would result in a way to find his wife, realizing now that it had to be Lord Fuller at the bottom of Lilly's disappearance.

"Maybe," Connal paused, "Maybe not. The doctor examining the body couldn't tell. Might have been his heart or the attack could have been provoked. Appeared as if a tiny scuffle happened in his room. Don't expect we'll ever know the truth."

"Where is Townsend?" Brady needed to know the location of all the players in this mysterious dance.

"A few minutes ago, he was seen sipping a pint at the castle. He's been there all day. As far as I remember all day yesterday too. He's taking advantage of the free hospitality. We all know if Claymore is dead, he no longer owes the man money."

"It has to be Lord Fuller who hit me and took Lilly. There is no doubt in my mind he wants her. Do we know anything about the man?" Brady asked striding to his horse, which was still hitched in front of the cottage. Following his wife, finding her, was most important

"Need to speak with Townsend. Perchance he can shed some light on the man as well as where he might take Lilly," Connal said. "Now, I know you want to take off. Look for Lilly but best to be informed before you start on a fool's mission. Let's talk with your cousin, Houston, as well. He would crave to be a part of this now, don't you think?"

Brady knew his father was right on both counts. Didn't help the turbulence he felt. They would need additional forces. Houston would be eager. The four men set off for the manor to make plans as well as recruit the cousin, Kit's older brother. As they rode the weather seemed to be taking a turn for the worse. Ever darkening black clouds dotted the horizon. He was afraid that even in his cat form he wouldn't be able to pick up her scent if the barely tangible traces were washed away by rain.

Fear rippled in Brady's soul, tripped in his mind, caused his gut to spiral in tight knots as he tried not to think of the fear Lilly must be feeling at the whim of Lord Fuller. The devil, but Fuller, if that was the man who took her, had an entire day's lead, a lead that was growing as they spent time learning about the man and where he might take Lilly. Unchangeable fear gripped him. Fear they might indeed be too late.

He had been a fool.

A bloody fool, arrogant, too, for thinking there would be no danger for Lilly if he was with her. Time to secure the area had not been taken. Lilly trusted in him. He betrayed that promise of safety he gave her. He succumbed too easily. Hit from behind, he didn't even know who inflicted the blow.

What Brady did *ken* was that Fuller wanted her, wanted her enough to forgive the debts of Stephen Townsend to have her. What man wouldn't want her? She was so very beautiful with a fine and charming wit. He was beginning to think Lord Claymore was just a rouse, in case something went wrong, another pawn in Fuller's dark game of deadly secrets coupled with the intrigue of purchasing a woman and to what ends?

Well, something did go wrong. Fuller was going to die. The aging Lord Claymore was already dead. If he had doubts before how Claymore died, he no longer had them. If Lilly bore even a scratch from this ordeal, the men who took her would die a torturous end at the hands of his cat. It would have taken more than just Lord Fuller to carry off this deed.

Once in the castle, Roby and Kit went in search of Houston.

The three men met up with Connal and Brady. Together they approached Lord Townsend.

Townsend looked as if he would jump from the table where he sat when he saw the five McKenna men striding toward him, hands fisted at their sides, expressions grim. He drank down the glass of ale sitting in front him. When he started to rise, Brady pushed a hand down on his shoulder. "Stay where you are. We've a few questions."

When they surrounded him, two sitting at the table by his side, Brady behind him and Houston in front, he choked on the tiny speck of ale left in his throat. His face turned a mottled red. His fists knuckled white around the glass.

"What do you want?"

His voice wavered with the fear that must have been coursing through him. He motioned for one of the servants to bring him another glass as if he could gain time.

"What do you know about Lord Fuller?" Connal asked, his hand holding Townsend's forearm to the table. "We aren't going anywhere until we're satisfied, until we've learned everything needed."

When he spoke Connal's eyes flashed silver, threatening.

There was nothing friendly about the gesture. It was meant to intimidate and threaten. His Adam's apple bobbed up and down with the question. "Wh-what do you mean?"

"Would Fuller have killed Lord Claymore? Or did you do it?" Roby asked, taking out his knife, running it the length of Townsend's quivering neck, stopping to insinuate the point at his throbbing pulse.

"No, no I didn't. Anything is possible." When the sharp point of the knife drew a small spot of blood. "If it would serve his purpose to have the old guy out of his way, yes. He could and would kill the man. Heard tell of other murders that he was a prime suspect for. His money always gave him an out or he bought off a judge or two. He could always buy a witness with threats of blackmail. He owns a goodly portion of London, the seamier side, if you get my drift."

"Did he covet Lilly as much as Claymore did? What made the two men coconspirators?"

Connal was sitting back in his chair now, his hands folded together on the table watching the man squirm.

"No, Claymore needed an heir. He understood that wasn't going to happen without help. When Fuller learned about this, he offered his assistance."

Townsend touched the blood Roby drew with his knife, which was once more sheathed in his boot.

"Is there anywhere he would take her? Does he have a place in Edinburgh or Inverness?"

Brady was standing now, pacing, his mind racing wildly with the need to leave to track Lilly to wherever Fuller took her. He pulled in a deep draught of air, searching for patience.

Townsend seemed to think for several seconds then a few more. "Claymore has a townhouse in Edinburgh, but I've heard Fuller talk about a secluded hunting lodge in the highlands."

"That could be anywhere," Brady gritted out, his mind reeling with the very real possibility they might never find her.

When they finally did, she would be a shell of the woman they knew now. He would use her force her to his will. She would fight. He couldn't let that happen yet time was racing away.

"Actually, I think it's north of here. Also heard him talk about the tale of the Kinnel Stones. That people disappear if they wander into them. The lodge could be nearby."

Connal's brows narrowed at the mention of the stones. "That's a start. We'll head that way."

"Start from the cottage," Brady said as his gaze transferred in that direction, realizing that would be the best place to catch her scent.

He would shift there. Breathe in the wind; touch the air surrounding the tiny home until he could track her. The four of them would follow whatever path he thought right. He understood that while she was in the carriage it would be difficult to follow her, trail her he would though.

The night was eerily silent when the four of them started out. Connal and Roby along with Kit rode their great horses while he and Houston shifted to their cat form. Three more horses were led by his father, one for him and one for Lilly when they found her, one also for Houston.

Brady inhaled long and deep testing his increased senses as he searched the dark forest for a clue. Her scent hovered faintly in the still of the night. Roses and Lilly. No stars lit the way along with a slivered moon. Only the oppressive black silence coupled with his raging, complicated emotions.

Dwelling on those simmering feelings would get him nowhere, would hinder the cause. Her rescue. He started out at a lazy pace unwilling to spend himself in a fevered dash. The night wore on, minutes turning to hours until pink shone through the dense trees. He found the spot where they had stopped for a few minutes pleased he had proof she was still alive and fighting her captors. Now he also knew the scent of the man. He discovered the food tossed carelessly from the vehicle, knew each place they halted their trip into the highlands for food and water.

Another night passed. With the coming of a newly pink sky, they came upon the abandoned vehicle. When he realized what had happened, he let out a scream that echoed through the hillside, bouncing off the rocks and craggy hills. The path wound through the heather clad knolls along dangerously raging steams. He caught the scent of her fear, the panic in her heart. He smelled everything she felt, the resounding pain.

With a newfound burst of energy, he raced forward, followed by the ever-present sound of horses. He pulled up short when he scented her tears, the smell of her blood, the terror. Here she gave up, drained of energy, accepting her fate as she saw it. Lilly didn't understand the evil of the man. Didn't understand all he was capable of in pursuit of his pleasures.

"Fuller drug her along the path. There are traces of skin and blood. What kind of demon would do such a thing?" Roby asked.

Brady couldn't think. Rage engulfed him.

"He is demented, mad," Connal spoke softly directing the next statement to Brady. "You may do whatever you wish when you find him. If you mean to rip his heart out, you may. No one will gainsay you. I've no qualms about his death or any man who helped in this horrid treatment of a woman."

"If you wish to tear him apart with your claws and teeth, none of us will do naught to stop you," Roby said glancing at his cousins for confirmation.

"If you wish to bring him in front of a judge and jury here in the highlands, we will follow suit. No judge could possibly be paid and bought for here," Connal said quietly in his soft-spoken voice. "Indeed, I will make sure it is someone of honor and trust who hears this case."

With a flick of his tail and a nod, Brady started down the path where Lilly was dragged. He knew the instant she fell prone, could no longer move to defend herself in any way. It seemed she no longer had the strength to remain conscious. He shook with the fury coursing through his veins, the very real and potent fear for her life. No longer did he worry about Fuller violating her. His fear was that he would find her dead.

Once more the scream that dissolved in the mist filling the highland air would set anyone who heard the desperate furious cry to run with fear. When he looked over his shoulder, the faces of his father and brother were grim, filled with an unmistakable determination.

Lilly...

I've only just found you. I can't lose you now.

Brady fought to hold back when his desperate need to race after her attempted to overpower his common sense. Exhausted from no sleep, he could ill afford to expend himself with a short-lived race one that would never take him the distance to the lodge.

They continued throughout the rest of the morning, winding between the knolls and valleys, skirting the craggy rocks, following a winding stream ever upward. With a feeling of deep satisfaction, he sat back on his haunches when the small hunting lodge came into view. She was in the cabin and she was strong. Lilly would survive this. The breath he sucked inside tore at his lungs while it ripped into his heart.

For several minutes he stared at the place. A curl of smoke rose from the chimney. Lilly was inside somewhere. Was she alive? He could only wonder and pray yet his gut told him she was and she was fighting. Rushing inside might not be prudent. That was exactly what he needed to do.

He found himself tempted to shift, knew he'd rather put the fear of God into Fuller when he burst into the room as a black panther. A burst of energy shot through him. He looked to his family who were gathered around him, Houston sitting on his haunches next to him as his cousin waited for whatever signal he would give.

He drew in another deep lungful of air, held the oxygen in his lungs until his body burned. Closed his eyes to listen to the sounds. Her heart wrenching sobs filled the silence between them. She was still alive. In pain, he was sure but alive.

Lilly would be in his arms soon. He would protect her, shelter her. Whatever had happened to her, she would heal. He would treat her with the love and kindness she deserved.

His need to kill Lord Fuller overpowered all his senses, all he held dear save the one to make sure Lilly would survive. His family gave him the knowledge he could kill if he wanted. *Nay*, Fuller should be sent through the Kinnel Stones to oblivion and beyond if there was such a thing. Lord Fuller would be ripped from this life he coveted, sent to a new destination where he had no power, where he had nothing.

In that case he might live. Life was too precious to be granted to that man. If he went to prison, he would rot there for the rest of his life.

He would still live.

No one truly understood what happened inside those stones. A person might die. Or a person might be sent to a different time. If that were the case, Brady prayed Fuller would be sent to a place so desolate and despicable it would be hell to him.

Ah, but one never knew what was in store for them, what waited for them beyond the place where they stood in the present. His father sent a man through the stones. Sent two men years ago, before his birth. Sent Wynnie's abusive father and his wife's betrothed through those stones.

The two men vanished without a trace. What happens beyond the magic in those stones? Be they good or evil? Did the character of the stones depend upon the character of the person among them?

Aye, he would terrify Lord Fuller then drag him to the stones, send him to whatever hell awaited beyond. It was fitting.

The moment was his. He let out another scream then raced behind the horses toward the lodge. Roby leapt from his horse to fling open the door.

~ * ~

Lilly woke to blinding pain encompassing her entire body. Her wrists still bound in front of her, she found her feet were also tied securely with leather thongs. Someone had taken her shoes before they tied her. She discovered then that she wore only her shift. Lying on a pallet in a corner of a bedroom, she heard the heavy tread of boots below her. Harsh voices raised in argument caught her attention.

Where was Lord Fuller?

What awaited her here?

With those haunting questions in her head, she scooted to a sitting position her back against the wall. The small effort drained her of energy. The single window let in no light. Night had fallen. When she squinted, she could see a few stars on the velvet blackness. What day it was she didn't know, wasn't sure if she cared. Brady wasn't here or if he was, there was no sight or sound of him.

Delicious smells floated through the floorboards. Warm bread caught her attention first coupled with the mouth-watering scent of bacon. She couldn't remember when she last ate. Her stomach rumbled discontentedly telling her she had little to eat over the last few days. All she could remember was a few crusts of dry bread coupled with sour wine. Fuller meant for her to beg at his feet. Was this a torment he would incite in her body? She would not beg. Never.

Surely, he wouldn't starve her.

What good would she be to him if she died? He certainly wouldn't collect on her father's gambling debts if indeed that was what transpired this sale of her to the man.

He would have to untie her to eat. He would have to take her to see to her physical needs soon or did he intend to...for her to embarrass herself? *Nay*, not even a man as vile as Lord Fuller would do such a thing. Still, she was trembling, the dark storm of emotions she held back all these days threatened to surface. Tears burned hot in her eyes. Her hands felt clammy and cold. She flexed them, sensations barely coursing through to her fingertips, fingertips that were numb.

She wanted to see Fuller. She didn't want to see him.

Brady would come.

Unexpectedly, the hinges on the door creaked a spine-tingling screeching sound that sent the small hairs on the back of her neck to stand on end. Her gaze flew toward the opening as her breath jammed her throat. The moment filled with unleashed tension. The man who stood framed in the opening was not Lord Fuller. He was tall, muscled where Fuller was not. His legs were long, his belly flat. His gaze traveled from her lips to her toes coming back to linger on her breasts. She felt as if he undressed her with the avid heat of his gaze.

She let out a tiny gasp of relief coupled with dismay. It was the man who carried her in front of him on the horse up the steep rocky path to this place. He held a tray of food and drink in one hand. In the other he held bandages.

For her scratches she supposed.

"Are you hungry, lass?" he asked, his voice surprisingly gentle.

Yet his eyes looked upon her with a hunger she couldn't deny. He wanted her, wanted her as Brady did, Fuller as well.

She pushed back against the wall until she could go no further. A gesture that would do her no good if the man harbored evil intentions. One look at him told her she could not fight this man and come out the winner. "Lord Fuller? Where is he?" her voice whispered into the room surrounded by the dark bleakness of her mood. Her fears she knew were evident in the trembling of her hands, the thinness of her voice.

"He is sleeping. The long trip exhausted him. The night is almost over. Morning is almost upon us. You should yield to him when he comes for you. Do as he asks. It will do you little good to fight. You will just harm yourself more as you did yesterday. He doesn't wish you harm. Only wants to experience pleasure in your arms."

"Never!" She could not say that one word enough times. She would never succomb to him. Never do as he insinuated. If he wanted something from her, he would need to take it, force it from her. She would not yield. He wanted his pleasure, not hers. He wanted to violate her in the worst possible way. *Nay*, nothing could convince her to yield.

The man grimaced, his heavy dark brows drawing together. He stared hard at her seeming to realize her intent. "Very well then, lass. Do as you wish. Fighting will do naught but harm you further. After he's rested, I'm sure he will be up to see you, check on your condition. For now, I'll untie you so you can see to your needs. Take these precious moments to consider what I just told you." He did so then, "I'll be back in a few minutes. Your wounds need tending to before they fester and get infected. Don't want you sick."

Frozen to the wall, she didn't move until the door shut behind the man. She heard a key turn in the lock, the sound grating against her nerves. Massaging first her wrists then her ankles, she stood. Her knees were weak but with a concentrated effort she was able to make her way gingerly around the barren room until her limbs began to work more smoothly. There was naught but a pallet along with a few necessities in the chamber not even a table or a chair. The tray of food the man brought rested on the floor.

Even as Lilly looked out the window, she noticed the sky changing color. Velvet darkness gradually grew lighter, turning colors as the sun rose to herald a new day. Birds tweeted their song in the trees.

She realized suddenly she needed to take care of herself first. The man said he would return. Quickly, she washed, using the cloth and water he brought to the room after that taking care of her other needs. When she finished, she sat on the pallet. The tray was heaped with bread and butter along with honey. Her stomach rumbled deeply. She was famished, her mouth parched from lack of food and drink. There was no water or tea but a large glass of wine. Mayhap Lord Fuller needed his women slightly drunk when he forced them.

She ate hungrily, sated herself far more than she thought she should. No doubt her stomach had shrunk from this ordeal. Leaning against the wall, she vividly recalled the tender caress of Brady's fingers. Imagined the way his lips molded so perfectly to hers. She would remember the blinding ecstasy he gave her when he loved her. She forced all the bad memories of Lord Fuller and his hated touch to the back of her

Before she knew it the man was back. He bent over her, pushing her hair aside with tenderness. Soaking the cloth in the water, he dabbed at her face cleaning the myriad of abrasions, pulling bits of thorns and plant matter from the scrapes. She knew she was horribly scratched, her face, her hands, all of her where her clothes were ripped from her body from the rocks she encountered along the trail, remembering the grueling ride as she was dragged through the hills until she fell unconscious.

"You've abrasions that need to be tended to, bruises over much of your body that will take some time to vanish. He won't take you until you're healed. Perhaps you would like that, hmmm? Perhaps you are such a beauty a few marks on your tender white skin won't matter to him. Time will tell I suppose. It would make no difference to me."

At his words, she closed her eyes, a spasm of relief gushed through her. If she could find a way, she would garner more bruises more scratches. She'd claw at the door until her nails and hand were bloodied and raw, filled with splinters that would have to be cleaned. So, she thought, if he didn't like the way she looked he wouldn't force her.

Her's was a fine idea, a fine idea indeed.

"He will come to see you though, check you out. You should be prepared. He will want to see you without any clothes. If you value your wellbeing don't shy away from him. I don't doubt he has other tortures in mind. Lord Fuller is a cruel man. As I told you before, humor him if you value your life, if you want to see your husband again. If you don't?" he shrugged his shoulders, "Do whatever suits you. I see you ate everything. Keep up your strength while you can." He picked up the tray. "You will be mine when he's done with you. If there is anything left."

Lilly nodded, ignoring the man's last words. "Guess I was hungrier than I thought." She would be surprised if she received anything more to eat for a while. She couldn't think of anything else the man could do to her besides starve her to make her beg him to force her. "Good girl, I'll leave the wine. You might need the false courage it will give you to make it through the next few hours. Or not. Continue to make good choices. If you do, you'll live."

209

"Thank you. Why are you telling me these things?"

She didn't truly know why she thanked this man. Possibly he could assist her in some way. She could promise him something, anything. He might help her escape.

His lips curved in a half smile, his eyes smoldering once more when his gaze rested on her breasts. "As I told you before, I would like something of you left for myself. If you die...well then all this will be for naught."

Lilly shuddered, turning her face away, unwilling to look at the leering grin now painted on the man's face. She inhaled sharply, her body searching for air.

She recalled what Fuller told her. When he was tired of her, he would give her to his men to do with as they pleased. No wonder the man was solicitous. He wanted her alive when Lord Fuller had his fill. Well, she meant to be alive. She also meant to find a way out of here before any of that happened.

Saving herself was up to her. Relying on Brady would be foolish. She didn't know if he lived. The blow to his head appeared brutal. He dropped to the ground so quickly. Didn't know if he could follow her when or if he came to his senses. Sometime the clan would miss them. They would look for him. She drank the rest of the wine. Leaning against the wall, her eyes closed. She was so very tired.

Her dreams were of Brady.

I want you.

She recalled his ardent declaration. Ah, but he only wanted her for his mistress until he realized she was his mate. He didn't love her then, still didn't. Her question to herself was if she loved him. It was so easy to recall his strong hard body, flush against her, his rod moving within her. She wanted to dwell on the images, on the memories so nothing Lord Fuller and his men did would dispel those thoughts.

The visions she saw that night he claimed her swept through her again. All the times she slept with him over the infinite years, he never looked exactly the same. *Nay*, one time he had red hair and a beard soft as a kitten's fur. His eyes had been a brilliant green instead of the silver-steel they were now. His body though was always hard and unyielding. She shivered with the overpowering surge of love for him, something suddenly very new to her.

She loved him, loved Brady McKenna with all her heart.

She didn't want to die before she could tell him she loved him.

No, she would find a way from the lodge, a way back to the castle. Her body slumped in blinding despair, her shoulders quivering, her hands clammy with dread. She didn't know the way. It would be impossible for her to find her way back to McKenna land.

Brady had to come for her.

"Wake up!"

A large booted foot prodded her in the side. She blinked a few times adjusting to the bright light of the day. The storm clouds from days before cleared to reveal bright blue sky.

"It's you."

Her apathy toward this man surprised her. She should feel disgust. He told her he would make her beg him for favors, perhaps just for the food her body craved. He had her tended to for his selfish motives.

She murmured softly, "Didn't expect to see you for a few days."

"You are quite unappealing right now. You know that don't you? If I didn't know better, I might have thought you caused this because you knew I wouldn't want you if you were ugly in any way. I'm here now because I wanted to see how you fared after a good night's sleep. Needed to see for myself how long it would be before you came to my bed."

"Just fine," she said sarcastically the tilt of her chin rising as she stared into his frosty eyes. Raising her hands, "As you can see. I'm not coming to your bed nor will I ever beg."

"Always the little princess. Nothing has changed. I used to appreciate that quality in you. Now it seems fitting that I should beat the haughty arrogance out of you. There are ways to do that without leaving a mark." He ran the back of his hand along her cheek, down her neck then across her shoulder. She winced where he touched her bruises. "You truly should not have chosen the punishment over sitting with me on the horse. I didn't want you hurt, you know. Your small act of defiance enraged me.

Had the greatest need to punish you. Suppose one could say I lost my power to think rationally where you are concerned. Don't make me angry, Lilly. It will not bode well for you if you do."

She bristled, trying valiantly to curb her rising temper. Words blurted from her lips without conscious thought. "You're hurting me just by keeping me here away from my husband. Do what you will but remember, Brady is no fool or a weakling. He will not give up what he deems his without a fight. You should run from here. Run before he arrives to seek his vengeance."

Her breath was nearly gone, her words indeed were. She wasn't sure how much of this was bravado to give herself courage or to make Fuller doubt. "He won't come alone."

Lord Fuller waved a dismissive hand in the air as his brows drew together in a straight line. "Forget Brady McKenna. He's long dead. Even if he isn't, he won't know where to find you. It would take years to search all of Scotland and England. No, he won't arrive anytime soon."

Talking to him would get her nowhere. He was too arrogant by far. Her lips thinned as she looked away, focusing on the window and what lay outside. Brady would be here. She believed that fact with all her heart. "I-I won't forget my husband," Lilly cursed, the weak tenor of her voice, the rapid breaths caused from fear.

"It a waste of your time to continue to hope for that which will not happen," he sneered fully confident in himself.

"You're wrong."

He would come for her.

"No, my dear, I'm not wrong about this."

"What is it you want of me?"

Her words came out breathlessly as all she feared seemed to be coming to fruition. Brady would never find her. There was too much land to search not unless he could somehow follow her scent.

He laughed as he lifted a strand of hair, ran it through his fingers, touched the nape of her neck. He trailed a finger along her shoulder, dipping slowly to caress the top of her breasts. "A bath first I believe. You smell horrible. Mayhap I'll watch. Does your husband enjoy watching you bathe? No, I can tell by the look on your face it is not something you do. I might even run the cloth across your body or better yet my hands lathered with soap. What do you think, Lilly? Would that be nice for you? Would it bring you pleasure?"

Revulsion deep and painful slid through her. *Nay*, he would not do such a thing. She forced the image from her head concentrating on her feelings, her needs at the moment. Continuing to believe in Brady was imperative. She should protest a bath understanding he didn't want her the way she was now. "I won't take a bath," she said while the very thought of hot water on her flesh sent a feeling of contentment flooding through her.

He lifted his narrow shoulders in the semblance of a shrug making tiny noises for a few seconds. "If you won't do it yourself, I'll have one of my men do it for you. I'm sure they will enjoy themselves. Their hands on your beautiful body. Since you're no longer a virgin it doesn't matter to me if they have you first. I will still enjoy your lithe, slim woman's body along with the sweetest nectar of your tight sheathe." He paused for several seconds, tapping his chin with a finger. "Perhaps I'll watch. Would you like that, Lilly? Would you like me to watch you with my men, all gloriously naked and panting for them?"

She hissed in a sudden gasp of air. "*Nay*."

He grinned, skimming his gaze over her body, resting on her breasts for a moment longer to see his fill. "Yes, yes, that sounds delightful. I'll watch the men as they take their turn with you. Although I don't want to see the nasty blue marks and scratches that mar your body. What should I do, put aside some tantalizing moments or put up with the marks on your delicate skin? What say you? It is of course your choice."

"I'll take a bath," she said quickly, too quickly because it caused more laughter to bubble up from the horrid man's throat.

He appeared pleased with her easy compliance, too pleased.

"Thought you would say that. Look at it this way, Lilly. You will feel much better after you're clean. Don't you think? When you are more yourself, I'll think of little ways that will make you beg for me. I've given this a lot of thought. The problem has kept me up at night. Rest assured I won't hurt you. I abhor men who treat their women to beatings. No, there are other ways to make you plead to have me between the sheets with your nakedness flush against mine. Oh, I forgot, you don't have sheets. Oh my, perhaps we'll remedy that or just do without."

She turned from him, presenting her back, hiding the fear in her eyes. He wouldn't allow it. Grasping her chin between his thumb and finger he forced her to look at him. "You need a clean shift. Would you like a gown to wear? If you do all I say, you can have a dress, one of your own actually. I had the pleasure of bringing a few with me. Would that please you? One of your dresses?"

"You know I would like something besides this to wear." She plucked the thin chemise covering her. The fabric hid nothing from anyone's sight. Her body was totally revealed.

"Then be a good girl. Take your bath."

He left. The door shut behind him with a booming click. His footsteps resounded down the hall. Lilly let out a long breath of air, relieved to be alone again. Thoughts tumbled around in her head.

She understood all too well he would return. Understood that taking a bath was so little to do to make him happy. It would also please her. She swallowed the lump in her throat, casting her gaze once more out the window.

Be a good girl.

Aye, if she were to survive this, she would have to do just that. What would it take? Only a few minutes passed before first a tub then the steaming bath water arrived. It was a different man who brought the hot water, the second man. She had a vague recollection of him. He was taller, thinner, tawny hair instead of dark brown. His eyes were narrow, slanted a little, his nose broad with thin lips. After he poured the hot water into the tub, he stood back watching, a leering grin on his face, his gaze focused on her breasts. To no avail, she tried to cover herself.

She didn't think taking a bath in front of this man was part of doing as Fuller told her. She gamboled with the next words. "You may go now."

The silent wait for him to leave seemed to go on forever. Finally, the man turned, his hand on the doorknob.

"You may think you're the high and mighty lady, but the time will come when Lord Fuller gives you to me and my friend. It will please me to bring you down a peg or two. You won't act the princess then." With that said he vanished.

Lilly inhaled a long-ragged breath that seemed to shudder all the way to her burning lungs. Just barely she kept her feelings in check. She wasn't going to say anything more than necessary to this man as she once again tried to reassure herself Brady would come for her.

When she no longer heard footsteps outside her door, she slipped from the chemise she wore letting it fall to the ground. Steam rose from the tub, inviting beckoning to every aching portion of her body. Once inside, her back to the door, the water swirled and simmered around her, easing her sore muscles. Where the liquid touched on her scratches, she felt the momentary sting. Eventually, that slight pain subsided. Slowly, she soaped her body, relishing this moment, not knowing if she would get another bath anytime soon. Mayhap this was to lull her into a sense of acceptance. Help her forget what awaited her outside the door to this room.

With her head on the rim, she closed her eyes lingering in the hot water until it began to turn tepid. It wasn't so much as to think about Brady but to ease the terror the future moments would bring. Before she was out of the bath, the door slowly creaked opened. The fine hairs on the back of her neck prickled. She covered herself with her arms and the small scrap of cloth left to her.

"Shy, Lilly? We will soon end that horrible affliction of yours. You will quite get used to wearing no clothing," Fuller told her, sneering as he stepped around the tub. "You have a lovely back. It's not bruised. I'm glad to see you agreed to the bath." After walking around the tub to face her, he held a gown up. It was deep sapphire blue. His gaze swept her, seemed to see beneath the water as well as the fragile barrier she held in front of her. "Does this meet with your approval? It matches the color of your eyes. The cut is too modest for my taste, but if you're with me very long, I'll have all your gowns altered to my specifications. I enjoy seeing what I've purchased so dearly."

Lilly nodded, her breath catching in her throat as she realized the intent of his softly spoken words. "Yes. The gown will do just fine."

"When you finish with your bath and dressing, come downstairs. I'd like to eat the next meal with you. Tonight, we can make it more romantic, a bit of candlelight to set the mood. Maybe spend an hour or two getting to know each other better. What you like as well as what you don't like is important to me. Ah, you don't want to know me better. I see it in the glimmer of your eyes. Too bad." He walked to the door, stopped after he opened it. "Ah, Lilly, remember a good girl is willing in all things. You will be too or you will pay the price. I'm working on your punishment if you disobey me."

When all she heard was silence, she quickly finished, her body shaking so hard she could barely stand. The water had turned cold, icy. The thought of one of those two odious men walking in this room, dressing her, sent more shivers wracking her body. Good girl, she reminded herself.

I can manage that. The alternatives are worse.

With her dress on, she inhaled softly staring at the door, wishing she could pinch herself and this would all be a bad dream, a nightmare she could whisk away with the bright light of day. She had trouble believing he could have this fashioned any lower. Her breasts would be bare to his gaze, her nipples prominent.

It was not to be.

She opened the door. To her surprise it wasn't locked nor was a guard standing outside to prevent an escape. She looked around, her heart in her throat, her pulse frantically hammering against her ribs. Silence overpowered her. The lodge was dead silent. Not one sound filtered up from below. With hesitant steps, she walked toward the stairs then down to the main floor.

Still nothing.

Where was everyone?

The front door was open, banging on its screeching hinges, a soft summer breeze floating inside coupled with the scent of heather. Tables and chairs were knocked askew. On the floor in front of her a lamp was shattered. She picked it up as well as the table nearby setting what was left of the lamp on the table.

Her hand at her throat, her breath stopped for a moment. What the devil happened here? When she was dressing, she thought for a moment she heard a roar. Dismissed the noise as her imagination. She walked into the dining room. Plates of food, dishes and other things were scattered around the room. It appeared as if Lord Fuller and his men raced from here panic struck. The devil himself must have been after them. The back door was also open on its hinges, slowly sliding open then closed. A hot rush of air swept through the lodge. Spilled across her face. She let the breath she'd been holding surge from her lungs.

Mindlessly, Lilly walked outside. She saw nothing. Sunshine beat down on the earth, warming her. A cloud of dust on the horizon caught her attention, men walking, men on horseback. Her breath caught in her throat, her heart stopping. The sight could mean only one thing.

A soft purring noise behind her had her spinning, skirts whirling around her ankles. The gasp of surprise caught in her throat. For a tiny second her heart stopped. She stepped inside the kitchen.

"Brady? Is that you?" A black panther sat on his haunches in front of her, nodding his head seeming to grin cockily.

Just like Brady.

Before she could process this or even blink, the big cat shifted, changing form in a matter of seconds. He stood before her stark naked, glorious. He held out his arms for her, a wide grin on his oh so handsome face. She ran into his embrace never so glad to see anyone as she was now.

"How?" she asked, staring into the steel gray of his eyes.

~ * ~

Connal protested when Brady decided to send Lord Fuller and his men to the Kinnel Stones without being there himself. He wanted to find Lilly, hold her. Make sure she was fine. He yearned to be alone with his wife if only for a short time before the others returned.

Connal understood the raging need to protect, surging urgently through his son. He would allow Brady to do what he deemed necessary. He would catch up to him once he discerned Lilly to be sound and healthy. Connal prayed she came to no harm during this ordeal.

For the time being Houston, Kit and Roby stripped the men of their shirts and trousers. When they made their way through the Kinnel Stones they would be stark, blatantly naked. Connal chuckled silently as he thought of the people on the other end, if there were people on the other side of the stones. For some inexplicable reason he thought there must surely be something else there. They would either be shipped to the past or the future. There were tales about this too, not just people vanishing but of some appearing out of nowhere.

"Where are we going?" Fuller was trussed up like a fat pig ready for the spit, his round belly shaking with fear, his eyes dark rimmed with what must be fear now that he was no longer in control.

"We don't know," Roby said, turning to wink and grin at the men behind him. "That's the fun of it. You won't know either, at least not until you get there. Where do you think you're going? Ah, Sassenach, you haven't heard tell the stories abounding about the stones, have you?

"To another place?

"To another time?

"One might have to believe in witchcraft in the dark arts as well as other magical things beyond your comprehension, mayhap even the black arts if one were to be superstitious."

"Together? All of us are going together?" he queried looking at his men as if somehow having company would make this easier.

It might but they weren't going anywhere together. Connal hoped they would all end up in a different place and time if any of the rumors could be counted as true.

"Again, we don't know," Houston said with a snide chuckle joining Roby in the unstoppable mirth they were all feeling. "Not going to send any of you together hoping you won't end up in the same place. That wouldn't be good. No, it wouldn't be good at all. The idea of all this is punishment not camaraderie."

"You shouldn't have kidnapped Lilly. Made us all angry to have one of our own hurt. The woman is a McKenna after all. Hurt one you hurt us all," Connal said unable to share the amusement his son and nephews found in the situation.

He was bitter as he thought of why the last two men were sent through the Kinnel Stones. It was much the same reason as Fuller and his unsavory cohorts. They'd hurt and abused two women he held dear. "Brady didn't want you to die. That's the only reason we decided on this punishment. He could have ripped your throats out quite easily. We all wanted to rid the highlands of you forever. Vanishing from this part of Scotland as well as this earth seemed fitting in your case."

Roby lifted his broad shoulders in an indifferent gesture, "Mayhap it won't be a punishment at all. You might be going to a better place. In this, one never knows what is to be."

"I will pay you whatever you want." Fuller said, his words shaking almost as much as his belly. His fear, sheer terror now, was so very evident. "You won't want for anything the rest of your lives. Whatever you want it's yours. Just ask."

"Truth of the matter is we don't need or want your money and we've already everything we could ever desire," Roby said softly, his brows drawing together as if he truly understood the wealth of his words as well as the value of life as he knew it. "You will go into the stones last. Perhaps Brady will have a chance to bring Lilly here to watch the process. You would like that wouldn't you? You would like her to see you naked, your belly bouncing with the fear of what will happen to you. Why your breasts are larger than some women's, not as shapely though. Why is that do you suppose?"

"It's not necessary to bring Lilly," Lord Fuller said, still having no idea where exactly they were going and if any of the words McKenna spoke were true or if they were just meant to terrify him.

Connal leaned on the saddle horn, pointing northward. "'Tis the Kinnel Stones where we're going. Straight ahead. See them standing straight and tall."

"I don't understand."

"Sassenach," Connal sneered. "Of course, you *dinna ken* what this all about. It is said when one walks into the stones they disappear forever. That's what is going to happen to you as well as your boys. You're going to vanish and never be seen again, at least not in the highlands."

Fuller's large jowls sagged. "You cannot mean to send me someplace like that. Besides it's not possible. Things like that don't happen."

"In Scotland they do," Kit said.

Roby wiggled his eyes brows his smirk large. "Naked. You will go to your future naked just as you came into this life."

"Anything is possible," Houston agreed showing a wealth of even white teeth as his lips parted.

"Do you *ken* fear now, Fuller?" Connal asked with derision. "We're sending you somewhere, we don't know where, naked as the day you born. You can start over with your life. Make yourself a better man if you want. What do you think? Think you'll like being naked in a new land with new people you don't even know? They might be people who enjoy a man with a large girth. You might even find a woman who likes your soft belly."

"Now wait a minute," one of his men finally spoke up sounding as if he objected. "You can't do this to us. It's, it's not right. It's cruel."

"Did you see the lass naked? Did you give her a choice? Did you think you were being nice?" Roby asked pleasantly his gaze turning to the stones then back to the men.

They were all shaking their heads as if they didn't have a clue as to what Roby said. "*Nay*," one protested.

"Of course, you did and of course you didn't. This situation is no difference. Always said the punishment should fit the crime. What do the three of you think? Does it do as we planned?"

Silence greeted his question as each of the men realized what was happening here was very real. They had no recourse but to accept their fate. At the moment they were bound, tethered each to one of the men. The sun beat down on Lord Fuller's tender white flesh. He might well find himself burned to a crisp before he walked into the circle of stones.

All the better.

After several more miles passed, they pulled to a stop in front of the mystical stones. A strange humming vibrated the air. As they drew closer the hum seemed to turn to a song, something that compelled as the sound drew one closer. Mist floated in and out of the stones, swirling fluidly. It was indeed a magical place. Something akin to the highlands smothered in mystery coupled with enchantment. Light danced within the circle, skipping and playing as if it couldn't decide on darkness or light. Perhaps the devil would take these men today. They deserved nothing less than to spend their days in hell. He didn't think anyone died when they went through. Even heard a rumor once of a woman who went through ended up in a different time. She found a way to come back.

Connal remembered the place well as he looked over his shoulder in time to see Lilly and Brady riding to meet them. "Guess they made it in time after all."

Roby leapt from his horse, pulling his knife from his boot. Fuller staggered back a few steps, his eyes wide.

"Nay! You said you wouldn't kill us."

Chapter Nine

In his cat from, Brady burst into the hunting lodge, Houston behind him, the others following. Lilly should have heard the gunshot? Searing pain ripped through his shoulder. For a moment he staggered a short pause in his quest to rescue the woman he loved, his mate. Neither the bullet nor the pain stopped him. When he saw Fuller, seething rage that had been a part of him for two days exploded in a burst of power.

He didn't wait.

Brady leapt high in the air coming down on top of the pompous Lord who dared kidnap his wife. The man was shaking, his face drained of all color. Brady's teeth hovered above Fuller's neck then grazed lightly drawing blood. He sat, holding the man down with the weight and strength of his paws as he longed to tear into him with his claws, longed to rip his clothing from him to rake his body, to see him bleed and suffer.

Fuller wept, cried out for mercy. It wasn't something Brady planned on giving him, not after the way he treated Lily. Did she plead for his mercy? Beg him to take her back home. Plead that she would never tell who kidnapped her? He grinned, his teeth showing more prominently. He didn't know if Fuller understood who he was, didn't know if he'd heard rumors of shifters deep in the highlands. Didn't care what the odious man thought or felt except sheer terror. Well, he just encountered a very angry shifter.

"Nay!" Fuller cried, tears coursing down his portly cheeks, his arms flailing, covering his face as if he could protect himself. *"Nay* do not do this thing. What have I ever done?"

Brady wanted desperately to taunt him with words. Unfortunately, that wasn't something he could do at the moment. Instead, he taunted him with the sheer physicality of his body, teasing him with his teeth and his claws, hinting at the man's possible demise as he grazed him over and over again with his claws. Slowly his cravat and jacket fell from his arms then his snowy white shirt became a tangle of white strips painted with his blood.

This sight pleased Brady.

"Stand up. Face your opponent like a man," Connal gritted out as he stepped between Brady and Fuller while he motioned for his son to move away from the victim.

One hand wrapped around what little was left of his shirt as Connal hauled him to a standing position.

Brady backed off, unwilling to kill the man. Death for murder that was something he did believe in. What he wanted was to put the fear of God into Fuller then give him a life that would hopefully be worse than death. A life of torture and fear. He would have no way of knowing it though.

He sat on his haunches, unmindful that blood dripped from his teeth, the lord's blood. Heedless of the dull ache in his shoulder where a steel ball plowed through his flesh. Lilly wasn't on the first floor. He prayed she was above and ready to see him. He wanted her in his arms.

"You finished with him yet?" It was Roby's voice Brady heard through a fog of rage he was contending with. "We can let you go at him a wee bit longer if you like. Whatever pleases you."

He nodded, moving backward, his gaze shifting up the stairs to where he thought Lilly might be. He needed to race to her. At the moment his attention was needed here.

"Is Lilly alright?" Connal asked, looking to the stairs then back to Fuller who appeared ready to lose consciousness from sheer terror.

"She was just dressing to come downstairs for the next meal," Fuller's voice shook even though Brady was no longer intimidating him. Indeed, Brady's attention turned to the steps leading upward.

"Did we decide what is to be done with the men?" Connal's voice rumbled through the interior as he looked to his son for an answer.

Brady nodded unable to speak. His panther screamed again, sending Fuller to such a quaking, he fell to his knees despite the tentative hold on his lapels. The other two men eyes wide with fear covered their ears.

"To the Kinnel Stones then," Connal cried.

"Find Lily. You can join us later. We'll take our time," Roby said his voice taking on a strange edge. "Promise you won't miss a thing."

Brady watched them as they left the lodge. Houston shifted quickly, donning his clothes then taking off after the others.

Brady was thankful to be alone here in the lodge. He needed time to gather his feelings around him, to talk to Lilly and ease any fears she might have, to find out if she'd been harmed in any way.

All he wanted was to hold her in his arms.

They had started that fateful day wanting to be alone, to have the much-needed privacy of a man and woman newlywed craved but also to keep her safe from the demons following her.

It had not worked out that way.

While he waited for the men to leave so he could shift, he listened to the world outside, listened to the sounds of the earth and the wind. It spoke of many things both bad and good. Lilly's name was whispered softly. He prayed that Fuller and his men would find a hell on this earth somewhere besides the highlands, a place where they could never return.

Finally, the sounds of his family leaving with the captured men disappeared. He knew he was alone with his wife. Understood their relationship might be fragile for a while. He prayed it would not. His gaze shifted above him to the stairs and beyond aching to see her walking down the steps.

Noises above him caught his avid attention. Water sloshed in a tub soaking into the floor. Light footsteps padded across the ceiling. Rose scents filled the air as well as his nostrils. She must have heard him roar. It was loud. He was loud with the terror he'd meant to set in Fuller to his very bones. He had not wanted to frighten her. Perhaps he didn't. Perhaps she didn't hear. Once more the scent of roses filled his senses, permeated his very soul.

Ah, Lilly, you always smell so sweet.

He imagined her dressing after the bath, her soft skin dewy and moist. Remembered the subtle sway of her breasts as they swung and moved unencumbered by clothing. He realized he should shift soon and don his clothes, which lay in a pile by the door. His human form was much preferable when it came to holding and kissing his wife. She wouldn't appreciate the rasp of his long tongue on her cheek or anywhere else.

Ah, Lilly, you are too quick by far. *I wanted to see you in your bath.* He watched mesmerized by her exquisite form as she regally descended the steps her head held high, as she looked from one corner to the next as she wondered what happened here. The puzzled expression on her face coupled with the pursing of her soft moist lips was endearing. Still, she didn't see him yet.

She picked up a shattered lamp and a table. Truly, he didn't remember any of this. Didn't recall the shattering and toppling of furniture. His rage blinded him to everything except his unyielding purpose.

When she first saw him, he felt the sudden burning of his lungs. Her body, what he could see of it, was covered in bruises as well as abrasions. His gut tightened, turned sour. Mayhap the stones were not a fitting punishment for these transgressions against his wife. The three men should be beaten to a pulp before sending them into oblivion.

He knew the minute she realized it was him standing in the kitchen. Saw the stark expression of relief. Did she recognize his cat? She'd only seen him once. They were all different, his brother, Houston, his father, Kit all of the clan who shifted. To many they would seem the same but to those who knew them they had their distinct appearance as well as personality. Any injustice to their woman, to those they held dear could be brought to a scorching fury.

For what seemed an eternity to him, she stared at him, her hands clasped in front of her, slender fingers white with the intensity of her grip. She'd seen the destruction of the rooms but she did not see that Fuller left here alive. Didn't understand that he would be punished for what the man did to her. A Lord of the realm, the man was no more a real Lord than a rat. Indeed, he was viler than a rat.

She stepped forward, her trembling hand outstretched, reaching for him. He needed to shift now.

Gradually, he felt the quivering of his body, the slow change starting from his feet continuing to his head. He closed his eyes absorbing all the distinct sensations as the transformation was taking place. This was something he reveled in, absorbed into his being. It seemed to him every time he altered form the transformation was different.

He stood before her, naked, his arms outstretched as he waited for her to run into his embrace. Her eyes widened. Her smile broadened. Recognition was stark and so very real. He felt as if he saw the sun glow brighter. She walked then she raced. Her arms wound around him tugging him closer. He felt her tiny hands run the length of his back, hovered on his buttocks. He chuckled at her audacity, something new to her. Something he would cherish forever.

He held her at arms lengths absorbing all he saw into his memories. Making sure to steal a look at all of her. "Suppose I should get dressed, hmmm."

Blessed hell but he'd like to make love to her this instant. He'd like to slowly take all her clothing off just to make sure she was not hurt anywhere else. He knew she was. Saw the scratches as well as the bruises. She would tell him she was fine even when she was not.

"You're bleeding." Her hand came away from his shoulder blood on her fingers. "I need to take care of this. You really must take better care of yourself."

"It's nothing but a flesh wound." Ignoring her tender concern, he kissed her nose then strode to the pile of clothes on the floor near the door that his father left for him. He pulled on his pants and boots.

Lilly was beside him then, a damp cloth in her hand gently dabbing at the blood on his shoulder. He laughed the sense of foreboding gone. All he felt now was joy and a heady contentment that they were both alive. There would be time to talk later. Now they had somewhere to be, somewhere that wouldn't wait, the Kinnel Stones.

She stepped back, "It's stopped bleeding for the time being." She dabbed a few more times. "I didn't know if you would come for me. Didn't know if..."

He silenced her doubts as he pulled her into his arms. His lips found hers, fashioned across them while she opened for him. She burned in his arms, a sizzling force he needed to claim. He found the hot darkness within her mouth, the dampness still salty from the tears she'd not shed. Her scent, roses filled him again. He tasted the wine she must have had. He pulled her against him, cradled her between his thighs.

"I'm here, Lilly. I will always come for you. Know that wherever you go, I will come for you. I promise. Remember always, a promise made is a promise kept." He wanted to learn what happened to her, needed to discover things she most likely would not want to speak of. He prayed that perhaps in time she would open to him. He understood the deepest secrets were the hardest for her to reveal. He prayed that in time she would come to trust him.

She pressed her head against his chest, ran her hands down his arms. "Kiss me again," she whispered softly. "I need you like I've never needed anything before."

Her eyes were wide blue pools, simmering with emotions. With both hands she held his face.

His lips touched softly upon hers, swept across the tender swell. He ran his tongue lightly across the upper then tugged gently on her lower lip with his teeth. The tiny sounds of pleasure enticed and intrigued spurred him to take more of what she offered so willingly. Taking this to a private spot was what he wanted.

It wasn't to be, at least not yet.

They both needed to see the disappearance of the man who kidnapped as well as threatened her. Needed to *ken* he would never hurt her again.

He pulled away, gently ran his thumb across the dewy softness of her lips. "I should get dressed."

She made a tiny sound of protest but stepped from his arms seeming to understand there was business to take care of before pleasure.

"I don't know why?" she said, a beautiful smile on her face. "I like you just the way you are."

Blessed hell but he wanted to stay this way, yearned to have her just as naked. "We cannot. Lord Fuller and his men are on their way to the Kinnel Stones. I for one want to see them disappear, the sooner the better."

Her head tilted a bit, her tongue swept across her lips. "I *dinna ken* what the Kinnel Stones are. Tell me why you take them there."

He wasn't at all sure what to tell her. "Fact and fiction," he murmured. "Rumors and very real happenings. They are a mystery unto themselves."

"What?" she queried as she watched him dress, her eyes sparkling with curiosity. "You speak in rhymes that tell me nothing."

He chuckled softly, pulling his arms through his shirt. "Let's just say, when a human walks into the circle of rocks they disappear. That is what is going to happen to the men who kidnapped you. They will vanish."

"It cannot be," she murmured. "What makes you think it is so?"

I can only tell you what has been told to me, the tales passed down from one generation to another. They are ripe," he chuckled. "What I can state as an absolute fact is that my father sent two men through the stones before I was born. They've never again been seen in the highlands or at his manor in England. They were bad men."

"Your father sent these men through?" she asked her blue eyes wide with a strange simmering glow about them.

"*Aye* he did. One was my mother's father. He abused her. Let other men have her. She ran from him; from her home she was so desperate to get away. It was my father's good fortune that she ran into his arms."

"It was fated," she murmured softly. "Somehow fate will always bring a McKenna his mate. Am I right?"

He smiled broadly, reaching out to stroke the long strands of her reddish-blond hair, letting them sift through his fingers as he watched them fall to curl around her waist. With the sun glinting off the strands they appeared to be on fire. "As I found you, Sassenach. One must have patience. McKenna men are not noted for this quality."

Her hands rested on his chest. Her dark lashes fanned her cheekbones while she seemed to be studying something on the floor. When she looked at him again, he saw the wealth of understanding in her eyes. "I'm glad you found me. I would not have liked being wed to Lord Claymore or Fuller."

"Come, father will only wait so long for us to follow him." He held her hand as he tugged her toward the door. "The horses are waiting for us."

While they rode, he wasn't at all sure what else to say. It didn't seem to him she wanted to talk of what happened with Fuller in the hunting lodge. In ways he didn't want to know. Still, he was sure she could put it in her past easier if she spoke of it.

He would wait.

They saw the stones. Saw the men gathered round. He heard the hum before he reached the circle. Awe in his voice, he asked, "Do you hear that?"

She nodded. Visibly stiffened as if fear swept through her. "What is it? It almost sounds like singing, words, but they are gibberish. Sometimes I believe I hear laughing."

Brady didn't want her to be afraid of anything that would happen here. This was safe for anyone who didn't venture into the circle. "Magic, I suppose. The voice or voices are calling to those foolish enough to heed them."

"The swirling mist is black. One would think it should be white, hazy and mystical," she said her gaze intense.

"Mayhap it is because they are evil men. If they were not, the magic would be good and true. The mist would be white."

"Black magic," she murmured. "Not too sure I can believe in all this. I am a skeptic."

"You believe in me." He reached over to take her hand within his. "It would be easy for you to deny the existence of a shifter."

She laughed softly, gracing him with a smile that left his heart scorched with longing. "I say to you. Remember? One can hardly deny the existence of something they've seen with their own eyes, now can they?"

He brought her hand to his lips. Kissed the back. There would be more of that soon but not at Fuller's hunting lodge. He would find an inn on the way home. Somewhere they could stay the night or two if that was what they wanted.

God how I love her.

I will have to tell her soon.

By the time they reached the men all three were naked. Houston and Roby held pistols on them. It was a sight Brady believed he would never forget. Lilly's eyes grew wide at the men standing so close to the stones, naked. He chuckled softly as her perusal turned away.

"I cannot bear to see him."

"*Dinna* like what you see, Sassenach? I wonder why?"

"Please, Brady. I *dinna* want to think of that man forcing me or the other two. Can we leave? Please?" she asked turning her horse without waiting for his response.

Brady was torn between something he wanted to see more than he ever thought possible and pleasing his wife. He had no alternative but to leave.

"Tell me everything," he murmured to his father as he turned to go with Lilly. "We will stay the night and perhaps another in the first inn on the way home. Don't want anything to do with the memories at the hunting lodge."

"This was no place for Lilly. Although," Connal seemed to pause to understand, "I might have thought she would have liked to see the men vanish."

"I believe it was his naked body more than anything that swayed her to leave." Brady looked up to see Lilly a distance from him. With a chuckle, "Send Fuller through first. Mayhap if I peer over my shoulder, I will see his pure white buttocks vanish forever into the black fog."

Slowly, he nudged his horse down the trail to follow behind Lilly. As he said, looking over his shoulder he watched as Fuller disappeared into the dark swirling mist. The hum turned to a light song. It seemed ethereal as wraith like humans wove in and out between the tall rocks. Black mist turned gray then black again.

It was good. All good. Perhaps Lilly could find a small measure of peace. Still there was Townsend to deal with when they returned home. There was no excuse for the man. A gambling problem by all that's holy, he sold his daughter because he couldn't stop himself from betting on a turn of a card or a horse.

He would deal with Stephen Townsend later. He pushed his horse to a faster gait.

~ * ~

The sky was painted brilliant shades of pink and orange when Lilly and Brady finally reached a small inn on the way home. The horizon was clear of clouds, something unusual for this time of year in the highlands. Lilly looked at her husband's broad back, watched him with avid fascination as desire welled within. He helped her from her horse letting the men from the stable behind the establishment lead the animals away to shelter for the night.

"We are here?" she murmured, as she let him slide her body down the length of his. She felt the hard planes of his strong masculine form, felt the hardness between his legs as he cradled her there for an instant before he let her feet touch the ground.

Lilly was exhausted and hungry. She wasn't sure she could respond to her husband, as she knew he hoped. The days of travel and lack of food had taken their toll on her physically. She didn't think she'd ever felt so tired, wearied to the depth of her core.

When he let go of her, she felt her head spinning the ground swirling beneath her feet. She reached out to him to steady herself, her hand seeming suspended in midair.

"Lilly!"

She heard the frantic concern in the tenor of his voice. It seemed to come from so very far away. She thought surely, she would hit the ground in a crumpled heap. Instead, his strong arms caught her up into his hold as he strode inside. Darkness descended. Her eyes fluttered closed.

When she woke, she was lying on a bed, a soft warm quilt pulled to her shoulders. She was surprised to realize she still wore the blue gown Fuller had provided for her to wear.

"What's wrong?" he asked so much concern in his voice. He was sitting back in the chair to look at her, gently brushing long tendrils of hair away from her face. "I was terrified."

She touched his hand, bringing it to her lips for a small caress. "Just over tired and hungry. He didn't let me eat much. Have you been sitting here for very long?"

"No. The bastard. Pray he starves before he finds any food wherever it is he's gone off to," Brady gritted out his jaw tense.

The knock on the door stopped him from speaking more. He called for them to come into the room. Servants arrived with trays of food and drink, more with a tub and steaming water. She thought of the bath she had earlier in the tiny room upstairs in the lodge, Fuller leering over her.

This one would be wondrous. She wouldn't have to worry as to who would open the door. This bath would help her wash the stench of Fuller along with his men from her body and mind.

"Thank you," she touched Brady's arm. "Thank you."

He helped her rise, assisted her with the gown she wished she would not have to don after the bath. When she was in the tub, he kneeled beside her, a strange smile on his face. His eyes simmered with the passion along with the desire for her she now recognized. Her body quivered in anticipation of his touch that was yet to come. Perhaps she was not as tired as she thought.

Brady picked up the lavender scented soap along with the cloth they sent. "Let me bathe you."

His softly spoken words were gentle nearly a purr. She thought of his strength of his power. He was a man of his word, a good man one who would do no harm.

She nodded, leaning forward so he could stroke her back with the tenderness she was coming to know so well. He cleansed her, all of her, stroked her breasts, between her legs, everywhere.

"I would kiss you in all the places I've washed you," he murmured softly, his eyes warm, gray flecked with tiny bits of blue.

I want you.

She recalled his words to her. It was true for her too. She desperately wanted Brady, needed him in so many different ways she'd never before thought possible. She needed his reassurance as well as the comfort only he could give. When she closed her eyes, she fought the demons Fuller created. Fought the demons her father spawned. She would need to rely on Brady to rid her body and soul of the blackness residing therein.

I will survive. Be stronger for it.

Now he washed her hair, massaged her scalp. The sensations earth shatteringly pleasant, so very delectable. She should have never let him do this. Washing her body and hair was something she certainly could do for herself. He was not her maid. Yet she had the distinct sensation that even if she protested, in this case, he would have acted on his desire.

Too soon, he was finished. She was bathed and rinsed, the bath sheet wrapped around her. He led her to a fur rug by the fireplace. Somehow, somewhere he found a comb. Gently he untangled her hair, painstakingly ridding the length of the mazes and snarls created over the days. Closing her eyes, she sighed in contentment. He placed a glass of wine in her hand before feeding her a tiny chunk of cheese. She tasted his fingers where they met her lips, touched them with her tongue.

"Drink, but not too much. Don't want you to get lightheaded again."

She heard his soft laughter. Gently, he kissed her across the back of her shoulders. They were light teasing kisses, meant to leisurely seduce. He would coax her into his bed with all the finesse of a well-practiced lover. She would let him, simply because it was all that she wanted.

Her eyelashes flew open when he suddenly left her. She was surprised. He must have heard the ever-present rumblings of her stomach. The bit of cheese was not but a teasing appetizer.

When he returned, he brought her a bowl of stew. "Eat first," he told her. "Then we can pursue other pleasurable activities."

The food was heavenly. Content, she settled into his arms, her back against his chest. He ran his nimble fingers along her arms. Her hands rested on his powerful thighs. She drew in a long-contented draft of air before slowly letting it go. The scent of lavender seemed to hover around her.

Lilly turned in his arms, the towel slowly slipping to her waist. Her breasts were pushed against his chest, the tips puckering tightly with the sensation. A tiny sound of pleasure bubbled from her.

"Do you want me, Sassenach?" he asked, his voice husky with what to her sounded like long pent-up desire.

"Take me to the bed. Help me to forget," she murmured softly, threading her fingers through the hair at the base of his neck. "I want you, Brady McKenna, now. Need you so much."

"*Nay*, I want to see the soft firelight play against your breasts and in your hair as well as weave the delight in the triangle that guards your feminine parts. We can make love in the bed later. This time I want to see your white flesh against the dark fur on the rug beneath you."

His lips formed smoothly, tantalizingly over hers. They were hot and moist, hard as well as soft. With her tongue, she touched him tentatively inside his mouth, the dark savory part of him, part of the mystery that was Brady McKenna. To Lily he was an enigma. Her fingers played and danced with the buttons on his shirt until the fabric slowly parted, lay open ready for exploration. She wound her fingers into the dark curling hairs on his chest then lower, the palms of her hands stroked across his tiny male nipples so hard and surprising to her, nearly as sensitive as her own. Hesitantly, she touched one with the tip of her tongue.

She reveled in the deep groan of raw hunger or satisfaction. Mayhap it was longing that rumbled up from deep inside his broad chest. For a moment, her breath caught in her throat. He wanted to talk to her, explore what happened in the minutest detail. She understood that.

And yet...

...She wanted to forget those two days. Did not want to relive anything that happened in the hunting lodge or on the way there. She understood she was lucky in that she was not forced. Brady arrived in time. Neither did she want to explore what would happen between them if the man had forced her. Nor did she want to condemn her father for his weakness. She saw it for what it was, a debilitating devastating sickness of his mind.

She gasped anew when his fingers touched upon her, stroked, bringing her a delicious sensation of pleasure, the ecstasy she knew only he could create within her. Her hands traveled lower, finding the fastening of his trousers. She unlaced them, discovering his pulsing rod beneath. She caressed him. Her hand clasped around his steel hard length.

"Perhaps that should be left until later." His words were a raspy breath of air as he rose above her.

Soon he was just as naked as she was. Fire glow caught the warm bronze of his hard male flesh. She ran her tongue across her lips, enjoying the wondrous sight of the man she loved, the man who saved her life. The shudder ripping through her had nothing to do with the moment. It was all about what might have happened if it was not for Brady McKenna and his family, for the timely rescue. If any woman had a knight in shining arm, she did.

"What will make you happy, Sassenach?" he asked as he lowered himself to lie flush against her body.

"To be in your arms," she murmured softly. "Forever and always, I don't want to be away from you. Yes," she sighed, "in Brady's arms forever."

His fingers tightened around hers just before he urged her mouth to his—then there was no need to compel her further. Her mouth opened under his, as if it was a rose beneath the blazing heat of a warm summer sun. This was everything a kiss should be, everything she wanted it to be, sweetly tender and wondrous, breath-stealing thorough. He made a sound deep in his throat. His hips were bound against hers. She felt the steal of his pulsing arousal cradled between her thighs. Lord, how she coveted him.

All she wanted was to forget the last few days while she made new memories, memories that would last her a lifetime. She closed her eyes as she absorbed Brady into her, felt the heat of his magic, the enchantment he generated within her so easily. He was her heart and soul. In truth she didn't know how she would survive without him.

As he said earlier, he wanted to kiss every part of her. He proceeded to do just that. His lips travelled from one breast to the other, coaxing each to a tight hardness that he laved with his tongue.

She arched her back as he sucked one then the other deep into his mouth. Tiny little cries simmered and rippled from her as she hoped to show him her delight. Her nails dug into his shoulders.

He winced at the pressure on his wound.

"You're hurt. I shouldn't," she told him, studying the jagged line of flesh.

" *'Tis* nothing. Forget that it happened. I have. We have other more urgent things to think about."

His strokes and kisses roamed more thoroughly than ever before. Tempest swirled and stormed hot and wild within her. Now, his hands were beneath her buttocks, lifting her so his lips met her most intimately. His tongue dancing with delightful play against the soft petals of her moist, hot folds.

"Brady..."

Her voice wavered stopping abruptly which each pass of his lips upon her. She didn't know how he always brought her to such an earth-shattering place where the heavens seemed to meet the sky, where stars collided with her heart and soul. Where tempest and calm vied to be the winner.

"Am I hurting you?" he queried tenderly even though she was sure he knew he wasn't.

"*Nay*, don't stop. Please don't stop."

He left her then, turning her over so his lips and teeth could stray along her spine, upwards to her shoulders, back down where once more he caressed her most intimately with his lips and tongue while he held her away from the soft rug beneath her.

She found herself on her back once more. He was kneeling,

between her legs pressing them ever farther apart. He could see her, all of her, all the private places only he should ever see. "Do you want me, Sassenach?"

His query was filled with male arrogance and certainty. He knew her answer before the question.

"*Aye*." She was writhing beside herself with the frantic need to have him bury himself deep inside her. She yearned to feel his hard length, the pulsing rhythm he would set that would bring her a shattering ecstasy.

She wanted to feel the steel texture of his rod, feel the lifeblood pulse inside. The tip of his shaft touched upon her swollen slick folds, teasing and taunting while he gave promise of more. She could feel the heat of him, smell the scent of Brady coupled with the spicy scent that always churned around him. The first tiny pulses of ecstasy rippled through her to her core.

He laughed, his head thrown back, his lips flattened against his teeth. He pulled back from her, brushing the tangle of hair he created with his fingers from her face. Once more she arched her back then let her hips rise to try to meet him in a silent invitation only he could accept. To come inside her and take her to paradise was all she desired.

"Do you really want me?" his laughter spilled from him, his eyes shining with amusement when he knew the answer.

Sunshine and light filled her.

Lilly punched him in the chest not nearly as amused as him. "You're truly a devil's spawn. I want you, Highlander. Please..." her voice died away with an echo of need and passion. "I cannot wait a moment longer."

Slowly, exquisitely he entered her. Her hips were bucking, trying to bring him deeper inside. He wouldn't allow it. It seemed he wanted to take his time, to taunt her more fully. Finally, he was sheathed to the hilt. He pulled out then slowly pushed himself inside. There was nothing hurried or frenzied. Indeed, he was doing this as it pleased him.

Once again tremors rippled the length of her core, sucked him deeper inside. She knew the wondrous spasms swamping her would ignite into the deliciously painful pleasure the fire would build until all control vanished. She would be completely his.

His face was taut from the strain of holding back from the slowness of their coupling. His eyes glimmered as molten steel and fiery passion swept through him. She wanted to cry out to him, to let it all happen now before she died from the anticipation. Yet the heat, the inferno continued to grow.

"Brady!" She did cry out as his strokes became harder and faster, deeper ever deeper.

She could not would not hold back. Her body set its rhythm to join with his. The wild pulsing inside her began slowly then grew with speed as his strokes inside her catapulted harder and faster. His thumb found the satin knot of her greatest pleasure, fueling, the storm inside her growing and writhing within.

It happened. She gave into the sweet and so very delicious ecstasy. The pulses increased until her mind seemed to spin and twirl in never ending pleasure. She lost all thought save the sensations bombarding her body. Above her he cried out her name, his body growing rigid for a moment as his seed emptied into her.

His weight settled upon her. He was slick with the sweat of the mating as was she. Her breath seemed to be held in her lungs until finally she let it out slowly. It was then that he braced himself on his forearms above her, staring down at her, an arrogantly confident smile on his face.

"Did I please you, Sassenach?"

She punched him again. He gave her an obligatory male grunt.

"You know you did," her words were softly spoken. She barely had breath to speak. "Brady?"

"Hmmm?" He rolled to his side pulling her with him. "What is it?"

"Did I please you, Highlander?"

She touched his mouth with her finger, traced the bottom lip. The softness there always surprised her when at times his kisses were hard and demanding.

"If you pleased me more, I'm sure I'd die of the pleasure, pass from this earth into heaven or hell I *ken* not which one. As it is, it seems as if there is always a moment in time that I lose."

"Then I better not please you more." Her lashes fluttered closed for a moment. She understood he would question her about Fuller. If he did so now, she was sure she would scream.

"*Nay*, I wouldn't die."

His warm smile spoke of more delightful pleasure still to come.

For a few more minutes, he held her close. The length of his body next to hers as his arm wound around her pulled her even closer. She tucked her head into the hollow of his shoulder. Sounds of the night spilled in from the slightly open window. A breeze, redolent with the scent of highland heather ruffled the curtains then she heard the clock chime. There were other sounds, other scents, but the clearest scent was of Brady and the finest sound was that of his deep even breaths. They soothed her.

He rose then. The soft padding of his feet across the floor, wine sloshing into the glasses, plates heaped with food, he was beside her urging her to eat and drink.

"You need to eat some more. We've still another round of lovemaking, on the bed this time," he murmured handing her a plate and a glass.

She sat up, his gaze focused on her breasts, still damp from the ardent attention of his lips and tongue. She knew he liked to watch them sway with her movements. The wine tasted good as did the food. It was too much though.

With a glint of mischief in his eyes, he touched the puckered tip of her breast then the other. Ardently, they reacted to his attention. His grin broadened until his beautiful even white teeth showed.

"Where do you think they went?"

Where did that unwanted question come from? She didn't understand why she asked. She vowed not to speak of Lord Fuller again, or think about him.

For what seemed like eternity, he looked out the window. She wondered if he was as loathe to speak of the man as she was. Still, she supposed he might have been right about talking this out. He rested an arm on his bent knee.

Before he answered, he drank long and deep from the glass of wine. "I don't know. Think that's why this is hard to accept completely. I have a burning need to *ken* what has happened to him." Again, he drank from his glass setting it on the hearth. "Are you tired? Your eyes have dark circles beneath them. As much as I would love to continue this, you need to get some rest. A good night of sleep should be our only agenda."

"I'm glad they are gone."

"As am I."

"I would not have wanted to see you kill him though." She knew he felt the silent shuddering of her body. "Murder."

"In my mind for the terror he put you through, I wanted him dead." Delicately, he brushed his knuckles across her cheek.

When she started to protest, he set a bronzed finger on her lips, stopping her. "Hush now, I'm not a murderer. I would not have killed him unless..."

"He killed me," she finished for him as she reached out to touch him.

"Yes."

"I understand. A life is too precious to take. He is sent away to some unknown place. We will never see him again. I suppose that will have to be good enough even though we will always have to wonder what became of him."

"Indeed, it will have to be good enough."

He lifted her from the rug. In a few easy strides they reached the bed. He set her down gently upon it, standing back to look at her, his gaze roamed the length of her body just as her gaze strayed lovingly over his.

He was hers.

She was his through all eternity and beyond.

His rod thickened, flourished before her very eyes, which seemed to grow wider and longer as she watched fascinated with the sight before her.

With a gravely harsh voice, yet she also heard a hint of amusement, "If you want to sleep, you will have to stop staring at me like that."

"Who said I wanted to sleep?" she murmured as she reached out to touch him, take him into her hands.

When Lilly woke, Brady was watching her though silver-gray hooded eyes. His dark brows were drawn tightly together. Worry lines creased his forehead. With his fingertip, he drew a line across her brows then down her nose.

"You're beautiful with the sunlight falling across your face, highlighting all the wondrous colors in your hair. Now that your eyes are open, the blue is light as a summer sky." He placed a chaste kiss on her forehead. "Breakfast is served whenever you want to get up."

As if the night before never happened, as if they had not made love several times before they were both so exhausted they could not keep their eyes open, Brady kissed her long and deep, his mouth playing wanton and forbidden havoc with hers. If she'd been standing, he would have had to hold her. It was at least another hour before they finally rose from the bed to eat.

The tray was filled with fresh baked bread and sweet butter. A pot of tea sat on the tray along with lemon slices and cream. A jar of honey and strawberry preserves were in other separate bowls.

Lilly ate until she could eat no more. She sat back finally feeling satisfied. "Don't know if I can move for another hour.

Brady wiggled his eyebrows at her, his smirk infectious. "We could work off our breakfast in bed."

"You're incorrigible. Is that all you think about?" she laughed.

Suddenly feeling green around the edges, she bent over grasping her arms around her middle. "I," she paused as she tried to hold back the bile threatening, "don't feel so well. Think—sick."

Brady rushed to find the bowl they used to wash from. By the time he reached Lilly she lost the breakfast she ate into the bowl. She groaned, closing her eyes and wishing...she didn't know what she wished just for this awful nausea to go away. It came on so very suddenly.

He handed her the cup of tea before her. "Swish it around in your mouth then spit it out. It will take away the bitter taste."

She did as he said, then sat back, looking at the tray of food again with a grimace. "I don't know why I'm so sick."

"Perhaps it just a reaction, a release of all the fear along with the exhaustion you've felt for the last few days. You've been through a lot. Your body doesn't know what to make of it."

He sounded concerned, worried. Yet she didn't feel as if the ordeal with Fuller would make her sick now. She should have lost her... Well, she didn't have anything in her stomach to lose when she was with the odious man.

Once again, she grasped her stomach before finding the bowl. When she was done, she sat back a sudden realization coming to her. She wasn't sure, wasn't positive but...

Lilly counted back the days to her last monthly flow. She tried to count. Honestly, she couldn't remember. It seemed to her Brady was doing the same thing as his lips spread in a wide grin.

"You're increasing."

She nodded, "I believe it's a very strong possibility."

~ * ~

"I'm Lord Fuller a lord of the realm. You can't do this to me!" He shouted as he was forced into the swirling black mist surrounding the stones. His fists clenched. He was determined to seek his vengeance.

Not for a second did he think he would vanish into thin air. He didn't believe anything the McKenna told him. Sounds of chanting, a strange humming floated through the whirling clouds of darkness, the faint impressions of a tune. Clandestine figures wove in and out, darting between him and the huge, intimidating stones, bumping into him as often as not. He felt sure they directed him, subtly pushing him in one direction. He tried to do the opposite. When he didn't move the way it seemed they wanted, they pushed harder, more methodically, more aggressively.

He found he was cold, freezing. Yet as he moved farther into the circle heat wafted through him stirred by intermittent breezes twirling around him before ceasing all together. Occasionally, he caught glimpses of the sun hovering in the dark shadows before disappearing again in the now stagnant darkness. He could barely breathe or catch air into his lungs, his heart thundering beneath his ribs.

Hell.

This is what hell would feel and smell like.

Covering his private parts with trembling hands, he continued, hoping that somehow he could reach the other side of the stones without Connal McKenna seeing him, without the weird figures sending him somewhere else. The swirling acrid scent caused him to choke.

Seconds seemed to turn to minutes, minutes to hours. Still he stumbled in the ever-changing mist. Now, when he tried to breathe, his very breath jabbed painfully in his throat before scalding his lungs. Sulfurous smells captured his senses, creating bile in his throat a sour taste in his gut. What the devil was happening to him? Lord but, he'd welcome death at this point.

Once more, he felt a subtle pressure guiding him, pushing when he faltered. He stumbled, his hands upon one large rock. Suddenly, a hiss filled his ears, pulled him with a swiftness that opposed time and space. He felt as if he was hurtled through the very rock his hand touched down upon.

Fuller didn't know how long the total blackness lasted. For a while the sensation of floating transposed him. His mind traveled through space and time. When he woke, the sun beat down hard on his naked body, grass prickled his skin. He hoped when he woke all the rest had just been a bad dream.

That was not to be.

His skin ached from the burning rays hitting upon him. His flesh was red, scalded from the harsh sun overhead. The Kinnel Stones loomed high on his right. A shudder cleaved through him all the way to the core. He sat on the grass, a field, stretching out around him as far as he could see. He understood he couldn't stay here. Also understood he might not have anywhere to go.

"I'm naked."

Once again bile threatened to erupt. He could hardly go anywhere in this state of dress. He couldn't stay here either. A glance to the stones set an idea in motion. Perhaps he could return from wherever this was to when he left. Surely, he had to try. He would still be naked but at least he would know where he was.

Fuller strode quickly to the bizarre rocks guarding the field. He walked inside. Waited. Nothing happened. There was no mist, no chanting, no dancing figures no scent of sulfur. He wasn't in hell. To him it seemed he must have imagined the entire happening. If he lost consciousness for very long, perhaps the McKenna's left thinking he did indeed disappear. He would get his revenge for this. As soon as he could find someone to help him, he would go back to London and regroup.

With a few vines and leaves he found, he fashioned a covering for his privates. It wasn't much but it would have to do until...until he found someone to give him clothing.

Until he found a way from this cursed spot.

Lord Fuller walked. The miles seemed endless, his feet scratched and bruised his muscles sore. His stomach rumbled as he thought of food and a place to sleep. He didn't ever remember feeling so very wretched. He never went without the comforts expected even though he kept them from others. Lilly wasn't the first woman he used to bend to his will.

Night fell. On the ground he slept a restless sleep. Images and dreams of the Kinnel Stones whirled in his head. When he woke the next morning, a frail gray mist hung low over the land. With a heavy sigh coupled with a strange depression he walked again. Another day and night passed. He found some wild berries to eat. He searched and ate until his body was covered with scratches and welts. For a while he didn't have the nagging hunger pains.

When he discovered a road, he rejoiced, confused and puzzled as well. Hesitantly, he touched the strange hardness. He jumped back when something extraordinary whizzed past him. He leapt out of the path quivering in terror, watching the peculiar vehicle disappear around a curve in the road. He held his breath, his heart raging a violent staccato. It took minutes to calm himself enough so he could continue on.

Several hours later, one of those carriages with no horses stopped by him. Three young women occupied it. When one asked, "Do you need some help?"

Of course, he needed help. What were they blind and daft as well? "Yes," he told them unwilling to explain just exactly how he arrived here almost stark naked afraid to ask question lest they think him mad.

The women were giggling and pointing at him, contradicting their noble gesture of lending aid. "Well, get in and tell us where you would like to go."

London was on the tip of his tongue until he drug the words back from his lips. "I've need of clothes and directions. My name is Lord Fuller. If you would be so kind, I'll see you compensated for your efforts."

"That would be nice if we could believe you," one of the ladies said unable to hold back her ear-splitting giggles. "I suppose we should see to some basic needs. Clothing first. The Thrift Store in town would be a great place to start."

"Thank you," he said, wishing he could fade away.

This was not the course he thought his life would take.

"You obviously don't have any pounds."

"Pounds?" he asked. "Ah, not with me but I've sufficient funds in my bank in London to take care of anything you might purchase."

He got in. The car took off. Fuller held onto a door handle, his knuckles turning white as they sped recklessly around one corner then another. Terror never truly held meaning for him until now.

"What happened to you?" One of the ladies eyed him, let her gaze roam down his naked body.

"You would not believe me if I told you. Let's just say I ran into a bit of bad luck along with someone's ill humor. Thus, I was left this way. What year is this?"

They all seemed puzzled but the driver finally answered. "Why, it is 2021."

He pulled in a startled gasp.

"Are you alright?" she asked. "You will have to get a covid shot as soon as possible

Bloody eyes, "Fine," he said in a soft whisper as he tried desperately to assimilate what he was told. What the hell was a covid shot?

"Suppose that has to be good enough for now."

A while later, they drove through a small village and pulled up in front of a store.

"Do you want to wait here or come inside?" After what appeared to be careful consideration, she said, "You should go inside. We wouldn't know your size."

"Well..." Reluctantly, Fuller agreed yet a few minutes later he was wearing what the ladies called jeans and a soft blue shirt. They also found him a pair of tennis shoes, which were surprisingly the most comfortable shoes he'd ever worn. Even if it was not what he was used to wearing, he was pleased. "Keep track of what I owe you."

"Pass it forward," one of the ladies told him as she handed him fifty pounds.

For a moment he thought he would weep. While he knew he had more than enough money in his bank, he was now also understood those funds might not be accessible in 2021.

He would have to make his own way in a changed world.

He felt both humbled and frightened. If he was ever able to return to his time, he would seek vengeance on the McKenna clan. The Kinnel stones would remain where they were. They were his path home.

Chapter Ten

A week passed before Brady and Lilly left the inn and returned to McKenna land. Still, he had not told her he loved her. It seemed they spoke of nearly everything but their feelings for each other. When he started to tell her, they would inevitably become involved physically, not that he minded.

Now, she waited for him at the crofter's cottage she first called home. With the danger to her gone, they wanted to start a life separate from his family. Connal agreed to give him the land surrounding the crofter's cottage with the promise that when it was time to become head of the clan, he would accept responsibility and return to the castle.

Hands around Lilly's waist, Brady lifted her from her horse. "You look tired, Sassenach."

Her laughter was soft. "Doesn't take much these days, Highlander. 'Tis your fault you *ken*. You must own up to the responsibility."

Yes, her condition was his fault, hers as well. If she wasn't so damn appealing, he never would have touched her, never would have learned she was his mate. He held her close, wishing to keep her in his arms a bit longer. Worried about her condition now that they were aware of it, all he wanted was to make sure the next months were easier on her than the last.

Her breasts were slightly larger, infinitely more tender and sensitive. When he rested the flat of his hand on her belly, he discovered a slight baby bump. Still, she didn't eat in the mornings, understanding if she did, she would lose what little she put in her belly.

He pulled her close for a quick, affectionate hug. "I'll see to the horses as soon as I get you settled. Want you to rest and eat before we do anything else."

Wrapping his arm around her waist, they walked toward the house.

With the door wide open, they could see well into the interior. "Someone must have put all the damage to rights," she said as he scooped her into his arms, walking with her across the threshold.

Once inside, he kissed her long and deep with all the passion and desire for her he felt. This was exactly what he hoped his life would be like. He should tell her he loved her tonight sitting in front of the fire, sipping wine.

When he set her away, her blue eyes turned darker from the kiss, her passion rising, giving him pause. He turned her to look at the home they would share. He had plans to put in a second floor enlarge some of the rooms on the first. The clan would help.

Hand in hand they walked through the rooms, leaving the bedroom for last. He thought it prudent to leave this one until after dinner. He did but he didn't want to end up there before they accomplished anything else, eating and relaxing to be exact. In the kitchen they found dinner served for them on a silver platter covered to keep warm.

"I think Crissie and mother played a role in this?" He pulled her against his chest, his hands settling on her still small belly.

"Do you want a boy or a girl?" she asked as her hands covered his.

The devil, but he yearned to know her thoughts. "Doesn't matter to me. A healthy child is all one can hope for pray for. I would like the child to be a shifter though."

"Do you?" She turned in his arms, touching his lips as she watched him with reverence in her eyes. "I thought you might. A little shape shifter, just like his proud papa."

"We shall see. Suppose he or she might not be since you are not. Should we eat now? Are you hungry?"

He wanted to put the thoughts of all the possibilities to the back of his mind. Waiting to discover all this would suit him just fine.

"I think I'm always hungry. Will be until after the babe is born."

He laughed softly, loving the feel of her ever-changing body. Could hardly wait to feel his babe kick within her. He drew in a long bliss-filled breath of air holding it in his lungs before expelling it. Life could not be better than this. "But of course, you are eating for two now."

It was her turn to gently scold. "Do I look like two people?"

"Not yet." He kissed her behind the ear then trailed kisses down her neck. "However, I will certainly find pleasure in your body when you are."

Snorting at him, she pushed on his chest. "Brady McKenna, behave yourself and open the bottle of wine. Then get yourself outside so you can take care of the horses as you said you would do. I will set the plates on the table."

"Already a little nag. Guess I'll have to put up with your not so sunny disposition at times. Don't know what I'll do with you?"

Don't know what I'll do without her. He laughed as he contentedly did Lilly's bidding. *Believe I could keep her in bed and beneath me all day and night.* Satisfied, he whistled as he left the house, heading for the stables.

I am going to tell her I love her tonight. Hopefully she will reciprocate the sentiment.

The chores taken care of he was back inside watching her as she slumped, her head lolling to one side in the large wing chair by the fireplace. The chair was new. A gift from his family he assumed.

There were dark circles beneath her eyes. She needed to sleep as much as she did to eat. He drew in a breath of air as he studied her, longed to pull her into his arms. Sex with his wife would have to wait until tomorrow morning. Then he would love her thoroughly.

Instead, he knelt down beside her. Touched her cheek with a fingertip. All the love he felt for her pouring forth. With a swift indrawn breath of air, he studied her, made a decision he wouldn't take back.

"Sassenach," he said fondly, any hint of sarcasm in his voice vanished ages ago.

Her face nestled against the palm of his hand, she slowly sighed. His smile was soft, filled with love. "Sassenach, you need to wake up.

Need to eat then give yourself to your husband who is waiting patiently by your side."

He didn't care if she gave herself to him only that she wake up and eat.

"You drive a hard bargain, Highlander. Don't *ken* if that's what I want. To eat. I'm just too tired to care about food."

"You have to eat now. As you well know in the morning you won't be able to keep anything in your stomach."

He was worried about her. He realized he was also concerned about the health and wellbeing of the new McKenna growing within her womb. The realization left him breathless, inhaling swift droughts of air. This was not what he expected, different sentiments churning within. A deep seething awakening into his future left him reeling. He'd always expected children, always understood he wanted a family, children he could call his own. This was so soon, sooner than he expected.

Now, the moment was at hand. He'd yet to tell the mother of his children how much he loved her. That revelation had been as startling to him as the knowledge he was about to become a father as well as when he realized Lilly was his mate. Yet, he paused to reflect, she was his mate. Of course, he loved her. Not too long ago he wondered how that emotion would feel.

Now he knew.

She stretched, her arms out, rising, pushing her breasts against him. All he could think of was lying down beside her, filling her with himself.

Blessed be, desperate to hold back the throbbing urge that possessed him, he said, "Let's have dinner, shall we?"

"I'm only hungry for you."

Her voice was throatily seductive, coaxing him to go against his better decisions. She appeared sweetly disheveled from sleep.

He groaned, couldn't help himself. "You need to think of the wee one. We cannot possibly make love right now."

Lord, but of course they could. They could eat later. He could tell her he loved her later.

Her brows drew together as her eyes blazed with wantonness he'd never seen before. "You accuse me..."

"*Nay*, I'm just reminding you to take care of yourself. You are..." he paused trying to think of the right words so her tender feeling would not be hurt. "You carry my, our, child. You must take care."

"I've more responsibilities than just to myself?" she asked one perfectly sculpted eyebrow lifting sarcastically to meet the heavens. "My, my, I never would have thought."

"You comprehend perfectly."

By the look in her eyes, he understood all too well he'd not uttered the right words, not conveyed his feelings the way he meant. This was all too new for him, uncharted territory. This evening, before it even started, was spiraling rapidly downhill.

"I don't believe I do," she told him pointedly. "Perhaps you should take this golden opportunity to explain yourself and what exactly you mean for me to do."

God all mighty, he didn't know if she was angry or testing him mayhap it was gentle tease. He was acting a bit ridiculous. Well, he'd never been a father before nor had he been in love, a besotted fool. He didn't know how to respond. His voice grew taut. He let out the breath he'd been holding. "I don't know what to say. Are you angry?" he queried hoping to get the argument he didn't want to have out of the way before heated words had the chance to ruin this night.

"We should eat. Perhaps that is why I'm acting so contrary. I'm simply hungry. Perhaps it's the baby."

He was thrilled she took responsibility. He could do the same. "I am also sorry I've said things that you take issue over. I didn't mean to imply you could not take care of yourself or our child. We are both tired and hungry. Go sit by the fire and I'll bring you food and drink."

To his satisfaction, she did as he implored. Holding the small of her back as if the muscles ached, she slowly walked to the wing chair she'd been sitting in earlier and sat. Her hands were folded in her lap as she watched the flames before her. It was a sight Brady wanted etched into his memory.

Chagrined, Brady pulled a small table between them. It was just large enough to set their plates and glasses upon. He handed her a fork and knife. Her smile was hesitant. Gingerly, she speared a piece of meat then ate.

Now, when she glanced his way, she bore a self-satisfied looking smile. He was sure she dared him to take issue with the amount of food she would eat. He vowed he would not. She sipped her wine, gazing at him over the rim her lashes fluttering closed for a brief moment.

He swallowed hard. The look in her eyes was anything but platonic. She beckoned to him, just as she did before the food.

"I believe the short nap I took when you were tending the horses has renewed my energy." She waved her hand in front of her face, unfastening a few of the laces holding the front of her gown together. "It seems I've grown *verra* hot."

Brady choked on his wine, droplets spewing in front of him as he watched her reveal the soft white curves of her breasts. The slightly swollen flesh calling to him as he fought the urge to sweep her from the chair and take her to bed. His body throbbed and ached to possess her. He could hold himself in check long enough to achieve his most important goal for this evening.

He bent close to her, used her fork to hold another tempting morsel of food by her lips. "You are not finished with your dinner," he told her his voice whiskey smooth and husky soft.

Her lips opened, parted slightly while her tongue traced the full bottom softness. He turned away, stifling the groan threatening to rip from him. When he swung back, "You're a little tease now aren't you?"

His finger followed the path her tongue traveled. He was pleased when her own purr of sexual pleasure rippled from her lips.

Satisfied that he managed to excite her as much as she did him, he sat back, replete with the scenario so far. Before he took her to bed, he wanted her sated with food and wine, ready for him, her most feminine parts begging for his caresses. Two could play at this game she started.

"Brady."

"Hmmm?"

"I cannot eat any more."

"Then there will be no bed play for you this night. You must take more into your stomach, a buffer for tomorrow morning." He grinned at her look of vexation.

"Truly I..." Once more she fanned herself, additional buttons leaving their holes to reveal more tender white flesh.

"You are a vixen, Sassenach, but I stand by my decision."

Once again, he forked a piece of meat, held it near her lips, beckoning for her to take the food into her mouth. She did. It was a tiny victory. He refilled her glass of wine. She sipped. This time she didn't watch him. Her lashes were lowered in a flirtatious gesture across her beautiful high cheekbones, light against dark. The contrast incited lust along with passionate desire.

In an attempt to reciprocate his actions, between two fingers, she picked up food from his plate then held it to his mouth. He opened for her. She placed it on his lips. He sucked both fingers into his mouth biting gently. Her little gasp of pleasure pleased him immensely.

He picked Lilly up, pulling her onto his lap. She nestled her head into his body, her lips discovering the pulse at the base of his neck as she licked and teased him there. He stifled the incredible urge to take her right then at this very moment. He could turn her. She could straddle him. In a second the pulse of his life would be buried deep inside her soft velvet core.

He had other plans that would have to come first. She purposefully tempted him, pushing against him. Once more buttons came undone. He smiled at her, refusing to give into the bait even while he stroked the hard tip of her breast that crinkled tightly beneath the fabric of her gown. Slowly, he ran his fingers along her ankle, rose slowly to find the tender spot behind her knee then rose higher to caress the folds that were hot and dewy with anticipation.

For a few seconds he stroked the satin bud, pleased when her hips jerked and her back arched with the pleasure, he gave her pushing her breast ever closer to his lips. Then he withdrew. Heard the tiny muffle of displeasure.

"Brady, please."

"Please what?"

"Don't stop touching me. I want you so."

Her voice was thready and so very thin he could barely hear her.

She reached a spot exactly where he wanted her. He would keep her needing him until he said his piece.

~ * ~

Lilly wanted Brady desperately. She hungered to feel his arms around her. More than anything though she yearned for him tell her he loved her. The elemental words were so important to her needs as she moved through this pregnancy.

I can say the words first.

Nay, what if he outright tells you he doesn't love you? What will you do then?

His hungry kisses seemed to devour her on the spot, spread a tender demanding fervor throughout. Into his mouth she moaned, her body beginning to writhe and twist matching the erotic dance of his fingers. Still, he kissed her, teased every sensitive spot she possessed. She cried out his name. His mouth absorbed the one word. Still, he kissed her again and again, nibbled lightly across her mouth, teasing and taunting, sending shiver after shiver of ecstasy through her.

He stopped. She whimpered with the need he produced. He laughed, holding the back of her head with one of his large hands. She found that her gown was open, her breasts spilling free. He made no attempt to stroke her there, no move to continue the seduction.

One bronzed finger touched her brows, traced a gentle line across. "We should not make love, Sassenach. It might hurt the child."

She swallowed the lump clinging to the back of her throat. "We should not? Why do you think that?"

Lilly wanted to yell at him, tell him how ridiculous his words were. He stopped her with a touch to her lips.

"Hush," he kissed her again, touched once more the silken hot folds guarding her core with his strong fingers.

"You're wrong, Highlander. This will not hurt our babe."

She was breathless from his kisses, stunned at his words.

"It will unless you let me speak my piece," he murmured unable to stop the light teasing kisses along her jawline culminating with her ear then the sensitive spot behind it.

"Can you wait to say what's on your mind until after you take me to our bed?"

Her wistful sigh sent a shudder into his body. She wanted to laugh. He was as affected by his love play as was she.

"*Nay*, I've tried over and over this last week to tell you what's on my mind. I forget after I've, we've, well you've let me become one with you."

Still, he was kissing her, stroking with every part of him. His fingers toyed with the tight bud of her breasts sending her to a heated fever.

With all the strength, physical as well as mental, she pushed away from him as she tried to keep him at arm's length. "Brady McKenna, tell me or stop teasing me. I care not what you decide. Pick one and choose or I'll walk out that door."

"*Nay*, Sassenach, you will not." He traced her lips with his thumb, smiling mischievously.

She had the sudden impression of their boy, their little boy grinning in the same manner. They would have a dark haired, silver-eyed son. She knew it beyond a certainty. Her fingers drifted to the swell of her belly.

"We are going to have a boy," she told him convinced after the tiny premonition. "He will be a shifter just as you wish. The two of you will drive me crazy with your antics."

"You think so?" One of his perfectly shaped eyebrows lifted in speculation toward the heavens.

With a proud smile, she beamed at him. "I believe so. Now, what was it you were going to say?"

"So, now you want to listen. I'm pleased, Lilly, so very happy.

Still, it matters not the sex of this babe." He joined his hand with hers atop her belly.

She stared at him. Expectant. Decided to say nothing more until whatever it was that bothered him was said.

"Lilly," he began softly his voice husky.

The sound sent a tremor of apprehension through her to her very toes. She was suddenly very afraid he might set her aside. "Yes?"

So unusual, he appeared tentative, hesitant to speak so very unlike his usual confidence. Her breath seemed to hold in her throat while her heart picked up its pace.

"I love you, Sassenach."

This was what she wanted to hear, what she waited so long to hear come from his lips. She touched the palm of her hand to his face.

"Well, you don't have anything to say?" he asked, sounding extremely perturbed.

She inhaled several times, faced with the moment, knowing he did love her. "I love you too, Highlander. I've loved you for so long. Even when you were so arrogant you thought to take me to your bed as your mistress, thought every woman would be willing to share their body with you."

He looked as if he wanted to roar. Instead, he swept her into his arms then carried her to the big brass bed in their room. "Brady, all I want is to be in your arms, for you to hold me and protect me for the rest of our lives."

"Yes, I want that too."

"In Brady's arms," she murmured softly. "Always."

"Into eternity and beyond."

Nobody but Walker

Walker Endicott, tenth Earl of Briarwood, sat atop his stallion staring across the meadow at the McKenna keep. Sun glinted off the battlements. A soft breeze flew the McKenzie standard. Above it, the flag of Scotland flew. Bittersweet memories assailed him, tormented him as he stared at the peaceful scene. For a moment in his life he thought he had found love here, a forbidden love. Crissie could never be his. Too much stood between them. Though he could see her one last time.

He'd been gone now for a year. His travels took him to Paris then the Bordeaux region of France, family business of a necessity he couldn't ignore even while his musing were of Crissie McKenna and this small part of the highlands where his heart belonged. When he closed his eyes, he could always see her lying in the dark green moss, her dark hair spread out around her, silver eyes shimmering with passion. His return was in question. While he'd written to her, he received no response in return.

He didn't like himself very well, the way he treated the lass the day he left the country and Crissie behind. What he'd willingly as well as eagerly taken from her a year ago had been hers to give. So many times he told himself it wasn't his fault. She practically begged him. Still, he should have been a gentleman and told her no. She had a way of bewitching him, her scent all woman coupled with the light citric aroma that was always about her enthralled every sense he possessed. Whenever he caught the smell of oranges or lemons, he was reminded of her, wrapped in the sweet memories she evoked.

He didn't, could not have told her no to save his soul.

No, he wanted her with an explosive need within himself he'd never felt before. His body succumbed to the months of denial he inflicted on himself. Never before in his life had he been celibate for so long. The truth of the matter was that he felt that way every time he saw her, stood close to her, caught the elusive scent of oranges and lemons. The silken length of her hair never failed to draw him, provoking him to touch. The soft curve of her breast always left his fingers itching to possess. That day she was a fire in his soul he couldn't battle. He could not tell her no when all he wanted for the last month or so was to possess her, claim her as his. She could never be his.

She ran after him.

Begged.

So he did.

Still, he wouldn't be starring at the keep situated high on the hilltop if he had not been forced into another mission involving the unveiling of the McKennas. He would never have returned. Because she never answered his letter, he assumed she didn't want to see him again. Perhaps she couldn't forgive him for taking what she offered, her innocence. It was his now. Maybe he couldn't forgive himself for the rutting bastard he was that day.

Refusal of the assignment had been first and foremost on his lips until he realized if someone else was given the task, they might well ferret out the truth about the McKenna clan a story best left untold. If the truth were to be discovered, he feared for Crissie. He had to get her out of the highlands even if she protested. He would find a way. The list of reasons in his mind to say nay to the assignment was short, but he felt if he'd given in to his superiors, they would have listened.

Ah, but he thought that perhaps he should take a room in the village beyond instead of assuming he might be welcome in the keep. He wasn't at all sure of the greeting he would receive from the McKenna lass or her brothers. Despite his resolve, he yearned for her, thought of little else when he was at rest than the feel of her lush curves pushed softly against his length. Lord, when he closed his eyes, he vividly recalled her naked, sunlight shimmering over the gentle slope of her hips and the ripe swell of her breasts. He remembered the lush fall of her dark black hair as he wound the silken length through his fingers.

Walker let out a long slow breath of air before hitching in another deep gulp. Prudence dictated he should avoid her. Should do everything in his power not to see Crissie McKenna. He couldn't do that. She stirred a fever in his blood, he couldn't douse. Even now when he tried desperately to put thoughts of her to the back of his mind, the image of her with moistly parted lips, her long hair curling down her back and through his fingers sent heat straight to his loins. He recalled the way her lush breasts with the rose tips pushed against his chest, the way her sweetly rounded buttocks felt beneath his hands.

"You're an utter ass," he mumbled, starting his horse down the trail to the keep not to the village. His heart hammering beneath his ribs, he knew he had to see her; could not rest this night until he discovered the truth of their heated parting. He would find a way to keep her safe from the intrigue he was forced to be part of.

She never wrote him. He wondered at that after he sent a letter to her at least once a week until he realized she did not answer back. But then, perhaps she decided what happened between them the last day was for her a mistake. Well, if she thought that way, she was right. It was tantamount to the biggest mistake she'd probably made in her entire young life. To him, he would never forget the feel of her body next to his. For the rest of his life, he would remember. He couldn't have her though. Couldn't do right by his mistakes.

If her brothers learned what passed between them that long ago day, he might very well be giving his life into their hands. She wouldn't say anything. It was, after all, her virtue at stake. Still, he decided he needed to stay alert to any pending situation.

The short distance, now that he was almost at his destination, seemed to go on endlessly. Beneath his chest his heart pounded, thundering against his ribs. As to what he would say to Crissie McKenna when he saw her, he didn't know. In his mind, he thought of a thousand different things. None of which satisfied him. Possibly, she would speak first taking the initiative, setting the stage for the direction of his comments. Sweat trickled down the back of his neck. Unending nausea settled in his gut.

Why didn't you write? was one of the first thoughts. Somehow he didn't think it prudent for him to blurt something like that out before he actually had a chance to find out what she was feeling for him after all this time. The only women he had encounters with were widows when he was out of town, his mistress when he was home. He never bedded virgins. Well, what they did that day in the secluded glen could hardly be considered bedding.

Bloody eyes, but she might have married someone in the last year. He couldn't fault her for that since he gave her no indication that he might want her for a wife.

He did.

He couldn't have her though. Couldn't ask her to wed him. That fact gnawed at his gut, churned in his stomach until it soured. The taste of that fact so bitter he couldn't swallow. To ask Crissie McKenna to be his wife and have his children was a dream that would never come true. He would have to live with that fact, accept whatever she was willing to give. She wasn't the kind of woman to become a man's mistress. In any case, neither her brothers nor her father would ever allow anything such as that.

As he approached the gate he was sure he heard a low murmur of voices rise around him. The sound so bitter and angry, he didn't understand. He wondered if it was because he was a captain in the English army. Now, for all practical purposes he was a civilian. Something hit him on the shoulder. Another missal hit him the small of his back. He found himself pummeled from all sides. Curses were spewed at him.

What the devil?

He sat up straighter, looking around for the assailant or assailants, knowing the English were still not liked around these parts. He had not expected this type welcome. After the battle of Culloden, he well understood the sentiments. This was far too brazen to be about that battle. It seemed personal to him. Hell, he wasn't even wearing the soldier's uniform. He was dressed in civilian clothing.

"Sassenach!" The jeer hit him hard. "Sassenach!" was called out over and over again. A tomato hit his face, juices sliding downward. Taking out a handkerchief he wiped it away.

"Bloody Englishman, go home!"

"Yer not welcome here after what ye did."

What I did?

He ducked the next pebble hurled at him, dismounting before handing the reins to a young man who suddenly appeared from nowhere. By mere inches he avoided another small rock directed at him. Beneath his breath, he swore as he headed toward the main hall. *Has everyone gone mad?*

"What the devil is going on?" he asked the lad, hoping the boy knew something he could pass on to him as he followed the lad into the stable.

"People around here don't like the English. You in particular have stoked their rage. Best you don't let either of the McKenna brothers or the laird see you. Doubt if you're welcome. Might not live to long enough to discover the truth. Secrets are never kept in small villages. Probably should mount on up and ride out of here if you value your life. Do ye want me to take care of your horse?"

"Yes." He wasn't going anywhere until he got to the bottom of this. "Don't go too far away though. I might be leaving sooner than I planned." A seething anger built inside as his long strides brought him closer to his destination. The building anger was directed at Crissie. She had to be the source of this debacle.

"They won't like you any better in the village," the lad went on to say. "Of all the McKennas, Crissie's one of their favorites. She holds a special place in everyone's heart."

Blessed hell, he would have never expected her to say anything about that day. He was more perplexed than ever. It was then he saw her. His heart caught in his throat, raw with emotion. Rushing after the few women who deigned to throw the pebbles at him, she was shooing them off with her hands. Her long dark hair was waving in the breeze, curling softly around her shoulders as it fell from the pins she used to hold the mass in place. He wished he could see her eyes, sure they were brimming with passion the burning hunger he so vividly remembered. The women seemed to get the idea, leaving as she bade them.

Walker turned his gaze to the savior, waving her arms, his protector. He stifled the chuckle welling up in his throat. When he caught her attention, she stopped, her hands falling to her sides. For several seconds she stared fixedly at him. She stepped back, her hands now clutched at her throat as if she just now realized who he was. A moment later her skirts were swirling around her ankles as she turned from him. Her pace quickened until she was running toward the hall.

Bloody hell.

His breath caught. She was more beautiful than before it that was possible. More than ever, he knew he had to talk to her, discover the truth about her strange reaction. By his estimation she should have been running to him not away. His strides were longer and faster than hers. He caught her arm, twirling her around. Her eyes were blazing pools of molten silver. By God, she was glorious in her anger. Never before had he seen her like this. The need to enfold her in his arms surfaced with a vengeance.

Yet, the fury she exhibited burned a hole deep in his heart. By the way her eyes shimmered and her body tensed he could swear what she felt for him at this moment was a deep-seated rage. He didn't understand. She was going to tell him if he had to tear the words from her throat.

"Let me go, Sassenach," she gritted out between clenched teeth while trying to wrench her arm from his grasp. "You don't belong here. Go home to your precious Englishmen. To Ireland, to wherever it is you come from. Leave me alone. I don't want you here."

Suddenly, his calm was held onto by the slimmest of threads. "No, not until you explain to me what is wrong with you, with everyone." With one hand, he gestured to the yard. "Why are people throwing rocks and soft vegetables at me? What the hell have I done? I haven't even been in the highlands for a year. We need to go somewhere private." Once more, he looked around the yard. It seemed they had an audience he didn't want. The people of the clan quietly fanned out around them, belligerence on their faces.

"Now you want to know? Now you care? Yes, it's been a year, a very long year for me at least." Her icy words were coated in sarcasm while she still tried to jerk her arm away. "Let me go." Her voice held steel.

"Yes, now I want to know. Yes, now I care. Would it be so hard to explain? I'll not let you go until I'm satisfied." He watched her sway slightly. She was thinner than he remembered, her breasts larger. She was just as beautiful, maybe more so than he remembered, her hair as black her eyes as silver. He struggled with a breath of air as his gaze traveled the length of her body. A slow realization coupled with a question formed.

"You've no rights here, Walker. Go back to England or Ireland or wherever it is you call home," she repeated as if he didn't hear her the first time. "I dinna want to see you ever again." She unexpectedly fell dead still, her eyes nearly crossing. Her voice lost the steel while she whispered, "Please..."

Suddenly, the top of her gown was damp, the wet stain growing larger as they stood in the hot noonday sun. A heated blush spread across her face. He watched with a fascination and wonder he didn't understand as he tried to piece together the reasons for this. The thought hit him full in the gut. Unreasonable anger simmered, escalated with a resounding force he couldn't put aside. His brain didn't work as quickly as the words tumbling from his mouth.

"By God, you little harlot. No wonder you don't want to see me. No wonder you never answered my letters." Unable to help the seething fury, he pushed her away from him. She stumbled. Her eyes blazing, the rage she now felt at his words evident in the changing color of her eyes. Christ, he shouldn't have said that. He didn't mean it although there was a shadow of a doubt in his mind.

"How dare you!" She turned, running full out away from him. Her skirts were hiked nearly to her knees so she could take longer steps.

He wasn't sure what possessed him. All his instincts kicking in told him to mount up and ride in the opposite direction. He understood he should put miles between them. Instead, without batting an eyelid, Walker followed her into the hall, matching her stride for stride then up the steps to the rooms above, oblivious to the possible scandal.

He didn't care.

Just wanted to glean the truth.

When she thought to slam the heavy wooden door in his face, he caught it with his boot. Pushing it open, he stepped inside fascinated by the scene enfolding in front of him. Slowly, he shut the door behind them. He leaned against the solid wood, his arms crossed in front of him as he surveyed the dimly lit room.

A baby was crying in a crib near her bed. He could barely see one tiny fist waving in the air. His gut churned over while his heart forgot to beat. Even though questions abounded, deep in his soul he knew the babe was his. She hovered over the crib, caressing the baby even while her shirt was slipping from her body then her sodden chemise.

Her milk-swollen breasts were naked to his gaze. Yes, she was indeed larger. He understood why. Now, she wore nothing from the waist up to her breasts swaying beautifully as she picked up the child. She didn't look at him. It seemed she pretended he wasn't there, in her room, watching her.

He forgot how to breathe.

It appeared she was more concerned about the babe than she was about her partial nudity. While he watched spellbound, she picked up a small blanket then the baby who seemed to stop crying the moment Crissie held the child. He was so intrigued, he couldn't move nor could he remove his gaze from the captivating scene before him.

Without sparing him a glance, she sat down in a large wing chair near the fireplace. The babe's greedy little lips fastened onto a nipple. His breath caught what there was of it, captured in the back of his throat. She didn't look at him though she must have sensed him watching her. The small blanket she'd been holding covered her a few seconds later, the child's head as well as her breasts.

Walker didn't understand the sudden rise of fury to his chest, didn't understand the compelling need to watch her feed his child or the protectiveness that filled him so completely. Abruptly, he didn't have a doubt in the world that this child in front of him at Crissie's breast was his.

Purposeful long strides took him to a spot in front of the pair. He needed to know if the child was a boy or a girl. Supposed he would have to wait until they finished with the meal. Wasn't sure if he possessed the patience for such a thing. All he wanted was to hold the babe in his arms, uncover his arms and legs, count toes and fingers.

Outraged at her audacity, he pulled the covering from the child's head. "The babe needs to breathe."

She gasped. Brilliant red heat flooded her cheeks, her dismay clearly evident in the narrowing of her eyes. For a second she looked down at herself before lifting her angry gaze to him. Still, she said nothing. He wanted to know what was going on behind those silver eyes.

"Don't want my child to smother to death while eating. Is the babe a boy or a girl? Crissie? Don't you think I deserve to know?" Even while he asked, he wasn't sure if she would tell him. Despite her reticence, he would discover everything. Now, she glared at him unspoken emotions glistening in her eyes. She had no reason to be angry with him.

"If I'm a harlot, you've no rights here. So, you *dinna ken* whose child this is, do you? Why should I tell you something you'll take exception to?" She didn't make an effort to cover herself. Her resentment was so very evident. He deserved what she tossed out at him. Somehow he would find a way to make amends.

In any case, she must know he wouldn't allow her to continue on that vein. True, he said something with no basis. He wasn't going to allow her to constantly throw it in his face just so she could continue the argument. She switched sides, her breasts lush and beautiful, swollen with the milk feeding his child. They swayed. He controlled his desperate need to reach out and caress the soft fullness revealed to him. An overwhelming rush of emotions nearly sent his knees buckling followed by an overwhelming fury that she never had the decency to tell him his child existed.

"Why didn't you tell me? You could have written. I would have been here for you. You didn't have to go through this by yourself." His voice was so very much calmer than his seething emotions.

"I did write. I wasn't by myself. I've my family. At least they don't burn hot then cold." She began to hum softly seemingly to the babe in her arms, ignoring him or perhaps ignoring the fact she was naked from the waist up.

"Nay." One hand slashed through the air. "Nay you did not. Don't lie to me. You wrote no letters. I received nothing in the mail." How dare she lie to his face? If she wrote to him, he would have arrived in the highlands before she could even blink. Would have cancelled all the business that seemed so important at the time. He would have been here for her.

A little bubble of milk appeared on the child's lips as the infant pulled away to stare at him with large golden brown eyes, his eyes. The lashes closed slowly then opened again when the babe seemed to notice him staring at him, noticed the caress of his finger along the soft cheek of the infant.

His.

"You can believe what you will. Roby, you know my brother, delivered them for me to Inverness. They should have been received." She rose, walking toward her wardrobe, the babe on her shoulder. With great finesse she managed to cover herself with a dry chemise. She walked around the room until a tiny burp issued forth from the baby.

With all his heart, Walker wanted to believe her. Every instinct he possessed cried out to him she told the truth. There was no reason for her to lie. Still, the facts were in front of his face. He received no mail from anyone here, from any McKenna. If he had, he would have replied immediately.

While he wanted to jerk the babe from her arms, he did not. "What is the child's name?"

She whirled, still clutching the baby to her shoulder, one hand cupped around the baby's head. "Now you care? Now after over a year you want to know details?" While she still sounded furious, her words were soft, hesitant as if she hoped for something more. Besides what he offered right now, his strength and support, all she could possibly hope for was for him to wed her.

He could not.

"If you had told me, I would have been here. Doubt it not," he reminded her, his voice soft. "I will take care of the two of you."

"If? If you say?" One of her finely sculpted dark eyebrows rose toward the heavens. "If is one pretty big word to be ignored for a year."

"Then the babe is three months old?" He was calculating backward from the day he left, the day he took her virginity. Blessed hell, but he wished she had bothered to tell him.

"Yes."

"The name?" He wasn't sure what demons drove him; fury, curiosity, possessiveness. The list could certainly go on. If he so desired, the name would be changed. She would not saddle him with some Scottish name that would haunt his child forever. A good Irish name would be appropriate.

She stared at him, tears brimming in her eyes spiking her lashes. "He's been baptized. *Ye* cannot change his name."

"Him? Then I've a son." His heart swelled with pride coupled with the fury he had not known before. He could never get back this time with his son. He felt robbed. Cheated. By God, he would not squander any more time with the babe. "His name?" he queried again trying to keep the tenor of his voice in check. If he had to shake the words from her, he would. Damn his good intentions.

She blinked a few times. He wasn't sure if the gesture was to rid herself of the evident moisture in her eyes or to infuriate him further. He was sure he was going to misplace all sense of patience. His hands fisted at his sides, he glared at her and waited. Hoping she understood in this he would not be denied.

Slowly, Crissie looked at him, a soft expression suddenly in her eyes as she pulled in a long breath of air. "I'm sure you won't like it. You have no say since the child is not yours."

"The hell he isn't." He never realized those long months he spent with her before their intimacy she could be so infuriating. Before, she'd always seemed so biddable, sweet natured.

This time her smile was soft and beguiling, tempting him with a promise. What that promise was he wasn't at all sure, retribution possibly. He had the uneasy feeling everything she told him before was a lie.

"Ian Walker McKenna." Her whisper reached his ears with a shudder and a sigh. "I'm sure you won't want another man's son with your name."

"Ian Walker Endicott," he told her, his voice countenancing no argument. He wished she would stop, remembering his earlier accusation. "The last name will be changed. You can count on that. You and I both know this boy is mine. He will be legitimatized. My heir."

"So, you say." She set the child in the crib. Turning her back to him she slipped out of the wet gown before quickly putting another one on.

Desperate to set this untenable situation to rights, he stabbed his hands through his hair thinking of the right words. After a few more seconds of watching her back while wishing he could see all of her, "I'm sorry I called you a harlot. There was no call to do something like that. I would take back the words if I could. I cannot." Once more he thrust his hands through his hair. "It's just that..." He didn't know what to say. One time. One time and he sired a child. It wasn't unheard of. He knew it happened, just not to him.

In his ecstasy, he forgot about protection, forgot she was untried in the ways of love and contraception. He'd been so shocked when she rode after him, stunned when she wanted him to make love to her. Lord, but the heat of the coupling, the frenzy, the desperate need she generated in his loins, he didn't have the good sense to withdraw. Didn't know if he could have done such a thing even if he thought of it.

He hadn't.

"Is there anything else you would like to know?" Her voice was soft in the stilted silence of the chamber.

He didn't answer. He was pacing the room, distraught by this, frustrated by the lost year, afraid he would lose his son if he didn't immediately rectify this situation. The boy was going to live with him. If she wanted to be part of the lad's life, she would have to come with them. Hell, from the beginning, he meant to take her with him. They were leaving now, this afternoon. Staying where her people despised him wasn't tenable. He didn't care who would try to stop them. They were leaving within the hour.

"No?" she asked seeming bemused now that she thought he would go without a fight.

"I'll be back in a few minutes. Pack a bag for you and Ian. We're going home."

Walker didn't wait for an answer or a comment. He left with every intention of speaking his mind to her father. He would return as soon as he set everything to rights. He heard her last comments just before the door banged shut behind him.

"Like hell I am. I'm already home."

Stepping back inside the room. "If you don't pack a bag, you'll be wearing that same gown from this moment until your things can be shipped to my home in Ireland. Your father won't, can't stop me from taking my son no matter how much he'd like to do just that. I'm sure you would like Ian to have a few things to change into from one day to the next." He stopped talking. His angry gaze bored into her. When he started again, "Of course, you don't have to come with us. It's your choice."

"You're talking to father?" Her fingers wove into the fabric of her gown, her eyes wide while drops of moisture spiked her lashes. "He won't let you take my son."

"I guarantee you, he won't say nay to this. A man should raise his son. You're father understands that."

"As should his mother."

He smiled at her. It was the first since he saw her in the courtyard. "So true. I'm glad we are in agreement. Of course, it is solely up to you if you accompany me. I won't force you. Your choice."

~ * ~

Crissie was so incensed she wanted to throw things at him. Yearned to deny him his son. She wouldn't. At this moment, she truly didn't understand what he was about. Why he wanted her to pack a bag. He wasn't going to take Ian from here. The right wasn't his. Deep in the farthest reaches of her heart, she knew her father would not stop Walker. Ian was his son. A wobbly breath of air slipped into her lungs.

She sat down next to the crib, stroking the babe's back, cooing soft words as she watched him sleep his little bum high in the air. Ian was her life. Once she thought herself in love with Walker. That emotion was why she threw herself at him that long ago day. Thoughts of Walker like this as an infant gave her reason to grin.

Nay, he was not so sweet now. There were no sweet bones, sinews or muscles in his body.

When she saw him in the courtyard less than thirty minutes ago, her heart stopped beating. He was everything she remembered, tall and powerful. His legs so long, thighs so heavily muscled his buff britches fit as if they were a second skin. His brilliantly polished black knee high boots shone in the sunlight. The shoulders she clung to so many times were broad. One strand of his tawny hair slipped to fall across his forehead, shielding his golden-brown eyes from view. In her estimation there was no one more handsome, more striking and commanding. Her pulse quickened at the sight. She ran from him, not because she was afraid of him but because she was terrified what he might think when he saw the child.

Her worst fears were confirmed when he called her a harlot. He thought she gave herself to another man. Heat stained her cheeks. One time. She got pregnant from one time with him. She never thought that would happen. Lilly, her brother Brady's wife, told her it was possible after the fact. Unfortunately, by the time she knew and confided in her, it was too late to take any precautions.

What was she to do now?

He said they were leaving, going to Ireland.

"*Nay.*" Her heart lurched to her throat. He was asking her to give up the only life she knew.

For a few tenuous minutes she struggled to breathe. Fought for control of her emotions as they splintered into a million shards inside her chest. He wanted her to pack two small bags. He was taking Ian, with or without her.

I have no choice.

Suddenly, she stood straight, racing around the room, desperate to complete what he asked before he returned. He wouldn't wait. Wouldn't give her two more seconds to finish putting their things together. So much was needed. She had to think. His determination coupled with the anger she saw in his eyes was terrifying. She didn't know he could be this way. He'd always been so gentle and sweet, given her anything she asked for. His kisses melted her heart. She turned to liquid in his arms.

She thought she loved him.

That was then.

This is now.

He was a dangerous formidable man. Not one to trifle with.

Tossing items from the armoire, she heaved a huge sigh as she stared silently at the items strewn on the floor. She didn't know what to take. She'd never been farther away than Inverness. Her father took her brothers to Edinburgh on occasion. She never went with them, content to stay in this tiny part of Scotland. The highlands were all she'd ever known. Tears ran down her cheeks.

He expected her to travel to Ireland.

She didn't think Ian was old enough to make such a journey.

An hour passed by then two. She sat in the wing chair watching the clock, her hands trembling, her breath shaky. The bags were set at the door. Still, he didn't come. It would be time to feed her son. He would have to wait to leave. If he objected, she would make him wait. After all a babe had to be fed. He might be cruel to her, never to the child.

She must have dozed. The sound of the door opening woke her. When she opened her eyes, Walker stood over her, hands on his narrow hips, his very presence commanding. She wanted to fight him, dispute his dictates. Taking Ian from this home was not something she wanted for her son. It didn't seem she had much of a choice though.

"Are you ready?"

She rose then nodded to the two bags resting by the door. "He will need to eat soon."

"When he does, we'll stop. Perhaps you can learn to feed him while we ride," he told her with no emotion whatsoever as he picked up the bags before holding the thick wooden door for her.

In her arms, Ian nestled against her breasts. His sleepy eyed stare so endearing she felt the twinge of her milk as it started to let down for him. "He needs to eat now."

Halfway out, he stopped. "Is this some ploy to keep us here longer. It won't work."

"If I don't feed him this instant, I will have to change my clothing. Lest you forget what happened last time. You understand I would not be able to go far without sickening if I was forced to ride in a wet gown."

"Very well."

She heard his impatient grunt before she turned her head to hide the smile. "It won't take long. Twenty minutes or so then we'll be on our way. You will not lose much time on this irrational quest of yours. Still, you will have to learn to deal with the needs of a babe. Your child. You will come to realize Ian comes first in everything. A new concept for you, I'm sure."

He sat down to watch. She understood all too well if she tried to hide from him, he wouldn't allow it. Resigned, she undid the front fastenings, smiling when Ian's tiny rosebud mouth latched on to her. She always felt such joy when he nuzzled into her, his lips sucking on her.

Some of her anger dissipated while Walker was gone. Now, it returned full force as she watched him, his gaze riveted on her breasts. He would allow her no privacy. She understood. Would have to accept. Those days before he left, she wanted him desperately. He sparked a desire in her no one else ever had. Still did. Even now, when he acted so very arrogant and condescending, she couldn't deny the inferno sweeping through her body. Somehow, she thought, if he would just kiss her, she could forgive him any and all indiscretions. She would willingly go with him anywhere without one objection.

Nay that was not true. She would not go willingly as his whore.

By the tight line of his mouth coupled with the narrowing of his eyebrows, she didn't for one second believe a kiss might be forthcoming. He was angry, furiously so. Absently, she stroked Ian's cheek, cupped the downy top of his head with her palm. This little boy was so very precious. She didn't understand how Walker could even think to take a three-month-old baby overland to Glasgow then by ship to Ireland. In her estimation he wasn't thinking straight.

Ian seemed to sense her mood. He looked up, his golden-brown eyes staring at her while his little fist was clenched on her breast. She switched sides with him, giving her the other nipple. He would be finished soon. They would be on their way. To what end would this unsolicited journey lead them. She doubted if it would lead to anything good.

"I would have thought my father would put a stop to this sudden nonsense," she said a curiosity began to get the best of her. Her father had not been angry with her when he finally discovered she carried a child within her. Though she knew he was disappointed. He and her mother supported her through the long trying months before Ian was born. The delivery had not been easy. She swore at the absent father, cursed him as the pains became too much to bear. Then the sweet innocent babe she now held in her arms came screaming into her life. Without a doubt Ian Walker McKenna was the most precious being on this earth. He was her sunshine.

"Connal understood a man's got to raise his child. I didn't force you." He stopped for a moment. "When we made love. Suppose I've got you to thank for that." His voice was a sultry soft murmur, showing none of the impatience she was sure he was feeling at the delay.

No, at the time I told father I loved you. Also told him you returned the love. I was a foolish child. No longer. I'm walking into this with my eyes wide open.

She lifted her shoulders, trying not to disturb the babe. "Everyone saw me race out of here to catch you. They also saw my slightly disheveled state when I returned more than an hour later. Never thought to hide it. Never thought there would be consequences."

"Guess you wouldn't." He sounded insincere to her ears.

Crissie remembered how in awe she felt, how strange to know the man she loved reciprocated her feelings. She was floating on air when she returned to the keep. Naivety led her to believe he loved her. He never said the words. Never would she was sure. All he wanted of her now revolved around the child.

"One might say I had absolutely no idea what happened to me. My feelings..." He did take advantage in ways though. She didn't understand at the time what she felt was lust not love. He alone spurred the fires in her body she didn't understand. He could do that to her. That day he stole her heart. Since then she'd been trying to take it back. Now, when she looked into his eyes, she was sure the feat would be impossible.

Roby, her older brother knew sooner than anyone else. She didn't know how he *kenned* she was with child. Didn't ask. He stood by her. Went with her when she told their parents. Connal's disappointment in her was so very easy to read in his eyes. If she could, she would have melted into the walls. Roby placed reassuring hands on her shoulders. Even before she told them, she thought to make some excuse to go after Walker. She was mightily glad she did not. These extra months without him near, gave her much needed time to think to vanquish him from her heart.

What was it about men that they needed to control every situation?

"What were your feelings, Crissie?"

"What were yours?" she shot back unwilling to put her heart on the line. She would never tell him how much she thought she was in love with him. Never tell him how broken she'd been when he never wrote. Or when he didn't care enough about her or her child when she told him of Ian.

"At the time, shocked. I'm not going to deny anything. I wanted you from the first moment I saw you. Made a promise to myself I would have you." For a few seconds he looked away. "No matter what."

Her laughter was bitter, strained to her limits. "It worked out for you then didn't it? You got more than you bargained for."

"Yes, but not as I planned," he spoke slowly, his gaze resting on her lips, moving lower to linger on her breasts. "I gave up my plan because you were too much a lady for me to take advantage of you. I knew you would never lie with me without benefit of marriage." He lifted his broad shoulders, the fabric of his shirt straining against the muscles. His smile failed to reach his eye. "Then you did."

"When I threw myself at you, you didn't have any trouble doing just that. Did you?"

"No. It was all I'd wanted since I was assigned here. Everyone told me I didn't stand a chance in Hades with you. I did woo you tenderly still hoping I would taste a small part of you. When I was called back to Ireland, I thought a few kisses was all I would get of you. Then I got more."

"A hell of a lot more." She thought she saw him wince. Probably because of her profanity not because of what she implied.

She so needed to end this conversation. Ian was staring at her, no longer nursing. "We should go now. If you want to get off before it gets dark, that is." Crissie rose. After burping Ian then walking him to sleep, she wrapped another blanket around the sleeping child.

With her back stiff, unknowing what was before her, she followed Walker Endicott, the tenth Earl of Briarwood from her chamber, from the keep where she grew up. In favor of a new one, she left her old life behind. They rode for a few hours. Her arms grew sore and stiff from holding Ian. Her back ached. She bit down on her lips in a feeble attempt to keep the pain at bay. He completely disregarded her, overlooked the possibility that she might be struggling in his efforts to get as far away from McKenna clan land as soon as possible.

He let her catch up to him. "Can you make it another hour to the inn or would you like to make camp here?"

Her jaw dropped at the two impossible decisions he presented her with. She hoped he would offer to carry Ian for her. Warring with the option of telling him the truth she blurted. "I cannot possibly carry him any farther without dropping him. There is no way I want a three-month-old child to spend the night on the ground in the wilds. Do you think of no one except yourself?"

His once mild features changed to anger, his brows narrowing. "You should have said something. Do you expect me to read your mind?"

His low harsh voice was a side to him she'd never seen. He reached for Ian, cradling him in his strong hold.

Tears pricked the back of her throat. Her arms tingled where the blood seemed to rush back into the numb limbs and fingers. She turned away from his probing glare trying to ignore him, fighting the overwhelming exhaustion. She didn't say anything simply because she didn't wish him to believe her helpless or weak. Before they started on this journey, she determined she would never complain or ask anything from him. There was coin in her pockets. She would pay her way. Owing him anything was unconscionable.

One of his tawny eyebrows rose in question. "Nothing to say?"

Well she had a lot to say. In this case biting her tongue was the most prudent choice. "Thank you for carrying my son. It seems I've been alone and doing that very thing for what at this moment seems a veritable lifetime. The inn will be much nicer than the forest floor."

His laughter sent a shiver of anger through her. Then he corrected her. " All prim and proper are we now? Remember. My son. My heir." He settled Ian on his shoulder before kicking his black stallion into a canter.

She watched his back, the smooth play of his body as he so easily rode away from her. He carried the babe with little effort. He wouldn't slow his pace. She understood. Still...

Still what? She urged her horse to a gallop until she caught up to him.

"Thought for a moment you weren't coming. Perhaps second thoughts," he told her, his voice bland.

Third thoughts too.

She gritted her teeth to keep the reply on the tip of her tongue from bounding forth. Instead of words that would do neither any good, she smiled. It wasn't a sweet smile, probably bordered on mocking. Try as she might she just couldn't conjure anything pleasant.

Less than an hour later, they rode into the yard of an inn. Rustic Inn was the sign above the door. Dear God in heaven, she prayed it wasn't too rustic. All she wanted now was a bath as well as food for herself and Ian. After that she wanted a nice warm bed. What she'd been through this day, she didn't think that was too much to ask for. She would pay for it if it was the only way to get what she needed.

Walker helped her down, held on to her waist for a few seconds while she struggled to get her legs back in working order. They had not been on the horses for more than a few hours. God in heaven what was she going to do tomorrow when he was sure he intended to ride all day? Walking with a slight limp while rubbing her thighs, she followed him inside.

He registered for a room before she had a chance to tell him she would stay in her own as well as pay for the separate lodging. When she moved toward the desk to do just that, he took her by the arm propelling her toward the stairs. For a second, she tugged on her arm. When he didn't release her, she let him have his way. He would anyway. She was too tired to argue over a room.

While he opened the door, she kept quiet choosing to keep her complaint private. When he handed her Ian, she smiled at him. "Where are you going to sleep?" Perhaps she shouldn't have said that. Maybe she should have waited a little longer to let him know her intentions.

His grin broadened to show his even white teeth behind the lips she so longed to touch, to kiss. "With you."

"We can't possibly share a bed, we're not..."

"Lovers?" he quirked, a tawny eyebrow lifting upward. "You're holding the proof that we are."

"No." Unable to look at him, she turned her back, doing the only thing she could think of to keep her emotions from escalating.

"We made a baby together, Crissie. We can obviously share a bed. Unless you forgot."

She didn't dare say what was on her mind as the door opened. She gasped in a sharp breath, knowing everyone would think they were married. Better than believing she was his whore, she supposed.

The innkeeper along with his staff arrived with a cradle along with a tub. Buckets of steaming hot water were carried in behind the man who smiled at her knowingly. Crissie couldn't help herself. She grimaced. Then she let out a long slow breath of air, feeling the momentary anger at this intolerable situation fade. She would make the best of this. Just the thought of all that hot water started to relieve her sore muscles. If she wasn't already halfway to hell, this was almost heaven. For the time being she decided she would ignore the sleeping situation. She could deal with it later.

Walker spoke to the man for a few minutes before he set Ian in his cradle. He turned to address her, his words tenderly spoken. "I believe the water is for you. If you don't take too long, we can use the same water." He busied himself with the fire, setting a few logs on it watching as they flamed to life.

She let out a long slow breath of air before straightening her shoulders. Understanding she needed to make her wishes clear, she said, "I suppose it's too much to ask for you to leave."

"Suppose it is. We've seen each other. I've kissed most every part of you, although there are a few places... Best you hurry. I've a feeling junior is not going to have a lot of patience if his mama doesn't feed him right away."

He sounded so agreeable, so sincere, so very condescending and presumptive. Crissie struggled with the need to argue, to vent her feelings. She understood he wouldn't bend in this. She comprehended he wanted her with no commitments attached. She couldn't do that, not to her son, not to herself.

Walker would do just as he pleased. He sat down stretching his long legs out in front of him after he poured himself a glass of brandy, something else he must have ordered before they found their room. His lashes lowered, fanning out across his cheeks.

"Water's getting cold."

Quickly, her back to him, she disrobed, her breasts so full and now unconfined they hurt with every small movement. It was time for Ian's feeding. Walker was right, she needed to hurry with her bath. There was little to no time to soak and enjoy the marvelous heat. Still, the water was everything she dreamed of. With a soft sigh she settled into the heat, allowing the warmth to soothe the soreness accrued today from the hours in the saddle. She permitted herself a few minutes with her eyes closed.

The tender touch to her cheek surprised her. Her lashes flew open. She stared into the honeyed eyes of the man she loved with all her heart. Months ago, she wished her feelings away. Thought for a few fleeting weeks she succeeded. Now that he appeared so suddenly into her life, she knew that love for him would never leave her.

I need to learn to deal with it, ignore the ache in my heart.

"*Dinna* touch me. You've no right," she whispered softly. Even to herself she heard no conviction in the words. How could there be when she wanted more than anything to feel the tender strokes of his large hands on her flesh. He'd kissed her so many times, lovingly caressed and held her. No matter her intentions or his, she could not let him have his way. Despite her past actions, sex before marriage was not appropriate.

"You cannot mean that, lass." His soft, wet lips followed the path of his long, slender fingers while his words whispered across her cheek. "What difference can it make now? We both want each other in the most elemental ways."

She jerked away, her body melting into the heat he offered as well as the flames he so easily fanned inside her. She could not let him do this to her. She needed to be strong for the sake of her son. Could not fall into his arms again. It was sensations just like these that had her racing after him that day so long ago. The day that changed her life forever. She couldn't allow him to coax her from her decisions, from her principles. While in so many ways she didn't regret lying with him, it had been a bad decision. If for no other reasons, her son would be brought up a bastard.

"Aye, I do. As you said I need to hurry. Ian will be screaming soon. Already he's making those tiny demanding noises that tell me he's ready to have his dinner. See, he's kicked free of his blanket. His chubby little arms and legs are waving in protest." She brushed his hand away then washed the rest of her. Tonight she didn't have the luxury of washing here hair. It needed time to dry. They would leave early in the morning.

To her amazement, Walker backed away, resuming his seat near the fire, sipping the drink he poured earlier seeming to brood. She let out a long slow breath, understanding this was just the beginning. He would not give up. Wasn't a man to forego his pleasures. Staying strong where his tender coaxing was concerned would be difficult. God willing, she didn't intend to stray.

Not now.

Not ever.

She finished with the soap. When she was rinsed, he stood by the tub, a huge bath sheet extended for her use. As she stepped from the water, he wrapped it around her. While he watched his smile broadened.

"I will give you time to get used to me," he murmured as he began to strip his clothing from his tall, powerful frame. "Soon you will want me as much as I want you."

Time to get used to him. What did that mean?

For a few seconds she observed, fascinated by the play of muscles across his naked chest, the tawny hair curling provocatively there. She remembered the feeling of it pressed against her breasts. Remembered how she twined it through her fingers. She swallowed hard, closing her eyes before turning abruptly away from the sight of him.

From her bag she pulled out a long white nightgown, one that buttoned to the neck. She picked Ian up from the cradle, cuddling him to her before she unfastened the nightdress far enough for him to suckle.

Just as she assumed, Walker viewed her. She kept her gaze on him wary of his every move. He seemed oblivious to her blatant perusal. Humming a tune, he washed then rose, the water sluicing down his long firm legs across his well-shaped buttocks. While they made love that day, she never really saw all of him. She touched and stroked him, held him in her arms but...

He was a perfect specimen of a man.

Walker pulled on the doeskin pants he wore that day. When the knock on the door came, he opened it making sure he took the tray from the servant before the person could see inside the room. The scent of the fresh baked bread and hearty meat stew sent her stomach into a tailspin.

"Are you hungry?" he asked smiling broadly, his eyes glistening. As he watched her nurse, he poured a goblet of wine for her, brought it to her. "This will help you relax."

"Famished," she murmured as she drank down a large portion. She did need to relax. Somehow she knew that while he was part of this room and there was only one bed relaxing was most likely not in her future.

"Did I ride you too hard today, Crissie? I was eager to get you away." He sat down beside her a bowl of stew for her in hand. She couldn't eat the stew until Ian was finished. The huge slice of bread he handed her that was smothered in butter and honey was perfect. She bit into it, closing her eyes, delighted with the warm yeasty taste.

"If you are asking me if I'm sore, I am." She bit off another large chunk of the bread, chewing contentedly as he dished up a plate for himself. "Not used to spending so long in the saddle."

"Yes, I am sorry for your pain. You have to tell me how you're feeling." He picked up Ian, holding him to his shoulder as he rubbed the child's back. The large burp made him laugh. "He likes his meal. Can't say I wouldn't like some of what he's getting also."

"You won't. Get what he's getting." With an exasperated sigh, she set the spoon down that had been halfway to her mouth. "What do want from me, Walker? I won't be your whore or your mistress. I've heard no words about marriage or love. All I've heard is the demand that you would take Ian from me. I could come or go as I pleased. What the hell do you want from me?"

His brows drew together, his voice suddenly harsh. "I cannot wed you or anyone else. You best come to understand that. My son will grow up feeling his father's love. His mother's also if she chooses to stay with him."

She gasped at his words, swore softly beneath her breath. "Can't or won't?"

~ * ~

Connal found it incredibly difficult to keep from looking at Wynnie and seeing the disapproval so blatant in her eyes. Walker presented no choices when he came to talk to him. There was nothing he could do to keep Walker from taking Ian. Hell, he could have insisted Crissie stay here. Walker certainly didn't look as if he wanted the mother to come with him.

"Tell me what happened this afternoon," Roby sat down on the opposite side of Connal, a glass of ale in hand. He didn't appear at all pleased with the situation. "You say Walker took off with Ian and Crissie? I can go after them. Bring my sister as well as the babe home. They don't belong with that Sassenach bastard."

"Aye, that he did. No, you cannot interfere in their private relationship." Connal didn't' want another argument. He spent most of the afternoon defending his inaction to his wife. Didn't need to have the same conversation with his youngest son. Brady would come along and a repeat of today's events would have to be hashed out.

"I could bring Crissie and the babe back," Roby offered once again, grinning as if he already understood what was happening. "Never did like that particular Sassenach."

"You liked him well enough until you learned he was the father of Crissie's child, until you understood how he took advantage of her," Wynnie said in a soft voice seeming to need to tell her youngest son to go after the couple and bring her child and grandchild home.

Roby's unfettered hand was fisted, the knuckles on his ale glass white. "He did take advantage even though Crissie said she was willing. She was innocent, naïve in the ways of men and women. She would have had no idea of the consequences of the quick dalliance. Walker did."

"Well, they are gone. He did explain to me why he couldn't wed her. The entire story is unsettling at best. Maybe in time, things will change in Crissie's favor."

"Why is that?" Roby asked, his voice harsh.

"He is already wed to another," Wynnie spoke before Connal could say the damning words. "Damn his everlasting soul to hell!"

"And you want me to believe that Englishman didn't take advantage of my sister?"

"Not me," Connal said softly, hands in the air as he slanted his wife, a look that only the pair understood. "Crissie wants us to believe her."

"That tale is hard to swallow at best. The Sassenach should be hung by his thumbs," Roby said watching the door as if he hoped Crissie and Ian would be walking inside as they spoke.

"Aye, it's hard to accept," Connal agreed. "In this case, Crissie made the only decision she could. Walker was hell bent on taking both of them away from here. Says we are all in danger but he didn't explain why or how. Said to be very careful. I got an ominous feeling from his words."

"So, what is it he plans to do with her when they reach his home? Keep her as his mistress or his whore? Set her up in a home nearby when he can visit at leisure? Use her when it pleases him?" Roby asked. "What is he planning on doing with the child? He still needs his mother. The bastard wouldn't dare hire a wet nurse with Crissie in such jeopardy."

Wynnie reached out touching her hands on both her husband's and her son's hands. "I believe that will be up to Crissie. I'm sure she is aware of his wishes by now. He's an honorable man. He will abide by what Crissie wants. I'm sure he won't take advantage of her again. Unless she's willing."

Roby let out an astounded chortle. "Honorable? You are far too naïve, mother. He will try to seduce her. Will do so until she gives in to his wishes. The way she feels about the man, he will achieve his desires with few difficulties."

"You've never bedded a woman?" Wynnie asked directing her attention to her son. "You've never coaxed and seduced until you got your way?"

Connal watched his youngest son squirm. "I've never gotten one with child, never an innocent maid. Don't intend to do so anytime soon."

"That's good to hear," Connal said reflecting on his past as well as his actions until he met his wife, his mate.

He did protest, did ask to speak with Crissie before they left. Walker refused. Connal supposed he could have argued and won that particular battle. Walker had been right, however in his conviction that what transpired was between the two of them and he didn't want interference to complicate things.

Walker didn't speak of love. Connal had a strong suspicion the Englishman did love Crissie. Wed to another. It was hard to believe. Walker told him it was a betrothal made by fathers when the children were born. Walker had been married nearing ten years now. He said he was nineteen at the time. Had never consummated the marriage to his wife.

No, Walker's marriage was not one of love. It was easy for Connal to read the truth in Walker's eyes. Easy to see how much he regretted that marriage. He suspected they lived in separate bedrooms. Connal could well understand Walker's need for a warm willing woman in his bed.

He just wished it wasn't Crissie filling that position. For he had no doubts that she would end up in the earl's bed again.

Other Books by Christine Young
Available at Rogue Phoenix Press

My Sweet Broc
Bad Boys Book One

He's a bad bad boy...

Broc Wallace is a fun-loving rake who never thought any beautiful woman could melt his heart. He lives life in the present enjoying the camaraderie of his friends and the pleasures of his mistress. When Bliss races into his life, he is ill prepared to deal with her secrets or give up the tenor of his life. When the truth is revealed, he finds himself unable to forgive and forget the betrayal.

... but she's sweet for him

Bliss MacTavish knows she's playing with fire when she refuses to tell this bad boy her name. He tempts her with sweet whispers of seduction knowing her innocent nature will be unable to refuse all he yearns to give her. Deciding to follow her heart, she finds the repercussions more than she bargains for when she gives herself to this bad boy.

Crazy for Cam
Bad Boys Book Two

He's a bad bad boy...

Lord Cam MacEwen, Viscount of Rosehill, tries his best to be proper and court the lady of his dreams in the acceptable way. The feat proves impossible when the lady in question uses every means at her disposal to tempt him. He fights his jealousy for another man as well as the need to make her his own, finally giving in to her irresistible passion.

... but she's crazy for him.

Chelsea MacTavish wants the bad boy she fell in love with and kissed just before her eighteenth birthday. With feminine wiles and irresistible allure, the sensuous lady plans to best Cam at his game of hearts and make him forget his need to court her properly.

Falling for Flynt
Bad Boys Book Three

He's a bad, bad boy...

Fascinated by Hope's loss of memory yet haunted by her sultry beauty, Flynt is irresistibly drawn to the stoic miss—and into her troubles with the sultan who wants her for himself. When he discovers she is the sister of his best friend, his pride keeps him from pursuing her and making her his.

... but she's falling for him.

Raised in a harem but now penniless, alone and without her memory, Hope must discover a way to remember all that she has lost. She finds a way to continue with her life as a servant in Flynt's home. The first sight of Flynt steals Hope's breath as well as her heart. Can she overcome her fears and give herself to the man she fell in love with.

Dancing With Donal
Bad Boys Book Four

He's a bad bad boy...

Once a bad boy always a bad boy, Donal Chamberlin's carefree ways come crashing down around him when he meets the ravishingly beautiful Daryl MacTavish, the innocent little sister of one of his best friends. He is determined to win her heart as he sets his sights on marriage and an heir. His past gets in the way of his quest when a woman he once loved threatens Daryl's life.

... but she's dancing with him.

Daryl has seen the control her sister's husbands hold over them.

She yearns for a life where she makes decisions for herself. No man will have power over her. But no man kisses her the way Donal does. No man can make her forget all her goals leaving her helpless to give up her dreams. Yet Donal is determined to dance through all the barriers she thrust in front of him, pursuing her until she says yes.

Loving Leslie
Bad Boys Book Five

He's a bad bad boy...

Leslie Stewart, Duke of Southcliff is stoic, set in his ways, a spy who is used to having his life well ordered. He expects life to continue on in this perfectly conventional fashion. He assumes his bad boy status while keeping mamas and debutantes at arm's length. An heir is needed but Leslie has every intention of finding a woman who doesn't covet his wealth and tittle. He is irresistibly drawn to the headstrong young lady who becomes more beautiful as she develops into a woman.

... but she is loving him.

When Leslie kisses Lacie MacTavish, she knows even at the tender age of fifteen this is the man of her dreams. Forced to wait until she comes of age, Lacie withdraws into herself. Now she is eighteen and Leslie has returned from a mission for the British Government ready to claim her as his bride. She refuses him and he must find a way to seduce her and in the process create a burning passion within her, which she cannot deny.

Pleasing Arie
Bad Boys Book Six

He's a bad bad boy...

Arie Demir has never been denied anything in his life. He takes what he wants. What he undeniably yearns for is the beautiful redheaded spitfire he sees in a restaurant in Glasgow. At every turn, she confuses him by disputing his power over her. Alison refuses to accept the fact he owns her. While Arie tries desperately with patience and tenderness to drive her wild with new sensations, his scorching kisses ignite the fires of her very soul to make her understand he is all she will ever want.

... but is she pleasing him?

Alison Fletcher never expected to find herself kidnapped and sold to a whorehouse then bought by a Turkish sultan to become his slave. She vows to never surrender to the arrogant man who believes he owns her. She is stunned by the magnificently handsome man who awaits her compliance. Unexpectedly, she finds Arie the lesser of all the evils. The hidden depths of his mesmerizing dark brown eyes hold her into their power; his muscular embrace makes her weak with desire. She is his to do with as he wishes.

Graham's Wicked Kiss
Bad Boys Book Seven

He's a bad bad boy...

Graham Chamberlin is stunned to find three young boys dangling from the trees lining the drive to Runningmead Manner. On further inspection, he is astonished at their obsession to protect a young woman who has been brutalized by her pimp. The woman he discovers hiding in a third-floor attic room is gravely injured. He takes the silver haired stowaway under his wing. Clearly, Graham's new guest is a lady with many secrets. He is determined to unlock all the mysteries surrounding her.

... But she can't resist his wicked kiss.

The years since Ria left the convent where she was raised have been a nightmare. Her secrets are dangerous—as is the powerful man determined to find her. Handsome Graham Chamberlin is clearly a gentleman with secrets of his own, but staying with him could mean the difference between life and death for Ria. With each passing day, her handsome host turns Ria's convalescence into an increasingly sensual escape. Now her greatest challenge may be imagining anything less than a future in his arms.

Feeling Etienne's Love
Bad Boys Book Eight

He's a bad bad boy...

Etienne Dubois is the son of a wealthy vineyard owner who craves the excitement of putting his life on the line. Working with the French government and as a confidant of King Charles X give him reasons for living. An encounter with a beautiful young woman in a plush bordello in Paris has him rethinking his roguish ways. Etienne never expects to become a father especially from one encounter with an innocent prostitute who whispers his name and has him rethinking his well-ordered life.

...But she can't help feeling his love.

Elisa Moreau, the only daughter of Angelique Moreau, the owner of an exclusive bordello in Bordeaux, France, has loved Etienne Dubois since she was six. Unfortunately, until an unexpected encounter at a brothel in Paris puts the two of them in the same room, Etienne doesn't even know she exists. Confused but wanting Etienne and this chance meeting to never end, Elisa gives herself to the man who has held her heart in hands for what seems like her entire life.

Foolish for Piper

The pickpocket...

Piper has spent her life surviving the streets of St. Giles Parish in London, a den of iniquity and crime. Masquerading as a boy she escapes the whorehouses the young girls are sent to as they come of age. The day she encounters Brett MacLachlan begins the same as every other one. When she picks his pocket, she has no idea her life is going to change irreversibly.

... and the mark

Handsome aristocrat Brett MacLachlan has come to London for his amusement only to find his world turned upside down by a thief and her dog. From the moment he spots her, Brett knows there is something intrinsically wrong. In his arms, Piper discovers passion and joy. Yet secrets of her past haunt her, and a scar will tell the true tale as well as her identity.

Taylor's Destiny

She traveled to another time and place to change destiny...

Enjoying a day of sailing, Taylor Maxwell never expected after a suffering a concussion she would wake up in another century. A resilient independent woman in the twenty-first century, the blond beauty is ill prepared for life in the 1800s. Her first sight of the naval captain who rescues her makes her heart stop, giving her hope for her future.

His life is transformed by a woman who appears from nowhere...

Born to a life of ease, Reid Stewart defies the dictates of those born to aristocracy and chooses a life of adventure in the navy and as a spy for the crown. When he discovers a nearly naked woman on the bow of small sailing ship, his heart warms. His love for Taylor and his need to protect her from a man who pursues her might cost him his life as well as hers.

Caitlin's Duke

She played a fiddle in an Irish pub...

Caitlin O'Shea Is the most beautiful woman Roc Leighton has ever seen. With her blue violet eyes and long black hair she captivates him. In turn he mesmerizes Caitlin. Caught in the power of his gaze as he watches her, she is wise enough to know he desires her but will never give his heart to her. Caitlin has vowed to never be any man's mistress.

And fell in love with an English Lord...

Roc knows the first time he watches her play the fiddle and dance around the pub, she will be his next mistress. Despite her protest, he will find a way to convince her that her place is with him. While Caitlin's determination to keep her vows, fate takes a cruel turn and she is forced to seek refuge with Roc.

Catching Meara
Book One in the McKenna Clan Series

Meara Thorton was a feisty, world-class computer hacker—cornered by the FBI and shockingly given the chance to be their newly acquired technical analyst. Brilliant and intuitive, yet aching with the loss of everyone she has cared about, her restless heart led her to discover a love she fought and a world she didn't know could possibly exist.

Sweet Sexy Sadie
Book Two in the McKenna Clan Series

From the first time Sadie's eyes met those of Brody McKenna in the hot Sierra Madre Mountains, theirs was a potent attraction—not gentle, slow, and easy, but hot, hard, and all-consuming. The daughter of a dysfunctional family, Sadie had dreams no man could wrench from her with hot sex and an all-consuming passion. She'd challenge this alpha male with all the strength she possessed. But her red hair, fiery temperament, and indomitable spirit obsessed Brody... and he knew he had to find a way to show her he was more than he appeared and convince her to make a life with him.

Sweet Misbehavin'
Book Three in the McKenna Clan Series

Cast adrift after fleeing the home of Jokul, the ice demon, Atantsi, a firestarter, grew to womanhood as she moved through time to keep the demon from finding her. Though stubborn and courageous, she was ill prepared to use powers she had not been taught. Her first sight of the intoxicating Carr McKenna left her breathless, and her second encounter gave her hope for a future she never thought she had.

A playboy, a second son and a shifter, a man who thought his life would be carefree, Carr McKenna was shocked to discover the woman he'd paid as an escort is a firestarter who is running for her life. He is the leader of all the McKennas around the world and that he has multiple powers. His passion for Margo and the need to defend her might cost him his life as well as hers.

Sweet Talkin' Sugar
Book Four in the McKenna Clan Series

Lyonesse McKenna, was dreaming, or was she? From the instant Lyn saw Deacon McClain across a black jack table in a crowed Las Vegas casino the unmistakable attraction sent Lyn's senses flying into overdrive. Her family of shapeshifters believed in soul mates. She'd always been skeptical yet she couldn't help but question the way her heart sped when he looked at her.

When Deacon appeared in Las Vegas he knew his first job was to save Lyn from a Sea Demon, but the next order of business was to convince her he would someday mean more to her than she'd ever expected. But her stubborn nature and unbendable spirit consumed Deacon... and he had to chase away all the demons real and imagined in order to win her heart.

Sweet Surrender
Book Five in the McKenna Clan Series

Ripped from her family at the top of Infinity Cliff, Kimi McKenna finds herself thrust somewhere into the future. Dark elements threaten to destroy the earth unless Kimi can work together with the white witch to stop the destruction. Confused by her mate's role in the conspiracy, she refuses to acknowledge the connection. But amidst raging fire and attacks on the people she is coming to hold dear, she allows Maska O'keefe into her heart.

Maska O'keefe has loved the beautiful shapeshifter for years. Unable to save her life years ago, he vows to watch over her as he is given a second chance to convince her that even though he is a witch and not a shifter, they are indeed soul mates. Kimi's divided loyalties between her family and the cause she is now a part of will determine their relationship. Only the part she plays as the messiah can bring this to a conclusion in the final battle.

Dakota's Bride
The first book in the Lakota/Pinkerton Series

When Emma St. John received her brother's letter imploring her to escape her stepfather's vengeful scheme and to trust Dakota Barringer with her life, she was willing to chance it. But the handsome, brooding riverboat owner Emma found in Natchez a danger of another kind. For Emma soon found herself surrendering to an unrelenting desire.

Raised by the Sioux when his parents were killed, Dakota had been betrayed once before by a white woman. He wasn't about to trust another, especially one claiming that her stepfather, a powerful U.S. senator, had framed her as a murderess. But he couldn't let Emma's intoxicating effect on him. Now Dakota would risk his very life to protect the innocent beauty who had seduced him with her tender love.

My Angel

The second book in the Lakota/Pinkerton Series

A BEAUTY IN BUCKSKINS

When her father decided to send her to a finishing school back East, Angela Chamberlain refused to be confined to stuffy drawing rooms. Instead, the daring spitfire who could shoot like a man and ride like the wind longed for a life of adventure and romance—and she knew exactly who could give it to her. Devil Blackmoor was a hired gun with a dangerous reputation. But Angela was willing to go to the ends of the earth to capture the handsome devil's heart.

A DEVIL IN DISGUISE

He'd come to America looking for excitement, but Devil Blackmoor got more than he bargained for when he encountered a beautiful rebel who answered his kisses with a wild innocence that touched his very soul. Yet standing between them were more obstacles than either ever dreamed. For Devil had strapped on a gun for the wrong man. And that made Angela his enemy. Now he'll have to choose between his duty and the woman he loves more than life.

The Locket
The third book in the Lakota/Pinkerton Series

The year is 1894. Seeking revenge for crimes against his family, Misha Petrovich follows a path that leads straight to Ariel Cameron's boarding house in Mist Harbor, Oregon. A family heirloom in Ariel's possession leads Misha to believe she is guilty. The locket has been handed down to the oldest girl in the Petrovich family for generations. Ariel is innocent of wrong doing, but her father is not. Misha is torn by his feelings for Ariel and his need for restitution against her father. Knowing that the relationship between them is fragile, Misha does everything in his power to protect Ariel's father. His efforts are to no avail when her father is shot. Ariel comes to realize Misha's steadfast courage and determination to protect her and her father despite what has happened to his family. Ariel's love and devotion heals Misha's heart.

The Talisman
The fourth book in the Lakota/Pinkerton Series

Running from a marriage that lasted one night, Dr. Moriah McKeown discovers the land she has settled on is coveted by determined and lawless men. Yet the proud young woman who once vowed never to abandon her home has second thoughts when her adopted children are threatened. Her only recourse is to enlist the aid of a dark, dangerous gun for hire.

Haunted by the past and a betrayal he will never forgive, Ian Civanovich uses his fast gun and his reckless courage to forget the faithlessness of a woman in his past. He will trust no female—nor will he rest until the threat hovering over Moriah McKeown is put to rest.

Forever His
The fifth book in the Lakota/Pinkerton Series

Struggling to come to terms with the part she played in Jacob St. John's death, Etta Barringer resigns from Pinkerton Agency and seeks peace and solace in a Rocky Mountain Cabin.

Jacob has vowed to discover the reason Etta has betrayed him, sold him out to his enemy and left him for dead.

Isolated in their cabin, they discover their love for each other and learn to trust. But the trust is shattered when Jacob learns she is married to his sworn enemy; the man who left him in the desert to die.

Allura's Secret
Twelve Dancing Princesses Book One

Allura McClellan is horrified by her father's decision to take out an ad in the Times awarding her to the man strong enough and smart enough to win her hand and uncover her secrets. She's an intelligent young woman who takes great delight in the freedom allotted to her by her father. She's well aware that marriage would effectively curtail the adventures she's shared with her sisters and cousins.

Hunter Gray is nothing like the other men who've arrived to vie for Allura's hand in marriage and everything that goes along with it. However, he is the first to refuse to concede defeat and pursue her despite her attempts to disguise her true appearance. It's her temperament that is of more concern to him than her looks. Hunter has worked all his life with the hope of someday owning his own land. Now that it looks like there's a very real possibility that everything he's ever wanted is within reach nothing is going to deter him – including Miss Allura's disagreeable disposition.

Amorica's Wager
Twelve Dancing Princesses Book Two

Amorica Hepburn was sent to London to find a husband. Finding a man was the last item on her agenda. With her two cousins, Amorica wagers she can dissuade her suitor before the others. Despite her efforts she discovers a chemistry that cannot be denied. Suddenly she is the arrogant man's wife, pledged to a marriage neither desire. But swept off to his ancestral home above the Dover cliffs and into his strong embrace, Amorica is soon possessed by a raging passion for the husband she had vowed to despise...

Damian Andrews couldn't afford to trust the emerald-eyed spitfire who happened upon his secret. Amorica's hatred of all men of his kind only inflames the war that rages between them. Still, he can not control the intense desire his stubborn bride inspires, or make her surrender to his will until he has conquered the headstrong beauty on the battlefield of love...

Ravyn's Marriage of Inconvenience
Twelve Dancing Princesses Book Three

A REGAL BEAUTY

When the duchess decides to wed her to a wastrel and a fop, Ravyn Grahm takes matters into her own hands and declares her engagement to another man. Instead of fessing up and telling her great aunt what she has done, she goes through with the pretense. Ariec Lakeland is the bastard son of an earl and has a dangerous reputation. But Ravyn is willing to do most anything to keep the duchess from discovering the lie.

A DEVIL-MAY-CARE SMUGGLER

He'd bought land in America, looking to put down roots and end his life of adventure, but Ariec Lakeland got more than he bargained for when he encountered a beautiful heiress who made a promise she didn't want to keep. But the promise could not be undone and standing between them were more obstacles than either ever dreamed. Ariec had made plans to spend the rest of his life in America and that was at odds with Ravyn's plan of living in England and running her father's estate. Now, he'll have to choose between his dreams and the woman he loves more than life.

Christel's Sunrise
Twelve Dancing Princesses Book Four

He Made Her An Offer...

Life has thrown Christel McClellan some experiences that could have devastated a less determined woman. Beautiful, self-assured and fiercely independent, she is trying to forget the loss of her stillborn child. But is the child alive?

She Couldn't Deny...

Life is carefree for Ryder MacLaren who loves to see what is on the other side of the sunrise. Laird of Clan MacLaren, he is wealthy, handsome and happily unencumbered... until stunning Christel McClellan enters his life. When he hears her story, he believes the child she thought dead has been sold to a wealthy buyer.

Storm's Passion
Twelve Dancing Princesses Book Five

SHE MADE A PROPOSAL...
Life strikes Storm Graham a shattering blow when she learns her father has bartered her to a man she detests. Storm is beautiful, self–assured and fiercely independent, and refuses to be a pawn in her father's schemes, yet she can find no way out of this bargain made in hell. Going on the offensive she asks the wealthiest man on the eastern coast of England to marry her, never believing she might fall in love.

HE TRIED TO REFUSE...
For Hadden Johnston life has provided everything he ever wanted, including a sanctuary for homeless children. He is wealthy, handsome and happily unencumbered... until stunning Storm Graham marches into his life and proposes a marriage of convenience. Yet this type of marriage to a woman who inflames his senses is far from acceptable. If he's going to be tied down, he will move heaven and earth to have this woman warming his bed.

Gotta Have Fayth
Twelve Dancing Princesses Book Six

A regal beauty with raven hair and piercing blue eyes, Fayth Graham is unwilling to parade herself in front of the wealthy Lords of England during the season. Seeking a means to dissuade any man wishing to wed her, she seeks a way to ruin herself for marriage. When she unexpectedly meets a man with sparkling gray eyes and an infectious grin, she decides this is the man who will keep her from agreeing to obey.

He returned from six months at sea, looking for a few nights of pleasure with a willing lass, but Jarret Kinsley got more than he bargained for when he met a beautiful debutant who responded to his kisses with a wild innocence that touched his heart. Yet the obstacles looming between them might rip them apart. Both had vowed never to marry, so when consequences of their dalliances got in the way, Jarret would have to choose between the life he's always desired and the woman he loves more than life.

Ella's Pleasure
Twelve Dancing Princesses Book Seven

A WHISPER OF PLEASURE

Ella Hepburn was an auburn haired debutant from the harsh Scottish coastline—a wild innocent to be seduced and tamed. A spirited beauty, she captivated Drake Montgomerie's jaded heart—while succumbing to the smoldering desire she felt for her unyielding suitor.

A WHISPER OF DANGER

In Drake Montgomerie's glittering world of money and privilege, young Ella discovered passion and desire could overcome everything she'd been taught to resist—entangling Drake, the heir apparent, in a lethal coil of aristocratic family intrigue. But grave peril would only nurse the sparks of a love that knew no limits and a magnificent ecstasy that would not be denied.

Eveleen's Seduction
Twelve Dancing Princesses Book Eight

A WHISPER OF SEDUCTION

A brutal attack on Eveleen Hepburn's cherished island off the Scottish coastline leaves her shattered and bewildered. Learning a man she once trusted can kill as easily as he can breathe even though the deed saves her life, creates questions that need answers. An innocent beauty, she enchants Logan Maxwell's cynical heart—giving in to the raging passion she feels for her mysterious suitor.

A WHISPER OF INTRIGUE

In Logan's Maxwell's world of espionage and privilege, young Eveleen discovers truths about herself she never expected, and a need for passion and love can overcome all her fears if she learns to accept certain truths. She finds herself entangled in a lethal battle for land that was once owned by French nobility, taken from them during the revolution and sold to Maxwell. But grave peril would unleash the flames of love that simmers, creating a magical union that cannot be refuted.

Tavia's Deception
Twelve Dancing Princesses Book Nine

WHISPERS OF DECEPTION

When her father decides to send her to London for her season, Tavia Hepburn resolves to see the world instead. The raven haired beauty decides to disguise herself as a lad and find employment on a ship bound for Barcelona as a cabin boy. But she never bargains on finding passion and love to a red haired sea captain who rescues her from certain death.

WHISPERS OF MURDER

For James Macmurra, the world is black and white until he meets a young debutante, who turns his world upside down. He's unable to deny Tavia's intoxicating effect on him. In a match tense with obstacles, unwillingness to divulge secrets, and unforeseen peril, irresistible desire and passion grows into undeniable love. James would risk his life to shelter and protect the innocent debutante who seduces him with her sweet love.

Larena's Fascination
Twelve Dancing Princesses Book Ten

WHISPERS OF FASCINATION

Fiery, free spirited Larena Graham never wanted to marry a duke. She is thrilled to be in love with the fourth son of an aristocrat, Gavin

Broon. But when it seems Gavin ignores her, she set her sights on politics and bettering human life. Unsuspecting intrigue and a plot against her, she continues her dangerous plans despite Gavin's wishes.

WHISPERS OF TRUST
Gavin has every intention of properly courting the beautiful Larena until he must leave the city in order to put his affairs in order. Returning to London, he finds the woman he means to make his own is embroiled in political protests that could lead to a prison ship. Larena must learn to trust the handsome Scotsman whose most pressing mission is to protect her and keep her from harm.

Tira's Education
Twelve Dancing Princesses Book Eleven

WHISPERS OF EDUCATION
Learning how to build ships is Tira Hepburn's only dream until she meets Jamie Lundin and her world is turned upside down. With her raven black hair and vivid green eyes, she tempts Jamie and pushes him to defy his vows. She never bargains on finding an irrevocable love and a passion to a man who cannot fulfill her dreams despite his burning desire for her.

WHISPERS OF A BARGAIN
Arrogant and self-assured Jamie is brought up short when Tira captures his heart. All his carefully made plans are put to the test when he decides to teach her the art of ship building if she will spend a week with him alone on his ship. He is unable to deny Tira's intoxicating effect on him. When Tira leaves him behind unwilling to live with him without the benefit of marriage, he races after her. Jamie will risk everything to shelter and protect the innocent debutante who seduces him with her sweet love.

Aidan's Love

Whispers of Love

Aidan McLellan has loved since she first set eyes on him as a young girl. Spontaneous, wild and eager to grow up, Aidan haunts his waking thoughts day and night, insinuating herself into his life. With her fiery red hair and sparkling sapphire eyes, she seizes Blade's heart even while he tries to resist the innocent child until she becomes a woman.

Whispers of Courage

Blade has waited what seems a lifetime to claim the woman who captures his heart as a little girl. Claiming his inheritance before his younger brother takes what is rightfully his, Blade must convince Aidan of his sincerity after years of avoidance and wed her before his father dies so he can return home, securing his rightful place. Everything is put to the test when his life as well as Aidan's is threatened by the man who once called him brother.

Twelve Days to Love

When Archer Steele shows up at Calanthe Durand's failing plantation with an alligator over his shoulder, Cali thinks she's never seen a more handsome man. During the war she had to defend herself and her servants from both union and confederate soldiers. Independent and self-sufficient, she vows to never marry.

But Archer Steele has different ideas. The first time Archer sees Cali in town, he feels an instant attraction. He decides he will do everything and anything to convince the beautiful Miss Durand he is worthy of her love. During the weeks leading up to Christmas, he gives her twelve gifts in hopes she will fall in love with him. Yet they are faced with challenges they must overcome before Cali can commit to a marriage.

Door to Heaven

Jessica Lawrence is the stepdaughter of a woman born in the twentieth century transported back in time to the year 1868. An acclaimed suffragette, she raises Jessica to believe in the equality of women. Jess Law believes everything she was taught, and when the time is right she becomes a private investigator. Courageous and impetuous, Jess finds danger in her quest to save all women from white slavery. Her passionate mission results in a wedding to Roc Newman, a man she knows can steal her heart...

Roc can't trust the sapphire-eyed spitfire who invades his home in search of secret papers and knocks him flat with her karate moves. Jessica's refusal to obey his wishes serves to inflame the war between them. Still, he cannot control the intense desire his reluctant bride inspires, or make her surrender her independence, until he has conquered the headstrong beauty on the battlefield of love...

Rebel Heart

HER REBEL SPIRIT DEFIED HIS OUTSIDERS SOUL... She was velvet and silk, eyes the color of a summer storm and amber hair. Victoria DeMontville, because of a promise and a codicil to her father's will, was forced to marry one man to protect her from another. She hated Cameron Savage with a fierce passion. But to hold on to her genetic research and find a cure for the deadly Signe virus, she must pretend to love the enemy at her door, come with weapons of fire to melt her icy heart...

HIS OUTSIDERS TOUCH IGNITED RAGING PASSIONS... He wore a mask, disguised as the Phantom, a true legend come to life. Even as war and debate over new genetic research engulfed them all, he would find his greatest adversary in the beauty who'd branded him an outsider and barbarian, the woman he was born to possess, his soul mate.

Safari Moon

Solo St. John, a wildlife photographer, is preparing for a trip to Alaska. Suddenly, Solo finds women of all sorts invading his privacy, his home and his office, all cooing nonsense words and blatantly throwing themselves at him. Solo doesn't know why, and he has no idea how to rid himself of the persistent women. He finally decides to beg a favor of his best buddy Nyssa Harrington.

In love with Solo for the past ten years and knowing he doesn't return her feelings Nyssa doesn't want to talk to Solo. She knows if she accepts his phone call, she will not be able to resist the temptation to hope again.

Straight to Heaven

Running from demons, Alexandra McMurdie stumbles into Forbidden Ground where up is down and elements of nature are contested. Though a strong independent woman in the twenty-first century' she is unprepared for life in the 1800s. Her first site of the formidable James Lawrence makes her heart skip a beat, giving her cause to reconsider her desperate need to find a way home.

Born with a silver spoon, James' life was torn apart during the War Between the States. Moving west he vows to put the life he once knew in the past. When he discovers a half-frozen woman near Gold Hill, his heart begins to thaw. His love for Alexandra and his need to keep her from a man who has pursued her through time might cost him his life as well as hers.

A Valentine's Anthology

The Lending Library-a fantasy by Christie L. Kraemer
Faeries try to fit into the human world when the forest where they make their home is destroyed by a mysterious enemy.

Chasing Rainbows-a contemporary romance by Genene Valleau

An eccentric aunt, an inventive uncle, a mother who wears poodle skirts, and a brother who wears pearls provide a hilarious backdrop for the courtship of a young woman who yearns for a "normal" family.

The Gift-an historical romance by Christine Young
A man and a woman on opposite sides of the Civil War get a second chance at love after one final battle returns soldiers to their war-torn homes to rebuild their lives.

A St. Patrick's Day Tale
Christine Young, C. L. Kraemer, Genene Valleau

Tumble through time...
...to Ireland in 1817, when tensions are high between Protestants and Catholics and fae people guide the fate of villagers. A lovely Catholic lass stumbles upon the weakly ritual fisticuffing between Irish lads. She falls into the lap of a handsome young Protestant. Family ties, grudges, and two conniving faeries threaten their budding love. But the faeries outsmart themselves when they hijack a time machine that has mysteriously appeared in their forest and are whisked to...
...Eugene, Oregon in the 20th century, amid a property feud between the local faeries and night elves. The conniving faeries from Olde Ireland try to stir up more mischief. However, a warrior gnome convinces the magic folk to control their own destiny, and forces the intruding faeries to take refuge in the time machine again, spinning their way toward...
...A modern day castle in western Oregon. An eccentric inventor is determined to reclaim his wayward time machine and save his beloved wife from her latest misadventure. If only they can travel safely past the black hole...

a May Day Anthology
Christine Young, C. L. Kraemer, Rosemary Indra, Genene Valleau

Highland Miracle — Christine Young

HURTLED THROUGH TIME, Sean Michael Sterling, landed in the midst of a May Day celebration he didn't understand, assuming the role of Laird Sterling.

ILLIGITAMATE CHILD OF NOBILITY, Reagan Douglas searches for a way out of her half brother's house.

Defying the Odds — C.L. Kraemer

The night elves on the hill aren't happy without their magic. They concoct a plan to punish those who were involved in the act that rendered them almost human. Meanwhile, Uther, the rogue night elf, has returned to woo the Librarian to be his eternal mate.

Love in Bloom — Rosemary Indra

When childhood friends reunite it takes two fairies and a matchmaking daughter to help them admit their true love for each other.

No More Poodle Skirts — Genie Gabriel

After drifting for years in the innocent age of the 1950s, a woman struggles to join today's world by finding a career and a new love, with some help from her zany family.

Once Upon a Christmas Moon
Christine Young, C. L. Kraemer, Genene Valleau

TWELVE DAYS TO LOVE

When Archer Steele shows up at Calanthe Durand's failing plantation with an alligator over his shoulder, Cali thinks she's never seen a more handsome man. During the war she had to defend herself and her servants from both union and confederate soldiers. Independent and self-sufficient, she vows to never marry. But Archer Steele has different ideas. The first time Archer sees Cali in town, he feels an instant attraction. He decides he will do everything and anything to convince the beautiful Miss Durand he is worthy of her love. During the weeks leading up to Christmas, he gives her twelve gifts in hopes she will fall in love with him.

BOOTS AND BLADES

An ancient evil from the old country has arrived in the high desert of Oregon. Gnome children are vanishing then re-appearing, showing various stages of traumatization. Tiamoon, warrior gnome, will put her skills to use alongside Killian, a handsome warrior, also in need of a cause.

CHRISTMAS PAWSIBILITIES

With their world destroyed and their space ship malfunctioning, the dogizens of Planet Canid have little choice but to crash land on Earth. They face tortuous experiments at the hands of the Geeks in Green... or they can trust an eccentric inventor and his zany family to deliver the Canine Queen's puppies and help them celebrate new lives.

www.ingramcontent.com/pod-product-compliance
Lightning Source LLC
Chambersburg PA
CBHW070652180626
46817CB00006B/2337